The Secret of Godspear

by

Dean Kinne

The Secret of Godspear is a work of fiction. Names, characters, places and incidents are products of the author's imagination or are used fictitiously. Any resemblance to actual events, locales, or persons, living or dead, is entirely coincidental.

ISBN: 9781734033236

The Secret of Godspear

For Bonnie. Without your endless encouragement this story would never have been written.

Acknowledgments

Though an author may set out alone to write a novel, many will join to aid in the endeavor. Without them, the journey's end could never be reached. A special thanks to those who accompanied me on this odyssey.

To my editor, Lisa Gilliam. Her keen eyes and meticulous attention to detail discovered errors and inconsistencies I had overlooked during my numerous reworks. This story wouldn't be the same without her.

To my best friend, John-Paul. On many a night he served me dinner and made sure I didn't become a starving artist. He epitomizes all I strive to be: giving and selfless, thoughtful and considerate, intelligent and pragmatic. J-P, you're a better man than I.

Without my beta readers and their feedback, I'd never have learned the strengths and weaknesses of this story. Bonnie, Cheryl, Dawn and Mike, I'm indebted to you and all the rest too numerous to list.

Full credit for the cover goes to Hollie Haradon. She is a true artist with saintly patience for dealing with me. Visit her at www.mischiefcircus.com.

To Tiffany, for making tangible the world in my mind with her magnificent cartography skills. See all her outstanding work at www.feedthemultiverse.com.

Without my family, I wouldn't be where I am today. Every one of them has contributed, whether knowingly or not. I firmly believe family is the strongest foundation one's character can be built upon, and it's because of my father, mother, siblings, aunts, uncles, cousins, nieces and nephews to which I owe such beliefs.

And to Kim, for tolerating my idiosyncrasies on a daily basis.

Last, but certainly not least, I'd like to thank you, dear reader, for giving this story a chance.

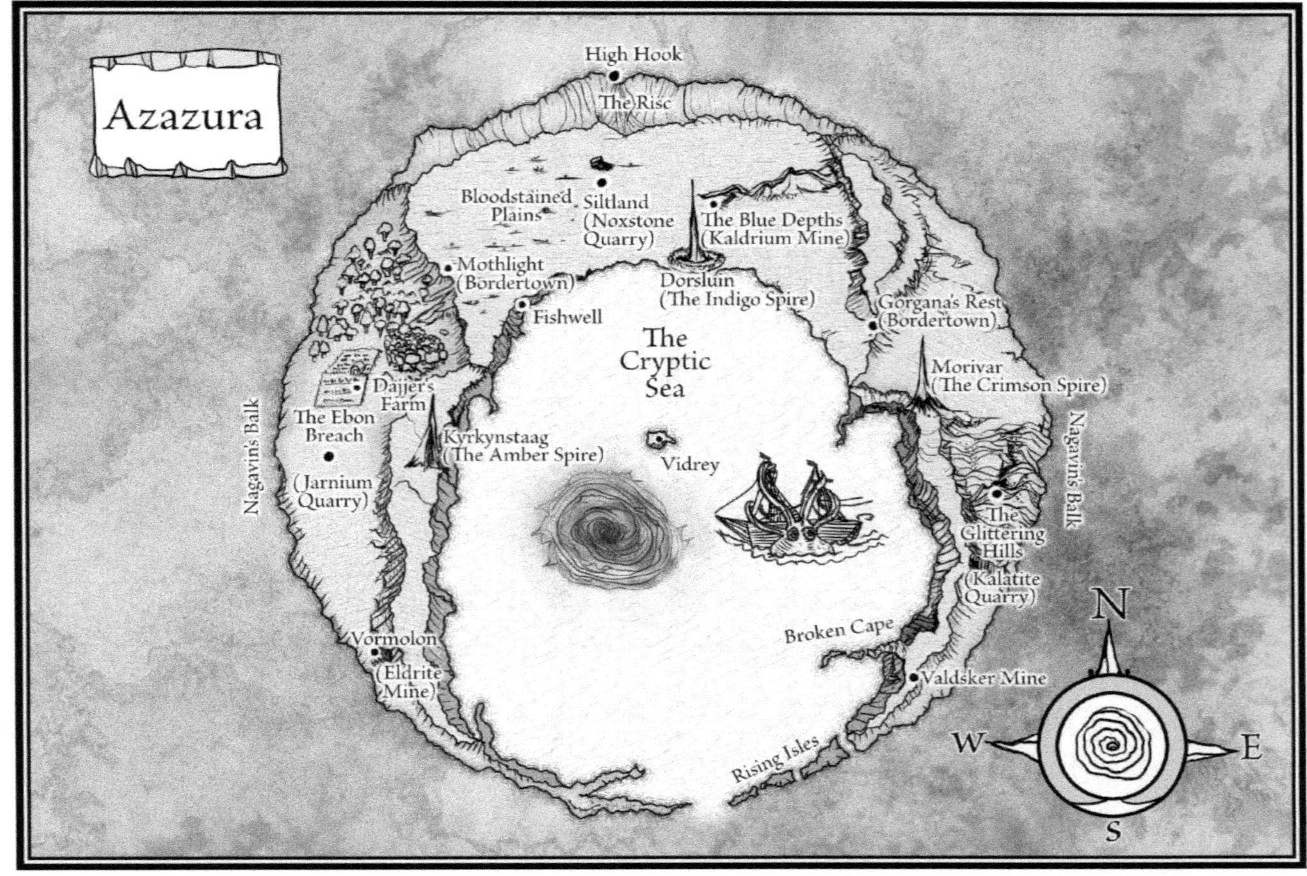
Azazura
High Hook
The Rise
Bloodstained Plains
Siltland
(Noxstone Quarry)
The Blue Depths
(Kaldrium Mine)
Mothlight
(Bordertown)
Dorsluin
(The Indigo Spire)
Fishwell
Gorgana's Rest
(Bordertown)
The Cryptic Sea
Morivar
(The Crimson Spire)
Dajjer's Farm
The Ebon Breach
Kyrkynstaag
(The Amber Spire)
Vidrey
Nagavin's Balk
(Jarnium Quarry)
Nagavin's Balk
The Glittering Hills
(Kalatite Quarry)
Broken Cape
Vormolon
(Eldrite Mine)
Valdsker Mine
Rising Isles
N
W
E
S

CHAPTER 1

Cyji was shaken awake. She lay against a tree as she had done while captive. Now no longer a prisoner, Cyji found comfort in nestling against the trunk of an aged elm. It reminded her of home and the many times she and Ralm sought solace in the forest where he stole kisses from her. A hand on her shoulder shook her again, and Cyji scolded herself for not keeping something, anything, within reach she may use for a weapon. The notion of threats and defenses against them was still new to her.

"Get up," Tulla whispered.

Cyji chased the fog from her mind as she asked, "Why? What's wrong?" She couldn't see Tulla despite being next to her. Absolute blackness enshrouded the forest. Stars peeked between tree branches overhead.

"Dajjer wants to speak to you," Tulla said.

Cyji rubbed her eyes. "Now? Can't it wait?"

"No. He means to leave before sunrise."

"Leave? For where?"

Tulla smacked her lips in annoyance, an unmistakable sound in the darkness. "I was told to get you, nothing more. If you want to know the why and where of it, you best get up so you can ask him yourself."

Cyji rose to her feet and steadied herself against the tree, still dazed from sleep. "Where is he?"

"I'll lead you," Tulla said, taking Cyji's hand to guide her along.

They moved slowly through camp. Tulla warned Cyji whenever there were tent stakes, rocks, stumps, or other obstacles to step over.

"Can you see in the dark?" Cyji asked.

"Of course not."

"How do you know where to go and what to avoid?"

"I memorized the camp's layout. I always do when we set up in a new place. Besides, we're not running through here, if you haven't noticed. Each step I take is careful. I feel with my feet as much as my hands."

"Like I do hunting," Cyji said.

"Yes, I suppose."

Tulla stopped at a dim campfire, almost all the wood burned to ash. Dying embers threw a feeble orange glow against the pressing dark.

"Cyji," came Dajjer's voice from the far side of the fire, his shape barely discernible among the night. "I mistook you for illkin when I first saw you, and because of it, you were bound and made our prisoner. That was my mistake, just as it was my mistake for going to the pool alone." At Cyji's side, Tulla grunted her agreement. "You saved my life, and that's a debt I've yet to repay."

"You already have," Cyji began. "You killed the men who were going to kill me."

"Hush, child. Don't interrupt me," Dajjer said. "You speak of your home and the trees there. You tell of a menace and needing help. Everybody in this camp has needed help, or is in need of help, and none are refused. Come with me this morning and I shall try to find the help you're searching for."

"I'll take any assistance you can provide," Cyji said.

They departed, jaunting through the dark forest. Tulla scouted ahead, slipping deeper into the all-consuming night. Dajjer led Cyji between trees, over hills and into forest dips. Night receded, yielding to dawn's granite-colored sky. At midmorning they stopped to eat a small breakfast before returning to their trek. As the sun reached its apex, they crested the peak of a long, sloping hill where trees grew spindly and sparse.

"There's the outpost," Dajjer said.

The ground dropped sharply before it flattened to become a yawning dale. It was a place devoid of trees, the ground more generous to smaller growth such as scrub grass and hardy brushes. A road snaked through the vale's center to be swallowed by the outpost—a simple building sheathed in pine slabs grayed from age and dry sap. Its roof sagged. A fence surrounded the outpost, constructed from young pines cut to a man's height, their tops sharpened to points. Any tree once populating the valley appeared to have been conscripted as part of the outpost's construction or ongoing maintenance, their stumps left behind, overtaken by course grass and stunted bush. At the gate an amber flag waved lazily in an arid wind.

"I count ten low guards, two high guards and one ascender," Tulla said, emerging from the trees to Cyji's right. It was the first time Cyji had seen her since breakfast.

Dajjer nodded as he studied the outpost. "There you are, Cyji. If you're looking for aid, the ascender stationed there reports directly to the ascendant, the most powerful person in the domain."

Cyji couldn't see the ascender, only men patrolling the fence. They reminded her of the soldiers she'd first encountered on the coast. She desired aid, but instinct warned this was not the place to find it.

"They're all like the ones we saved you from," Dajjer said, as if sensing the cause of her apprehension. "If you go down there, you'll probably never have a chance to explain who you are or what you want. They'll see you as illkin and treat you as such. They'll either capture you and take you to High Hook, or, if you're lucky, they'll kill you on sight."

"How's being killed luckier than being captured?" Cyji asked, her gaze following the guards.

"I've heard rumors about High Hook. Strange things happen there. Bad things. If only half of what they say is true about that place, you'll be begging for death within a week."

Tulla edged closer to Cyji. "I'd go down there with you, but I'd fare no better. I'm an outlaw. They'd kill me, or demand a proxy, but not before they did horrible things to me."

"Horrible things? Like what?" Cyji asked. "And what's a proxy?"

"It doesn't matter," Dajjer said. "The choice is yours. Go there and take your chances, or not."

Cyji sighed. "What choice is there? I need to find a cure, and I need to find the ones I love." She took a step forward.

Dajjer grabbed her by the elbow. "Hold on, there. You're daft, girl. Simply daft. You're not supposed to go. You're supposed to realize it's a dangerous and foolish proposition and you'll never save anything or anyone by going down there."

"If it's my only chance, I have to take it. No matter the risks." Cyji jerked her arm free of his grip.

"This is only one choice," Dajjer said. "There are others, though no more promising. But they're less dangerous."

"Why bring me here?" Cyji asked, her voice laced with irritation. "Why waste my time if there are other ways?"

"To show you all possibilities. And to warn you of the Ascendancy. You're no prisoner of mine. You're free to go where you please, but understand if you go down there, if you ever cross paths with anybody from the order anywhere, you'll be a prisoner. I mistook you for illkin. They will too. The difference is, they won't let you go." Dajjer's stare drifted upward to a cloud blotting out the sun. "We need to get moving if we plan to put some miles behind us before nightfall."

They left the rim of the valley, heading west and into the cover of forest again. There were no roads to follow, only occasional trails made by woodland creatures. Birds chirped on branches above. Squirrels chased each other up and down trees. The forest was a constant reminder of Vidrey and the trouble there. It served to quicken Cyji's pace until she found herself abreast with Dajjer rather than following him.

That evening they made camp in a small glade. Tulla returned with a rabbit she killed while scouting. Cyji didn't know how; Tulla carried only her knife. When asked, Tulla simply shrugged and muttered something about thrown blades being quicker than crafty hares. Over a fire the rabbit sizzled, its aroma rumbling the stomachs of those gathered around. Mosquitoes whined in Cyji's ears, threatening to sting. Sometimes she swatted them, sometimes the campfire smoke shifted to her direction and chased the pests away.

The next morning they breakfasted on rabbit bones before returning to their journey, and within a few hours Dajjer slowed the pace from a brisk walk to a skulking crawl where the forest sloped and ended at an expansive field. They lay prone, surveying the land. A farmhouse and barn stood in the field's center, two grim structures of neglect—exposed clapboards, roofs missing shingles and foundations sinking. Vegetables grew from pale green bushes in the surrounding field in uniform rows, tended by men and women in soil-laden clothes. They plucked ripe vegetables and dropped them into baskets slung across their shoulders. As they toiled, Low Guard watched from atop horses. When a worker paused to stretch her back and drink from a waterskin, a low guard pushed his steed into a gallop, his attention fixed hard on the loafer, and raced by, whip cracking in the farmer's general direction.

"A family once owned this farm," Dajjer said. "Food grew in abundance, enough that the farmer and his family could survive and still have plenty to sell so taxes to the Ascendancy could be paid. One year came a severe drought. The crops withered, but the Ascendancy still wanted its money. The farmer and his family were forced to flee when they couldn't pay. The order seized the land for taxes owed and brought in people to work it. Someday, when the land is barren, they'll sell it to some fool who'll try to work the soil. Someday he too will owe the order, and the cycle will start again."

"It's a strange concept…owning land," Cyji said. "On Vidrey, we share the island and all it provides."

"On an island, you must. There's not much land. Things are different here, Cyji."

She wouldn't dispute his comment. Char and chalk, indeed. "Why did the farmer not stay and work off his debt?"

"The farmer could never repay it. If he worked three hundred years he'd still owe. The order designed it that way. Those people"—Dajjer pointed to the workers in the field—"aren't slaves, but they aren't free, either. They, like the farmer, owe the order. They work to repay their debts. Unfortunately, few see that day. The order charges them rent to live in the barn, while low guards sleep in the house. The workers are charged for food they eat. See how thin they are? They choose to eat less. They can barely stand or work because of it, but the less they eat, the less they're charged and the closer they are to repaying their debts. In such a weak state, many die from working too hard. Death doesn't absolve debt, however. The order finds family and holds them responsible for what's owed. If a father dies, his daughter may find herself dragged here soon after to fulfill his obligation. Besides, how can you expect the proud farmer to work soil he no longer owned? Better he disappear and live as an outlaw."

Tulla sniffled. A lone tear streaked down her face. She quickly wiped it away. In that simple gesture, understanding struck Cyji. Dajjer wasn't telling just a story, he was telling his story.

"The farmer was you," Cyji said. "You and Tulla were the family."

Dajjer nodded solemnly. "Our home. The order came to collect. They wanted to shackle us. Fedik refused. He gave Tulla and me time to escape while he fought the Low Guard. Tulla and I fled into these woods. Fedik came later, battered and bleeding. But we were together, alive and free. Farm or not, being together is all that matters."

Tulla stared at a barn on the verge of collapse. "Do you remember, Father, when I climbed onto the roof and couldn't get down?" Cyji thought she almost saw Tulla blush at the memory.

"I do," Dajjer said. "Fedik had to climb up and get you. We had no ladder tall enough to reach the roof. How you managed to get up there in the first place, I still don't know."

"I don't know either," Tulla confessed. "I just remember putting one hand over the other until there was nothing left to grab."

Dajjer chuckled quietly. "You always were on the move. Never sitting still. And always finding trouble. My little mouse. Do you remember? I called you that."

Tulla's bent lips reflected both sorrow and joy. "I remember."

"You nearly sent your mother to the grave with all the trouble you found," Dajjer said.

"And every night she gave me the same threat," Tulla said.

And both she and Dajjer imitated in unison, "Keep this up, Tulla, and I'll drop you at the orphanage."

Father and daughter exchanged winsome grins at the shared memory. Cyji smiled too. It was good to see them remembering fondly despite the bitter reminder spread before them of what had been lost. She cherished being part of their moment.

Dajjer cocked his head toward Cyji. "So, you see, this is why the Ascendancy is my enemy. This is my problem. Not yours. It doesn't make them your enemy. But you must understand how they operate. How they are. They take and take and demand more and more. They have power, and they use it to keep the weaker under control. I was diligent in paying them, but the one year I struggled they offered no leniency. In my vulnerability, they stole my life."

In the field, a worker tugging weeds straightened and wavered. A beige dress frayed at the edges hung loose from a body worked too hard and fed too little. Her basket slipped off her shoulders as she swooned and collapsed under a blistering sun. The nearest low guard dismounted from his horse and marched to her, riding crop gripped tight in hand. He beat her exposed legs with it again and again as she howled in agony. Cyji readied to spring to the woman's defense when Dajjer stopped her.

"Stay still and stay quiet," he whispered harshly. "Or you'll get us all caught."

"We can't just watch."

"We can and we will. What do you think will happen if you go rushing in there? Do you think you'll save her? You'll only make her punishment worse, and that's only after every low guard surrounds and kills you. What good will you be, then? I don't like it either, but there's nothing we can do. This is the face of the Ascendancy, girl. Look and see the brutality. We can't help that poor woman. I want to, as much as you, but to try will get us all killed."

Dajjer tugged hard on Cyji to remove her from the hilltop. She planted herself, unwilling to ignore the woman's torture. Tulla finally coaxed her to leave. For a while, the plight of the godspear was forgotten, along with the fate of Ralm and Lavak, replaced by a simmering hatred for the Ascendancy and the suffering it caused.

"It's about time," Rosh said, sitting before a small fire. "When you said you'd be delayed, I wasn't expecting to wait three days."

"The wait did nothing for your temperament," Dajjer said, leading Tulla and Cyji into the small clearing Rosh was settled in.

"Made it worse, that's what it did," Rosh grumbled.

Fedik was there also. He rushed to Tulla and kissed her passionately. "I missed you," he said, staring wistfully into her eyes.

"It was only a few days," Tulla said.

"A few days are too many," he said. "A few days feels like a few years."

Their exchanged affections reminded Cyji of Ralm and how they behaved together. She wondered if she'd ever feel his embrace again.

No tents were pitched, but blankets lay on the ground. The small fire would do for cooking but fail in lighting the area at night or casting much warmth. No stack of seasoned firewood was present, only a small bundle of branches by the fire.

Two other men were in camp. Cyji recognized them from her time in captivity: Chep and Jerin. Chep was barely a man, perhaps in his fifteenth year, but he was anxious to prove himself like all boys his age. Jerin was his opposite. He'd entered manhood decades before Cyji was born. Moving with a deliberate gait, each step he took with profound measure, his lean muscles on the cusp of emaciation. Cyji glanced from one to the other, noting the contrasts: Chep's rosy cheeks, yet to sprout whiskers, and the deep lines carved into Jerin's gray-bearded face. The youth's eyes were bright with life, hope and a lust for the uncertain, while wisdom and suspicion had hardened Jerin's dark orbs.

"Everything ready?" Dajjer asked, inspecting the bubbling contents of a pot sitting in the coals.

"All is ready." Rosh gestured over his shoulder to where several bows and quivers, a dozen arrows in each, leaned against a tree. Some arrow shafts shimmered in the firelight. Enchanted arrows. The array of blue and black lusters was mesmerizing.

Dajjer stirred the broth with a spoon. He raised it to his lips, blew softly on it and slurped. "Needs salt."

Rosh said, "If it pleases you, my master, I'll go fetch some from the biggest salt boulder I can find. Then I'll skip over to the Pastry Forest and cut down a tart tree. Shall I scoop the topping from the raspberry or strawberry stream?"

"We'll leave at midnight," Dajjer said, setting the spoon down and ignoring Rosh's sarcasm.

"Leave? Where are we going?" Cyji asked. They only just arrived. She had been traveling for days, and though her companions appeared unaffected by the daily rigors, she was fatigued and in need of a good night's sleep. One only moved so far on an island before arriving on the other end, but Azazura was a place where a person could walk for days and never see the same place twice. Her body was well suited for felling trees but unaccustomed to such ceaseless treks.

"We need supplies," Dajjer said.

"What about the help I need?" Cyji asked.

"All part of the plan. The supplies are the first step in getting you help," Dajjer said. He studied her for a moment. "Do you know how to use a bow?"

Cyji strolled to the tree and held up a bow. It was a head taller than her. Short bows were best for hunting deer in the forests of Vidrey. The island offered few long shots. If the wind was right, she could stalk a deer to within a few paces before shooting. A pluck of the bow string produced a serenading thrum, which promised every arrow loosed would fly true with speed and power. Drawing the string, the yew flexed nicely, though stiffer than what she was accustomed to with her own shorter bow. "Of course I do. What are we hunting?"

Dajjer didn't reply. Neither did anybody else, but they all wore expressions telling of grim work ahead.

They ate, and afterward Cyji fell asleep against the bosom of a hemlock tree. It seemed she had only closed her eyes for a moment before Tulla woke her, but the stars had crawled across the cloudless sky enough to tell Cyji she'd slept for at least a few hours. The group gathered their belongings, each claiming a bow and quiver before departing. Tulla and Fedik scouted ahead and disappeared into the enveloping night.

As the first beams of sunlight touched the land, they entered an expanse of gentle hills veined by murmuring brooks. Occasionally, Rosh stopped at a water's edge to hunt frogs and crayfish. "Mmm, breakfast," he said, stuffing his catch into a makeshift creel. Cyji wrinkled her nose in disgust; not from the thought of eating frogs or crayfish, but because the poor creatures last moments of life were in the presence of Rosh's stench. "Ten or so more of each and we'll have a feast," Rosh said as he snatched a crayfish from the sandy bed of a brook. Once Rosh caught what he decided was enough frogs and crayfish, he settled beside a small pool, gathered all the twigs within arm's reach and struck a fire.

"We're close," Dajjer said. "The smoke may alert somebody. And we're late. We should be preparing."

Rosh tossed crayfish into a small pot of water. "We are preparing. We've been following our feet all night without rest or food. We'll need the energy." He finished with the crayfish and moved on to the frogs. "I'm drained. I need to eat."

Cyji sat beside the small fire and inspected her wound. It was nearly healed. Only a faint trace of pink circumscribed the scar. She touched the skin around it, feeling firm tissue but no discomfort. Pulling her shirt down, she glanced up to find Rosh grinning at her.

"Not to worry, lass. You're still pretty to me. I like women with scars. Shows they're tough." He slid two frogs onto a spit he'd fashioned from a twig.

His words did nothing to comfort her.

They ate and continued the journey. It wasn't long before they reached a hump with sharp, angular rocks jutting from it. There they crouched, hiding behind the prominences as Dajjer pointed to what lay beyond.

"Jarnium Quarry," he said.

Cyji didn't know what a quarry was, but she guessed it had something to do with the work happening about two hundred paces away. The bounding hills and sudden dips of the countryside were interrupted by a broad tract of land bared and hewn. The ground was deeply excavated. Tiers of onyx stone descended to a bottom unseen from Cyji's position. Upon them, men and women swung hammers and pick axes and deposited the results into nearby pails. Shanties clustered the lip of the uppermost step. One structure towered over the rest: a hopper, fed with the contents of pails hauled up via a series of ramps. At the base of the hopper, teams of men laboriously turned a wagon-wheel-sized millstone, their efforts producing a fine, ebony dust collected in barrels. All about the quarry, Low Guard patrolled.

"What is that stuff?" Cyji asked, watching a withered man seal a barrel.

"Jarnium," Dajjer said flatly.

"What's it for?" Cyji asked. Having never seen a quarry before, she wanted to know every detail. To scar the land so severely, the powder must certainly be important.

Dajjer shook his head. "I'm not sure, but the Ascendancy finds it valuable."

"That makes it all the more intriguing," Tulla said, using a hand to visor her face from the sunlight.

Some workers waited in line at a cauldron. Each cupped a bowl in their hands. When it was their turn to be fed, they held up a finger. The cook nodded with clear disdain on his face and poured a ladle's worth of soup into the bowl.

"What are they doing?" Cyji asked.

"Being fed," Tulla said. "Isn't it obvious?"

"Why do they hold a finger up?"

"They're telling the cook how much they want to eat," Dajjer said. "One finger equals one ladle."

Cyji turned to him. "They can eat more? But they look to be starving. I can see their ribs. Their arms and legs are thinner than pine saplings. Why don't they eat more?"

"Each serving of food is added to their debt," Dajjer said. "Just like at the farm. The more they eat, the more they owe. Workers eat only enough to survive. The rags they wear, the shoes on their feet, are bought at the storehouse over there." He pointed at a ramshackle building at the far edge of the highest tier. "They even have to pay for their tools. And the supplies aren't cheap. The Ascendancy inflates the prices, double, sometimes triple, the item's actual worth. The people don't pay up front. They take what they want or need and it's added to their debt. It means working the quarry longer, breaking stones and breaking bones. So the less they eat, the sooner they're freed. Of course, like the farm, their chances of paying off the debt before they die are slim."

It was the strangest, most corrupt notion Cyji had ever heard. In Vidrey, if somebody needed a tool, food, or clothing, they could take it from the storehouse without consequence. All work benefited the island. Debt had a different meaning there. If one owed another, it was usually a small favor. Many debts on Vidrey went unpaid and were often forgotten altogether after a while.

Cyji rested the bow on the ground beside her. "Are we going to liberate these people? Is that why we're here?"

Dajjer gave a quick snort. "No. Look at that place. It's full of Low Guard. I count twenty, and that's just what I can see. More could be in those buildings, or deep in the quarry beyond our sight. To attack would be suicide. We might kill a few, but the rest would run us down. We don't have the numbers for that kind of madness."

"Why are we here?" Cyji asked.

"For that," Dajjer said, pointing to a wagon being loaded with sacks.

With each sack tossed into the wagon, dark dust wisped out to be swept away by the wind. Men loading the sacks coughed harshly, but none paused in their work while guards with coiled whips glared from a few paces away. When the last sack was thrown onto the wagon, a low guard took his place at the reins and urged the horse forward. Four mounted Low Guard escorted.

Dajjer craned his neck and motioned to the road leading from the quarry. "The road drops behind a hill, out of sight, and forks. One leads east to the spire. The other heads south and ends at Vormolon. Jarnium is taken there and loaded onto ships headed for Morivar and Dorsluin. If it turns east, our trip is for nothing."

"And if it turns south?" Cyji asked.

Dajjer stared intently at the hill and the road rounding it to come in their direction, but he did not answer.

"What if it turns south?" Cyji repeated.

The wagon appeared from around the hill. It had turned south.

"Here we go," Dajjer whispered, excitement in his voice. "Tulla, take Cyji, Fedik and Chep. You know what to do."

"Come on," Tulla said as she sprinted away.

"Where…what…are—" Cyji started, confused.

"You better hurry," Dajjer said.

"I'm not going anywhere until you tell me what this is about," Cyji said.

"I already told you, this is about getting what we need to get the information you need. Do you still want help or not?"

"I do," Cyji said.

"Then, go. NOW! No more questions," Dajjer said.

Not wanting to be left behind but still uncertain what was happening, Cyji followed Tulla and the others. They headed in a direction opposite the quarry, dashing between hills to avoid being seen at distance before stopping atop a ridge overlooking the southern road. There, Fedik and Chep crossed to the far side and took positions behind a rock spur. Tulla crouched behind similar cover and pulled Cyji down beside her.

"What are we doing?" Cyji asked.

"Waiting."

"Why?"

"In a few minutes the wagon will pass by here. We're going to ambush it. Fedik and I will target the soldier riding the wagon. You and Chep will kill the front escorts. My father, Rosh and Jerin will attack from the rear."

"Kill the escorts?" Cyji hadn't planned to kill anybody. Now she understood what they were hunting. It wasn't deer or rabbit, but men, though the reason was still unclear. The thought of taking a life—regardless if it belonged to a low guard—didn't rest well inside her. She had killed once before: the watcher in the Cryptic Sea. It was self-defense and Cyji felt no guilt for it, but this was different. These deaths could be avoided. "Why not capture them? And what does this have to do with me and my needs?"

Tulla turned to Cyji, her features hardening. "Don't believe these men to be innocent. They've all done horrible things. They won't hesitate to kill you. Have you already forgotten what happened on the shore where we saved you?"

"No. I haven't."

"As for your needs, that'll be made clear soon. I assure you, this is a vital part of Dajjer's plan. Shh. Listen."

Thudding and creaking from up the road announced the wagon's arrival. Cyji stiffened, her heartbeat quick in anticipation and fear of what was about to happen.

"Get ready," Tulla said, drawing her bow. "Remember. Aim for the front riders."

If Cyji had more questions, they wouldn't be answered now. As the wagon passed between where the four ambushers waited, Tulla fired, the bowstring's twang the only warning before her arrow struck its mark. The low guard on the wagon let out a shrill cry, clutching the arrow buried deep in his side. Another arrow, shot by Fedik, sped through the air to strike the wagoner in his neck. The forward escorts raised spears and shields. At the rear, Low Guard shot arrows blindly at the hills.

"SHOOT!" Tulla barked as she nocked another arrow. "SHOOT!"

Cyji fumbled for an arrow with trembling hands. A forward escort snarled upon spying her, spurred his horse and charged with spear poised to thrust. Panicked by sudden, oncoming danger, Cyji let loose the arrow. It missed, flying far over his head. She raced to draw another arrow, fearing she'd be overrun first. Tulla fired, her aim true, and the guard slumped off his horse. Dajjer and the others arrived along with volleys of arrows. Soon, all the enemy were dead.

"Is anybody hurt?" Dajjer shouted as the group gathered about the wagon.

"Chep's been shot," Jerin said.

They rushed to the fallen boy. A lustrous red shaft jutted from his arm. It wasn't a lethal shot, but the boy was dead. Dajjer yanked free the arrow and tore the cloth from around the wound to reveal red, blistered skin.

"How could he be dead?" Cyji asked.

"Fire-felt," Dajjer said, examining the arrow. "Hit by one of these, any wound is fatal. The fire spreads through the body, burning flesh inside and out."

His words were true. Though Chep was dead and the arrow removed, the blistering continued to spread outward from the wound. New pustules sprouted from the skin, growing, rising, changing from scarlet to pink to white. A revolting reek soon followed, and all covered their noses in disgust.

"What is that?" Cyji asked while resisting a sudden urge to vomit.

"Burning flesh," Dajjer said.

Even Rosh shielded his nose. "You mean cooking flesh. He's being cooked from the inside out."

Flesh surrounding the wound turned brown as if roasting over an unseen fire and spread outward. Blisters popped and oozed milky pus. And still the wound spread up Chep's neck and face and throughout his body. Brown skin blackened. The stench intensified until it was unbearable. Tulla stumbled to the road's edge and gagged. In all her years hunting, all her chance discoveries of dead and decaying animals in Vidrey's forests, all the fish washed ashore to rot before seagulls reaped them, Cyji had never smelled anything more unpleasant than what she experienced now. It was an odor she'd never forget.

"We'll wrap him up. It's the only way to mask the smell," Dajjer said. He glanced around. "Nobody coming down the road. For now. We need to act quickly. Jerin, use a saddle blanket to cover Chep. Then put him on a horse. Rosh, help him."

"I don't want to," Rosh protested. "He stinks."

"So do you," Cyji said. "Now you know how the rest of us feel."

Rosh said, "I don't want to use an order's horse. If we're caught with a branded animal we'll be strung and hung."

"That'll happen if we're caught with or without the horse. Now, quit delaying," Dajjer said. "The rest of you get to work on what we came for."

It wasn't the sacks the party gave attention to, but the dead soldiers. They pulled armor and weapons from the corpses and rummaged through clothes for anything of value. When they finished, the treasure was displayed on the ground by the wagon. Dajjer crossed his arms and smiled.

"Enough for ourselves and to trade," he said. He produced a pouch and poured black dust in until it bulged. "Scatter the rest of the jarnium. Anything that deprives the Ascendancy, supports us." Sacks were sliced open and the contents broadcast across the road and into the nearby countryside.

"This was your plan?" Cyji asked. "Banditry? You tell me the Ascendancy took your farm and you repay them by killing their men and robbing the bodies?" Her outburst caused the others to halt their efforts.

"Easy, child. You're a stranger to this land and my motives," Dajjer said. "You'd be wise to stay your tongue if you expect my help."

"You offer help, but so far I'm the one expected to murder without reason. And for what? Loot?"

"The jarnium will not reach Morivar and Dorsluin now. It's no good to anybody, especially the Ascendancy. We've hurt them, though not with wounds of the flesh, but by commerce." Dajjer's voice was even and calm. "And I don't understand your refusal to kill. You said yourself you killed an ascender."

"In defense. It was either me or him."

Dajjer shrugged. "Was it any different today?"

"Yes. Yes it was." Cyji stepped toward him, arms stiff at her sides, fists white-knuckled. "This whole thing could have been avoided. Nobody needed to die, especially this boy. He was young, with a full life ahead of him. Now it's gone." A few years older and he would've been Lavak's age. "You don't mourn his loss. You care only for the spoils. What kind of man are you?"

Dajjer raised a hand as if about to slap Cyji, but he refrained. Veins bulged in his neck. His cheeks and forehead flushed. Cyji didn't flinch. She stood before him, defiant, challenging. Hand dropping heavily to his side, Dajjer released a long breath. "I will mourn for Chep. But now is not the time. Soldiers patrol this road. We must leave, now. Later, we'll remember Chep's sacrifice and celebrate his life." He locked his eyes on Cyji. His tone took a harder edge. "You need to be more grateful for what others do for you, girl. These are more than spoils. Some will be used to barter for information. The kind of information you seek. Knowledge comes at a price, either in blood or trade. I suppose things are quite different where you come from."

"Quite," Cyji said. The more she learned of Azazura, the less she liked. Char and chalk, indeed.

CHAPTER 2

"Here. I want you to have this. You've earned it," Dajjer said, holding forth the armor, a spoil from their recent ambush near the jarnium quarry.

Cyji admired the finely crafted godspear. Although the wood was black as pitch, the splinted armor shimmered pearly white as light danced across its surface. All eyes in camp turned in her direction. Those nearby gave approving smiles. Cyji didn't understand why.

"I didn't kill anybody," she said. "I didn't earn anything."

Dajjer shrugged. "Very well. You didn't earn it, but I want you to wear it anyway. You should have protection. You don't want to get killed, do you?"

Cyji accepted the armor. It was surprisingly light. The amount of godspear required to make it should have weighed twice as much. "Magic?" she said while examining it.

Rosh gave a hearty laugh. "Magic? Of course it's magic."

Cyji narrowed her eyes at the man. She didn't appreciate being patronized, especially by Rosh. There was still much to learn about Azazura and magic and a large sum of other matters. Her gaze slid to the mound of fresh dirt at the outskirt of camp. Chep's body lay beneath. Upon their return to camp, the horse was removed of its burdens and released to eventually return to the order. It was too dangerous to keep. By the time Chep was interred, the reek of cooked human flesh pervaded the camp and surrounding forest. All were affected by it, and dirt was hastily and unceremoniously thrown onto Chep's body to cover the odor. Appetites were lost because of it. In the moments before Chep was buried, Dajjer had removed the emptied sack from his face to bid a final farewell. Chep was unrecognizable. His entire body was black, but unlike Cyji's, and unlike illkin, his was charred like overcooked meat.

She insisted a tree be planted at his grave. An elm was uprooted and transplanted to the head of the grave. It was a young tree, like Chep, but would one day mature into magnificence, a chance Chep would never have. At least his death served to nourish the elm.

The thought gave her little comfort. A young man was dead and he didn't have to be. Cyji was partly responsible for it. Her need for information initiated the ambush, though Dajjer had reassured her several times on their trip back to camp it wasn't so, that the attack had been planned weeks before her arrival and what happened to Chep would've happened regardless, but his words did nothing to lessen her guilt.

"Go ahead, try it on," Dajjer said, drawing her attention from the grave.

She let the bow slip from her hand to fall gently onto the ground. Dajjer had told her to keep it and practice so she would be ready if another situation arose where she needed to defend herself. Cyji was already skilled with the bow. She could pin a squirrel to a tree at thirty paces if she wanted and was likely the best shot in the group, but she lacked the will to slay men. These bandits held that advantage over her.

Cyji slipped the armor on. It rested awkwardly on her body, riding uncomfortably on her breasts and hanging too high above the midriff. It was clearly designed to be worn by a man and not a woman. Tugging at the ends, she tried to adjust body to armor and armor to body, but no matter how she wiggled, the armor didn't fit well. She peeled it off. "I can't wear it."

Dajjer frowned. "A pity. You're in need of protection. Those buckskins won't stop an arrow."

"I'll make do," Cyji said. She saw Fedik standing there and his need of protection. "Here, take it."

Fedik stepped back. "No. Thanks, but no."

"Please, I want you to have it. You don't have armor, and I think it'll fit you." Cyji thrust the armor at him.

Tulla stepped between them. "Fedik doesn't trust magic. He never uses it. Never touches it."

"It's a tool of the order," Fedik explained. "And the less I share with the Ascendancy, the better. It's a personal choice."

"I see," Cyji said. "I'm sorry. I didn't know."

"If she ain't having it, I'll take it," Rosh said, his greasy fingers groping the armor.

"It's Cyji's to do with as she likes," Dajjer said. "Whether it fits her or not, she owns it."

Rosh gave a black-and-yellow-toothed grin. "C'mon, dear. What about it? A little gift for old Rosh?"

Cyji jerked the armor out of his reach. "No gift. However, I'll trade it for something."

"A trade? What is it you want? Maybe a kiss from Rosh?" He puckered his lips.

"Your ax."

Rosh's jesting quickly dissolved. "My ax? But I've had it since I was a lad. It's as much a part of me as my arms. I can't part with it."

"No ax, no trade. I'll keep the armor."

"No. Wait." Rosh hefted his ax and stared at it with forlorn eyes and quivering lips. "It's like parting with an old friend," he said with a sigh and passed Cyji the ax.

"Now you've a new friend." She almost felt guilty for parting Rosh from his beloved ax. Almost.

Rosh took the armor, grousing something only he heard, his

words passing lips arced in a heavy frown. Cyji's hands wrapped around the ax, a familiar feeling that comforted and homesickened her. The shaft, worn smooth from a lifetime of use, ended at a piece of steel forged into two crescent blades opposite each other. It was an impractical tool, ungainly to use in a manner suitable for felling trees. This was no woodsman's ax. It was meant for battle. She examined the edges, discovering nicks and dings possibly brought on from battle, but the ax was also a victim of Rosh's neglect. Chips on the blade and pocking on the face told the story of an ax that had served its owner well, but may have served better had some care been given to it. She ran a thumb across the blades. Both were in dire need of sharpening. She swung it a few times and found its balance different than the axes she was accustomed to using. Still, it was an ax, a better defense than her knife and a more reliable weapon than even her bow.

Tulla stepped close beside Cyji and whispered, "You know he lied to you? It's not true about the ax. He found it about a year ago on the roadside."

"That explains its condition," Cyji said. "But why lie to me about it?"

"To make it seem more valuable. You just traded magic armor for a simple ax. If he told you as much, would you've traded for it still?"

"I like axes. I can use axes. I couldn't use the armor." She studied Rosh a moment, now standing outside earshot by a campfire. He held the armor high, inspecting it, a wide grin on his cracked lips. "It won't fit him, either, so I don't see what use he has for it."

"He'll sell or trade it," Tulla said. "And it'll fetch a far higher price than your ax. I'm afraid he's duped you."

"I think it was a good deal."

"I suppose that's what's important."

"Now that's settled, let's move on," Dajjer said. "Cyji, I want you to check the snares. Trapping is a useful skill you should learn."

"I know how to set traps and snares," Cyji said. "Back home, it's something I did regularly."

"Good. It means you'll know how to reset them. If anything has been caught, bag it for dinner." Dajjer handed her a sack.

With ax in one hand, bow in the other, Cyji trudged into the woods, mumbling profanities that surprised even her. She still wasn't past Chep's death. As the forest curtained the camp behind her, Cyji's temper cooled. She needed some time alone. If she stayed at camp and dwelt on Chep, she'd likely say or do something regrettable. Besides, it was only fair she do her part in the group. After all, she'd eaten their food and shared their fire. Tending to snares wasn't the worse chore she could be given. She'd seen the toils of some of the others in camp: digging squat holes and scrubbing pots. Neither task appealed to her, and she could use this time to find a sharpening stone for her ax. Perhaps she'd do a bit of exploring as well.

The trapline was easy to locate. She hadn't been the one to set the snares, but years of trapping small game made locating them effortless. Setting snares was as much about location as it was about the snare. They could be made by just about anyone, but if it wasn't located where animals traveled, meat would never reach the table. At an early age she'd learned the skills of traps and snares and where to best use them, placing them along subtly worn paths no wider than two fingers, or around breaks in the underbrush. A diligent trapper checked her lines twice a day. This ensured she could end any struggling animal's life quickly. It also reduced the chance of another forest dweller, be it man or animal, from happening by and earning a free meal.

The first snare in the line hadn't been triggered, probably because it had been set carelessly. The sapling it connected to, meant to spring upright once the snare was triggered and suspend the captured prey, was too small. It wouldn't straighten under the weight of a rabbit or similar game. Damage to the tree was certain. After the snare was removed, the tree would suffer deformity. If it was fortunate, the tree might live to maturity, but on a gusty day, its leaves would catch too much wind and it would fall to the ground. All because of a simple, misplaced snare. A moment of grief rippled through Cyji. She wanted to relocate the snare, but she decided to leave it. The tree was already damaged. She adjusted the snare for it to catch smaller, lighter game.

At the next snare, she shook her head in frustration. It was another spring snare, not triggered, set to a more resilient sapling. The attempt was commendable, but the location was not optimum. It lay in a path used by small animals. All the signs were there, but had the snarer scouted the path only a few more feet, he would've discovered it joined with two others. Overturned leaves and disturbed soil indicated well-traveled routes. If the snare was set somewhere after the three paths converged instead of before it, Cyji would be bagging dinner right now instead of relocating the snare. As she finished setting the snare, Cyji glimpsed a flash of white from the corner of her eye.

She crouched, her keen senses sharpening as hunting instinct took command. Ears pricked at sounds of the forest: birds chirping and leaves rustling; but there was another noise as well. Stamping. Slow and deliberate. A scent teased her nose, almost familiar yet still foreign. Cyji struggled to identify it as she peered through branches and brambles of the forest weave. A deer, but it was no island deer. This animal was as tall as she, with a deep brown coat instead of the reddish fur native to her island. Antlers splayed from the top of its skull, tines curling forward. Cyji gawked, counting ten points. Vidrey bucks grew little more than nubs, incomparable to the grand crown of the magnificent beast before her. Its white tail, which initially caught her attention, flicked.

The wind shifted. Cyji adjusted, prowling behind the deer to remain downwind. If the deer caught her scent, it would spook and flee. Mindful her clothes carried odors of campfire and her own perspirations, Cyji dug her fingers into the ground, releasing the earthy scent trapped below its surface. She rubbed handfuls of rich soil onto her arms and chest to mask her smell. The deer browsed, unaware of her presence. It may be larger than deer back home, but it behaved the same, finding edibles and chewing them with its head raised in search of predators. Cyji crept from tree to tree each time the deer lowered its head to forage, its vision of her obscured by surrounding terrain. She couldn't be seen, or the deer would bolt. Hunting was about patience, and though her heart raced with anticipation, she'd long ago trained herself to quiet the urge to strike prematurely. Haste, more often than a poor shot, resulted in vegetable soup rather than venison stew.

She loved the hunt. In Vidrey, she spent many mornings tracking deer and rabbit. It didn't matter if the table needed meat. She scouted the woods unarmed sometimes just to test her skills. Cyji found new ways to challenge herself, like hunting during the dry season, when everything on the ground crunched underfoot, forcing her to move more stealthily than usual.

The deer entered a small glade, drawn to the lush vegetation growing in the center where ample sunlight nourished the forest floor. The buck lingered there, its head down as it tugged at a grassy patch with its teeth. This was it, her opportunity to slay the animal. This creature, with its marvelous crest, was hers for the taking, though Cyji didn't desire the antlers for a trophy. No. Foremost was the meat. There'd be enough venison to feed the entire camp for days. She could work the hide into buckskin. The antlers, however, would make great mementos.

Kneeling behind a tree, Cyji set her ax down and readied an arrow. She drew back the bowstring and aimed.

The buck's head jerked upright. Ears twitched. Nostrils flared. Large, dark eyes scanned the forest. Cyji stiffened, ready to make the killing shot, waiting only for the moment when the buck relaxed. The moment never came. It was alarmed, alert to danger, though Cyji had taken great care to conceal herself from all the deer's senses. The buck grunted and bounded away. For an instant, all Cyji saw was the white tail bobbing as the deer attached to it fled deeper into the woods in swift, graceful bounds. Then it was gone. Cyji slowly eased the tension on the bow before sighing her disappointment. Perhaps she was mistaken about Azazuran deer and they possessed senses superior to their smaller Vidreyan cousins.

The softest of sounds reached her ears: footsteps on forest litter. Somebody else was out here and probably the reason for spooking the deer and her failed hunt. Cyji drew back the arrow again, this time at a target she'd yet to see. Branches snapped. Movement to her right; a staggering illkin less than thirty paces away emerged from behind a tree.

Cyji stiffened. It was her second encounter with this kind of creature. The first was by the pool, when she'd saved Dajjer. Back then, everything had happened so fast. There was panic in the shadows and then the illkin was dead.

This illkin hadn't noticed her, so Cyji studied it like she would a creature to hunt. To learn the habits of an animal was to know its behavior, and understanding prey helped guarantee a successful hunt. Not that she planned to hunt illkin, but she was curious about them. The illkin before her was male, perhaps thirty years in age. His clothes appeared to have been well kept once but were now torn, ragged and heavily soiled below the knees. Yellow, vacant eyes contrasted leathery, gaunt skin as dark as Cyji's. The illkin stumbled and fell, released a raspy moan and clambered to his feet. He lurched for a moment before wandering in Cyji's direction. She hunched to hide herself.

Another few steps and the illkin paused. He raised his nose and sniffed, moaned again and proceeded. He tripped on an exposed tree root, fell, rolled onto his side and climbed back to his feet before smelling the air again. He appeared to be seeking something and relying on scent to guide him. The illkin shambled onward, pausing every few moments, sniffing the air before moving again. What was he searching for? Snatching a dry twig from the ground, Cyji snapped it, the sharp crack announcing her location. The illkin didn't react. She broke it again. Still no reaction. She rose out of hiding, revealing herself clearly to the illkin. The man gave her no regard, though his blank stare crossed fully over her. "Hey," Cyji called, and still the illkin didn't respond. Perhaps the illkin was blind and deaf. He sniffed at the air again.

Movement behind her raised the hairs on Cyji's neck. So engrossed was she with the illkin, her awareness with the rest of her surroundings had lapsed. She spun and aimed, ready to let the missile fly. Tulla emerged from the forest veil.

"You shouldn't be sneaking up on me," Cyji said, shaking the bow in her grasp. "I might have mistaken you for something else and planted an arrow in you."

"Dajjer told you to practice with it. Part of practicing is knowing your target."

"I don't need practice. I know how to use it and when. Why are you out here?"

"I've been looking for you. You were supposed to be checking the trapline."

"I was, but then I saw a deer. I was hoping we'd have venison for dinner tonight."

"Did you kill it?"

"No. Something scared it off."

A grating scream erupted behind Cyji, followed by breaking limbs and heavy footfalls. The illkin was charging her, heedless of brambles hooking his face and arms and drawing blood from countless instant scratches. Tulla gasped as she fumbled for her bow, the illkin mere paces away. Cyji fired. The arrow pierced the illkin's skull, dropping him with a sudden spray of blood. He lay motionless less than three steps from them.

What was he? Cyji wondered. He resembled a Vidreyan, though he certainly didn't behave like one. Did she just kill a man? Or something else? She glanced to a trembling Tulla, the flame-haired woman's eyes wider than Cyji had ever seen them before.

"Illkin," Tulla managed to say after a few moments. "Illkin."

"I was studying him when you came," Cyji said. "I'm sorry. I should have warned you." She knelt beside the twisted form on the ground. "It's strange. He didn't care about me, until…" She glanced at Tulla before pressing a hand against his skin. It was hot, as if he had been suffering an intense fever. "Tulla, do you have any magic on you?" Cyji waited for a response, but Tulla had yet to regain her wits. "Tulla!"

She started at the sound of her name.

Cyji asked, "Why are you so shaken? You've seen illkin before."

Her eyes met Cyji's. "I never had one attack me. His eyes…"

"Do you have any magic?"

"Yes, a little." Tulla slipped off her quiver and plucked two arrows from it. One was iron-like, the other fire-felt.

"So that's it," Cyji said. "They seek magic. They hunt it by smell. I don't have magic. That's why he wasn't interested in me. It wasn't until you got near that the illkin changed. He wasn't attacking me. He was coming for you. I happened to be in the way."

"Everybody knows they hunt magic."

"As long as I'm away from magic, illkin are not a threat."

"Correct. But magic is useful. The gains outweigh the risks."

Cyji rose, conflicted if she should bury this man and plant a tree at his grave. Despite his current condition, he was still a person. As she considered, she asked, "What brought you out here?"

"Dajjer sent me to find you."

So, this was no chance meeting. Tulla had been tracking her as Cyji stalked the deer and illkin. "Why?"

"Dajjer has arranged a meeting with a trader. Well, more a smuggler than trader. Dajjer wants you back at camp in case he needs any information you can provide to give the trader."

"Information? What can I give this trader?"

"Details. Descriptions of your brother and husband so she knows what to look for and what to ask others during her travels."

"Come on, what are we waiting for?" Cyji grabbed her

belongings in a fluid motion that didn't interrupt her stride as she darted to camp. She left the illkin unburied.

The prospect of finding Ralm and Lavak drove her at a relentless speed which no forest obstacle would impede. Cyji leapt across a brook, its banks slick with mud and moss, but she didn't stumble. Her balance was true, her footing sure, her goal certain. Only when she glimpsed camp did she slow to a brisk walk. Tulla came up beside her, breathless.

"How? How can you move so quietly?" Tulla asked. "I've been practicing since I left the farm, but I can only move quietly when I focus. You can do it at a sprint."

"Hush," said Cyji. This wasn't the time for unimportant matters. On her approach, Cyji listened for unfamiliar voices and searched for unfamiliar faces.

"They're not in camp," Tulla said.

"They're not? Then why bring me back? Where are they?"

"Dajjer doesn't trust many people, and our camp's location is always kept secret. He wouldn't bring a stranger to the campsite. If he needs you, he'll send Fedik."

"Take me to them. I'll give any information he needs."

Tulla gripped Cyji's arm. "Hold a moment. Don't forget, you've the look of illkin. That's enough to put anyone on edge. We may know you aren't, but everybody else will see you as a threat. If you go up to this trader, she just might run for her life and you'll lose a chance at finding your family. And worse, she might find the nearest low guard and report you. It's best you wait here."

They entered camp and huddled by a fire. Cyji sat down with a moan of disgruntlement while Tulla spooned stew from a pot resting on coals into two bowls. She gave one to Cyji, who accepted grudgingly. Cyji stirred the contents absently. She wasn't hungry. She was too anxious about dealings and discussions happening elsewhere without her, and dinner was as unappetizing as usual. Root and tuber stew, again. She thought of the deer. It would've been nice to dine on venison today. Even something snared, like rabbit or squirrel, to flavor the pot. Roots and tubers sustained but hardly satisfied, no matter how much spice was added to the broth.

So Cyji waited. She watched Tulla blow on each spoonful of stew before eating it. When she finished her meal, Tulla yawned, stood and brought her bowl to a stack of others waiting to be cleaned. "I've got watch tonight. I'm going to get a nap in while I can. You'll be all right here?"

"As best as I can," Cyji said.

"Good. Be patient. Fedik will come for you if needed. He may even return with good news." Without a backward glance, Tulla slipped into her tent.

Cyji had no plans concerning patience. What information could Dajjer give this trader? He'd never met Ralm or Lavak. How could he describe them?

Setting her bowl down, Cyji sprung up and casually strolled to the perimeter of the camp and began circling it. With every pass, she edged a step further away. Others in camp paid her no mind; they tended their own pursuits. Her attention alternated between Tulla's tent and the ground where she searched for markings only the land could show. So close to camp, everything underfoot was upturned by everyday activity: scuffs from children playing games of chase and deep impressions left by men hauling wood to the fires. Every expanding circle held fewer disturbances. The muddle of traffic gradually disappeared, revealing a faint trail leading into the forested west. People had gone that way. It wasn't Tulla. She was too lithe to leave signs. Dajjer, however, lacked his daughter's grace, and Rosh wasn't at camp. Both burly men were the sort to trample and mar the land without care.

She surveyed the camp. Tulla was still in her tent. Now was Cyji's chance. She dashed down the near invisible trail. Signs wove through the forest randomly. It must've been Dajjer's effort to keep the camp hidden by traveling a route that didn't lead straight from it.

The forest thinned. Hardwoods yielded to sparse and stunted

white pines rooted in increasingly dry and dusty loam until only a boulder-strewn landscape lay before Cyji, where only tufts of brittle grass and thorny bushes were allowed to root. Cyji's skills at tracking excelled in the woodlands, but the loose soil did well to hold prints in places the wind didn't reach. The trail passed between two massive boulders smoothed by weather and time. Rocks pierced the ground like fangs, sharp and chipped. She climbed an ever-steepening grade locked between a deep gorge. Risk came with each step as pebbles rolled underfoot, threatening to unbalance Cyji and send her tumbling down the hill. She crawled the last few paces, the ascent too steep to overtake upright. The ground leveled again. Sheer cliffs penned her. As Cyji rounded a bend, voices from somewhere ahead bounced off the stone. She scurried for cover behind a nearby boulder before darting to another, then another, tracing the voices back to their source. Peeking around a bend, she saw Dajjer ten paces away in a wide span of open ground, Rosh and Fedik at his side. A woman stood opposite them, a cumbersome pack strapped to her back, pots and bleached bones dangling from it.

"These are quality items," Dajjer said. He gestured to a heap at his feet, purloined from the recent ambush. "Not like the substandard fare you usually procure."

"They may be," the woman said. Her skin was tanned and wrinkled like neglected leather. Inked into the skin on her neck was a six-pointed star. "That's the problem. They've a good quality, which marks them. I won't be able to sell these easily."

"Don't give me such fables," Dajjer said. "We've known each other for too long to banter such things. You can sell these. You have in the past."

The woman shrugged, causing the load on her back to jangle and clank. She carried her burden with the ease of somebody half her age and twice her strength. "Things are different lately. The Ascendancy is more attentive. They're watchful of traders. Many I once dealt with are gone now because they were caught with contraband."

"If you can't use them, we'll keep them. I'm sure we'll find somebody else who'll trade with us."

"Now, now. I never said I didn't want them. I can take the smaller fare, but not the larger items. Keep the spears and bows and the like. For the rest, I'll pay you half what's common."

"Half?" Rosh exclaimed. "We risked our hides for these. It's a bargain at what we're offering and still you're trying to steal from us. Do you have any idea how many enemy bodies were between us and this magic?"

The woman cackled. "Bodies made dead by you, stinky man. Bodies with records of what they were issued. Bodies stripped of their magics, magics the Ascendancy will be looking for. You think it's easy to trade such things, stinky man? My troubles begin after we trade. I know collectors, and they know forgers. When I have what a collector wants, he buys it, then he hires someone to forge the proper documents of ownership. None of that is your problem, or mine. What is my problem is getting these enchantments to the collector without hassle. It's not cheap, stinky man, and I'll not lose profit because of it. Half is my offer."

"Half is fine," Dajjer said calmly. "Now, onto another matter." He unhitched a small pouch from his belt and tossed it to the woman. She opened it and scooped out a handful of powder. Her eyes gleamed.

"Jarnium. What do you want for it?" she asked.

"Information."

"I've that in excess. What kind of information?"

"There are rumors of people in Azazura. People who look like illkin, but are not. They speak as we do. Act as we do. They're not tainted by the magic, but wear the dark skin. I want to know their whereabouts."

The woman's features twisted with confusion. "Illkin who aren't illkin? Absurdity. I've never heard of such people, and I've never heard anyone else speak of them, either. I think your mind is going soft."

Cyji groaned quietly at the news, or lack thereof.

"Rumors, that's all I heard," Dajjer said. "But is there any truth to them? I'll give you half the contents of that pouch. In exchange, all you need do is keep your ears and eyes open for any information. If you find any, tell me."

The woman nodded. "Agreed, but I think you're wasting time and jarnium for nothing."

"Perhaps, but all the same, I want my curiosity sated."

"I'll keep my eyes and ears open," the woman said.

They shook hands and exchanged goods. For all the trader received, she only gave Dajjer a handful of gold coins. Cyji's eyes widened at the bedazzling metal, fascinated so little gold equaled so much magic, even at half the price Rosh expected. Still, it seemed an insulting sum compared to what Dajjer had traded.

He had, however, fulfilled his promise in seeking information regarding Ralm and Lavak, though the trader's reaction left Cyji more hopeless than ever. If there was any hope to cling onto, it was the possibility this trader may discover some information during her travels and relay it to Dajjer.

Cyji wanted to confront the woman alone, to demonstrate how she resembled illkin in appearance but not behavior. The insight might aid the trader in her search. Cyji's chance wouldn't come today. Dajjer, Rosh and Fedik soon parted ways with the woman and headed back to camp in a direction bringing them directly past where Cyji hid. She darted away before her presence was discovered.

Tulla was waiting back at camp, waiting and pacing.

"Where have you been?" she asked.

"I was looking for berries. Something sweet for a dessert. The stew is rather bland," Cyji lied.

Tulla studied her through narrowed eyes. It was possible Tulla, upon exiting her tent and finding Cyji gone, had searched for her. It was just as likely she tracked Cyji, or at least knew which direction she'd gone. If she knew the truth, or suspected it, her following words eased Cyji. "I know. You can only eat gruel for so long and stay sane. Have any luck?"

"No, but I'll keep looking," Cyji said, trying hard not to show her relief.

Dajjer and company strolled into camp soon after. "Cyji. Good news. I've someone searching abroad for your family."

Of course, Cyji already knew. She had spied on them, after all, though that was her secret, and perhaps Tulla's.

CHAPTER 3

Lavak couldn't decide which was more interesting: the beetle feces or the lenses used to study them. Fragments of the broken jar lay piled near the corner of the table, providing him a variety of curved glass. Viewing through different thicknesses of glass resulted in increased or decreased magnification. Details unseen by the naked eye were revealed under the lenses. Hidden worlds full of intricate patterns and minute lifeforms became exposed. He scrutinized everything in his lab: leaves, insects, clippings of his hair and fingernails. Everything. Under the glass, godspear wood fibers wove tightly between the grain, and in a pinch of sand hundreds of tiny fleas lived and died, never venturing beyond their minuscule domain. Magnified, the beetle appeared more menacing with enlarged barbed legs and its monstrous, sawlike mandible, offering some insights to the creature's anatomy but nothing further on how to stop the pest.

When Kuldahar and his grackles were last in Lavak's room, they had ravaged the place. The setback to his work was painful, but the lenses had been a worthwhile serendipity. Lavak had swept the glass into a pile, and as he went to collect it to throw away, he noticed a distortion in the floor beneath where two glass shards lay together. Fascinated, he handled a piece in each hand and peered through both as he varied their distance to each other. The results were extraordinary. Everything he viewed through the two lenses was magnified. The application for such a find was immediately apparent, and Lavak set to work using his new discovery to further his search for a cure. Though extremely useful, it was bothersome holding the glass pieces with both hands while trying to study his subjects. Someday after a cure was found, Lavak vowed, he'd design a device to eliminate the problem, but he'd be reluctant to share his design because of the rumors he heard about inventions being illegal in Azazura.

Beetle droppings were intriguing under the glass. To his touch it felt like silky powder. Behind lenses, another truth was revealed: the texture was coarse. Among the frass were crystals, almost unnoticeable even under magnification, their presence announced by how they glittered in the light. Lavak tried separating them from the dung, but he lacked precision tools necessary for such a delicate task.

His tormentors approached. Lavak detected the savors before he heard their voices: Jaquista's ice-kissed, Eberan's fire-felt and Kuldahar's still unidentified savor. Of all, his savor most mystified Lavak. He yearned to know its enchantment, if only to satisfy curiosity. The grackles entered their usual way, without invitation, barging in with snide and mocking words spilling from their mouths.

"Each time I see you, freak, you are lazing about. Such an easy life you have," Kuldahar said, glaring at Lavak from across the table. He held a thick book under one arm. "Not everyone in the spire has such luxury. We all work. Except you. You've mastered the craft of lagging."

Lavak didn't meet his gaze. He remained staring at the pile of droppings. Of the two, he preferred looking at beetle excrement over Kuldahar. "Perhaps if you didn't intrude on my privacy, you wouldn't be subjected to such sights."

"I'll go where I want," Kuldahar said through his teeth.

"Does that include the supreme's chambers?" Lavak risked

the other's wrath with the question. It was a delicate topic, but if Kuldahar visited his bullying upon Lavak, there was no reason the favor couldn't be returned with a verbal jab.

"When she summons me," he said. "It hasn't happened since your arrival."

"Is that so?" Lavak asked.

"You're her new pet. I've been tossed aside because of you."

"Is that how you want to be regarded? As a pet? Shouldn't you aspire for more?" Lavak prodded. So far, Kuldahar and his cronies had been all bluster and no action. They tried hurting him with words. Amateurs. He'd graduated from spoken to physical abuses by grackles on Vidrey when he was still a sprig.

"Check the place," Kuldahar ordered.

Jaquista and Eberan searched the room, tossing books on the floor and opening containers. They investigated under the table and chair before frisking Lavak.

"What's this all about?" Lavak asked, sitting again after Eberan finished patting him.

Kuldahar grinned. "An enchanted cup has gone missing from this level's kitchen. At first it was thought misplaced or forgotten somewhere, but it hasn't been found. I believe you stole it."

"Ridiculous. Why would I do that?"

"Primitives like shiny things. Or maybe you hoped to sell it."

"Which is foolish," Jaquista said. He and Eberan now flanked and crowded Lavak. "Everybody knows you need certification to sell magic."

"Only legally," Eberan said. "The freak probably hoped he could get a few rounds for it somewhere outside the city."

Kuldahar shook his head. "We never had a problem with theft in the spire until he arrived, but I don't think he's smart or ambitious enough for either. Still, no cup here. He probably hid it somewhere. He'll slip one day, and I'll catch him. I'll be watching."

Every ascender in the spire could search his room, and none would find the cup. All that was left of it was dust, and it had been brushed off the table and scattered across the floor. Lavak had planned to return to the kitchen and steal another cup, but with Kuldahar's suspicions raised, his scheme was now jeopardized.

A quick snap of pain erupted from Lavak's scalp. He shot a glance over his shoulder, finding Eberan grinning as he pinched a few of Lavak's hairs between his fingers. His tormentors had elevated to physical abuse, albeit currently only a minor annoyance.

Kuldahar leaned against the table and crossed his arms. "You've no understanding of the way things work in the spire. You're here because the supreme believes you've some kind of power. When I look at you, I see a primitive. A termite. No power. No talent. Your place here is undeserved." Kuldahar withdrew a small chunk of godspear from inside a robe pocket. "I've heard rumors. The supreme thinks you've a gift for communing with godspear. That's preposterous." He rolled the godspear in his palm, as if measuring its weight, before dropping it onto the table. "Make me believe. Talk to the wood. Tell me what it says to you."

"It doesn't work like that." Lavak tried to stand, but Jaquista's and Eberan's hands landed firmly on his shoulders, forcing him to remain seated. "This isn't a living thing. It's part of something that was once alive, but no more. And if it were a tree, I still wouldn't be able to commune."

"You admit to your lies? You confess before three witnesses?" Kuldahar said. "Just as I thought. You're a fraud."

Jaquista and Eberan chuckled behind Lavak.

Lavak carefully chose his words. "I admit that power hasn't emerged yet. I admit it may never emerge. The supreme is aware of this. I've not deceived her, or anybody else."

"You're a fraud and a freak."

"If labeling me helps ease your mind, so be it. I don't want to be here any more than you want me here. Were it not for the beetles, I'd be home right now and we'd both be happier for never having met."

Kuldahar sneered. "There it is. You don't belong here. You

agree you've no powers. Nothing makes you special."

"I can't commune with godspear trees," Lavak said. Nobody, especially Kuldahar, need know his other developments with magic. Let Kuldahar and the rest believe he was a fraud. "I agree with you. I don't belong here. If you want to be rid of me, there's a way to hasten my departure. Let's work together to find a cure. If you and I, and you two"—he tilted his head, acknowledging Jaquista and Eberan—"make a concerted effort, we can solve the problem quickly. Then, I can return home and you'll never see me again."

"I wouldn't help you if the supreme commanded it," Kuldahar said. "If I was appointed prime with the only requirement being to help you, I'd refuse."

Lavak sighed. "Why do you hate me? We both agree I shouldn't be here. We both want to see me gone, yet you still insist on hating me. Why?"

The book Kuldahar had kept tucked under his arm was now in his hand. He dropped it heavily on the table. Dust within its pages shook loose to wisp in the air. "Read this and you'll know why."

It was as thick as Lavak's hand was wide. The words *Collective Journals of Supreme Ascendants Regarding the Origins of Starwood* were embossed into the leather cover. He regarded it impassively, not wanting to give Kuldahar satisfaction despite Lavak's interest. "If I have a chance. I've more pressing concerns right now." He pushed the book aside and returned to studying the beetle frass.

Kuldahar grumbled. "If you have any sense, you'll read it soon. The reason I dislike you is in those pages, but there's more in there you'll find compelling. You'll probably thank me for it before you're finished. Not that I want your thanks, freak."

Kuldahar strode from the room, Jaquista and Eberan trailing him. Their footsteps faded, and Lavak was left alone again. He questioned his logic for traveling to Azazura. Would he have served his people better staying on Vidrey?

The book teased him, but Lavak refused to open it. Whatever it contained, Kuldahar seemed intent on Lavak uncovering the information. He doubted the ascender was being helpful. Kuldahar wanted him to find something specific. Something jarring.

"What are we?" a voice more hushed than a whisper asked.

Lavak stiffened, alarmed by the unexpected presence. He glanced behind him to find nobody there. He searched beneath the chair and table and every corner of the room, wondering if somebody had slipped inside without his knowledge. Nobody. Peeking into the hall, Lavak expected to find Kuldahar or one of his cronies pranking him. The passage was deserted. Was his mind tricking him? Was fatigue affecting his thoughts?

His focus returned to the book. If he was hearing voices, he needed a distraction. His curiosity of its contents became irresistible. Lavak yawned as he sat and pulled the book closer. "One page," he said. "I'll read one page."

CHAPTER 4

Ralm awoke disoriented, but he was becoming accustomed to waking in unfamiliar places. All his life he'd risen each morning to the known: his bed, sunlight creeping through his window, Cyji beside him. Years of routine. Of complacency. Of comfort. Of security. Yet in recent days he'd known nothing familiar, including sleeping both in a swamp and an old mine converted to an asylum. And now here, another place as foreign as the last. But where was here?

His eyelids pried open to blurred vision. He lay on a thin rug spread across a wood-planked floor. A usual discomfort greeted him: an aching back. Life on the move brought its own hardships. Soft beds were scarce, making stiff muscles plentiful. A small pillow supported his head. A thin blanket covered his body. If he were in Vidrey, he'd certainly not have been on the floor, even if he'd been so stupidly drunk as to not find the bed. Cyji would've helped him to it, though she certainly would've scolded him the next morning for his foolish intoxication. But Cyji wasn't here and he wasn't in Vidrey, or in a bed. He was on a floor. It just wasn't his floor.

Ralm's vision cleared along with his clouded mind. Crooked shapes towered around him. Books. Stacks and stacks of them. Near enough that Ralm merely needed stretch an arm to touch some. It was fortunate he wasn't a restless sleeper. A stray kick might have sent one or two or all of the stacks tumbling onto him. An embarrassing death indeed, to die under an avalanche of books. Were he a librarian, it would be a fitting end, but not for the former overseer of Vidrey. The stacks reminded him of where he was, a place slightly familiar.

He was in the sitting room of Zirrin Paladas's home. The night prior he'd arrived and met his host and family. Zirrin and Ralm spoke deep into the night, and when it was over, Zirrin offered the room for Ralm to rest. Zirrin explained there were no other accommodations, apologizing repeatedly for the lack of, which Ralm assured there was no need for and he was grateful for shelter of any sort. And indeed, Ralm was. In Vidrey, he lived a comfortable life, sleeping under the stars on occasion as a lad, but as he grew older, the softness of a bed became too appealing to forfeit. Sleeping twisted in a cramped boat at sea, on land with rocks poking into his back and in a swamp where even his dreams were soggy had humbled Ralm. Sleeping on a floor was luxurious by comparison, despite the aches visiting him upon waking, but he now appreciated the simple pleasures a bed provided.

Shadow bathed the room. Through the window the sky was a darkening blue. Twilight approached. Confusion nipped at him. How long was he asleep? It was night when he retired. Night was drawing now. Had he slept an entire day? More?

Murmurs from another room arrested his attention. A woman, her voice familiar. Memories drifted about his mind as Ralm sought a connection. Hilni. Yes, that's who was speaking. Zirrin's wife. He stood and stretched his stiff back, the long, loose-fitting nightshirt draping him failing to prevent a cool draft from snaking up his legs and thighs. Ralm shivered. Yawned. Then followed the voice. He left the sitting room and stumbled through the narrow hallway leading deeper into the house. Aromas of baking bread greeted him as he entered a warm and welcoming kitchen. Hilni tended a kettle over a fire brick while speaking to Neva, who stooped in the corner, long hair shrouding her face.

"Good evening, Ralm." Hilni smiled.

Ralm had heard only her voice and wondered if she carried the conversation for both Neva and herself. He'd yet to hear the girl speak.

"Evening? How long have I been asleep?" asked Ralm, squinting at the light.

"All day." Hilni carefully pivoted with the hot kettle before gently placing it on a trivet set upon the table. "I hope we didn't wake you."

"No, not at all. I'm sorry for sleeping so long."

"You don't need to apologize. You've had a strenuous few days. I'm sure you needed the rest." She retrieved a mug from a cupboard and set it beside the kettle. "Please, sit. Have some dinner. Or breakfast. However you want to view it."

Although Ralm vaguely remembered Zirrin explaining to him the night before his appreciation for clutter, it was contained to the sitting room. The kitchen counter was clean, the floor scrubbed and the dishes orderly. Hilni kept it tidy. Ralm sat in a chair at the table while Hilni poured tea into the mug. She sliced a loaf of bread on the counter before spreading berry preserves on the piece and presenting it to Ralm on a plate. He bit into the bread. It was warm and soft and sweetened by the spread.

"This is delicious," he said between chews.

"Thank you. The berries are only in season a short while. I preserve them so they last until the next growing season."

Ralm finished his bread and washed it down with a gulp of tea. "We have mostly raspberries in Vidrey. Some blueberries, too. And bloodberries, though they're poisonous to eat." He was reminded of Cyji's fondness for coloring the tips of her hair with a dye she created from the berries. What he'd give to see Cyji and her red-tipped hair now.

"I love raspberries," Hilni was saying. "But there aren't many bushes around Dorsluin. They're almost as expensive as magic when they're available."

"Back home, they grow in thick brambles at the edge of the forests. During the peak, there are so many it takes half the village to pick and barrel them."

"Sounds like a lot. Who gets to keep them?"

Ralm puzzled at her, one brow raised. "Everybody."

"Everybody? The berries must belong to someone. It's on somebody's land. They have rights to it."

Wiping a stray crumb from his lips, Ralm said, "In Vidrey, we all work together. The island belongs to all of us and none of us."

"I like that. Your way of life seems to benefit all your people."

"Everybody shares the harvest. We share all the land provides. No person claims it as their own."

Hilni shook her head. "That's fascinating. It's not like that here. People own things. If somebody wants what another has, they buy it. Everything is owned by somebody. The Ascendancy owns most of all."

"Scalamar told me as much. It's a strange system, this money. It seems unnecessary to use when bartering is more practical."

"Well, yes. Bartering is useful." Hilni prepared another slice of preserve-covered bread and handed it to Ralm. "But the order doesn't allow it. It still happens outside the city, but if someone is caught they're punished. The Ascendancy likes to control the flow of money."

"My money." Ralm's hand fell to his waist. His purse was gone.

"It's safe with your other belongings. That reminds me. Neva." The girl was still standing quietly in the corner. "Would you fetch Ralm's things? His clothes are on the drying rack upstairs. The rest are beside it. And check on your sister while you're there." Neva said nothing as she exited the kitchen. There was a soft thumping as the girl climbed a flight of stairs somewhere else in the house. "You'll need to excuse her," Hilni said before sipping her tea. "She's a…special child."

"That's all right. There is one like her in Vidrey." Ralm's

thoughts centered on Lavak. What had become of him? The question haunted Ralm. Since departing Vidrey, he'd lost Lavak, Cyji and his naive view of the world. Back on the island, more godspear were likely being lost every day. Loss, it seemed, was becoming commonplace in his life. Another loss was the sight of his host, which prompted Ralm to ask, "Where's Zirrin?"

"Working. He'll be home soon. He also planned while he was out to speak with some of his contacts who may help you, so he may be late."

"What work does he do?"

"He's a money lender. He loans to people who need it. And there are plenty who need it. When they repay, it's what they owe plus a small amount of interest. That interest is the money we use to live."

Iron skillets hung from pegs on the kitchen walls, herbs dried over a window, the table and chairs sturdy yet simple. All practical things, all lacking any hint of wealth. If Zirrin was a rich man, his modest dwelling hid it well. Ralm shook his head. "Money lending. Interest. Repayment. It all seems a strange way to operate. I don't mean to criticize Zirrin's livelihood. This whole system of money is something I'm still trying to understand."

"Not to worry. After hearing about life on your island, I understand your confusion. There is some bartering involved. Sometimes, people can't afford to pay Zirrin back. Most other lenders will threaten their borrowers to get their money. For every day or week a payment is missed means another day or week of interest or confiscation of possessions or even bodily harm. Zirrin is different. He forgives interest in exchange for other things. Sometimes goods. Other times, it's services. It's how he makes contacts. People owe him. They pay him back with information a price can't easily be put on. Sometimes, even with magic." She motioned to a rectangular box in the corner Ralm had overlooked until now. In the light, it cast an almost undetectable shimmer of blue. "That's maybe the best repayment Zirrin has ever brought home. It keeps food fresh for months. There's a raw slab of meat that's been in there for weeks. It hasn't spoiled yet, and as long as the lid stays on, it won't. Well, not until the magic begins to fade. Yes, Zirrin's methods have proved quite beneficial to everybody, except the order."

"Because of the bartering?" Ralm's mind swirled with the confusing fundamentals of commerce.

"Because for every transaction, the Ascendancy receives a portion of it. Zirrin must record every exchange of money, and each time he is repaid, part of the interest is given to the order. That is why bartering is outlawed. The order can't easily impose tax on it. With money, they can. So, Zirrin trades. And he alters his records so if the order ever investigates, all will appear legitimate. I only know some of the workings. Zirrin can explain it better than I."

"Is that why he hates them so much? Because they take some of his earnings?"

Hilni grimaced. "That. But something else." She bit her lip and averted her eyes. There was pain in those eyes, but Ralm was hesitant to pry.

Neva returned. In her arms were Ralm's clothes, neatly folded, his purse and knife atop the pile. She wordlessly placed them on the table.

"Thank you, Neva. Is the baby still asleep?" Hilni asked, any hint of anguish now gone. Neva nodded slightly, only her subtly swaying hair suggesting motion. "Very well, dear. Go to your room for now. I'll be up in a while." The girl skulked away. Hilni glanced at Ralm's knife. "Be careful who you show that to."

"Why?"

"Weapons must be registered." She tapped the knife she'd used to slice bread. "This is registered. It's considered a weapon. Although it's for the kitchen, it still can be used to kill somebody."

"Anything can be used as a weapon." He nodded at the kettle between them. "This could kill somebody."

"Yes, that's true. But it's the obvious weapons the order wants registered. And the cost is high, even for a simple kitchen knife. To be caught with an unregistered weapon is to be jailed and fined."

"It seems jails and fines are the order's answers for everything. The Ascendancy must be wealthy and its jails full."

"Those are truer words than you realize."

"In Vidrey, we've all manner of what would be considered weapons. Knives. Axes. Bows. There's no fear of them being used to kill. They're simply tools."

"And you have no Ascendancy to fear them. That's the difference. It seems your people work together for a common goal. That's enviable. Here, the order works toward its own means. If the population is armed, they might revolt and unseat the Ascendancy. If the order controls who has weapons, they stay in power by limiting the amount in the city. Registering a weapon is expensive, so they also make a hefty profit."

Sounds of the front door opening and shutting came down the hallway. A moment later, Zirrin entered the kitchen, a leather satchel slung over one shoulder. Features weary from a long, exhausting day revived upon seeing his wife and Ralm.

"Ah, my dearest love and my newest friend. A pleasure to behold for a working man." He slid the satchel off his shoulder and hung it on the back of a chair. "I see you're up and moving, young Ralm." He grabbed a bread slice and spread a generous helping of preserve onto it. "Feeling better?"

"Yes. Thank you."

"Good." He bit into the bread, chewed it ravenously and swallowed. "I could barely sleep last night. After all you told me, my mind was busy with thought."

"Did you speak to your contact? The one who could pilot the De' laNir?" Ralm asked.

Zirrin shook his head. "He isn't in the city. Off on some business. He's due back in a few days. I did, however, hear a rumor somebody in the city is impersonating an Ascender. I wonder who it could be?" He smiled and winked at Ralm. "If nothing else, that'll stir the Ascendancy up."

"And Ralm, if he goes out in disguise again," Hilni added.

"True. Quite true," Zirrin agreed before stuffing more bread into his mouth. "Not that it was preferable to begin with. It may be a disguise, but trotting around the city as an ascender is risky. I'd have protested future outings anyway, but now it's a certainty. That disguise of yours is no good anymore, Ralm."

"How do they know?" Ralm asked.

"Know what?" Crumbs escaped Zirrin's mouth as he spoke. "That you weren't an ascender? Witnesses marked you leaving a scene where dead soldiers lay. That's enough to alert the authorities something is amiss. Ascenders are nothing if not slaves to protocol. Never mind you handled an orphan. Ascenders wouldn't do such a thing. It's beneath them. Then, there was your exchange with another ascender at the third gate. You left quite a trail. It didn't take them long to piece things together."

"I didn't know how to act like an ascender. If I knew more about their nature, I'd have adopted it for my disguise."

"Hope you personally never learn their true nature," Zirrin said. "Supposedly, there was a fresh cairn outside the city and the body inside wasn't a soldier. The theory floating around is that corpse and this impostor were acting together to kill Low Guard."

"Wirgan," Ralm muttered. "Were it not for him, I'd never have made it here."

"So you both killed those soldiers? He'll be the lucky one if the order finds you out."

Ralm shifted uncomfortably in his chair. "I, well I—"

Zirrin smiled, exposing bits of bread and berry seeds wedged in the gaps of his teeth. "You needn't explain to me, or feel ashamed. I've no compassion for those in service of the Ascendancy. I also don't judge you for what happened. Killing isn't something I wager you take lightly."

"I did have a part in all of it."

Zirrin's expression turned grim. "There's something else. I

didn't want to tell you, but you must understand the severity of your situation."

"Tell me what?"

"Ralm, this Wirgan who helped you. Tell me, what was he like?"

"Wirgan?" Unease crept over Ralm at Zirrin's unexpected question. "He was a wild man. And deaf."

"Was he husky? Broad in body?"

"Yes. Why are you asking?"

"And his face, was it round with a wild mane of hair?"

"Yes. Why?"

Zirrin pressed his back into the chair cushion. "Ralm. I wasn't going to tell you, but you've a right to know. There's no easy way of saying this." Zirrin paused, as if struggling with how to deliver the rest of his findings. "Wirgan's body was exhumed. Soldiers removed it from the cairn, dragged the body to the city and mutilated it. They tossed it into a mass grave outside the city, but not before they cut off the head. They put it atop a pike outside the gate as a warning to any who might betray the Ascendancy."

Ralm's stomach churned, threatening to reject the bread inside. His skin grew clammy. He dizzied. Were he not already sitting, he'd have likely fainted. Wirgan was nothing but kind to him and had lost his life saving Ralm. The man didn't deserve to die, and he certainly didn't deserve the indignation of having his body desecrated or his head displayed.

"I'm sorry, Ralm. I didn't want to tell you, but I felt you should know because if you're found to be involved, you'll share the same fate."

"We need to do something, Zirrin. He deserves better. He helped me. I need to help him."

"No. That's impossible."

"Why?"

Zirrin reached under his shirt and withdrew a gold emblem hanging from a chain around his neck. The medallion was circular with the number eight in its center. "You need this. It allows passage between circles. With this, I'm allowed to travel between the ninth and eighth circle. The lower the number on these, the more places you can go. Everybody has one, and everybody is required to carry it."

"I recognize it. While looking for a way into the eighth circle, I watched an ascender check people for them. A man didn't have one and was beaten."

Zirrin nodded. "Leaving is easy and usually without scrutiny. Going inward is the difficult part. You cannot pass through an inner gate without showing one of these to the gatekeeper."

"I did."

"As an ascender," Zirrin said. "They go where they please."

"Then I will wear the robes again to go where I must."

"Absolutely not." Zirrin shook his head vigorously. "You'll not get past the gate. You may not even get far down the street. The order is looking for somebody impersonating one of their own. If you're caught, you'll join Wirgan. You need to stay out of sight. No going about in those robes. And being dark-skinned is enough to draw half the city guard, along with the screams of any citizen who sees you." Zirrin slapped the table lightly. "No, my friend. I'm afraid you're stuck under this roof until we find a way to get you home."

Ralm sighed. "I don't like the idea of Wirgan being up there. He risked his life for me. I should at least risk capture to make his sacrifice not one of shame."

"And if you're captured he'll have spent his life for nothing. Tell you what I'll do, Ralm. I'll see if I can arrange for him to disappear one night. He'll have a proper burial. A private burial. But I'll do this only if you promise you'll clear your head of anymore thoughts about going out."

Ralm groaned his dissatisfaction. "It's the best I can hope for in a bad situation. I promise."

"Good." Zirrin ate the last of his bread, licked the preserve from his fingers and prepared another slice. "In the meantime, Hilni will do what she can for you when I'm not here. Won't you, dear?"

"Of course I will," Hilni said. She laid a hand over Zirrin's forearm and squeezed gently, a smile touching her lips. "Hopefully, he won't be too bored with a wife's life."

Their subtle exchange ached Ralm's heart. Zirrin and Hilni reflected a devotion Ralm shared with Cyji. Many a time he'd spent wondering about their future. He'd daydreamed of how many children they'd have and what they'd be like. He imagined once the children were grown, he and Cyji would spend evenings holding hands by the fire watching the flames dwindle, passing each day together until death and they were joined eternally in the ground, with godspears marking their graves.

But there was another grave to fill first, without a godspear to commemorate the brave wild man to whom Ralm owed his life.

CHAPTER 5

The room was located mid-spire, with walls as thick as a horse was wide. Its location was an almost tolerable distance for Zenteezeee to travel from his chambers atop the spire. At his age, walking more than twenty steps was an arduous journey, fraught with the dangers of bone-breaking stumbles and crippling falls. He cursed the designers of the spire for their lack of foresight with the lift. Certainly, it was a marvelous piece of equipment for bringing the supreme from the base of the spire to its peak, but that's all it could do. Moving between any other floor required using the winding steps. Applying a shred of sense into the design and incorporating at least a few more stops mid-spire for the lift would've increased its usefulness and eased Zenteezeee's routine struggles.

For trivial matters, he usually sent his prime, avoiding the cramped muscles and popping joints sure to plague Zenteezeee later, when only a hot bath (a risk to enter and exit in its own right) may soothe his decrepit frame. But for affairs of torture, the ascendant willingly chanced his health. He enjoyed torture; that is, he delighted in being the torturer. He'd yet to meet a person who enjoyed being tortured. Whores in the outer circles satisfied the proclivities of men (and some women) who dabbled in carnal sufferings, but that brand of pain was playful and safe and ended when a particular word spoken signaled participants had reached their willing limit. Those upon Zenteezeee's table weren't there by choice, and the torment they experienced was neither playful nor safe and no word (and many had been uttered, screamed and blathered within these walls) slowed Zenteezeee's cutting hand.

Walls of blocked stone did well to stifle screams escaping the room, but sometimes Zenteezeee preferred the ravaged be heard by his underlings. There was no better reminder of the price for insubordination than audible torment. Currently, the door was closed. Torment was trapped inside. He wouldn't share with subordinates tonight. They'd not be reminded the dangers of failing their supreme. Torture could be public display or an intimate experience; tonight it was the latter. Zenteezeee desired privacy.

After learning at the conclave of the imperiled godspear and the missing islanders, Zenteezeee sent spies seeking any information concerning unusual encounters with uncharacteristic illkin. Never trustful of Basara or Volstrysa, Zenteezeee ordered his spies in their domains report as well. Combing the border towns of Mothlight and Gorgana's Rest yielded no results. When agents disguised as traders met a woman asking peculiar questions concerning illkin not acting like illkin, she was arrested.

Now, she lay before him. She'd been somewhere between unwashed and filthy when captured in Kyrkynstaag, reeking of odors collected during her time abroad. Zenteezeee ordered her stripped, washed and bound naked on his table. The unpleasant stench no longer clung. Her body shivered, either from the chill air, cold table, promise of torture or being exposed and vulnerable before a scabby old man. All were reasons for her to worry, and worry she did, evidenced by wide, fear-saturated eyes tracking him as he shuffled between two pedestals located on either side of the table, horrific devices of pain displayed upon them.

"Why am I here?" the woman asked, her words tremulous.

Zenteezeee ignored her. He wouldn't allow her to ruin the moment he relished more than actual torture. He fondly examined every instrument in turn: wicked contraptions and sinister blades, reflecting on the many times he'd set them to work before. This was the most satisfying moment, when Zenteezeee presented every cruel and menacing mechanism in his repertoire to his victims. He stoked their fears and had yet to draw blood. Imagination was wonderful to exploit. Show a fisherman a hook and he'll think it was to catch fish. Show the same hook to somebody on the slab and they'll not know its purpose while simultaneously conceiving every possible atrocity for which it could be applied. Such sweet torture. No popping of joints, no poking of kidneys, no pulling of teeth compared to the delicacy.

And so effective. Just the sight of his instruments spilled many a confession. Zenteezeee had heard the gamut of depravity: murder, theft, rape, incest. Crimes committed and crimes considered were freely admitted once the subject fully realized his or her dire situation.

He never made eye contact with a subject during these delicious moments. It heightened the fear when he ignored them and focused on his tools. He needn't see them to know horror was affixed upon their countenance. Often, quite often, they begged for mercy. Some were more defiant than others, spitting and cussing at him. Others trembled, like this woman, becoming so terrified their bowels released. Her bowels held. For now. She was hardy. A trader's life was an uncertain one, especially for a woman. Behind any corner might hide a bandit, or inside a dark building a rapist could lurk. This peddler, with tanned skin, coarse raven hair striated gray and a star tattooed upon her neck, was more undaunted than many of her predecessors. She hadn't yet uttered a plea or begged for release. She was brave, despite her quivering body suggesting otherwise, but bravery always vanished once the cutting began.

A single lamp hung from a chain over the table, shedding enough light for Zenteezeee to perform his macabre task but lacking strength to illuminate walls where bizarre furniture sat dark and dormant. He preferred his private chambers be fully illuminated to aid his failing vision, but here, gloom served as its own torture device. Chained to the wall in one shadowed corner, a slumped figure lay quiet and motionless, the product of Zenteezeee's previous session. Usually his subjects received only one torturing, but that pitiful flea was of special interest to Zenteezeee and so he'd receive special attention. Again and again, if necessary.

The farrier's nippers on the pedestal were especially effective at removing tips of noses and ear lobes, but it wasn't their new purpose which attracted him. They were mementos of his youth and a time when he could easily mount a horse and ride across the countryside, despite protests from fellow ascenders who scoffed at any conveyance not attached to a coach. He missed the thrill of riding. The freedom.

Zenteezeee settled for an old favorite, a simple cutting instrument with a short curved blade. He sidled along the table and hovered the blade close to the woman's face. Her eyes widened further as she struggled against the thick leather straps holding her wrists and ankles firm.

Watching his victims wiggle, trying to free themselves of their bindings, he read in their eyes the horror and denial and realization. "This can't be happening," or "I'm having a nightmare," or "If only I could turn back time and do things differently." It was always the same, and no matter a person's status, or how much wealth they amassed, they were the same as everybody else once flesh was peeled away. Torture was, if nothing else, a humbling experience.

"Please," she managed between a stifled sob and a whimper.

Appraising the condition of her body, Zenteezeee estimated she was in her fifth decade. She was lean from years of roaming, but her skin was beginning to sag under the arms and chin. The ascendant remembered his own body in that state many years ago, when his youth had abandoned him and the menace of old age drew nearer and faster each passing day. What would he give to be her age again? His position as ascendant? The spire? All of Dorsluin? Yes. He'd give everything. And more.

If this poor woman hadn't been caught, she'd probably have

enjoyed another thirty years of life. Thirty years Zenteezeee envied. Thirty years of his gone, along with another fifty. Memories of his time as an aspirant were as clear as if they had happened yesterday. His whole life was ahead of him then, an eternity to play out. Old age was a long, long time away to be troubled with when it arrived. If it arrived. Youth was tethered to a sense of invincibility. Problems of the aged didn't concern the young. Naively, he'd expected old age to happen suddenly, but time was a slow, steady and stealthy trickster which stole not in gulps but sips. Days piled upon days, and now all of Zenteezeee's were stacked in years he'd never regain.

The trader woman didn't appreciate her life, or else she wouldn't have gambled it on illegal activities. Fifty years gone. Fifty years Zenteezeee would've paid any price to have. Fifty years she was about to pay for squandering. She sickened him, like all those younger than he, all those who'd still be alive after he was gone.

He pulled the blade away and leaned close to whisper in her ear. "I'm going to ask you some questions. You will answer them. What happens after depends entirely on if I believe what you tell me. If I don't think you're telling the truth, that's when the pain begins. Do you understand?"

"Yes," the woman said, her bottom lip quivering as the word slipped past it.

"Good. Let's begin with a simple question. What is your name?"

"Dessa Nuanuun." The words spilled from her mouth in a sudden release, as if they had been perched upon her tongue waiting for the right moment to flee.

"I believe you," Zenteezeee said. "Now, something a little harder. What is the symbol on your neck?"

Her brows furrowed as she considered the question. "I don't know. It was just a design I liked."

A quick flick of his wrist and the blade sliced a short gash into her cheek. Dessa squirmed and grunted as Zenteezeee withdrew the blade.

"I don't believe you. Tell me the truth. What is the symbol?" His question slid out calm and soothing.

Dessa whimpered her response. "It's a sign, to let bandits know I'll trade with them."

He waited through several of her panicked breaths before speaking. It was another layer of torture: building the uncertainty. Finally, Zenteezeee gave a hushed, "I believe you." She was being honest. Zenteezeee had seen the symbol before, or others like it. She wasn't the first on his table with the mark, or the first to admit its meaning. "Why do you deal with bandits?"

Her eyes flitted about, trying to look anywhere but Zenteezeee's demanding stare. "They pay in gold."

"Dealing in gold and silver is outlawed. There should be no transactions involving either. Anywhere."

Dessa's body stiffened, her every muscle tense with anticipation of pain Zenteezeee was ready to give, but no lick of the blade came. Instead, he posed another question to her.

"You were found with undocumented magic in your possession. Did you acquire it from bandits?"

"No," Dessa said. "I found it…on the roadside. I planned to give them…to the proper authorities."

Another bite from the blade, this time slower, more malevolent, leaving a long tear running across her stomach. Blood wept in the blade's wake. Dessa spasmed and screamed, her only defenses against the agony.

"You say you planned to turn it over, but you were seen leaving the border town of Mothlight where ascenders and Low Guard congregate. Yet, you never approached them." The hair on Dessa's legs stood up. Fear and suffering prompted such fascinating reactions from the body. "If you didn't plan to turn the magic over to the order, what were you planning to do with it?"

Tears pooled in her eyes, overflowed and streamed down her temples. "Nothing. Like I told you, I was going to give them back."

He dragged the blade perpendicular to the freshest incision, forming a bloody *X* across her stomach. Dessa writhed, her shrieks deadened by the thick walls. Zenteezeee waited until her cries reduced to uncontrolled sobbing. "Look at me. I'm not a gullible lad, and I'm not easily swindled. Tell the truth and the hurting will end sooner."

Dessa's breaths came rapid through clenched teeth. She turned away. "No."

"No?" Zenteezeee smiled. He enjoyed defiant ones the most. Breaking the spirit was far more satisfying than wrecking the body.

He set the blade down and chose a narrow hook at the end of a short handle as its replacement. "Do you know what this is? It's a simple device used to scratch at exposed nerves, like those in the cuts I just gave you. The sensation is…overwhelming." He probed the slice in her cheek with the hook. Dessa released a tormented scream before Zenteezeee applied full pressure.

"Buyers. Collectors," Dessa stammered. Her complexion went deep red. Facial features scrunched together.

The hook wavered in Zenteezeee's frail grip. "I'm most curious about the jarnium you were found with. Where did you get it?" Dessa pressed her lips together tightly, refusing to speak. "I've more instruments you've yet to experience. Tell me what I want to know and you'll not learn of them." Still Dessa remained silent. "Very well," Zenteezeee said with pleasure. Better she not tell the truth too soon. There was still fun to be had. He set the hook on the pedestal and chose a small wooden box the size of his palm. In its bottom was a hole. Through the top a capped rod protruded. "This is one of my favorites," he said, shuffling close to Dessa. He held the box over her face. "I set this over an eye. You see that hole in the bottom? See what happens when I press the plunger on top." He did, and from the hole a metal rod telescoped out with flukes at its end. He released the plunger; the rod sprang quickly back into the box. Dessa flinched. "It plucks out your eye. So quick you won't know it happened until your sight goes black. I've not used it in a while and fear the innards are rusty from disuse, so the operation may not be as smooth as it should be." He slowly centered the box over her eye.

"No! Please. Wait. I'll tell you. Please, let me tell you." Dessa's voice was hoarse. "It was a man. A bandit."

"Who?"

"I don't know his name."

"Where did you meet him?"

"Not in his camp. Someplace isolated. In Kyrkynstaag."

Zenteezeee moved the box away from her eye. Banditry, though occasionally bothersome, was swiftly eradicated by the order. Basara's neglectfulness of his duties strayed beyond his lack in choosing a prime. Elements were traded between the spires alone, their purpose in enchanting godspear a closely guarded secret. The fleas believed ascenders could touch stars and harvest their magic. If the truth was ever revealed to be otherwise, the masses would question the ascenders' power and challenge the order. Revolution would follow.

For Basara to allow bandits a chance to steal the valuable ore suggested his failing in office. Zenteezeee savored the moment only briefly. He'd enjoy nothing more than seeing the brash and arrogant ascendant fall, but doing so might endanger all the order. Basara had always been an ambitious man, striving for power at an early age. Why falter now? Had he grown so complacent so quickly he was no longer amused with ruling? Or was Basara so smug he considered such matters as banditry trivial and beneath him?

"The folly of youth," Zenteezeee said aloud in response to his own thoughts, drawing a perplexed, bloodshot stare from Dessa. He didn't oblige an elaboration to her. "Why did you accept this payment? What good is jarnium to you?"

"I just wanted to have some."

"Jarnium is for Ascendancy use only. It's used for making the colorful glass windows in the spire." The lie dated back centuries.

"I know. But…I've a nephew." Dessa's mouth twisted, as if she said too much already, and she fell silent.

"Go on," Zenteezeee said, hovering the box over her eye.

"He enjoys working with glass. I thought…maybe…if he got some experience with using some jarnium, he could one day work glass for the Ascendancy. Please, sir, please don't hurt him. He'd nothing to do with this. He doesn't know anything about what I did. He's a good boy."

"I'm sure he is," Zenteezeee said. He'd no interest in the nephew, just as he'd no interest in the nephew coming to the spire to work glass. Those jobs were reserved for low level ascenders, which the boy in question certainly was not. "I won't seek him out, but only if you're honest with me."

"Yes. Anything."

"What else can you tell me about this bandit you met?"

Dessa stared at the box, dread hardening in every crack of her features. "You'll think it lunacy. I thought it lunacy."

"Tell me."

"In exchange for the jarnium he wanted information, but it was a strange sort. He wanted to know about illkin."

"Go on."

"He was looking for illkin, but not illkin, talking sensible like. It's lunacy. I told you it was."

"Yes. I suppose it is." Zenteezeee set the box on the pedestal and straightened his curved spine as much as his brittle body allowed, his gaze drifting about the room before resting on the shadowed form in the corner. Stray islanders weren't Zenteezeee's only concern. Recently, somebody had infiltrated his city disguised as an ascender. He didn't know who but planned to find out. He did know the mask, however. Low Guard who encountered the impostor all gave similar descriptions of it. Its lack of features made it unique. Only one person had ever worn such a featureless mask. "Why was this bandit searching for illkin not behaving normally?" he asked Dessa, his attention lingering on the body in the corner.

"He didn't say. Please, can I go now?"

Zenteezeee's gaze drifted to one of the pedestals where six slivers of godspear lay neatly arranged on a small silver tray. Each sliver held a different luster: white, black, green, red, blue and purple. They were narrow like a sewing needle, but lacked an eye to pass thread through. They wove a different tapestry, one of madness and fear. "I'm going to release you," he said.

Dessa's tormented expression turned hopeful. Such sweet torture, Zenteezeee mused. She was probably in disbelief, wondering if she'd heard him correctly as her mind shifted to freedom, forming plans to seize missed opportunities and start anew. Perhaps she'd seek out long-estranged loved ones, or right her wrongs. Zenteezeee could almost hear her thoughts as he read her expressions, a series of new vows at better living that, until a moment ago, were unreachable. Hope was now restored, and with it, a new appreciation for life.

Oh, the sweet torture he was about to impose.

"Before you're released, you must make a choice. This will be the most important choice of your life, so think carefully. If you do not choose, I will choose for you."

"Yes, Supreme. Anything." Her words jumbled together; she couldn't speak her accord fast enough.

"Good." Zenteezeee carefully lifted the silver tray, keeping his fingers far from the sharp points, and presented it to Dessa. "You must choose which enchantment I'm going to inject into you." The slumped form in the corner groaned an objection. Zenteezeee ignored it. "You might want the airy. You'll be quicker than your prey. You'll easily overtake them. Or perhaps you'd prefer the fire-felt. The rage that will grow inside you will make you fiercest of all. Or the suspension, granting you the ability to remain motionless for days. Perfect for waiting for some unsuspecting oaf to pass near before attacking."

Hope drained from her face along with the blood. This torture he prided himself in most of all, cutting deep into a person's will by first lifting their spirits high, then slamming them down. No blade or device could equal such devastation.

"Please, Supreme," Dessa said. "Not this."

Zenteezeee continued without regard to her appeal. "The iron-like will harden your skin. You'll be near impervious to mundane weapons. The ice-kissed is a particular favorite of mine."

"Please. None of them. Please." Tears gathered in widening puddles on the table beneath her. "Kill me now instead." A new puddle formed, this time between her legs as urine released.

"Or how about the most severe of them all?" Zenteezeee watched with amusement as urine snaked to the table's edge and dripped onto the floor. "Influence. A sudden dip into madness followed by an even quicker demise."

"I'll tell you anything. Ask me and I'll tell you," Dessa said. She raised her head and locked stares with Zenteezeee. "I'll do anything for you. Anything to you. Anything."

He believed her. Torture had a way of swaying a person, and the threat of becoming illkin motivated them to make outlandish promises. He'd heard the offers countless times before: betray friends and family, serve the Ascendancy in some capacity, even kill children if Zenteezeee so wished. Some—and Dessa seemed willing to join these numbers—offered their bodies for Zenteezeee to use as he wanted, whether to serve in the kitchen or the bedroom. Indeed, strange promises were spoken under duress. The tongue flapped wildly when the body was in danger. In his youth, he'd often spared the lives of women in exchange for romantic company, only to finish their torture after he'd grown bored of them. Physical desire had faded with age, but not his lust for giving pain.

Zenteezeee frowned, unmoved by her temptations. "Since you'll not choose, I will. I'm afraid you won't have a quick end. I've plans for you, and they require you stay alive for a short time."

He set the tray back on the pedestal, took up a mallet and smashed the fingers of her left hand.

Dessa wailed until her voice cracked. As her cries turned to moans, Zenteezeee used forceps to pluck the purple sliver from the tray.

"No. Please. Don't. Please," Dessa begged and sniveled.

Zenteezeee pinned her mangled fingers, now sanguine with bursts of purple and black, and jammed the needle under her fingernail. Dessa squirmed, her breaths coming fast and shallow through gritted teeth. Using the mallet, he tapped it in until the needle was completely embedded beneath the nail. Zenteezeee stepped back with a satisfied smile as Dessa sobbed uncontrollably. Her reaction was sudden awareness of a coming doom, heralded by a plunge into insanity, followed by a constant, insatiable hunger for magic. Her life, as she'd known it, was over.

What delicious torture.

A soft rapping at the door tarnished Zenteezeee's moment of delight.

"What is it?" he said irritably.

"Prime Tendarin. I've news you'll want to hear," a muffled voice came from the other side of the door.

"Come in," Zenteezeee said harshly, his pleasure soured by the intrusion.

The prime entered and closed the door behind him. Zenteezeee watched a troubled man approach. He'd known Tendarin long enough to understand when something was bothering him. Tendarin glanced at Dessa with indifference. He'd seen Zenteezeee work many times before. He'd assisted many times as well.

"I don't enjoy being disturbed here," Zenteezeee said as he examined Dessa's finger. "Whatever news you have better be paramount."

Tendarin gave a curt nod. "It is, Supreme. Our spy in Morivar has finally reported in."

"And?"

Tendarin hesitated, glancing at Dessa.

"It's fine," Zenteezeee said. "She won't repeat anything you say."

"I won't. I promise. I won't. I won't," Dessa croaked.

"You were right. The transcendent is with her. She has him

locked away in the spire."

Zenteezeee stepped away from the table. The transcendent. He'd always hated the name, given to an undeserving whelp for no reason other than his skin color. He was supposed to be special, a harbinger of change, yet so far there was nothing exceptional about him. Some in the order wagered a great deal on the flimsy theory Lavak's appearance signaled a change in species. Fanciful attentions wasted on a cowardly boy. "Let the Dark Mistress have him for now."

"What if he talks of his home to the wrong person? What if the island becomes known?"

"I doubt even Volstrysa would be so incompetent to permit that. She has as much to risk as any of us. Send word back to our spy to continue his monitoring."

Tendarin bowed. "As you command, Supreme."

"As for this one." Zenteezeee pointed casually at Dessa. "Is the kennel in need of hounds?"

Tendarin glanced at Dessa's mangled finger. "There's an abundance of suspension already. I'd have preferred airy. We've a dearth of those right now. Unfortunate I wasn't consulted prior to your…endeavors. I'd have informed you of the kennel's needs."

"I don't consult you, Prime." Zenteezeee emphasized the title, its inferiority to his own. "You consult me. Remember that."

"Forgive me, Supreme."

Zenteezeee ignored the inauthenticity of the other's apology. "Take her to the prison. Keep her there until she turns. Then, put her to use for as long as she's able. Afterward, she'll make good sport for the Low Guard. I'm sure they'll welcome the chance to engage something other than thieves and prostitutes."

"Should we release another illkin so soon after the last?"

"It never hurts to remind the people there's a price to be paid for tampering with magic and bartering with bandits."

"Most wise, Supreme." Tendarin bowed again before leaving.

Zenteezeee was enlivened. The thrill of torture had that effect on him. He was eager to continue his malice. His gaze fell on the slumped form in the corner: the perfect candidate. With box in hand, he shuffled close to the figure. "I've more questions for you, Scalamar."

CHAPTER 6

Ralm stared blankly at the chip-brick as it burned. It was a gradual burn, unnoticeable in change without a lengthy passage of time. The brick's charred and rounded edges framed an ember of glowing orange veins which were, to Ralm's benefit, entrancing and entertaining. It mirrored his current situation: tedious, uneventful, a life slowly burning away.

He sat at the kitchen table, slumped in a chair. Boredom. Within the four walls of Zirrin's home, a steady nothing passed with exhaustive lagging. Since youth, Ralm had always been active. Following his father, performing chores and running errands all had kept him busy. Even his retreats into the forest where he spent time doing nothing were hours gone quickly by, and after his arrival in Azazura, there was little time for idleness except for his brief stay in High Hook.

All that changed when Zirrin told him to stay inside and out of sight.

The sitting and waiting was maddening.

"Wasting the day watching the fire I see," Zirrin said, entering the kitchen. "I've done it on a few occasions myself. It can be quite relaxing."

"Every hour is such an occasion," Ralm said. "There's nothing to do. I've read your notes about Vidrey, corrected some and added a few. I've been through every journal."

"Every journal? That's wonderful." Zirrin's voice teemed with delight.

"It helped pass the time, if only for a while. My insanity is delayed by a few days because of it."

"I understand. It's not easy to do nothing, especially when there are things in need of doing." Zirrin slid a chair beside Ralm, its legs screeching across the kitchen floor, and sat.

"Some of your records about chip-bricks were wrong," Ralm said. "Specifically, the process in making them. When a tree is chosen to be felled, it's tapped a year earlier and the sap is collected. Wood scraps, shavings, sawdust and bark are ground up and placed in molds. Sap is poured in and left to harden. The results are chip-bricks."

"Fascinating. I've always wondered how they were made. The process is simpler than I imagined."

"Simple but effective. In Vidrey, a single brick can last well past a year if no bellows are put to it."

"That's impressive. Godspears truly are extraordinary trees. Nothing from them goes to waste."

"As little as possible," Ralm said. "It's irreverent to drop such a magnificent tree and not use every bit of it."

"You're a wise people, Ralm. Wiser than many you'll find in Azazura." Zirrin stared at the chip-brick for a moment and smiled. "It's still the most profitable payment I've ever collected."

"Hilni said that box is." Ralm gestured lazily to the corner of the room where the faintly glowing box rested.

Zirrin chuckled. "She would say that. From a practical view, she's right. It can keep food from spoiling for a very long time. From a financial view, I'm right. One of my borrowers owed me two hundred rounds. When he couldn't pay, he offered me the brick, which was unused at the time. New chip-bricks cost three to five hundred rounds, if you can get them. So, you can see how much more profitable the chip-brick is."

Ralm thought for a moment before replying. "If the box keeps food from spoiling, you can store anything in there and not have to worry about eating it right away. That means less waste, less visits to the market, less rounds spent on food." It was as much a question as an argument. He was still trying to comprehend economics.

Zirrin nodded. "That's true. But consider my savings from not buying firewood for eight months because of this wonderful little brick."

"I find the idea of paying for firewood strange. Doesn't everybody share?"

"Azazura is not communal like Vidrey, Ralm. That's especially true in the city where resources are scarce. If you haven't noticed, there aren't many trees around. Just as I do my job, there are people whose job is to go out into the country, cut and split wood and bring it back to the city to sell. Everybody has something to do, and they all do it for a price."

They stared at the chip-brick in silence for a while.

"Any word from your contact?" Ralm finally asked, already knowing his host's reply. If there was news, Zirrin would've already told him.

"Not yet."

Ralm sighed. "What's it been? Two weeks waiting so far?"

"Five days." Zirrin smirked. "Only five days. Though, I'm sure sitting here has felt like two weeks. He'll return soon. He's detained, for one reason or another. You must understand, we aren't in Vidrey. Traveling can take a long time, much longer than crossing your small island."

"I'm just restless."

"I know, Ralm. I'm doing all that I can. I haven't heard anything from him, or anything concerning your wife or her brother. It doesn't mean they aren't alive, it just means nobody knows of them or their whereabouts."

"I hope they're safe."

"I hope so too." Zirrin stabbed the chip-brick with a poker. "I do have some good news."

"I'll take all the good news I can get right now."

"Your friend, Wirgan."

Sour bile slid up Ralm's throat at the mention of the name. Wirgan had frequented Ralm's thoughts these past several days. The idea of his head on display sickened Ralm. He dared not envision its worsening condition, yet horrible images still managed to flash in his mind. Guilt over his death and current state paired with a sense of helplessness plagued Ralm, and at the peaks of his doldrums during his confinement, Ralm considered breaking his promise made to Zirrin he'd stay indoors and sneak out to try to remedy the situation.

Zirrin continued. "I arranged for his head to be removed and rejoined with the rest of him."

"How can you accomplish this?"

"Remember, people owe me. If they can't repay me in rounds, they do so in other ways. Sometimes with information, sometimes in favors. A gentleman responsible for cleaning horse dung from the streets happens to be a debtor. I paid him a visit and made an offer. In exchange for what is due, he'll, let's say accidentally, tip over the pike while he's working and the head will find its way into his cart. Any watching Low Guard will think it nothing more than the clumsiness of a doddering old man cleaning the streets. Then, like he always does, he'll leave the city to dump the waste. Wirgan's head will rejoin his body."

Zirrin's idea of good news greatly differed from Ralm's own. He was relieved to know Wirgan would finally be interred, albeit not respectfully, but the manner to reach that end seemed immoral. "Wirgan will be carted off in a pile of horse dung?"

"I know. Not very dignified, but still better than atop a spike."

"I'm grateful, Zirrin. I truly am. I just wish the circumstances were better."

"I understand. Now you must understand something as well, Ralm. The Ascendancy cares only about preserving its power. If you're discovered, you'll likely share a similar fate, regardless of your origin. That's why they tried killing you at sea. They didn't want you to know the truth. Trust in knowing Wirgan died for a greater good. He died to save you."

"I'm not worth saving."

"I disagree. And I think your people would disagree, also."

"I bet they wouldn't, considering how I left them."

"You did what you had to, Ralm. Don't ever let somebody convince you otherwise."

Silence returned. Neither Ralm nor Zirrin spoke, allowing the moments to drift past while thoughts occupied each of them. A feeling of being watched prickled the hairs on the back of Ralm's neck. He peered over his shoulder to find Neva standing there. "Oh, hello, Neva."

Zirrin snickered but didn't turn from the fire. "Neva can be as quiet as a mouse when she wants to be."

She's already as silent as one when it comes to speaking, thought Ralm.

Neva touched his shoulder lightly with a finger, pulled away, then touched him again.

"I'm not sure—" Ralm began.

"She wants to show you something," Zirrin said, still attending the fire. "Go with her, if you want."

It was the first time since his arrival Neva had given Ralm anything resembling acknowledgment. Anytime they had been in the same room, she had kept her head down, remained silent and ignored his presence. Hilni had called her shy, and Ralm accepted it for her personality. Now, she not only regarded his existence, she requested his attention. "Go with her, if you want," Zirrin had said. *Of course I want to go,* thought Ralm. The reason for Neva's change in attitude was too compelling to dismiss. He rose from his chair, legs wobbly from the past few hours of disuse.

Neva spun and left the kitchen quickly. Ralm followed. In the hall, she opened a narrow door painted to match the wall. Ralm had passed the door dozens of times as he paced between the sitting room and kitchen during his confinement. He knew it led upstairs but never dared open it. Zirrin hadn't invited him upstairs, and polite manners meant not asking and not snooping. The staircase was narrow, only a few inches wider than the span of Ralm's shoulders. He climbed, following Neva ascending with ease, before entering an equally narrow hallway at the top. They passed a room, its door partially open, and Ralm glimpsed Hilni sitting on a bed rocking the baby, Brella. If she knew Ralm was there, she made no sign. She cooed and smiled lovingly at the child. His thoughts darted to an obscure series of questions involving how any furniture (especially a bed) could have been brought to the second floor through such a narrow passage. Piece by piece, he imagined. Neva opened the door at the end of the hallway. She paused briefly, tilting her head in Ralm's direction as if to confirm he still followed, and entered. Tentatively, Ralm entered, too.

Paintings sheathed every wall, overlapping in many places. A collage of portraits, some familiar: Zirrin, Hilni and Brella, mingled with faces he didn't recognize. Simple household objects: spoons and flowers, that despite their mundane nature, were made wondrous in paint. Scenic landscapes of sweeping vistas under lavender skies and ships upon turbulent waters encroached the room's only window. On the floor, artwork four or five renderings thick leaned against every wall. Pictures crowded the ceiling, the few uncovered patches revealing the white plaster truth beneath. Scattered about the room stood several easels. Each held a portrait, giving them the appearance of strange, three-legged creatures with oversize faces but lacking arms and bodies. All about him were masterpieces, some finished, others in various stages of incompletion. The only suggestion of the room's intended purpose was the bed wedged into one corner, blanketed in both canvas and linen.

Neva ambled to the center of the room. She didn't turn to Ralm, or speak, or make any gesture, or hint as to what she wanted from him or why she brought him here. To Ralm, it was a secondary consideration at the moment. He was too awestruck by the art surrounding him to reason Neva's intentions. Ralm scanned them all, trying to absorb every image's detail at once.

"Neva, did you paint all these?" he asked.

She nodded.

"I don't know what to say. They're incredible. You have extraordinary talent."

Neva lifted an arm and crooked a finger, beckoning Ralm closer. She pointed at the nearest easel, which was facing away from Ralm. Resting on it was a portrait. His portrait. Ralm gaped. The detail was impressive. She had matched his complexion perfectly, along with his eyes and the shallow wrinkles at their corners, even the stray whiskers in his beard. It was lifelike.

"I'm flattered," he said, the words catching in his throat. "I don't know what else to say. Thank you."

At the easel was an assortment of jars, each containing a different colored paint. Beside them lay a palette and several brushes of various sizes and shapes. Neva opened some of the jars and dripped paint from each onto the palette. Using a brush, she mixed the paints, working them for a few moments, dabbing a glob, adding more from a jar, back and forth until she blended the colors to her apparent satisfaction. She gestured to Ralm, and after a moment he understood she was asking for his hand. He held it before her. She stroked the brush over it, leaving a trail of peach-colored paint on his palm.

"Why did you do that?" he asked, a bit harsher than intended.

She brushed his hand again.

Ralm flinched. "Why do you keep doing that?"

Neva stood there, slightly more hunched than before, long hair masking her face. Ralm guessed if that hair were to part, he'd find a girl scowling at him in frustration, but he didn't understand what she was trying to communicate. Neva's head rocked side to side, as if involved in an inner debate. After a moment, she stopped and turned to his portrait. She slashed her brush at it, marring his likeness with a pale streak.

"What are you doing?" Ralm couldn't believe it. Why would Neva spend time to paint his picture, only to bring him up here and destroy it? Was this why she was so quiet? Did she harbor some evil resentment for him? Did she delight in his suffering?

Another stroke to his portrait. She dipped the brush into the paint before turning on Ralm and attempting to swipe his face.

His hand wrapped around her delicate wrist, keeping the assaulting brush away from his face. "What's wrong with you?" he asked.

As she tried wriggling free, Ralm glanced at the painting again, saw the color of his skin and the contrast of the freshly applied paint and the tone of Neva's skin against his own. The paint on the brush matched her skin color.

Comprehension struck hard, but not as hard as the guilt for his ignorance of her intentions. Ralm released his grip. "Neva, I'm sorry. I understand now." Neva stepped back, lowering the brush. If she was hurt or mad, she didn't display it. "Forgive me for being so thick." She swayed and nodded. "You're a genius. A genius." She'd found a way for him to move about the city without wearing robes, masks, or showing his true identity. She could paint Ralm as if he were a canvas. A living portrait. "Neva, can you paint me now?"

She dabbed the brush in paint and brought it to his face. Short, quick strokes. Fanning. More quick strokes. The wet paint was cool on his skin and tightened as it dried, an uncomfortable feeling, but he soon became accustomed to it. She blended the paint into the skin under his beard, parting each whisker with patient artistry. His ears, neck and hands were covered, until all exposed skin was given the same pale tint. She added touches of light pink on his knuckles, earlobes and cheeks and shaded around his eyes. Neva stepped back and nodded, her way of telling Ralm she was finished and satisfied with the outcome. Without a reflective surface, Ralm couldn't see his appearance, but if his hands were any indication, he was assured Neva had done well.

"Thank you, Neva. You've no idea how much this means to me."

Anxious to try his new identity, Ralm hurried downstairs, finding Zirrin and Hilni in the sitting room. They were engaged in conversation, their words terse and rigid, their faces locked in concern. Whatever he was interrupting was important, but it was too late for retreat now. They turned as he entered, their discussion suspended momentarily, their hard expressions quickly changing to amazement.

"Spiders in spires," exclaimed Zirrin as he stared at Ralm. "Were it not for your clothes, I'd never have recognized you."

"You look like us now." Hilni said, smiling. "Neva did a wonderful job."

Ralm edged into the room. "You knew about this?"

"No, but it isn't difficult to figure out what happened," Hilni said.

"Can I go outside now?" Ralm asked gleefully. He sounded like a child asking permission from his parents to go play now that his chores were done, but he didn't care.

Zirrin and Hilni both laughed, lifting the air of seriousness stifling the room.

Husband glanced at wife, who grinned and nodded her consent. "Let's go, Ralm. I'll show you some of the sights while there's still some daylight left. Put on that coat hanging in the corner, though. I'm afraid buckskins aren't common dressage within the city walls. Light-skinned or not, going out in those will give you almost as much unwanted attention as resembling illkin."

Ralm slipped the coat on. It was heavy and warm and hung down to his knees. He started sweating almost immediately. Zirrin limped to the door, donned his own coat and a brimmed hat, grabbed his cane propped in the corner and led Ralm beyond the four walls that had enclosed him these past many days.

Outside, the street was alive with activity. From the sitting room window, Ralm had passed time watching people walk by, wondering their stories: who they were and where they were going. Now he was among them, and though he still may not know who they were, he now saw where they were going and went without regard for him. So far, Neva's disguise was a success. He passed homes hedging the curved street, noting their similarity to Zirrin's and ignoring their disrepair, content with the new views no matter how dreary they may be.

"This is the eighth circle," Zirrin said with an all-encompassing wave of his arm. "Also known as the Hillside."

"I see no hills," said Ralm.

"No hills in the literal sense." Zirrin grinned. "This circle is called the Hillside because people are either climbing up or down it socially. On the other side of that wall"—he pointed to the outer ring—"are the slums, the poor, the forgotten. They're also the folks who do the work others find least desirable. Hard labor, or foul but essential needs such as cleaning the middens."

"Yes, I traveled through it to reach you," Ralm said, remembering the squalor.

Zirrin pointed at the inner wall. "And beyond there in the seventh circle, you'll find the sculptors, philosophers, musicians and similar sorts. In the sixth circle, the more respectable likes of society inhabit. Gentlemen and ladies aspiring for propriety. They pursue work that is less, um, hands-on. But here in the Hillside, you have the trades. This is where commoners make their homes. Merchants, carpenters, masons. Without these people, the rest would fall apart."

"Why, if this place has an abundance of carpenters, are all the houses so…"

"Dilapidated?" Zirrin finished Ralm's question. "Because repairs are costly. Tradesmen do well enough to not starve by selling their services to others, but there's little leftover for their own needs. When somebody from an inner circle needs a statue for their garden, they hire a local sculptor, but it doesn't mean the sculptor has funds to make his own."

A pair of Low Guard approached, their faces as rigid as the

glowing axes in their hands. Ralm breathed through his teeth, his body stiffening as he awaited their reaction. They paid him no attention. Their gaze met his own for a brief moment, before they stomped by without a second glance. Ralm sighed in deep relief. The first real test of his disguise was a success.

"So, it's called the Hillside," Zirrin continued, oblivious to the passing guards, "because those wanting to improve their social standing must climb through here to get there, and those losing their status fall here and sometimes continue to roll until reaching the ninth circle."

"How does a person go from one circle to another?" Ralm asked, baffled by the entire concept of societal classes.

"By magic, of course," Zirrin said. "The more magic, the more prestige. Those in the ninth own nothing enchanted. However, if they come into possession of some, they can move into the eighth circle. As long as they own at least three enchanted items, they're allowed to own or rent in this circle. If while here the amount of magic owned goes under three, they must return to the ninth circle. If they work hard and obtain five enchanted items, they can move into the seventh circle. The more magic one owns, the further into the city they can live." Zirrin waggled his cane, and for the first time Ralm noticed there was a blue shimmer to it.

"What about theft? Can't somebody steal magic to elevate their status?"

"No. All magic is registered. The order knows who owns what. There are records for each transaction. They're stored in the spire. If somebody is found with magic not belonging to them, they're punished. Sometimes prison. Sometimes exile. Sometimes death."

Ralm was beginning to understand the system and how much power, control and wealth the Ascendancy gained by it. Magic was currency. It was status. It was coveted, desired, lusted. Citizens competed for it, traded for it, cheated for it. The city, perhaps the country, was built on those principles. While the masses were busy striving for dominance, the Ascendancy rested easy and profited from it all. Divide the population through competition and any hostility festering in the people against the order is forgotten.

They meandered down the street, the homes gradually thinning, replaced by busy markets and barking merchants. It was harder to walk here. Crowds swelled and dispersed like flocks of birds turning into and against the wind. Shops were of better standing than the ninth circle, with sturdier, better-maintained buildings, though faded paint and warped wood alluded to ongoing neglect. Checkered teal, blue and purple storefronts lured patrons away from those duller areas, inviting them to browse and spend beyond the colorful facades.

"Stop! By order of the supreme!" a shout came from ahead.

Ralm's heart hammered in his chest. He peered past the crowd, trying to discover the speaker, expecting he was discovered and somebody, or many somebodies, were coming for him. There was a disturbance, too far ahead and too obscured by the mass of bodies for him to see any detail other than a few helmeted heads bobbing. The crowd parted as a scraggy, shirtless man bolted through, pursued by four Low Guard. He bounded left and right around citizens. He was fast and agile and gaining distance on those chasing him. Clearing the densest throng, he sprinted down the street, directly at Ralm and Zirrin.

Three of the guards continued pursuit, but the fourth halted. He spun a sling over his head and released. A purple blur streaked through the air before impacting the fleeing man in his back. He dropped with no attempt at breaking his fall. The man simply went stiff and toppled with a heavy thud like a bag of wet sawdust.

Something tapped Ralm's foot, drawing his attention momentarily away from the downed man. The sling bullet rolled to a stop by his toes. Ralm snatched it and closed his hand tightly around it, hiding the enchantment as the guards reached the prone man. They hauled him to his feet, his eyes and mouth open, but neither moving, his face and hands striped crimson from scraping the road.

"He's broken laws one, two, five and seven," one low guard said to another.

"One?" Zirrin gasped. "Oh, no."

Ralm glanced around. Nobody was watching him. All focus was on the unfolding excitement. He opened his hand and examined the acorn-sized projectile. It was polished and perfectly round, its purple hue dim in the weakening sunlight. He stuffed it into a coat pocket.

"What are the laws he mentioned?" he asked.

Zirrin recited as if reading from a book. "Law two: assaulting an Ascendancy member. Probably resisted capture and struck a guard as he fled. Law three: evading capture from the Ascendancy. Law seven: theft of magic. Any of those are enough to see him executed."

"What about law one?"

"One?" Zirrin's thoughts seemed to be elsewhere. "Absorption of magic. That means consumption or some other way of putting magic into the body. They'll proxy him for that."

"Proxy?" Ralm waited for a reply, but Zirrin was fixated on the immediate happenings. "Maybe we should leave."

"Too late for that now," Zirrin said. "We're caught up in this."

"What do you mean?"

"We're witnesses. We have to see this to the end. Now, stay quiet."

Joining the other guards, the slinger addressed the curious onlookers. "The lawbreaker is captured. The supreme protects you. Let us take this man before an ascender for judgment."

The crowd parted, allowing guards and prisoner to pass, the latter's feet dragging behind his still motionless body, and melded again as people joined the dire procession. Ralm and Zirrin were swept along the current of bodies. Nervous whispers swirled around Ralm. He couldn't hear any words clearly, but he saw an abundance of faces heavy with fear and tearful eyes casting wary glances. The guards halted at the gate leading into the seventh circle.

"We require the ascender's wisdom and judgment," one of the guards bellowed at the gate.

A bell tolled somewhere beyond the wall. The crowd stirred and hushed. Ralm stood on his toes, peering over the many heads separating him from the activity. A gray-cloaked figure appeared at the gate, the gold mask hiding his face an abhorrent visage of exaggerated features, a luminous red staff carved into a serpent's likeness in his grip.

"You're about to see the true nature of the Ascendancy," Zirrin whispered to Ralm.

"State his crimes," a gravelly voice came from behind the mask.

"This man is suspected of possessing illegal magic, unregistered and presumed stolen," a guard said as he signaled those holding the prisoner to hoist him up. The prisoner moaned, head lolling as he blinked several times, as if waking from a deep sleep. "When I asked for a writ of ownership, he shoved me, a servant of the order, aside and fled."

"Serious charges," the ascender said. "Where is this stolen magic?"

The guard wrapped his hand around the prisoner's fingers, squeezing them together in a twisted bunch and displaying them to the ascender. "Here is the evidence. His nails are blackened by the enchanted splinters beneath them." A torrent of disapproving murmurs rushed through the crowd before quickly dying. "Not only is this undocumented magic, but he's broken the first law and implanted it into his body."

The ascender nodded. "The evidence is irrefutable. Guilt of magic absorption alone warrants imprisonment at High Hook. However, theft of magic and attacking those in the supreme's service is considered undermining his will, and therefore punishable by death. Prisoner, choose your proxy."

"No. No," the captive whimpered. He squirmed, his body no

longer succumbed to the magic's stiffening effect.

"Choose one, or I will choose five," the ascender hissed.

The guards holding the prisoner faced him before the crowd. Nobody moved. Nobody spoke. A palpable dread settled onto Ralm, though he didn't know why. All eyes fixed on the scraggy man. He held a trembling hand up and slowly straightened a bony finger. "Him," he said with regretful eyes and quivering lips.

Gasps escaped some of the spectators as two unhindered guards seized the chosen man. "Please. No," he begged while being brought before the ascender.

The guards turned him toward the people and forced him to his knees. In the ascender's hand gleamed a dagger. A chilling memory resurfaced in Ralm at the sight.

"For your crimes, you are ordered to execute your proxy," the ascender said as he handed the dagger to a guard.

The accused was brought to stand behind the kneeling man, so that he too faced the crowd. The guard forced the dagger into his hand. Dazedly, the prisoner closed his grip around the hilt, his formerly rigid body now trembling.

"Know what all know." The ascender raised a hand. "An offense against the order is an offense against everybody."

The dagger wavered in the man's grasp. Before him waited the kneeling man, with eyes flicking back and forth, chest heaving from rapid, panicked breaths. The prisoner hesitated, and the guard grabbed his wrist as if to steady and guide the blade.

"Do it now, or more will die for your crimes," the ascender said harshly.

The prisoner's gaze met the accusatory, unsympathetic and scornful stares in the crowd. For a brief moment, Ralm's and his eyes met. Ralm wanted to rush forward, to declare this event madness, but feared his own life would be in jeopardy for defending the prisoner, a man who risked and lost and was now forced to kill another for his crime. The prisoner's guilt for causing another man's demise would stay with him the rest of his sane days.

In that moment of heightened anticipation, it occurred to Ralm the contrast between Vidrey and Azazura. On his island, he was overseer. The people looked to him for answers. He was the focal point of most discontent. Here, the Ascendancy succeeded not only shifting the people's resentment away from it, but directing it on one of their own.

Blade lowered to vulnerable throat. The prisoner's eyes twitched with unbidden tears. "I'm sorry."

Ralm couldn't be certain if the words were spoken to the kneeling man or the spectators. Perhaps both. The dagger's edge rode across the man's neck. A line of red trailed the slicing blade. Blood spurted from the wound, spraying those closest to the slaughter. The proxy gurgled as he vainly covered his gushing throat before falling forward, dead. It happened in moments, though time felt to have stretched into an hour. Some of those assembled vomited. Ralm, too, felt squeamish witnessing the execution, his stomach twisting with threats to eject its contents. The guard pulled the dagger from the prisoner's shaking hand, wiped it clean and returned it to the ascender. The crowd began to disperse. Somewhere among the horrified masses, a woman sobbed uncontrollably.

Zirrin tugged at Ralm's elbow. "Let's go."

"Wait. What happens next?" Ralm asked.

"He's illkin. He's supposed to go to High Hook."

"At least Scalamar will take care of him."

"If he makes it."

"What do you mean, if he makes it?"

Zirrin glanced about. The crowd had thinned, leaving them exposed in the middle of the street. "The Ascendancy wants people to believe he's going to High Hook, but he'll never leave the city alive." Zirrin paused as two low guards dragged the corpse off the street. One called for a wagon to come and take the body while another shackled the prisoner and led him down the street and out of sight. "The Ascendancy isn't going to waste men and resources on an illkin by trotting them through the Risc. He served his purpose.

He showed the will of the order by executing his proxy."

"They brought me to High Hook."

"An outland patrol took you. That's their job. They patrol the land for illkin and bandits, among other things. Chances are, they had nothing better to do, otherwise they'd have carved you up and left you for the crows and maggots." The low guard with the sling was speaking to the ascender. He glared suspiciously at Ralm and Zirrin. "Let's go. These are matters best discussed in private." Zirrin tugged at Ralm and led him quickly from the area.

They returned home to find Hilni lighting the evening lamps to keep the gathering dusk at bay. "Tea?" she asked as Zirrin hung his hat and coat and leaned his cane in the corner.

"Mead, if there is any," Zirrin said, hobbling into the sitting room. "Ale, if there is none."

"Oh," Hilni said. In her simple response Ralm detected an understanding forged between the couple after many years of togetherness. "I believe we have some mead. Ralm, would you care for some too?"

"If it's no bother," Ralm said.

"No bother at all, dear," Hilni said as she disappeared into the kitchen.

"And fetch my pipe and leaf," Zirrin shouted down the hall.

"I will," Hilni's voice came from the kitchen faint and with a note of concern.

Zirrin fell into a chair and sighed. Worry rode hard in the lines of his face. His brow furrowed downward, his stare fixed forward. Ralm sat beside him and neither spoke until after Hilni returned with the mead, pipe and leaf.

"Here," she said, laying another pipe down on the table. "That's for you, Ralm. It's rather plain, but it smokes well."

Ralm examined the pipe. It was simple and made from applewood. "It's exactly like the pipes we use back home. Thank you."

Hilni smiled. She glanced at Zirrin, her features turning

troubled, and left the room. Zirrin said nothing until finishing his mug of mead in three deep swallows.

"I need another."

Ralm slid his mead in Zirrin's direction. "Here. Take mine."

Zirrin nodded his gratitude and drank, but left half the mug full. He set it down, wiped the liquid clinging to his lips and proceeded to pack and light his pipe. He didn't speak again until he'd taken several pulls from his pipe and the air was heavily scented by the burning leaf. "The Ascendancy. To the bottom of the sea with all of it."

Ralm leaned toward Zirrin, his elbow driving into the chair's arm cushion. "What did I just watch? What happened back there? Is that Ascendancy justice?"

"The order learned a long time ago what not to do: provoke the people. Centuries ago, people were imprisoned or executed for crimes. The problem was, hostility, no matter the wrongs of the condemned, was directed at the Ascendancy. Protests. Rebellions. All fueled by the people's outrage. The order learned from this, and a new form of justice emerged. It's what you saw today."

"All blame for misfortunes rest on the people. They're responsible for the consequences."

"A citizen executed by the lawbreaker assures it," Zirrin said. "And the Ascendancy remains untarnished by the deed."

"It's not right. Why should an innocent die for another's actions?"

"Just because something is law doesn't make it right, Ralm. Is it right sick people in the ninth circle can't enter the inner circles to be treated by physicians? Is it right to defend myself and my family, I must first seek approval from the Ascendancy to own a weapon? Laws don't always benefit the many, Ralm, and too often go unquestioned and unchallenged."

"But some laws have the people's interest in mind. Like that prisoner. He absorbed magic. He'll turn illkin and endanger people."

Zirrin puffed his pipe while Ralm spoke and continued to

puff long after Ralm went silent. He stared blankly at a pile of books Ralm had neatly arranged the day prior, allowing the silence to thicken before finally speaking. "Are you sure he willfully absorbed magic?"

"Well, no. But his fingers—"

"His fingers were blackened by magic, certainly, but have you stopped to consider why? You've seen illkin at High Hook. Didn't Scalamar tell you how they get that way?"

"He said they use magic as a means to gain power, but in the end all it does is destroy them."

Zirrin nodded. "That's true. It's also true there's magic out there small enough to swallow and it's enough to change a person." Ralm's hand fell into the jacket pocket harboring the sling bullet. He rolled it between his fingers, but left the treasure hiding inside as Zirrin continued. "What bothers me are those splinters under his nails."

"They were enchanted," Ralm said.

"Yes, but why not ingest them? Imagine the pain of hammering a splinter under each fingernail." Zirrin paused a moment to sip his mead and draw his pipe. "There are two questions pounding my thoughts right now louder than the rest. How did he get that magic, and why did the Ascendancy bother to enchant splinters in the first place?"

Ralm shrugged. "Are there purposes for enchanted slivers?"

"None I'm aware of. The order wouldn't waste its time. It cares about weapons and armor and practical goods to sell to the people. Slivers are impractical. They serve no purpose."

"Perhaps they weren't slivers at all, but sewing needles. We were too far away to know for sure."

Zirrin rubbed his chin as he thought a moment. "It doesn't make sense. The ascendant wouldn't approve sewing needles for magic. Its frivolous. There's nothing an enchanted sewing needle can do better than a non-magical one. Still, the question remains on how he acquired them."

"Stolen. Theft was one of the charges against him."

"Ten needles, one for every finger and thumb. He managed to steal the exact amount? It's too convenient. And imagine how difficult, how painful, it had to be finishing the second hand after the first was full of those things."

"Power. Isn't that why people do it?"

"I travel the city, especially the outer circles, a lot. I know that man. I don't know him on a personal level, but I've seen him before many times. He's a farrier. Or, was a farrier. A good one. Reputable. Honest. Hard-working. On several occasions he'd stand outside the stables and tell anybody willing to listen about the injustices of the Ascendancy. One day, he wasn't there, and I hadn't seen him since. Until today, almost a month later. What I don't understand is why a prosperous man disappeared for a month only to reappear haggard and inflicted by magic. It makes no sense."

"What are you suggesting?"

"I've heard rumors."

"Rumors? What sort of rumors?"

A tendril of smoke climbed from Zirrin's pipe, snaking its way to the ceiling. "Rumors of people gone missing. Rumors the ascendant conducts experiments on them. Rumors his experiments are how some illkin are made."

"Isn't tampering with magic in such a way illegal?"

Zirrin cocked an eyebrow. "It is for you, me and everyone but the ascendant. He's above the law. What happens inside the spire, only Zenteezee and his kind know for certain."

"If those rumors are true, how did the man escape the spire?"

"Maybe he didn't escape. Perhaps he was set free."

"Why would the ascendant free him?"

"What better way to remind the populace the perils of deviance than by showing them?" Zirrin said. "It's how the order keeps control. Parade an offender before the masses and judge him. Illkin appear in the city regularly, and all are dealt with similarly. Of course, this is all speculation. We'll never be certain."

"There's one way to be certain," Ralm said. "We can find where the prisoner is being held and check his fingers ourselves. Maybe ask him some questions."

"You're as mad as illkin," Zirrin said. "We can't stroll into a prison for a visit. Assuming he's not already dead, which he probably is. Quite likely lying in a ditch beside the proxy whose throat he cut."

"Let's go there then. Take a shovel, dig him up."

Zirrin drew hard on his pipe, the orange ember inside glowing bright enough to illuminate eyes filled with intense consideration. "They'll burn his body outside the city tomorrow, but there's a chance they hauled him and the proxy out there already to keep the rats and flies away. If we go, it has to be tonight."

Ralm grinned. After five days he now had a chance to escape the house a second time. His hand slipped into his pocket. "At least I have a souvenir," he said, taking the bullet out and pinching it in his fingers.

"Where did you get that?" Zirrin asked, his tone turning harsh.

"I found it in the street after the man was hit by it."

"Foolish boy." Zirrin's sudden change in demeanor startled Ralm. "Didn't you learn anything from today?"

"What do you—"

"It's magic. It's not yours. That means it's stolen."

"I didn't—"

"The Ascendancy will be looking for it. They're probably searching right now. Did anybody see you take it?"

"I don't think so."

"It's city property. Ascendant property. When it can't be found, the order will start searching homes. There'll be a lot more proxies until its return. It needs to go back, tonight."

"I'm sorry. I didn't know."

Zirrin released a long breath. "I know you didn't. I apologize for scolding you. I forget, you're not familiar with the laws here.

Having that is considered theft of magic from the ascendant himself. You'll not have a trial, or a proxy. You'll be tortured over and over before you die. And, if they find out who you truly are, well..."

"I'll return it before we go find the body."

Zirrin shook his head. "No. It's too risky. If the Low Guard are out, and they certainly are, you may be questioned if they see you."

"It's my fault. I must take responsibility, no matter the consequences. Boles and poles."

"Eh? What's that? Boles and poles?"

"It's an abbreviated expression for bent boles make poor poles. It has something to do with lacking foresight in a decision and the results of it. If you use a crooked piece of wood to make a pole, you'll get a crooked pole. What's a crooked pole good for?"

"Nothing, I suppose."

"Exactly. Boles and poles."

"Boles and poles," Zirrin repeated as if testing how it worked on his tongue. "I rather like it."

"Let me do this. I'll be careful."

"If you're caught, I won't be able to help you. You won't be able to help your island. You'll be gone. Forever."

Ralm nodded.

"You can't leave the Hillside, anyway. You won't be able to get back in without one of these." Zirrin gestured to the golden medallion about his neck. "Besides, it's best if I go find the body alone. If I'm questioned, it'll be easier for me to explain why I'm out so late. You return the bullet. Put it somewhere easily found by the Low Guard and get out of there. We'll meet back here. Be sure you don't get caught. And especially not followed."

Ralm shrugged. "It's a simple task. Go down the street, drop the bullet and come back. How hard could it be?"

CHAPTER 7

There came a knocking at the door. Volstrysa rose from her chair and straightened her robes. She ran her hands down the front and sides, forcing away any wrinkles or bunched fabric. The knocking came again. She ambled from her place behind the desk and stopped a few paces from the iron-like door, its black sheen made darker by the dim lighting of her study. She adjusted her hair until it cascaded over her shoulders evenly. Presentation was important in all aspects of life.

"Come in," she said.

The door slowly opened to reveal Lavak standing on the other side. He bowed his head, his gaze at her feet. "You summoned me, Supreme?"

Volstrysa held her hands out, beckoning him to enter. She smiled invitingly. "I did, but you don't need to be formal. Please, call me Volstrysa. Vol, if you like, though only privately. Supreme is a title and a term of respect by those beneath me. You, Lavak, aren't beneath me. We're equals."

Lavak slouched, giving him a meek disposition. He remained by the door, hesitant to enter her quarters. Volstrysa strode to a small table where two filled wineglasses waited. She took a glass in each hand and offered one to Lavak, hoping to lure him into her room.

"I don't drink alcohol," he said.

"Please, I insist. Today we celebrate, and I refuse to drink alone."

Lavak stepped cautiously through the doorway. This was his first time entering her chambers. He accepted the wine but didn't drink. "Thank you." He held the glass awkwardly, as if fearful he'd spill its contents. "What are we celebrating?"

Volstrysa tapped her glass against his in toast and sipped. "Today begins your schooling in enchantment. It's a skill required by all ascenders. They must learn how to imbue godspear with magical properties."

"I'm no ascender."

"True. You're more than that. You're the transcendent."

"For years in Vidrey, the watchers told me I was the transcendent, but they never gave an explanation. I don't understand what it means."

"You're different. You know this already. It's not just skin that separates you from other islanders. You're smarter than they are. And you've a gift. We may not have unlocked it yet, but I assure you, it's inside waiting to come out."

"I think you're mistaken. You waste your time on me. I'm undeserving of your treatment and attention."

Volstrysa smiled. "No. I'm certain you're gifted. You're special. Especially to me." She brushed her fingers across his cheek. He was a man, but still a boy in many ways. Aware of the world, yet ignorant about it. Determined, but lacking confidence. So innocent. So naive. So malleable. With enough time, she'd shape him into whatever she desired.

"I should leave," Lavak said, shrinking into himself like a shy child in a room of scrutinizing adults. "Finding a cure is my foremost priority."

"How long have you been seeking a cure?" Volstrysa asked. "Weeks? And still nothing? I've my best ascenders searching for the answer. If there's a cure, they'll find it. You've more important matters to address." There was a strange air in the spire. News of the trouble on Vidrey had spread quickly among the order, leaving every ascender and aspirant questioning a future no longer certain. All available minds were set on finding a way to stop the beetles and preserving the Ascendancy's dominance. Volstrysa sensed an approaching inevitable change. Nothing lasted forever, not godspears or governments. If efforts to save the trees failed, she needed to secure her status by other means. Her power needn't last forever, only until the end of her days. Otherwise, she may be deposed and forced into manual labor, or, if the mob ruled, executed. Lavak was vital in protecting her interests.

"Nothing is more important than saving the godspear," Lavak said.

"That's why you're here. I know if anybody will solve this problem, it's you. Lavak, you're more intelligent than my best ascenders, but without vital knowledge, you're at a disadvantage. I believe if you understand the nature of godspear and its magical properties, it will assist you in finding a cure."

"It seems an unnecessary distraction," Lavak said. "The problem is with the beetles. They attack the trees. How will learning enchantment aid me?"

Volstrysa frowned. Lavak was the keystone in her still-forming plan. If the godspear was truly doomed, its absence would cause a schism among the Ascendancy. Godspear and its magic was the foundation of the order's power. Without magic, the order was impotent. Fleas would question and challenge the current regime. Revolt would ensue. While her ascenders and those from Dorsluin and Kyrkynstaag worked to save any healthy godspear on Vidrey, she'd be a fool to believe the order's source of power was infinite. If the godspear perished and the order's control was jeopardized, Azazura might see a new era ruled by a new power. Basara and Zenteezee would fall, perhaps be torn apart by enraged fleas, but such a horrific fate was not for her.

Lavak was magic incarnate. He'd exist after the godspear were gone. People would look to him for inspiration. Volstrysa may not be supreme forever, but she refused to be less. She'd groom Lavak to become a new kind of ruler. He'd be respected and feared. All would bow to him. So would she, in public. Behind closed doors she'd manipulate him. She'd influence his decisions, prod him to action and nudge him to eliminate those questioning his authority. Lavak would be her puppet. But first, she had to attach the strings. It was why he was in her company today. Lavak still thought of the present, of finding a cure. He likely believed once a cure was discovered, he'd return to Vidrey and life for him and his people would return to normal. Things were different now, changed irrevocably for ascendant and Vidreyan alike. Each passing day proved a cure improbable, and even if one was found, the beetles' toll on the godspear already affected the order's future. Supply had diminished. Magic and power were lessened because of it. Lavak couldn't see that yet. Determination clouded his foresight. He was still unaware of his greater role. To secure her plan, Volstrysa needed to change his reasoning.

"I assure you, it's quite necessary. Knowledge of enchanting will aid you. We've tried feeding magic to beetles. They show no interest for it. The insects want only raw godspear. Why do you suppose that is?"

"I don't know."

"Which is why you must learn enchantment. Perhaps the cure is to be found there."

Lavak nodded. "It's possible, but I still think it's a waste of time. However, I am curious of the enchantment process."

"Good. Come with me."

Volstrysa relieved Lavak of his untasted wine and set both glasses on the table. Taking his hand in hers, she led him into the hall to the door for the lift. She opened it and slipped inside. Lavak joined her in the dark, tight space. Volstrysa leaned in, pressing her bosom against him as she pulled a rope. Far below, a bell rang. A moment later the platform jerked into descent.

"There are six enchantments godspear can be given,"

Volstrysa said in a sultry voice. She kept her body close to his, though it was unnecessary. Despite the cramped space, there was enough room in the lift for them to stand comfortably apart. His breaths tickled her neck. She felt him shift, nervous and uncertain from her flirtations. "Fire-felt, ice-kissed, iron-like, airy, influence and suspension. Only one type of magic can be imbued to any given object. Combining multiple elements results in an explosion during the heating process.

"Once imbued, godspear will never be stronger. The magic will only decrease. As it drains from the wood, godspear weakens both magically and physically. When all the enchantment is gone, the godspear disintegrates." The lift rocked as ropes slipped in the pulleys. Volstrysa exaggerated the motion to bump against Lavak. She rubbed her body against his. "Some enchantments are passive, such as the door to my chamber. It's iron-like. It does nothing but hang in place. Eventually, its enchantment will diminish and the wood will become so brittle, simply knocking on the door will cause it to crumble to dust. Other items use magic actively, such as weapons and wands, and the enchantment they contain is discharged with each use. A wand enchanted with fire-felt will discharge more rapidly than a door because its energy is transferred from object to target. Some magical objects have been known to crumble in a user's hands as the last of the magic was tapped from them. By comparison, that same wand could sit never used in a desk drawer and still lose its power eventually from magic seep and wood decay. Magic has a life span. The more it's used, the quicker it goes."

"How long do enchantments last?" Lavak asked.

"It depends on the skill of the enchanter and the frequency the magic is used. Some ascenders have a wonderful talent for imbuing strong enchantments. Their work is sought by many. Some creations have lasted years. Other less practiced ascenders yield magic acceptable only for sale to commoners. Not very powerful or enduring, but those items are still helpful in keeping the circulation of magic ongoing. Those pieces don't fetch high prices, allowing even the most impoverished a chance of owning some. And since they typically don't last long, the demand for magic is constant."

"It seems a conundrum," Lavak said. "To use magic means to benefit from it at the expense of losing it quickly, or stash it and lose it still, if only more slowly."

"Which is why passive magic is most desired by people. Arrows and spears work well for Low and High Guard equipment, but commoners have little need for them. An iron-like strongbox that deters theft, fire-felt plates to keep meals warm or an airy ladder for chimney sweeps to carry with ease are more prized than a full suit of armor."

The lift jolted to a stop at another door. Volstrysa swung it open and guided Lavak into the base of the spire, past the winch, its attendants and the ostentatious receiving chair before going outside. They strode across the courtyard to a two-story building sheathed in huge slabs of shale bound together with gray mortar. At the door, a pair of high guards stood, their armor of splinted wood lustrous white.

"This is where godspear is shaped. When it arrives in Morivar from Vidrey, it's brought in from the docks through a tunnel and stored beneath here."

"Do the tunnels make transporting easier?" Lavak studied the ground, as if trying to see beyond it to the godspear and tunnel below.

"Yes, but that's not the reason. When the ship arrives from Vidrey, we wait until dark to move the godspear. The tunnel prevents commoners from seeing the wood. They don't know where it comes from. The Ascendancy has perpetuated the belief it creates godspear. Here in Azazura, it's called starwood. People believe we stand atop the spire and collect it from the stars themselves." Volstrysa chuckled. The absurdity of it and the gullibility of the everyman always amused her.

"To give the illusion you have the power to harvest it. By doing so, the people consider you magical as well."

Volstrysa grinned. Lavak was a clever one. His insight to the designs of the Ascendancy was remarkable despite his isolated life on an island. "That's correct. Here, let me show you the workshops." She glanced at one of the guards. A thick-fingered hand grasped the door handle and pulled. Volstrysa sauntered inside, Lavak close behind.

The first room was small, square and unremarkable. No furniture occupied it, but along each wall leather aprons and robes hung from wooden pegs. A few staffs of various lusters shimmered against the walls.

"When you come here to work, you'll hang your robe and wear an apron in its place," Volstrysa explained. "The work can be messy, and there's no reason to sully proper attire." She moved to a door opposite the entrance and opened it. A cadence of hammering and sawing greeted them. "Do the sounds remind you of home?" Lavak nodded slowly. "Come. What's inside should be more of a reminder." She led him into a large room with a high ceiling. Lamps hung in many places, leaving no place for shadows to gather. Dozens of sturdy workbenches lined the walls, all replete with every tool needed for woodworking: hammers, saws, chisels, awls, rasps, clamps, files and more all hung in careful arrangement from nearby racks. At some of the workbenches, ascenders and aspirants busily fashioned godspear, its rich scent hanging heavy in the air. Curls and chips of wood littered the floor and were in process of being swept up by one of the younger aspirants. At the workshop's far end, an ascender worked a lathe, his foot pressing a treadle, which turned a spindle. As the block of wood spun, he passed a chisel lightly across the surface, slowly rounding his workpiece. Tucked into a corner, an aspirant sat before a pile of dull tools. Currently, his focus was on a saw blade, running a file along each of its teeth until they gleamed sharp. Beside him, a grindstone sat idle.

"Much like your home, yes?" Volstrysa raised her voice over the noise. She didn't like to; it was unbecoming of her station.

A slim man glowering over an ascender's shoulder noticed

Volstrysa and Lavak. He marched to them, arms stiff at his sides, a frown carved in his lips. The many scuffs in his leather apron suggested a lifetime of service. He'd been master of the workshop since Volstrysa was an aspirant.

"Supreme." Drudylan gave a rigid bow. "My apologies. If I knew you were coming, I'd have arranged the place to be more presentable." His voice boomed over the noise of industry. Drudylan was accustomed to carrying conversations in the loud environment.

Volstrysa waved a hand. "This place should always be presentable. Let's go where it's quieter."

"Of course, Supreme." He bowed again.

They returned to the small room with pegs and aprons, where Volstrysa introduced Lavak to Drudylan.

"Our master craftsman, Drudylan," she said. "And this is Lavak, of the island Vidrey."

"Yes, I've heard about you." Drudylan's voice boomed as if he was still in the workshop. Years of exposure to loud sounds in enclosed spaces had diminished much of his hearing. "The transcendent." He gave Lavak an appraising stare. "Knew your father, Veren. He was a fine cutter. Did my time on Vidrey before you came around. Your sister was born just before I left."

"Cyji," Lavak said. "She's every bit a…cutter, as Veren."

Drudylan grinned. "I'm sure she is. And if she wasn't born to it, your father likely made certain she learned, eh?"

"Something like that." Lavak shuffled his feet. "I'm not much of a cutter."

"Perhaps, but you're the transcendent, and that's something else entirely."

"Drudylan," Volstrysa interrupted. She didn't want this particular conversation to go further. If Lavak was to be coaxed into his position as transcendent, she didn't need Drudylan's graceless tact to interfere. Lavak was wary, she could sense it. Every mention of him being the transcendent seemed to only dissuade him. He was uncertain of his role and probably lacked confidence in his abilities.

In his fragile state, the last thing she needed was Drudylan rattling him. "Lavak is to learn the art of enchanting, so he must craft an item here first. I expect you to teach him personally."

Drudylan smiled. "Certainly. Every aspirant coming here gets my attention. I'll be sure to double it for Lavak." He leaned toward Lavak and winked. "But don't believe just because you're the transcendent, I'll be giving you special treatment. You'll go through the paces like all the others. I'll start you with something simple. Special or not, you've the basics to learn first, just like everybody else."

Volstrysa regretted not announcing her visit beforehand. A private conversation with him was needed to still his wagging tongue before she'd allow him time with Lavak, else her master craftsman may masterfully craft an indomitable reluctance in her prodigy.

CHAPTER 8

Ralm clung to the dark. Only when certain nobody was about did he cross the occasional pool of light cast by a streetlamp. Streets were deserted at this late hour; the citizens had retreated to comfortable beds and warm hearths, leaving men tasked as night sentries to meander lanes with halfhearted interest. Occasionally, they'd stop and chat with each other for a while beneath a lamp before leisurely returning to their duty. They thrust torches into dark recesses and behind leaking rain barrels, intent on illuming work deemed unfavorable by the order. Ralm tucked between a home and a wall in hope the passing guards were not suddenly inspired to probe the depth of the alley where he sheltered. They didn't, and after they disappeared around the street bend, Ralm slunk from the shadows and onto his destination.

The street seemed twice as wide without the congestion of people. Another pair of guards leaned casually against a gate ahead, conversing about matters important to guards. After a moment, they drifted through the gateway and out of sight. Ralm slid from the shadows in search of a place to lay the bullet, somewhere neither entirely hidden or in complete view, so it could be easily found tomorrow and considered overlooked today.

A booth with an open awning overhanging a broad stoop caught his attention. A perfect location. Ralm skulked close and lingered for a moment as he decided where best to drop his burden. He glanced about. Nobody was in sight. Then he heard whimpering coming from the shadows to his right. Ralm peered into the alley where a woman hunched, her back to Ralm. Her silhouetted form swayed and twitched.

Ralm edged closer. "Are you all right?"

She stopped swaying. Her head jerked in his direction. "Pain," she rasped.

"Maybe I can help." He extended a hand. "Maybe I can get you some medicine."

She sniffed like a dog catching a scent on the breeze. Slowly, she turned to Ralm and crawled out from the dark. Yellow eyes were cradled in a gaunt ebony face. Illkin. "I smell it." She snarled, and between her curled lips were teeth worn to the gums. "I smell it on you. Give it. Now!"

She lunged at him with growls, hisses and a flurry of claws. Ralm stumbled back into the street, arms raised to shield his face. The illkin tackled him, gnashing as she scrabbled Ralm. Her strength, her ferocity, surprised him. The illkin wailed as she pinned him down, sniffing his body until her nose hovered over his pocket. One black hand scratched inside and yanked the bullet free, tearing the pocket with it. She fell away from Ralm and curled up on the street, clutching the bullet. Ralm shakily stood and prepared for another attack. None came. The illkin moaned softly. She sniffed and licked the bullet and stuffed it into her mouth and tried to swallow it. The illkin gagged, the bullet lodged in the back of her throat. After coughing it out, she gnawed at it. Her nub teeth cracked and popped under the strain, the sound amplified and sickening in the hushed evening air. A tooth broke and shot from her mouth and was lost to shadow. Blood spouted from the socket the tooth once occupied. The illkin continued to chew, undaunted by the evicted tooth. All focus was on the magic.

Ralm stepped back, transfixed on the creature before him with tangled hair and a strange six-pointed star tattooed upon her neck, barely discernible amid the black skin. Dried blood at her fingertips arrested his attention. Like the man tried and punished near this very spot earlier, the woman also had godspear slivers embedded beneath her fingernails.

Their scuffle had attracted the guards. The stomp of boots echoed down the street, but the guards were not in sight yet. Ralm's body urged him to flee, but his mind bid him to collect evidence. He cast a glance down the street. Still no guards in sight. Ralm knelt beside the illkin. She growled like a dog protecting its favorite bone but otherwise showed no aggression as she continued to futilely chew on the enchanted sphere. Ralm pinned her hand and deftly extracted a sliver, though his attempt was made difficult by the illkin's squirming. The thud of boots was loud now. Shadows played on the walls, cast by men holding torches as they rushed to the source of the disturbance. Ralm slipped into the shadows and fled further down the street, his heart pounding, his legs wobbly from the encounter. He paused and turned back to see what awaited his assailant.

"Illkin!" a guard shouted.

Two guards cautiously approached the woman. With weapons drawn, they circled her. The illkin remained unaware of their presence, still bent on consuming her prize.

"Slipped away from the handler, I see," the guard said. "He'll be strung and hung if the supreme finds out."

"Keep your voice down," the other guard said.

"What's that she's got?" the first guard asked with no effort to lower his voice. "I think it's the lost bullet."

"She must've found it somewhere we missed."

"See? These illkin are good for something. Sniffing out magic. Too bad they're useless for everything else. Can't even train them, not that they live long enough to put any training to use."

A bell pealed, shattering the still of night. Four additional guards appeared from the gate and cordoned the illkin.

One of the newly arrived guards approached the illkin and

asked, "What's going on here?"

"This hound sniffed out the lost bullet. She's got it right there in her mouth."

The new guard approached her, his hand outstretched. "C'mon. Give me that bullet."

The illkin growled and recoiled at his advance.

"Give it here," he said more firmly.

"She doesn't understand you," the first low guard said. "The hound will never give it up willingly."

The new guard stepped forward and landed a swift and solid kick into the illkin's midsection. She screeched a sound no sane woman was capable of making, bolted upright and slashed defensively at those surrounding her. The guards reacted with wild swings, beating her with fists and clubs. The illkin howled as she punched a guard in the chest. Another guard grappled the woman from behind, arms squeezing tight around her. Two more guards inflicted a series of blows to the illkin's face and chest. She spat at them. Blood launched from the void a tooth once occupied to spray eyes. She wriggled free of the hold, spun and bit into the man's neck. With teeth sunk in, she reeled, tearing free a chunk of flesh. Blood from the wound squirted upward like a macabre fountain. He screamed and fell to the ground, quaking hand clutching a blood-sodden neck.

The illkin hissed at the remaining soldiers as they encircled her. While three stalked her sides and front, another moved behind. He inched close and brought his club high before swinging down. The weapon struck the top of the illkin's head with a loud, nauseating crunch. The illkin dropped to the ground in a twitching heap. All the Low Guard stomped her under their boots and didn't cease until no more twitches or groans came from the body.

Ralm fled.

He was more careless returning to Zirrin's home than wisdom advised, risking premature departures from harboring refuges before fully surveying each length of street for possible threats. His encounter with the illkin had shaken Ralm's nerves and rattled his sensibilities. He desired only to distance himself from the illkin, the Low Guard and the ringing bell.

Back at Zirrin's home, Ralm sank into a sitting room chair. His heartbeat slowed. His mind cleared. His breathing calmed. Zirrin wasn't there. In the late hour, his house was eerie with its placid atmosphere. Hilni, Neva and the baby were certainly asleep. Occasionally, Ralm thought he heard noises coming from outside. He peeked between the drawn curtains and found only a dimly lit street beyond. No Low Guard passed on patrol and none approached the house.

His time in High Hook hadn't prepared Ralm for the illkin's attack. While aiding Scalamar as he tended to the illkin, Ralm had been in relative safety. With Scalamar and Ditron's experience, along with certain safeguards, Ralm never felt to be in real danger. Tonight was different. Without bars to separate him from illkin, with nobody there to help him and no mixture of soothing herbs to sedate the deranged, Ralm had fended the illkin's terrifying assault alone, though he realized now he was never the target. The illkin held no malice to him. She wanted only the magic he carried.

The front door squeaked open. Zirrin hobbled into the sitting room, his eyes and face showing the weariness of a man deprived of his usual bedtime and of untold rigors endured during that lost slumber.

"What happened to you?" Zirrin settled into a chair. He pointed at the side of Ralm's face. "You're bleeding."

Ralm touched his cheek. A swirl of white and red stained his finger. Paint and blood. The scratch lacked pain or irritation. "I brought back the bullet, but there was an illkin there. She attacked me."

"Are you all right?"

"Yes. She took the bullet from me." He gestured to his torn pocket. "The Low Guard came."

"The Low Guard?" Zirrin leaned forward. "Did they see

you?"

"No. I was hiding before they arrived. I think they believe she had the bullet all along."

"If so, that works to our benefit." Zirrin offered a reserved smile.

"Not to hers. They beat her, Zirrin. Beat her to death."

Zirrin shook his head. "Not entirely unexpected. Low Guard can be every bit as savage as illkin. More so, I think."

"I found this under her nail." Ralm laid the sliver on the table between them.

Zirrin studied it briefly. "Looks identical to this one." He removed a handkerchief from his pocket and unfolded it. A sliver rolled out and landed beside the other.

"You found the body?"

Zirrin nodded. "It wasn't easy and quite disgusting. Hope you never wade through a pile of bodies. It's a gruesome experience." He leaned over and studied, but didn't touch, the pair of slivers.

A thought occurred to Ralm. "Aren't these considered stolen magic? What happens if we're found with them?"

"A good question, but I'm not worried. These are evidence, and I plan to hide them where they'll not be found by anybody. I'll not risk losing the only proof we have."

"Proof of what? We have two enchanted slivers. That's it. There's no connection to be made between them and the supreme."

"That's true. We can't make declarations on flimsy theories."

"So, going to the grave was pointless?"

"Not necessarily. Don't you think it strange the order would allow the man to be thrown into an open grave with magical slivers still in his fingers? Magic is valuable, even if it must be pried out of a body. You'd think the Ascendancy would remove the magic beforehand, if only to keep it from getting into the wrong hands." Zirrin grimaced. "Sorry. Poor choice of words."

"Maybe the guards forgot to take them out," Ralm said.

"Unlikely. Considering he was killed for absorption of magic, I doubt even low guards would be so dumb as to forget so quickly about the enchantments."

"If they didn't forget, why did they leave them?"

"A good question. Unfortunately, I don't have an answer."

Ralm thought for a moment before saying, "Maybe the order wants them to be found."

"Eh? What do you mean?"

"If the supreme is making illkin, there's a reason."

"Zenteezee may not need a reason beyond his own sinister delights."

"Before the Low Guard beat the illkin, they were talking among each other. They called the illkin 'hound' and were commenting on how it sniffed out the magic. What if the supreme is making illkin to find magic?"

"A hound?" Zirrin's eyes lit with interest. "As in, a dog?"

Ralm nodded.

Zirrin sprang from his chair with renewed vigor. He knelt before one of the many stacks of journals. "Not this one," he said, looking at the topmost journal. He tossed it aside. "Not this one." The next journal was unceremoniously deposited atop its rejected twin. "No. Not this one either." Another journal was evicted from the orderly stack and relocated to the growing disarray. "Ah! Here it is." Zirrin returned to his chair and flipped through pages. The journal's cover was identical to the others. How Zirrin could differentiate it, Ralm didn't know. "Here." Zirrin stabbed a page with his finger. "I recorded this years ago. I remember at the time thinking it was peculiar and later dismissed it as my own brand of foolish conspiracy, but now that you've mentioned it."

"Mentioned what?" Ralm asked, his confusion mounting.

"The hound. See? I wrote it here. I overheard an ascender and a low guard speaking of hounds and how useful they were at finding magic. I thought they were training dogs, but I never heard of any dog, or any animal outside of illkin, capable of detecting magic. I thought I misheard them, or if I heard them correctly, that the order figured out a way to teach dogs to sniff out magic. But I've never seen dogs used before or since, except as guardians and attack beasts. With your story, it all makes sense. Illkin are drawn to magic. What better way to find a missing enchantment?" Zirrin rubbed his chin. "What other use does the Ascendancy have for illkin? The clues are stacking up, Ralm."

"Didn't Scalamar tell you about illkin being used this way?"

"He told me a great many things, Ralm, but there were many things he didn't say. Our time together was brief, too short for him to explain all that happens in the order." Zirrin tapped a finger on his chin in thought for a moment. "Maybe that's why the slivers were left in. If Zenteezee made the illkin you encountered, it's reasonable to believe he's made others. What if he planned to set loose an illkin to find the slivers?"

A series of images passed through Ralm's mind, beginning with a dark figure unchained from the spire and ending with it finding the slivers. He shuddered. The illkin he encountered tore through his pocket to gnaw on the bullet. It was a beastly act. What would another illkin do to reach magic wedged under a fingernail? Eat human flesh? Tear the nail off? Either act was stomach-churning. Ralm managed to keep his nausea controlled and said, "Scalamar and I discussed the possibility of illkin being created by another. Why would the supreme do that? Seems more work than necessary. Why not have the Low Guard do the searching instead?"

"Perhaps Zenteezee likes the fear illkin spread. The order wants people dependent on it. What better way than by creating a threat which is easily controlled? Illkin run amok in the streets. People become frightened. The order eliminates the illkin. The people view the order as protector. It makes sense. That's how the Ascendancy has kept revolt limited for so many years. Sure, it arises on occasion, but not as frequently as it should considering the multitude of wrongs the order is responsible for. It's because the order has cleverly manipulated the people into believing they are safer because it protects them from illkin. When in truth, it's the order creating them."

"One thing I don't understand. What happened to the magic when it struck the man?"

"It paralyzed him."

"Yes, but wouldn't that be absorption of magic? What makes an illkin? Putting magic into the body, correct?"

"I'm not following you, Ralm."

"When that bullet hit him, the magic went inside and paralyzed the man. He absorbed the magic."

"In a way, I suppose he did."

"Isn't that enough to make him, make anybody, illkin? Putting slivers under the fingernails is one thing, but wouldn't absorbing a hit of magic be the same?"

"Ah. I see. I'm no expert on the subject, but I believe it's a matter of duration. When that bullet struck, the release of magic was sudden. All at once. It entered his body and shortly after, exited him. With the splinters, the process is much slower. Magic acts as a poison rather than an attack. The body can shrug off a hit, but the slow action of a poison isn't so easily overcome. It worms into the system and takes root and is impossible to remove once it does. Whereas, the suspension in the bullet was a quick burst the man expelled after a brief time. Of course, only suspension works that way. Were it ice-kissed or fire-felt, well, let's just say there would've been no need for a proxy.

"What if he was hit with suspension every day for a year? Would he become illkin then, being slowly poisoned?"

Zirrin shook his head. "I don't have an answer for that, Ralm. I'll tell you this, however. The contradiction to it all is influence. A person wearing it is prone to suggestion. The magic is working them constantly."

"So they're being poisoned? A person wearing it will eventually become illkin?"

"That's the contradiction. I've never heard of such a thing

happening."

They discussed deep into the evening until Zirrin finally yawned and said, "It's late, Ralm. My body is tired along with my mind. I can't think clearly on the matter anymore tonight. Let's get some sleep and try again in the morning when we're refreshed. Goodnight."

Ralm listened to stairs squeak softly under Zirrin's weight and the groan of boards as his host made his way to bed. Soon silence ruled again, but Ralm's mind wasn't quiet. He stared at the magical slivers: black but without the sheen of other enchantments. These held the dull ebony of rot and were stained by the blood of their wearers.

Proof. What good was this proof of the order's deceptions, and how would it aid him in saving the godspear? Or finding his family?

Ralm shifted in the chair until he was comfortable. His eyes refused to stay open as thoughts gradually turned wayward and unfocused. Long after a rooster crowed somewhere in the distance, Ralm finally drifted to sleep.

CHAPTER 9

For three days the caravan traveled the rugged terrain of Tolina's Rends. Passage through the maze of gorges was slow, tedious. Rockslides littered many of the dry riverbeds Dajjer and his followers used as roads, often blocking the way entirely. Rather than turn around and seek an alternate route—usually, a time-consuming endeavor—wagons were emptied and disassembled. Dajjer barked orders. People formed a line under his command. Piece by piece the wagon was carried across the obstacle, to be reassembled and reloaded on the other side. Nobody voiced objections or displayed aggravation. They obeyed Dajjer dutifully. All, including children, participated, each with his or her own job, which they performed with surprising efficiency. People negotiated each hindrance with minor difficulty, clambering over jagged and flaking stone. Horses, however, neighed their reluctances at overcoming every sharp and abrupt hurdle, no matter how hard bridles were tugged or flanks shoved. After the horses were coaxed over and hitched again, the caravan resumed until another obstacle was encountered, which could be hours away or around the next bend.

Cyji felt useless during these times. While everybody else hurried to complete their appointed tasks, she stood back and watched. She wanted to help, she tried to help, but only succeeded in disrupting efforts. The people operated fluidly, and when Cyji attempted to assist, the flow stuttered. She stood back, feeling inept, feeling like the outsider she was. Uprooted by the Ascendancy, these people were made wanderers, bandits. They looked to Dajjer for guidance and protection. A farmer once, now a leader, he was followed without question, because he was the reason they were alive and free. Cyji wondered how long they would remain displaced and dispossessed. How long before they settled roots again? How soon before she returned to her roots?

Dajjer assured the network of gorges and ravines was a safer route than any road. He avoided roads whenever possible, and with the exception of the ambush weeks earlier, he hadn't traveled any to Cyji's memory. Despite Dajjer's confidence in the chosen path, his eyes constantly scanned the gorge's overlooking brinks. When rocks tumbled inexplicably into the gorge with echoing clatters, the entire procession halted. Weapons raised, women and children huddled around wagons, and men fanned out to investigate and defend. Only after it was determined there was no threat did the caravan continue and anxiety lessen, though Dajjer's raking gaze never ceased.

Tulla and Fedik slipped away to scout and returned at regular intervals, reporting to Dajjer on the terrain ahead and possible sightings of Ascendancy servants. A patrol of four Low Guard was spotted, miles away and riding in the opposite direction. Dajjer listened to Tulla's reports, intensity in his eyes, nodding his acknowledgments.

The more northward they traveled, the moister the riverbed became. First, sand clung to the bottoms of boots and hoofs. Wagon wheels sank into soft ground. Surface water appeared, a slender tendril in the middle of an otherwise parched riverbed. Further upstream it widened into a brook, forcing the caravan to skirt rugged banks.

"We'll be leaving the ravine soon," Dajjer announced. "Fedik reports the water is wall to wall ahead. Impassable, unless we have fins. There's an egress not far from here."

His words were true. When the water deepened to the knees,

they veered and climbed a steep trail out of the ravine to the land above. Tulla and Fedik waited at the top, vigilant of potential dangers. Cyji was last to ascend. For all her inabilities to aid the people during their trek, she felt compelled to stay behind and guard the rear until all were safely away. It was a self-appointed duty Cyji took pride in assuming as her own.

Out of the ravine, the vast network of deeply carved furrows comprising Tolina's Rends spanned every visible distance. How Dajjer managed to avoid becoming lost while inside the natural maze was a mystery. Tulla and Fedik certainly played a part in it, but ultimately, each decision for course had been made by Dajjer.

He pointed northward. "We'll follow the high ground until nightfall. The ravines stay far enough apart from here. We won't be crossing any more."

Cyji's gaze followed his finger. A dark shape gloomed the horizon. "What is that?"

"The Risc," Tulla said, as if it was all the explanation needed.

Not content with her answer, Cyji pressed. "What's the Risc?"

"A swamp. An enormous swamp. It covers most of Azazura's northern region. It's what feeds these ravines. Water from the Risc finds its way here. During heavy rains, the Rends flood. Traveling them as we did becomes impossible."

Cyji gawped. She quickly shut her mouth, ashamed of her awe. Never had she thought a swamp could be so enormous. Vidrey had a swamp. Located on the western outskirts of the godspear forest, it was barely two hundred paces wide. Calling it a swamp henceforth seemed silly compared to the Risc. "It looks to go on forever."

"It doesn't. On the other side of the Risc is the Balk."

"The Balk?" Azazura held many places with names strange to Cyji's ears.

"It's a precipice surrounding Azazura. Impossible to climb, but people still try to scale it. They've all died."

Danger seemed to be everywhere in Azazura. If she wasn't

being stabbed by watchers, she was being threatened by Low Guard, or fighting illkin. Why should a wall be any different?

The caravan trudged north, between two ravines, staying far from the brittle edges in danger of crumbling with the slightest weight brought upon them.

"We'll camp here tonight." Dajjer held an arm high, halting the procession. The sun hovered on the skyline.

"I don't like it," Tulla said. "We're too exposed."

"Whether we camp here or a ways farther, we're still in the open," Dajjer said. "Our advantage here is we have natural defenses on three sides. No tents or fires. We'll eat and sleep cold tonight."

The horizon swallowed the sun. Trails of magenta and pink smudged the sky until the first stars appeared. Without crackling fire, nighttime sounds loudened. Loss of sight raised other senses, with hearing at the forefront. Chewing of food, satisfied belches and water babbling in the surrounding ravines were all obtrusive in the dark calm. A serenity enshrouded the camp, the people at ease despite being hidden in the open. Serene, but not festive. No tales were told. No jokes were said. Voices and laughter carried, with or without fire. Night engulfed, revealing dim, tiny lights dappling the eastern horizon.

"What's out there?" Cyji asked.

"Mothlight," Dajjer said from somewhere near a wagon. "It's a border town. People from Morivar and Kyrkynstaag go there to trade with each other."

"Trade goods?"

"Yes, and the order is taking its share from every transaction. Twenty percent, last I heard. Thievery."

"Information? Do they trade information?"

Dajjer chuckled softly. "Yes. Information, too."

"Is that where we're going tomorrow?"

"Absolutely not. Didn't you hear what I said? That place is filled with Low Guard. Probably an ascender or two as well. That's company I want no part of."

"But somebody there might have information on Ralm and Lavak. We can't not go."

"We can and we will." Dajjer's tone grew stern. "Why do you think we don't take roads? Why we travel treacherous routes like the Rends? The order knows of us. It may not know our faces, but it knows enough details about us. We live an outlaw life, and that life is one of solitude. Going into a place like Mothlight is asking for trouble, and trouble is something I avoid unless I'm the one making it."

They sat in awkward silence, the darkness a barrier between them. After a few moments of staring at the lights, Cyji asked, "What did you get in return for the magic, besides information?" She had seen the trade, had watched as the trader filled Dajjer's palm with gold, but Cyji was still naive to its value. The idea of trading so much for so little intrigued her. She may glean some information from Dajjer and, at the same time, soften his mood through idle talk.

A light jingling sounded at Dajjer's hip. He was fiddling with his fattened purse. "Gold. It's something of value. It can be traded anywhere for anything. Well, almost anywhere and almost anything. The Ascendancy wants it all and expects the people to trade their goods for magic. To the Ascendancy, magic is the currency of choice. They want people to chase it. Not everybody can afford magic. But gold, anybody can get."

"And you use it to buy things?"

"Yes, where it's permitted. That town, there's trading going on there, but not with gold. That sort of thing happens away from the order's eyes."

"On Vidrey, everybody borrows and lends. The idea of ownership is more loose than it is here. If you have something somebody else needs, you lend it to them and they return it when finished. The only time we trade is when the ships of Azazura come for the godspear."

Dajjer grunted. "That may serve on an island, where if somebody takes something they can't get far, but on the mainland, things loaned are often things lost."

The stars glided slowly overhead as Dajjer and Cyji sat quietly across from each other. Around them came the rustling of bedrolls as people settled in for sleep.

"It's time for sleep. We've another long day tomorrow," Dajjer said.

"I'll get to bed in a while," Cyji said. Her attention lingered on the twinkling lights in the distance.

Dajjer retired. Cyji waited. When his light snoring reached a predictable rhythm, Cyji stalked from camp. Rosh was on watch somewhere along the camp's outskirts, likely about to join the others in slumber after consuming too much wine. His bad habits seldom faltered, including his lust for the drink, his passing out and his startling himself awake before his watch ended. Fortunately, this pattern hadn't yet allowed ill-doers to slip into camp. Tonight, however, his drunken napping would allow one of the camp's own to sneak away.

Cyji shed her ax and bow as she appraised the distance of the lights. Two miles. Perhaps three. She needed to move quickly. Weapons would only slow her down. Giving one final glance at the camp and the shadowy mounds sleeping about, she sprinted for Mothlight. Mindful of shallow trenches and sudden drops, she used starlight to navigate the treacherous land. Cyji easily leapt across narrow gaps and was forced to carefully descend into and climb out of the broader ravines. She slipped on greasy ground and stumbled over rocks cloaked by night and fell often onto her rump as pebbles slid from underfoot. Water proved hazardous. Deeper and swifter than she'd expected, Cyji was soaked to her chest by her second crossing. The surprisingly strong current threatened to carry her downstream. Only her Splinterfist strength gave Cyji the chance to reach the other side, though even with traits bestowed by her ancestors, she still struggled.

Drenched and mud-stained, she clambered out of a ravine, chest heaving with labored breaths. Mothlight appeared no closer than before. It was almost midnight, and there was still a land's width to traverse. Behind her was absolute dark. Without a campfire, she'd no idea the group's location. She noted a cluster of stars in the sky, guessing the camp somewhere beneath. The constellation may aid in finding her way back, but turning back now would be foolish. Although Dajjer refused to go, she needed to investigate Mothlight. Perhaps somebody there did have information. If so, she'd find them and return to camp by sunrise. With time fleeting, Cyji bolted onward.

The lights of the border town took shape, changing from indistinct flickering blobs floating in air to windows glowing amber. Silhouettes leaned against the backdrop of night: sloped roofs of buildings. When she heard voices, Cyji slowed to a walk. Gibberish in the distance, each step brought more clarity to the words. Laughter erupted. Singing abounded. Even at this late hour, people were still awake, still lively. It was a marvelous revelation.

Iron braziers scattered along the trodden road splashed light into alleys and against buildings. Cyji crept down a deserted street, drawn to the revelry happening deeper inside Mothlight. Shops hemmed the road, closed now, their windows shuttered and doors locked. Shingles hanging from rusty hinges whined in a gentle breeze, their painted images announcing the shop's expertise: mortar and pestle, tongs and hammer, flame and blowpipe.

Movement in the street ahead. Figures milled around the braziers. Laughter. Jeers. Shouts. Pale faces shone in the light before melting into shadow. Mugs raised in cheer. Music gushed from a brightly lit building, while a persistent stream of patrons flowed through its doorway. Cyji's eyes absorbed every sight and discovered reminders of the Fall Festival everywhere she gazed.

A frail man separated from the other merrymakers. He offered a few boisterous farewells before staggering in Cyji's direction. With cup in hand, its contents sloshing out with each clumsy step, the man slurred a song as he approached Cyji without apparent awareness of her presence. As he drew close, Cyji stepped before him.

"Excuse me, sir," she said. "I'm looking for somebody who may have information."

His concentration had been on the ground immediately before him, with all focus on remaining upright. As Cyji spoke, the man raised his stare with sluggish effort, and when he finally beheld the one addressing him, his eyes widened as he reeled and fell back.

"Illkin," he said with a heavy note of disbelief. "I don't have anything. Leave me alone. Illkin. Illkin!" He screamed before rolling onto his stomach and scrambling on hands and knees back the way he came. "Illkin! Illkin!"

All noise from carousing went silent as startled faces turned in Cyji's direction. In the next moment, Low Guard were filing out of doorways unseen in the shadows, tromping into the street with weapons bared. It happened fast. Cyji hesitated, uncertain what to do.

"Look! Over there!" A low guard pointed at Cyji. "Illkin!"

His words dispelled Cyji's paralysis. She sprang down the street, desperate to escape. A javelin rattled as it skidded along the street next to her. Driven harder by the threat of impalement, she fled into night's embrace.

Shouts behind her as more Low Guard gave chase. Cyji didn't look back. With heart hammering her chest, she fixed her sight on the constellation from earlier. Cyji needed to reach camp. She needed safety. She needed—

The ground fell away, and for the briefest moment, Cyji floated in air. The next moment she tumbled into a ravine, a black mass of nothing rising fast to swallow her. She struck hard. A sharp pain surged from her ankle as Cyji rolled helplessly down over rock and sand before sliding to a stop at the water's edge. Immediately, she tried to stand. Agony exploded from her ankle. Cyji bit her lip to keep from wailing. She fell onto the embankment and tried crawling, but every subtle twist of her ankle was a scream to her nerves.

Voices pierced the night. And they were coming nearer.

CHAPTER 10

Lavak sat on a polished stone bench near the rotunda's entrance. Marble pillars stood in crescent formation before him, supporting a domed ceiling. Sunlight breached its many windows, flooding the cavernous space with warm brilliance. Beyond the glass panes, the spire towered like an ever-vigilant chaperon, its crimson pennants sinuous in a passing breeze. The rotunda functioned as a hub for its two adjoining wings: the dormitory and the academy. Ascenders and aspirants crossed its floor with hurried regularity.

He pretended to read a book taken at random from his lab. Splayed open on his lap, it served well at concealing his true intentions. Ascenders might question his presence in the rotunda if he simply sat there and did nothing, especially if they knew (and they certainly did) he'd been tasked with finding a cure and been given a personal lab. He wasn't an ascender, wasn't one of them and certainly didn't belong there. With a book, his prop, they might believe he'd left his windowless sanctuary for a while in favor of a more open space to study and enjoy some sunshine.

An ascender exited the dorm in a rush for the exit, his robes swishing on the marble floor. As he passed, Lavak closed his eyes, focusing his other senses to catch any hint of savor. It wafted from the ascender and introduced itself to Lavak with a quick flush of heat: fire-felt magic. It was robust, suggesting the enchantment powerful and crafted recently by experienced hands. Possibly a wand tucked in the ascender's sleeve or under his belt. The ascender exited the rotunda, along with his savor.

Lavak had been feeling stretched thin the past few days. If he wasn't in his lab, he was enchanting under Drudylan's guidance. Although each task consumed him and he enjoyed the work, he grew increasingly anxious for escape. The need to find a cure constantly taunted him. He felt guilty when he wasn't researching, but his thoughts recently began to dull. Ideas were no longer spontaneous. Rather, Lavak struggled for any degree of conception. He was overworked and overtired. A respite, though time-squandering, was necessary if he were to continue his efforts with any earnest.

Earlier that day, Lavak followed the many steps down from his lab to the spire's base and into the courtyard, where he watched High Guard perform their morning drills before commencing with some aggressive training. Though relieved from their posts until the next evening, they could not yet rest.

"Come at me with it," High Guard of the Tenth ordered. He pounded his chest for emphasis.

High Guard of the Seventh studied the ax in his hand with nervous uncertainty. It was odd for Lavak to see the confidence of any high guard shaken. "What if I accidentally hit an exposed area?"

"You are High Guard of the Seventh of the Crimson Spire," the other said. "You should know where every blow you make will land. If you doubt yourself, then you don't deserve the rank or title."

The two high guards were surrounded by the remaining ten elite warriors tasked with protecting nightly each of the spire's landings. Rank was directly related to elevation in the spire, with the highest guard marked as twelfth and the lowest first. Lavak was most familiar with the ninth, who guarded the landing leading to his lab and who was currently among the spectators.

"We all know what will happen," the seventh said. "I don't see a need for this demonstration."

The twelfth scowled. "It's no demonstration, but a

reinforcement of surety. Something you clearly lack. If you're attacked, I don't want you flinching when the fool with a mundane weapon swings it against your armor. And if you're ever fool enough to lose your own weapon, I want you to understand the futility of attacking a magically protected opponent with an ordinary weapon."

The seventh glanced at his weapon again. It was an ax. A simple ax with no enchantment.

"Come at me!" his superior barked.

The seventh did, with mustered aggression. Taking two strides forward, he swung the ax into the twelfth's black-and-white meshed breastplate. The ax hit with a hollow ding but inflicted no damage. The twelfth stood there, unflinching, unharmed and smirking.

"You see?" he said. "See how ineffective your weapon is against starwood?" His gaze swept over the other high guard. "Remember this. If you must defend your supreme, I don't want to see any of you hesitate when facing an inferiorly armed opponent. You do and I'll throw you from the top of the spire."

Lavak watched awhile longer as magical shields clashed their ordinary cousins. High Guard used them to slam each other over and over until the mundane shields cracked, crumbled or otherwise fell apart while the enchanted shields remained intact and undamaged. He soon grew bored and meandered to his intended destination: the rotunda.

As he sat pretending to read, Kuldahar emerged from the dormitory entrance. He traversed the rotunda's interior expanse with the haste of somebody pressed for an engagement. Likely an appointment to polish Welnaro's staff, Lavak mused. Kuldahar's savor escorted him and tingled Lavak's lips. Suspension. The revelation didn't surprise Lavak. Kuldahar enjoyed an audience, and if there was a way to captivate one, he'd utilize a means to do so.

If he'd noticed Lavak, Kuldahar made no effort at bullying him. The ascender was alone and, like most grackles Lavak had experience with, wouldn't engage his victim without an audience. His dominations required witnesses, or at least lackeys, to encourage his behavior. Lavak was tempted to confront the ascender, to see how Kuldahar reacted while isolated. Instead, he allowed Kuldahar to pass by without interaction. Kuldahar's attention never strayed in Lavak's direction.

Surprisingly, the book Kuldahar gifted to Lavak contained the most intriguing reads. Magic and enchanting and Ascendancy history recorded in the other tomes at his disposal were interesting, but the equally cumbersome and ambiguously titled *Collective Journals of Supreme Ascendants Regarding the Origins of Starwood* captivated him. Within its pages, Vidrey's history was chronicled, from its discovery by the original three explorers who would eventually establish the Ascendancy to the shocking truth about Lavak's people.

Regarding the former, these men sailed from Azazura into the uncharted waters of the Cryptic Sea, happening upon the island only three days out. Drawn to the godspear easily spied from their boat, the trio attempted to fell one of the mighty trees. Although they failed, the men managed to cleave a single limb, which they returned to Azazura with and studied. It wasn't long before they realized the special properties godspear contained, though they still hadn't discovered its ability to be enchanted. That occurred later, by serendipity. During the interim, demand for the unusual wood grew rapidly as people throughout the land learned of it. To protect the island's location, the men named it starwood and claimed it had fallen from the sky. Subsequent trips to Vidrey yielded more wood and more wealth from those with the means to purchase it at exorbitant prices. The three men's excessive riches allowed them to purchase all of Azazura along with a fleet of ships to surround the island and deter any future explorers.

As for the Vidreyans, Kuldahar had been right. The information gleaned from the book was enlightening, especially concerning Lavak and his appearance. If Kuldahar had given him the book to dissuade him, he'd made a mistake. It only served to strengthen Lavak's resolve.

An aspirant entered the atrium. Lavak recognized him as one of the boys who had brought him samples to study the day his lab was stocked. The prime had slapped the back of the aspirant's shaved head, leaving a red handprint. His weak savor reached Lavak slowly. A slight chill tingled his spine: ice-kissed. Likely, the aspirant carried his first attempt at enchantment and it lacked imbued potency. The boy scampered to the academy with the panicked expression of somebody tardy for a lesson. Any hint of Welnaro's scolding had since faded from his bare pate.

No order member regarded Lavak with more than a flitting glance or refrained scowl. These gestures alone told him enough. He was an outlander. A primitive. A freak. He didn't deserve to be there. He didn't deserve his own room in the spire, or to be lauded by the supreme while they competed for her praise. They may not have been as vocal as Kuldahar in their opinions of him, but Lavak sensed it as strongly as he sensed the savor bleeding from the enchantments nestled under the folds of their robes. Only one of their peers showed him any kindness. His heart fluttered in step with thoughts of her.

Melindi.

The sun balanced on the tip of the spire when she appeared. Lavak sensed her magic before seeing Melindi, a metallic taste in his mouth, the signature of iron-like enchantment. He wasn't certain what she carried, but he'd forgotten about it once she smiled and waved as she left the dormitory, a large bundle cradled under one arm.

"Have you been waiting long?" she asked.

"No. I just got here." *But I'd wait an eternity for you.*

"Good. I was afraid I'd be late. I was teaching some of the younger aspirants how to sew. One of them pricked a finger. I had to tend to him. Not much more than a drop of blood, but for a boy of six, it and the pain were life-ending. I had to bandage his finger and kiss it better before he was convinced he wouldn't die. You know how children can be."

"Actually, no. Not in that way," Lavak said. He did know children could be cruel, however, as they'd been to him his entire life. "You teach the children to sew?"

"Of course. Aspirants are expected to mend ripped drapes, torn tablecloths, whatever may need it. We learn to hem our own robes at an early age, though some aspirants have no knack for it. Even Supreme Ascendant Volstrysa learned to sew when she was an aspirant, I think."

They left the rotunda and were greeted by the day's rising swelter. Between the academy and spire were gardens, a gated and guarded refuge reserved for members of the order, where they could enjoy tranquility without interruption and breathe fresh air without wearing masks.

Melindi giggled as she skipped to the garden entrance, glancing over her shoulder frequently at a trailing Lavak. Her laughter was infectious, and Lavak realized he smiled more in her company than he'd ever smiled in his entire life. His time with her was no longer a pleasant distraction. Now it was a delightful addiction. There was a glow about her, invisible yet comforting. It made him happy, and in times past after they had parted, Lavak found himself smiling from the lingering joy of her company.

The garden was a series of intertwining paths of river stone hemmed by verdant life: shrubs, trees and a prismatic array of flowers. Ferns clustered alongside a man-made stream. In the garden's center, dogwood trees surrounded a shallow pool populated by orange fish mottled black. It was a perfectly serene sitting spot. Melindi knelt on the thick carpet of grass beneath the dogwoods and unrolled the bundle. She neatly arranged the bread and cheese that was hidden inside along with a bottle of honeyed milk. The blanket she'd used to carry the picnic was spread out so she and Lavak could sit on it. They spoke quietly of small things and trivial matters, hushing and grinning to each other whenever a high guard wandered by on patrol and laughing aloud once he was well out of sight and earshot. After they ate, Lavak lay beside her on the blanket, letting his meal digest, content with simply being close to Melindi as the dogwoods' limbs swayed gently in a passing breeze. Lavak was reminded of an old island song: "In the Shade with My Darling." He hadn't appreciated the lyrics until now. He hummed a few lines of Vidrey's favorite ballad.

Melindi's hand brushed Lavak's thigh. It was an innocent, unintentional gesture, but Lavak's heart raced at her touch anyway.

"I've heard the ascenders speaking to each other," Melindi said as she stared into the dogwoods' tangle. "Some of them are really frightened about what's happening to the godspear. They're afraid a cure won't be found in time. They're not sure what's going to happen to the order. Even Kuldahar is trying to find a solution."

"Kuldahar." Lavak scoffed his bully's name. "He wants to find it first just for the glory. But if it means saving the godspear, he can have all the glory and my praise with it."

"There's other talk in the spire, about you. People are wondering what it's like talking to the godspears? What do they say?"

"I don't know. They don't speak to me."

"Some in the Ascendancy believe you've a gift for communicating with the godspears. It may not be talking the way people talk, but they think you can feel what a godspear feels by touching it. They're hoping you can learn things about them."

"If it's true, I must be doing it wrong. Every year on Vidrey, a new group of ascenders arrives, and each prods me to commune with the godspears. We've a tradition of burying our dead and planting a godspear at their grave. The ascenders believe some of the person's essence transfers into the tree and I should be able to hear them through the godspear. Quite ludicrous when you think about it. I don't understand how they can believe such a silly notion."

"They do, and they believe in you."

"Because of my skin. Because I'm different. They're all certain my powers will develop, but nothing has happened. I see they're disappointment. Yet each year they insist it will eventually happen." He was gaining powers of a kind the Ascendancy hadn't anticipated. Lavak wasn't certain of his still-manifesting abilities and less certain of sharing the information with anybody, including Melindi. She was safer not knowing.

"That's not true. What about your sensing of magic?"

Melindi's knowledge of this worried him. If she spoke of it to the wrong person…

"Let's keep that between us," he said.

"All right, but it's still incredible. Nobody else can do it, except illkin."

"Maybe I'm illkin," Lavak said lightly, but inwardly it was a serious concern. He'd learned much about illkin through his readings. One particular trait they possessed was the ability to smell magic. Since learning of it, Lavak wondered if he was somehow tied to them or the shared sense was mere coincidence.

Melindi sighed. "It's too bad things aren't different. If I was a bit older, I'd probably have already been sent to Vidrey. Maybe I'd find a cure while there. And maybe I'd be the one to help you unlock your powers." She nudged Lavak.

"I'm glad it's not different. On Vidrey, the entire village would watch as we sneaked away."

"We'd have trees to hide behind. Here, all the spire's eyes are on us. Ascenders and aspirants are forbidden from having relations. Being together here, now, may be viewed unfavorably."

Lavak rolled onto his side to face her. "So, you admit we're having relations?"

Melindi blushed and averted her eyes. "I'm not admitting to anything." She pushed him playfully, and Lavak rolled onto his back again, giggling.

"You'll be in Vidrey one day. You'll see the godspears," he said, but his confidence was hollow. Would there be any godspears left to see?

"I hope so. My rising to ascender is over a year away, but I know I'll become one. Last year, I went to Kalatite Quarry. I saw how kalatite is extracted. Oh, it's a wonderful place. You'll probably think I'm foolish for saying, but the quarry is beautiful. It's in the Glittering Hills. Do you know why it's called the Glittering Hills?" She paused only long enough for Lavak to shake his head. "When the sunlight hits the stone, it's dazzling. Sparkles everywhere. It's a magic all its own. Before I rise, I'm required to see the Valdsker Mine, but I don't think I'll like it much. I hear it's dark and hot and you're deep underground. That's not for me. I need daylight."

Lavak grinned. "My people would have no understanding of how to handle you."

"What do you mean?"

"Every other ascender who's been on the island has been distant and, well, grumpy. You're neither. To have somebody like you on Vidrey would shock the natives."

"Maybe they need that. And maybe, I'll change the image of watchers. They'll all be expected to smile and be polite." She slammed her fist into the palm of her hand, making the decree official.

Laughing, Lavak said, "Careful. They'll have you in the mine for that kind of behavior. A few years in the dark will sour your mood until you're like the rest of them."

Melindi stabbed a finger into his side. "I won't do it. I'll run away and swim to Vidrey and live among the godspears."

"Yes, and stories of a strange woman leaping branch to branch would be told by my people. They'd venture into the forest hoping to glimpse the beautiful tree creature."

"You think I'm beautiful?"

The word had slipped from his mouth before he considered the weight it carried. Lavak didn't regret saying it, but the truth behind it wasn't something he was ready to share with Melindi. "Of course you are." He struggled to keep his voice steady. There was a long, awkward silence as they stared at dogwood branches. Lavak wrestled with something more to say, but each string of words formed in his mind seemed inadequate to convey his feelings. Melindi finally broke the silence.

"I like you, Lavak. I enjoy being with you. But…we can't be together. Not in the way you want. It's impossible. I want to be an ascender. If we were together, I'd be expelled from the order."

His chest tightened as if an invisible hand had reached inside and slowly squeezed his heart until it shattered. The moments following passed for what seemed an eternity. He gathered his fragmented heart and managed a response. "I understand. It's your dream to rise in the spire. I'd be wrong to deny you that." Lavak forced the words through a constricted throat.

"If I can reach ascendant, I may be able to do some good in Azazura. Shelter the homeless. Feed the hungry."

Lavak nodded. Those were righteous ambitions. Melindi's compassion may lend in fulfilling her dreams, but would the Ascendancy allow her goals to be realized? She was sincere, her motives pure. The order suited the corrupt and power hungry. She was neither. Could she adapt? Or be consumed by its nature? Grim reservations aside, Lavak offered a comforting lie. "If anybody can, it will be you. It'd be selfish of me to keep you from doing so much good."

"Besides, I think the supreme wants you for herself," Melindi teased, but an underlying caution clung to her words.

"Volstrysa? I thought all in the order were forbidden to have relations."

"Well, she is the supreme. I suppose when one reaches that status, certain benefits apply, though they still must be conducted in private."

Her words brought no revelations to Lavak. He may have lived on an island and was inexperienced with females, but even he couldn't mistake Volstrysa's obvious advances. He didn't want her. He wanted Melindi. Volstrysa was attractive for her age, which was well twenty years beyond his, but age wasn't the problem: it was the personal connection, or more accurately, lack of one. His heart didn't beat for her the way it beat for Melindi. Taking the opportunity to lighten the moment, he said, "Well, that settles it. We'll need to make you supreme. Then you can do whatever you want with whomever you want."

Melindi giggled. "Don't say it too loud. Such talk might be deemed conspiratorial. Then we'd both be in trouble."

"At least we have a plan now."

She unclasped the necklace from around her neck. "Here, I want you to have this." She held it up. Carried on the necklace was a godspear pendant, carved into the crude shape of a diamond. "This was my first enchantment. Iron-like. I chose it as a reminder to always be strong."

"Melindi, I can't. This is special to you."

"And you're special to me. That's why it's fitting you have it. If we can't be together romantically, we can at least be friends. I want this to symbolize our friendship."

He'd have preferred romance to friendship, but took the pendant, knowing that for now, he'd rather have Melindi as a friend in his life than as nothing. "I'll cherish it forever," he promised, knowing the enchantment was weak and the pendant likely to be disintegrated within a year. Still, every day of that year he'd prize. Slipping the necklace over his head, Lavak was careful the pendant didn't contact his skin.

"What are we?" the voice again, the same hushed presence he'd heard in his room the night Kuldahar gave him the book. Lavak hadn't heard it since and dismissed it as imagination. Unexpected and uninvited the voice returned, interrupting his time with Melindi to curdle his mood, with nobody nearby to blame for its trickery. Lavak ignored the voice's sobering affect. His day with Melindi wouldn't be ruined, by voices imagined or otherwise.

"Melindi, can you feel magic?"

She rolled over to face him and looked at him with bright eyes. "Feel magic? Do you mean when it's used against me, like if somebody used an ice-kissed staff to freeze me? Yes, I'd feel that.

Anybody would."

"No." He dangled the pendant, holding it by the necklace, careful not to touch the enchantment directly. "This here, can you sense the magic emanating from it?"

Melindi's brows furrowed as she shook her head. "No, I can't."

"You don't know of anybody who can? The supreme perhaps, or the prime? Have you heard any of the ascenders talking about their ability to sense magic?"

Again, she shook her head, confusion lingered in her features. "No, though I don't hear everything they speak of. But I've neither heard or read of anybody who can do that except you and illkin."

"What about tapping into the magic, to draw an enchantment into the body and use it?"

Melindi chortled. "Now you're just being silly. That's impossible. Why are you asking these questions?"

"Just curious. Never mind." Her words confirmed his suspicions. The Ascendancy had been right all along. He did have a gift, but it wasn't communing with godspears. He was attuned to the magic within the wood. In all of his reading at the spire, he'd never found any mention of someone possessing the ability. He was, as he always was, alone. Only he had the power, and the prospect caused him to tremble. Should Volstrysa or the other supremes learn of this, he'd be viewed as a threat, or a tool to further their own gains. He was treading into dangerous territory. This secret mustn't be shared with Melindi. Lavak dared not risk endangering her, no matter their relationship.

They lay together in quiet contentment. Birds warbled from behind the dogwoods' rustling leaves. The serenity of the gardens invited peace, but a tempest of thought and emotion assailed Lavak's mind. Many troubles stood before him: the beetles, finding his sister and his fulfillment as transcendent. Lavak shut his eyes and calmed the storm brewing inside him. Enough time to tackle those problems later. Now was the time to enjoy Melindi's company.

CHAPTER 11

"Any sign?" Tulla asked as she wrapped a binding around Cyji's ankle.

"None yet," Dajjer said. He paced the ravine's edge, his eyes fixed to the east. Every footfall landed hard, loosening pebbles which cascaded down the slope to gather at the base of the ravine wall. "Worry about her leg. I'll worry about what I see up here."

The dawn of a new day found Cyji propped against a rock at the water's edge of the ravine she'd tumbled into the night before, her leg pained, her pride marred and her regret inescapable. Half her body was dry, the other half wet from where she rolled to a stop along the bank. Fortunately, her loss of momentum kept Cyji from plunging fully into the water. Otherwise, she may have easily drowned. Her ability to swim with an injured leg was questionable.

"You're lucky," Tulla said. "It's only a sprain. It could've been far worse. You should be completely healed in a few days, as long as you don't put too much weight on your foot."

Dajjer snorted. "Lucky. Foolish is more like it. Foolish girl. Going off to Mothlight by yourself, rousing the guards and running straight for camp. You could have led them straight to us. Foolish girl. Foolish, foolish girl."

"Still no sign?" Tulla asked again.

"None yet. And I told you, let me worry about up here,"

Dajjer said. "Foolish girl. Foolish, foolish girl." This time, Cyji wasn't certain if he meant her or Tulla.

"Then she hasn't led anybody to us yet."

Dajjer halted to glare down on Tulla. "Not yet, but that's not enough to hang a hope on. Maybe they're searching the town? When they can't find her, they'll look further out."

Tulla shrugged. "If they choose to pursue. I don't think they will. Not for one illkin. They'll probably decide to let her go, thinking she'll return eventually, drawn by magic, and catch her when she does. Low Guard aren't going to waste much time looking for one illkin."

"Spiders in spires! What if they do?" He resumed pacing, his gaze locked again on the distant border town. "You've upset my plans, girl. Instead of heading directly north like I wanted, now I'll need to seek an alternate route. I'll never understand the mind of a woman." Dajjer shook his head, hands hooking onto his belt. "You know you look like an illkin. You know how people react to your appearance. And yet, what do you do? You stroll into town like you belong there. What were you thinking? All I can say is you're lucky it happened at night. If it had been during the day, well, it would've been much worse. For you and us."

"I'm sorry, Dajjer," Cyji said. "I just thought I could get some information on my own. I wasn't expecting this to happen."

Dajjer grunted but said nothing as he continued to pace.

Tulla leaned close and whispered, "He's just ranting. Let him have a few minutes to get it out. He'll soften up in a little while." She finished dressing Cyji's ankle. "How's that feel?"

"Snug but not constrictive," Cyji said. "A perfect dressing, but my ankle is getting cold."

Tulla smiled, reached into her medicine bag and withdrew several splints. Most were of ordinary birch, but two shimmered blue while three others held a red luster. "Not all magic is for weapons. Some can be used for healing. I wrapped three ice-kissed splints around your ankle. They'll help keep the swelling down until we get your leg elevated. You hurt anywhere else?"

Cyji was, but nothing serious enough to warrant attention: a bump on her elbow, bruises on her legs, various scratches and scrapes, and her back promised to be sore and stiff before the day was over, but the biggest injury was the blow to her pride. She shook her head.

"She's ready," Tulla said to Dajjer.

"Good. The sooner we move, the better." Dajjer navigated his way down the ravine. He slid to a stop beside Cyji and extended a hand. "Come on, girl. Time to move."

Cyji took his hand and was pulled onto her good foot while favoring the other. She slung an arm over Dajjer's shoulder. Rosh appeared at the ravine's lip, his smug grin cutting through the gray morning. He followed the route Dajjer had taken, his burly frame negotiating the steep wall with little grace. Rosh and his foul stench joined Cyji at her side. She wrinkled her nose and, with great reluctance, put her free arm across his shoulder. A large part of her wanted to shove Rosh into the water, if only to dampen his stench. A simple dunking wouldn't remove his odor, but it might lessen it, if only for a while.

Rosh gave a patchwork smile. "Now don't be trying anything funny, lass. I've a reputation to keep. I know all this was a clever scheme for you to get the feels on me."

Tulla crested the ravine and scanned the landscape. Rosh and Dajjer carried Cyji up the slope, struggling at times to find sure footing and stumbling whenever the ground slipped beneath their feet. Once out, they laid Cyji on a litter and carried her back to camp. Upon her return, Cyji felt the weight of disapproving stares from the other men and women. She'd endangered them all with her recklessness, and though no words were uttered by any of them, none were needed. The disappointment hanging thick in the air was unmistakable.

"Maybe I should have kept you tied up after all," Dajjer said with a grunt as he and Rosh hoisted her into a wagon. Provisions and supplies were heaped against the wagon's sideboards, allowing room in the center for Cyji to rest. "But I suppose there's no need for it now. That ankle won't have you getting too far or into much trouble."

Rosh snickered. Spittle escaped his cracked lips from the effort. "You learn any lessons, lass? Maybe, watch where you're going and don't fall into anything deep?"

"You might have stopped me if you hadn't fallen asleep on your watch." Cyji winced in pain as she and litter were wedged into place.

Rosh's cocky grin vanished, his eyes suddenly wide from guilt under Cyji's accusation. He glanced warily to Dajjer, who was studying him with all the intensity of a cat watching a wounded bird flutter on the ground. Rosh stammered, trying to give an explanation, but Dajjer's subtle shaking of his head stilled his tongue. Another layer of disapproval was added to the laden air. Dajjer said nothing to Rosh. He spun about and strode away to bark orders at everybody to gather their belongings and ready to depart. Breakfast would be eaten en route.

"You've too big a mouth," Rosh hissed at Cyji.

"And you've too big a thirst," she snapped back.

Rosh snarled and tromped away. The rising sun's brilliance chased any lingering gloom away, but the dour mood in the camp remained, impervious to the light's effects. Women rushed by Cyji, as if sharing her air was an onus. They cast scathing, contemptuous and sidelong glances in her direction. Cyji lay flat in the wagon, wanting to sink deeper, to blend with the wagon's planks, or better still, be swallowed by the wood entirely. Neither happened, and she was left to stare at a brightening sky as guilt darkened her spirit.

Tulla appeared at her feet. She removed the cooling splints and gently propped Cyji's leg on a blanket roll. "Comfortable?"

"My leg is," Cyji said. "But I'm feeling very uncomfortable around everybody right now."

Tulla frowned but offered no reassuring words and

disappeared as quickly as she'd come.

Soon the caravan was underway. The wagon driver found every bump and dip (whether intentional or not) to steer the wagon into, adding to Cyji's discomfort. Each jostle reminded pain to her ankle and grew her back sorer. Children following the wagon averted their eyes and kept their heads down. Shame settled thick upon Cyji. She had betrayed these people's trust, and in doing so, endangered them.

Crossing a road, the wagon bounced over ruts. Pain shot through Cyji's ankle, but it was duller now because of the ice-kissed splints. All eyes scanned the road westward, then easterly where it stretched into nothing on its course to Mothlight. The road would be busy with traders soon, but it was still early and no signs of movement were glimpsed in either direction. Travelers were still eating breakfast in their homes, lodgings and camps. Only the caravan blemished the landscape's solitude.

The Risc loomed, no longer a dark obscurity on the horizon, instead a distortion of greens and browns, of tangled trees and lichen clinging to bark and branch. Unseen animals chirped and chattered within, their concealments betrayed by the occasional shaking limb or sudden splash of water. Turning west, the caravan followed the swamp's edge. The dark backdrop helped conceal the group from any eyes gazing from afar and promised cover to flee or hide should the need arise.

Tulla walked alongside the wagon, just returned from one of the day's many scoutings. Her first priority upon rejoining the group was to check on Cyji. She was an attentive caregiver. "How are you feeling?" Of the entire group, she seemed the least offended by Cyji's impetuousness.

"Fine," Cyji said. Physical pain she could tolerate. Disgrace, however, was difficult to endure. Unfortunately, the two were linked. Every jolt of the wagon visited a jolt of pain to her ankle and every pain was a reminder to Cyji of her foolishness. "How can a swamp so big exist?" she asked, hoping a change of subject may deflect her thoughts.

"Water comes down through the Balk, flows into the Risc and out into the land, eventually finding its way to the sea."

"The sea reaches Vidrey," Cyji added. "All is connected. Water, land, air, fire and life. I suppose in a way, water links Azazura to Vidrey."

The Balk materialized behind the Risc, an enormous, endless wall of jagged stone. Its massive form breached the skyline with an indomitable presence, ominous in its silent authority. As the caravan meandered in a southwesterly fashion, details were slowly revealed. Jutting ledges caught sunlight and cast shadows. Shallow cracks and deep fissures were everywhere. Elevated caves swallowed any daylight daring to enter their depths. In Vidrey, godspear were revered for their size, but their stature couldn't rival the impressive heights the Balk claimed.

The sun sank behind the horizon, and the caravan pushed onward. Unusual. Camp was always established by now. Did fear of pursuit by Low Guard compel Dajjer to drive further? There had been no sign of them the entire day, but it wasn't until night fully gripped the land before the caravan stopped to make camp. Wood was gathered at the Risc's edge. There were no reserved piles here. The sodden firewood was reluctant to burn, but with ample kindling it took the flame and served to prove Dajjer's uneasiness about pursuit had diminished.

Cyji slid out of the wagon and propped herself against the back of it to watch dinner prepared and eaten. Those huddled close to the fire gave her no attention, focusing instead on the warm bowls in their hands and the steaming contents within. If their contempt for her had lessened, Cyji didn't sense it. The atmosphere was still thick with unspoken condemnation. Nobody offered her food, drink or company. She was neither hungry nor thirsty, but some conversation would've been welcome. Cyji limped to the fire, earning stark glares from those nearby.

She felt no warmth from food or fire. Instead, the icy regards given chilled Cyji. It was an unaccustomed feeling. In Vidrey she was liked by all, at least openly. Boughleans smiled at her coming, and the oft bitter Maplequakes bid her kindly greetings whenever she passed by them.

Hobbling back to the wagon, Cyji grabbed her ax and limped to the Risc's edge. At the firelight's furthest reach she hacked two suitable branches from their parent trees and returned to the wagon where she trimmed them to length and wrapped some old rags she'd found in the wagon around the crotch of each limb. She'd crafted plenty of items from wood in the past, but crutches were a first for Cyji. Her armpits settled onto the thin rag padding. She took a few short, exploratory steps. Movement was slightly awkward and the rags cushioned her underarms only a little, but the crutches served the precious purpose of mobility. For now, it was the best she could expect.

The next morning she awoke to find Dajjer leering down at her. "Wake up." He nudged her good leg with his boot. The morning was bright, but his eyes were dark in their deep settings. "Wake up, girl."

Cyji rubber her eyes and rose to a sitting position. She had fallen asleep against the wagon wheel, the only position where her ankle felt the least bothered, though she still had a fitful slumber. Every time she'd shifted, her ankle stung, shooting her awake.

"Get up, if you're able," Dajjer said and turned, walking a few steps before he stopped, keeping his back to her. He was waiting on her.

Cyji used the wagon to pull herself up, hopping on her good leg. As her bleary eyes cleared, she discovered the entire group stood behind the wagon, faces lacking any hint of emotion. What were they doing? Was now the time they would separate from her, to leave her there, alone and wounded in an unfamiliar place?

"Everybody. Listen." Dajjer turned so he faced both Cyji and the group. "Cyji made a mistake and, because of it, endangered us all. But I feel we are free of that danger, just as I believe Cyji recognizes not only her mistake, but the consequences of her rash decisions. Therefore, I ask all of you to forgive her and accept her again as one of us, as I have forgiven and accepted her." His hard eyes softened.

The people nodded approval, their tightened lips loosening to reserved smiles. Dajjer hugged Cyji, the gesture unexpected, but she returned the embrace. He stepped back and grinned. Each member of the group approached and hugged her. Children accompanied parents and wrapped sapling-sized arms around Cyji's knees, each mindful not to upset her ankle.

"It looks like you'll get a feel of me today," Rosh said as he wobbled close. His odor preceded him, an invisible cloud of sweat, smoke and a dozen other unidentifiable scents to wrinkle the nose. "Just this time, I'll let you." His thick arms went around her, and he pulled Cyji close. She summoned every shred of composure to keep from gagging.

They all ate breakfast. The mood was lighter, more festive and friendly. Laughter was again heard among conversations, and children hurriedly devoured their food so they could run and play at the Risc's edge while ignoring the adults' terse warnings about venturing too close to the swamp.

"You think you can walk a bit?" Dajjer asked Cyji as she was finishing her meal. "I've someone for you to meet. He may be able to help you."

"I can walk. But if he can help me, I'll run to him." Cyji brought herself upright.

"Running isn't necessary. And neither was sneaking into town for information, if you'd just been patient."

"If you told me about this someone sooner, I wouldn't have gone into town in the first place."

"I never reveal my plans. I keep them private and prefer they remain fluid. That way, when a reckless girl mucks them up, they can be quickly and easily altered." Dajjer withdrew two enchanted spears from the wagon, the last of their spoils from the ambush.

"Follow me," he told Cyji, Rosh and Tulla.

They left camp and traced the Risc's edge. The swamp thinned and narrowed along its southernmost border until it converged with the Balk. A slender path cut between, with rock on the left, and murk to the right. Moss covered the path, but beneath the spongy growth was stone; solid and unyielding. Ivy snaked from the Risc, crossing the path to climb the Balk's steep jaggedness, gaining purchase among cracks and shelfs to ascend far overhead, beyond the Risc's canopy, beyond sight of the men and women trampling it below.

"You want me to carry you, lass?" Rosh asked with a devious grin.

"I'm doing fine without you," Cyji replied, trying hard to hide the difficulty she was having. The crutches with their narrow bottoms found more soft than firm spots and sunk fast into moss-hidden depressions, making Cyji's progress labored and slow. She refused to accept any help, especially from Rosh. Surprisingly, the Risc's odor was more offensive than the one latched to Rosh.

The path continued to tighten, forcing Cyji to sidle awkwardly. Then it abruptly ended. Sagging tree limbs blocked their way. Dajjer pushed them aside, revealing a narrow cave entrance in the Balk's face. He sidestepped into it. Rosh cursed the thin gap instead of his bulky frame and squeezed in with a series of grunts. Tulla followed with little effort. Cyji, becoming more accustomed to walking like a crab, entered the awaiting gloom.

The narrow passageway was, to Cyji's relief, short. It opened into a lamp-lit cavern with two tunnels leading deeper into the Balk. Stalactites hung above like menacing teeth, while below, rhythmic dripping disturbed puddles with ceaseless ripples. Benches, chairs, a table, cupboard and two beds pushed against the cavern's slanting walls to lay crooked and leaning. Somebody lived in this dark, damp place, under stone, without the scent of pines or the shine of stars. It seemed a dreadful existence.

"Grodin!" Dajjer shouted, his voice echoing down the

tunnels. He waited a moment and called again. "Grodin! Get out here! You've guests!"

Dajjer's call was answered with the rattling of a chain from somewhere deep down one of the tunnels. A soft light chased the darkness away in the passage's distance. The light came closer, casting a vaguely humanoid shadow against the stone.

"Guests?" a shrill voice said. "Guests are to be invited, and I've not invited any. How about you, Trask? Have you been inviting guests without my knowing?"

"We've magic to trade," Dajjer said, his voice lower now.

"Magic? Well, that's an entirely different matter." Grodin's voice lowered as well, though it was no less shrill.

The light was close now, near the cavern's edge. A pale hand held onto a chain fastened to a lantern's top. Light splashed onto a soot-smeared face. A bone-white beard dangled from deeply lined cheeks, so long it swept the ground with each step the elderly man took. He glanced at each of his guests in turn, eyes slit with suspicion. They widened upon finding Cyji.

"An illkin? You brought us an illkin? Get it out of here. We want no part of it. Come on, Trask." He spun about and began walking back into the tunnel from which he came.

"She's no illkin," Dajjer said. "This girl is from an island. An island where the starwood grows."

Grodin halted and almost stepped on his beard. "The rumors are true?" He turned to face Dajjer. "Or is this a trick?"

Dajjer shook his head. "No trick, Grodin. Let's trade. Magic for gold and information."

"Information, eh? What do you think, Trask?" Grodin cocked his head slightly and directed his question to nobody standing at his side. For a moment, Grodin said nothing, but nodded intently, then smiled and returned his attention to Dajjer. "Trask makes some good points."

Cyji wanted to know more about this Trask she couldn't see, but another question prevailed. "You're not afraid of me?"

"Afraid of you? A girl?" Grodin's laughter bounced off the cavern's walls as he turned to the unseen and unheard Trask. "Did you hear that? She thinks we should be afraid of her." His laughter ended as fast as it had begun. "Of course, I didn't mean to offend her. I know. I know. It was impolite to behave that way. Now, Trask, you listen to me. You were laughing too. No, I don't think she would agree." He carried on the conversation for a few minutes, Cyji and the others privy to hearing only one side of the exchange. Finally, he turned back to the visible and audible persons in the cavern, his gaze resting on Cyji. "Trask is right. I must apologize for laughing at you. No, we're not afraid of you. For a long time there have been rumors of a people dark as illkin, but without the insanity. These tales are told by sailors and are often dismissed by simpler folk as fables told by seafaring drunkards. For the wiser of us, those who listen as much as hear, we find some truth in their stories, however scant it may be. You may not believe it, but I was young once and this beard was much shorter and much blacker. Before I met Trask, I spent many nights drinking my day's wages, often at some tavern by the sea. The sailors frequenting these places often loosened their tongues after a few drinks, but only when their captain wasn't around, because captains tolerated no such prattling from the crew. Sailors spoke of voyages and of an island where they delivered goods and received cargo of starwood. They spoke of trees large enough to poke holes in the curtain of night and that's the reason we have stars now. Sailors also spoke of islanders, with skin the color of charred wood.

"When I first heard the rumor, I dismissed it, as most people do. But after being in several inns on several nights for several years, hearing the tale retold a dozen different ways, but with all the same key elements, I started questioning how much was actually untrue. Whenever I pressed the sailors for more information, they would always go quiet and give each other nervous looks, as if they said too much. Eventually, the familiar-faced sailors disappeared, replaced by new men. Men who drank less and didn't talk at all. I've wondered what happened to those other sailors. I don't think they were replaced. I believe they were killed. It's how the secret of starwood remains. Dead men don't speak. Dead men spill no secrets.

"That is what the Ascendancy prizes most. It guards the secret fiercely. It does everything in its power to keep people from knowing the truth. They persist lies of the blockade protecting Azazura from invaders from far off savage lands, or sea monsters able to devour a ship in one bite. Anything to keep people yoked. It's why I came here. The knowledge I gathered was dangerous and the tunnels of the Balk were my only refuge. There are others here, hiding in the maze of tunnels or in the Risc because it's safer than being among the order. It's how I met Trask. He's annoying at times, but he's fair company. If you were wise, child, you'd hide here as well. If the Ascendancy becomes aware of your presence in Azazura, it will do anything to stop you because you know the truth and truth is one product the Ascendancy doesn't deal in."

"Speaking of dealings," Dajjer said, his tone light and playful, contrasting the seriousness of Grodin's words. "Are you willing to do some trading now?"

Grodin's gaze remained fixed on Cyji a moment longer before drifting onto Dajjer. "Very well. Let's see what you have." Dajjer held forth the spears. Grodin passed the lantern over them, its light catching their luster. He regarded each for a moment and shrugged. "Native magic. Nothing impressive here and nothing worth our time or money."

"Native magic?" Cyji asked.

"Yes. Yes. Native magic," Grodin said, a hint of irritation in his words. "Each domain has native magic. Kyrkynstaag has iron-like and fire-felt. Dorsluin has airy and suspension. Morivar, influence and ice-kissed."

"Why?" Cyji asked.

"I don't know. Something to do with the particular stars they harvest the wood from." Grodin's annoyance was becoming more evident in his tone.

"But they don't. Godspear, um, starwood, doesn't come from

the sky. It comes from Vidrey," Cyji said.

"I don't care," Grodin said, now fully irritated. "Just come back when you have some airy or influence."

"Not so easy to get these days," Dajjer said. "What about this?" He slipped the sack of jarnium from his belt and opened it.

Grodin rubbed his hands together and licked his lips. "Jarnium. We can always use more of that."

"I thought it had no purpose," Cyji said.

"I told you I didn't know its purpose," Dajjer said. "Grodin has theories, though."

Grodin nodded vigorously. "Yes I do, and I'll gladly take it." He reached for the sack.

"Not until we settle on a price," Dajjer said.

"Price? Of course. What do you think, Trask? How much is it worth?" Another round of half-heard conversation ensued. "We'll give you a quarter of its weight in gold for it."

"That's all? Grodin, you insult me." Dajjer cinched the sack and tied it to his belt. "I can do better elsewhere."

"Others would eagerly accept my offer. I may be in a cave, but I'm no fool. Jarnium isn't so easy to sell."

"It isn't so easy to get, either," Rosh said. He'd been unusually quiet and inoffensive until now.

"And how many others are coming here to trade?" Dajjer asked. "Not many."

Grodin glanced to his left, listening again to something or someone only he could hear. "Trask counts three in the past year, including yourself."

"So you haven't a lot of supply for your experiments?"

Grodin snapped his fingers. "My experiments. I'd nearly forgotten. I was just about to perform another. Come with us. We'll show you." He turned and headed back down the passage, not waiting for Dajjer or the others to follow. "Come along, Trask. You know I can't do this without you."

"He's gone mad," Tulla whispered at Cyji's side. "I suppose

living alone in this place will do that to a man."

"Mad?" Grodin asked over his shoulder. "Perhaps. The labyrinths of the Balk are a sanctuary for Trask and I. Here we can live without the order's meddling. Here, Trask and I have no need to wander, unlike you. Someday you'll understand and appreciate my brand of madness. You'll tire of being a vagabond and settle in your own cave."

"Not me," Tulla said. "Give me fresh air and stars overhead."

"Someday, you'll be caught by the Ascendancy. You'll see no stars from a prison cell," Grodin said. "Then Grodin won't seem so crazy."

"I'll die before I'm caught," Tulla said defiantly.

"No stars for the dead," Grodin mumbled. "No fresh air, either."

They rounded a corner, and the tunnel expanded into another large cavern. The walls and ceiling were braced with heavy timbers, while thick ropes wove through a pulley system supporting a massive boulder hanging a man's height off the ground. Beneath it lay a single arrow, its blue luster swirling in the lamplight. How this man, with imaginary friend or not, managed to raise a boulder into the air was perplexing to Cyji. The elaborate system reminded her of the efforts it took to move godspear after it was cut and bucked and the equipment required for such feats. Grodin may have been crazy, but his ingenuity was impressive.

"One of your competitors brought me that," Grodin said as he walked beneath the boulder and knelt, holding his beard to one side while using his free hand to adjust the arrow so it teetered on a small rock. "One of my theories is, and Trask agrees, starwood and its magical properties aren't created by the Ascendancy. Your companion, Dajjer, is already proof. Now I pursue to debunk it entirely. The Ascendancy are purveyors of magic, nothing more. What's intriguing is the magic itself, and we strive to discover its source. That's what this contraption is for. To study magic in its unrestrained state."

As Grodin adjusted the arrow, a fragment of color among the otherwise gray and beige of a rubble pile to her left drew Cyji's attention. She nudged Tulla and subtly motioned to it. The color belonged to a scrap of red cloth, the tattered remnants of a sleeve. Concealed beneath and partly interred by stone were the distinguishing bones of a human forearm.

Tulla gasped. "Trask."

"He's real? Or, was real?" Cyji whispered, glancing nervously at Grodin. He still fiddled with the arrow and seemed unaware of what was happening behind him. "I thought Trask was imaginary, somebody Grodin invented to keep him company in his isolation."

"We've dealt with Grodin and Trask before," Tulla said. "Trask was alive the last time we were here."

She turned and beckoned Dajjer to come near. When Dajjer saw what they'd discovered, he sighed and frowned. He knelt and removed some of the rocks, unresting a fetid stench of latent decay into the air. Cyji and Tulla covered their mouths to stifle gags, but Dajjer simply rose and returned to where he'd been standing before. Cyji and Tulla joined him once their composure was regained.

"That sack of jarnium you have. I think it's part of the enchanting process," Grodin said, unaware of what had transpired behind him. "The Ascendancy does well in preserving its true purpose, but it can't hide its value. Why do they mine it? Why does Kyrkynstaag ship it to Morivar and Dorsluin? These are questions in need of answers. But answers are not given by the order, so we must discover them on our own." He stepped away from the arrow and returned to the others. "Oh, the Ascendancy says it's for the stained glass in the spires, but have you seen the spires? They have windows, but not many. And not all are stained glass. Certainly not enough to warrant the need for a mine. So why all the jarnium?"

"Grodin," Dajjer interrupted. "What happened to Trask?"

"What do you mean?" said Grodin, gesturing to his left. "He's right here."

"Were there any accidents?" Dajjer asked. "Any problems?

Did Trask get hurt?"

Grodin blinked several times before bursting out in laughter. "There are no accidents with experiments. Just findings. And Trask is quite well, as you can see."

Dajjer nodded. "Yes, I see."

"But—" Tulla began.

Dajjer turned sharply, his stare bearing down on her. It was a look warning her to make no mention of Trask's fate. Grodin was certainly insane, but still functional—to a limit, but it hinged on him believing his companion was still alive. It was Grodin's version of reality, hanging by a slender and frayed thread. If the thread was cut, Grodin would likely plunge fully into the depths of madness, never to return.

Grodin rubbed his hands together. "Now, if you're finished with the odd questions, I suggest you all go and hide behind that wall. What happens next is not something you want to witness without cover."

The wall wasn't a man-made structure. Rather, it was a cluster of stalagmites grown close together over the centuries. Their tips were missing, as if blasted away, to leave sharp-edged caps. Behind the natural wall, a taut rope climbed into the darkness of the cave overhead. Cyji and the others moved behind the stalagmites and crouched. Grodin joined them, urging Trask to hurry with his fine-tuning of the experiment.

"Get ready." Grodin gripped the rope. "As soon as I pull, everybody duck."

He gave a quick tug and the boulder dropped, landing squarely on the arrow and snapping it in two. Whether it was the sound of the boulder's impact, or something else, Cyji couldn't be sure, but the succeeding boom was deafening. A gust of air struck her with sudden and powerful force. Overhead, timbers and stone cracked and groaned. Stones fragments shook loose above, raining on Cyji and the others. Cyji feared the cavern would collapse, but the reinforced timbers held strong. Choking dust filled the space as a silence settled. Lamps swung from posts, their light cast on the ground, the ceiling, the ground and so forth until they stilled. When calm returned to the cavern, Cyji turned to the others.

They all shivered violently.

"What's wrong?" she asked.

"Cold. So very cold," Tulla said, her teeth chattering.

Dajjer wrapped his arms around himself. "Don't you feel it?"

"No. Just the blast, I think," Cyji said.

Grodin rose and shook off the cold. "Interesting. The same effect each time. The energy contained within the arrow was released in a magnificent explosion. Wouldn't you agree, Trask?" He waited in silence for a moment. "Well, of course it did. Can you see any shards sticking out from under the boulder? The arrow is completely and utterly destroyed."

Cyji hobbled to the boulder, inspecting the area for any sign of the arrow. Nothing. "What happened to the arrow?"

"Disintegrated," Grodin said flatly. "When something magical is broken, all that magic is released at once. The energy of the reaction destroys the starwood in the process."

Dajjer joined them, his shivering now gone. "Lucky I've brought more magic for you to experiment with." He shook the spears in his hand.

Grodin nodded. "And you're lucky I was working with ice-kissed today. Had it been iron-like, you'd have been slammed against the wall. Or stuck in place if it had been suspension. Destroying a thing is easy. It's magic's creation which intrigues me and Trask. But you're right. I need more to experiment on. What's your price for the spears and jarnium?"

"For you, half their weight in gold," Dajjer said.

"Half? Outrageous!" Grodin cocked an ear. "Eh? What's that, Trask?" He listened intently to a voice only he could hear. "All right, Trask. All right. All good points." Grodin's attention returned to Dajjer. "You'll need to excuse Trask. He gets rather excited at times. Very well. I accept. Though, what good will jarnium do us without raw starwood?"

"Raw starwood?" Cyji asked.

"Yes. I believe jarnium is used in enchanting starwood. I'm not certain how, but I've some theories, mostly what I've gathered from rumors. Obtaining raw starwood is impossible. I don't suppose you brought any with you from your island."

Cyji's hand moved to the pendant beneath her shirt and pulled it out. Grodin's eyes sparkled with lustful fascination.

"That's starwood, isn't it?" He edged closer to her, eyes fixed on the pendant. "Raw starwood? I've never seen anything so beautiful." Grodin stared, mesmerized. "I'll pay you well for it. Enough for you to live your days without want." He pawed at the pendant. Cyji backed away, out of his reach.

"It's not for sale or trade," Cyji said.

Grodin slouched and pouted. "May I touch it at least." Reluctantly, Cyji removed the pendant and handed it to Grodin. He cooed as the godspear fell into his palm, and made soft noises of glee as he ran a gnarled finger over it. "It's so smooth. So solid. Look at the grain. Like no other wood I've seen. It's marvelous, wouldn't you agree, Trask? The closest I have to raw starwood are rounds. I've tried experimenting with them, but the order does something to them during the minting process. They char them, I think, which alters the starwood's composition, making them unreceptive to enchanting. I've had more than a few disasters while attempting to enchant rounds." His eyes flicked briefly in the direction of the rubble pile where Trask's body lay.

Cyji held her hand out, drawing Grodin's attention back to her.

He gazed upon her with sorrow-drowned eyes. Reluctantly, he returned the pendant to its rightful owner. "If you ever decide to part with it, my offer stands. That pendant would go far in helping to understand the enchantment process."

"While you're waiting on that, how about we settle?" Dajjer shook the spears for emphasis.

"Yes, I suppose we can do that," Grodin said, his words still laden with disappointment. "Let's see, we agreed to one quarter their weight in gold."

"Half their weight," Dajjer corrected. Despite his dubious faculties, Grodin's shrewdness in the deal hadn't wavered. "Plus information."

"What knowledge do you seek? Neither Trask nor myself venture far from the cave these days. I'm afraid we're quite ignorant of the goings-on in Azazura."

Dajjer gave a brief nod of consent to Cyji. She explained to Grodin the events leading her to him: the godspear plight, her voyage to the mainland and her journey with Dajjer and his group. Grodin listened, casting the occasional concerned glance to his side where he believed Trask to be standing. When Cyji finished, Grodin released a long breath.

"All troubling news," he said. "If the starwood, um, godspear, is truly imperiled, then the Ascendancy will be more dangerous than ever. It'll do all it can to protect itself. I'm afraid neither Trask nor myself can offer any insight about curing your trees. I've no knowledge about beetles. But thank you. What you've told me about your home has given me great insight I'll apply in my experiments."

"You want these or not?" Dajjer asked.

"Certainly," Grodin said. "Let's return to the front. There you can enjoy some mushroom wine while I get your payment."

Returning to the furnished cave, Grodin poured the promised mushroom wine into two cups. "I lack accommodations for so many guests. You'll need to share," he explained. He passed the first cup to Dajjer and the second to Tulla. "Drink as much as you like, I'll be back shortly." With lantern in hand and presumably Trask in tow—or perhaps Trask remained to see after the guests—Grodin disappeared into the second tunnel.

Dajjer sipped from the cup. "Not the worst wine I've had, but not the best by any length."

Tulla sipped and spat it out. "It's disgusting. Like drinking mud." She handed the cup to Cyji with a grimace fueled by the wine's aftertaste.

Cyji sloshed the contents of the cup. The liquid was gray and cloudy, with a strong resemblance to the water in a tub after washing dirty buckskins. She sipped. Tulla was right. It was disgusting. Bitter. Dirty washtub water had more appeal. Rosh, however, had taken Dajjer's cup and consumed all its contents.

"I like it." He poured himself another cupful and gulped it down. "Here, lass, give it to me." Rosh snatched Cyji's cup. He grunted as he stared into the tunnel Grodin had entered. "Fool of a madman. Talking to nobody and thinking he can do what ascendants do. He deserves to be in here. He's as crazy as illkin." Rosh's gaze wandered the cavern before falling on Cyji. He smirked. "That necklace of yours is quite the prize. Nice and valuable." His stare hovered in the space between the pendant and Cyji's bosom.

Cyji ignored him. "Where did he go?"

"To get the gold," Dajjer said. "Rumor has it back there is an abandoned mine and Grodin has access to a vein of gold."

Rosh took a step toward the passage. "Maybe we should go see for ourselves. Maybe we should help ourselves, too."

Dajjer's hand fell on Rosh's shoulder. "Hold, Rosh. We may be bandits, but only against the Ascendancy. We're not thieves and cutthroats to the good people of Azazura."

Grodin returned with a chunk of gold half as large as the hand holding it.

"Well traded," Dajjer said as the spears and jarnium left one hand and gold dropped into the other.

Grodin's eyes sparkled in the dim light. "Well traded, indeed. Come back when you have more exotic magics." His eyes found Cyji. "Or raw starwood."

Outside, Fedik was waiting for them.

"I've news," he said between a grin. "A caravan of godspear is crossing Kyrkynstaag. Lightly guarded, with riches too great to ignore."

CHAPTER 12

"That's some fine work. As fine as I've ever seen," Drudylan said, leaning over Lavak's shoulder.

Lavak sat at his workbench and finished etching the piece in his hand. Carefully, he scribed a pattern committed to memory. Drudylan shifted behind him. The master craftsman's presence was distracting, but a few more nibbles with the awl and the piece was finished. Lavak set the tool on the workbench and admired his work.

"Fine job," Drudylan said. "But I'd expect nothing less coming from a Vidreyan. You all know how to shape godspear."

"Not all of us," Lavak said. In his palm rested a beetle carved from godspear. Spanning the width of his hand, it was a larger representation of the scourge affecting his home. He turned it over and searched for imperfections and found none. "My father, my family, are all cutters. They swing axes all day and never tire. As for me, I can barely lift an ax. There's no cutter inside me."

Drudylan came around to the side of the workbench and faced Lavak. He thrust his hands out, revealing palms and fingers toughened by years of callouses. "See these hands? They're not for shuffling papers. They're not for commanding people. These are working hands. Hands meant for labor. I'll never be supreme, or prime, and that's all right. You know why? Because I'd rather be here, making things. Sawdust in my hair is a whole lot better than ink on my fingers. What I'm trying to say is, never think just because you're different, you don't belong. We all have strengths and weaknesses."

Lavak smiled at the clarity of Drudylan's advice. To hear the simple yet profound explanation was refreshing. His gaze wandered from beetle to mentor. It was surprising where great wisdom was found.

"You may not be good at swinging axes and doing the rough kind of work," Drudylan continued, "but you've a talent for intricacy. It's rare to see such craftsmanship come from a novice. That'll help in the enchantment process. What you do here, in this workshop, is the foundation for all the steps which follow."

Hammer tapping interspersed Drudylan's words as aspirants around the room attended their own works. His back was to the rest of the shop, but Lavak knew who else was there. He could sense them, or more precisely, he sensed the magic they carried. He didn't know the names of those working, but their enchantments identified them. Weak fire-felts, robust iron-likes and moderate suspensions all marked the wearers clearer than any name. Each time an order member entered or left the place, Lavak knew who without looking, by the presence or absence of a magic's savor. Only a few lacked any savor, and those were the youngest of aspirants admitted into the workshop.

Sometimes the mixture of magic overwhelmed him. Flavors and smells of enchantment assaulted Lavak in constant waves, forcing him to leave the workshop and clear his senses. He often found his way upstairs to where money was made. There, ascenders operated lathes, rounding lengths of godspear into one of four sizes of rods. These rods were cut into disks, with the smallest about the size of Lavak's thumbnail and the largest as wide as his palm. Every disk was scorched and emblazoned with the denotation of the Ascendancy, officially marking it as currency. Even without enchantment, the Ascendancy had managed to make godspear coveted, for all people of Azazura desired wealth.

"Just one question," Drudylan asked. "Why a beetle?"

"As a reminder of why I'm here and the trouble still plaguing my people."

Drudylan nodded. "Interesting, to make from godspear the creature which destroys it."

"I suppose."

Drudylan rested a hand on Lavak's shoulder. "I didn't mean to offend you."

"You didn't. The pendant reminds me of home. Most of my life I wanted to leave the island, but having been gone so long now, I find myself wanting to return."

"Homesick? I've never been homesick for the orphanage. You're lucky to have people who miss you."

Drudylan's words gave little comfort. It was doubtful anybody back home missed Lavak. Who did he miss? Not many. None, actually. Not even his own family. All he missed was the island itself, because despite being an outcast among his own kind, the island was home.

"You'll get back there someday, and you'll have the cure in hand when you do. Until then, let's focus on the present. The supreme is on her way. She expects me to have taught you a few things. So, let me give you a test on the subjects you studied during your week here, unless you want her to hang me by my neck from the top of the spire."

"Of course not." Lavak set the piece down and spun on his stool to face Drudylan. "Test me."

Drudylan rubbed his hands together. "Me and my neck thank you. Question one. Is suspension recommended for arrows?"

"No. Suspension works best through blunt force. An arrow pierces, which may be suitable for suspension of a target, but not ideal. Items such as sling bullets, cudgels and war hammers are better for that enchantment. It disperses along the body better."

"Very good," Drudylan said. "Question two. Is a staff superior to an ax when enchanted?"

"That's a trick question," Lavak said.

Drudylan cocked an eyebrow. "Oh? Are you questioning me?"

"A staff has more wood by volume. Therefore, it contains more magic. However, with an ax, only the handle is enchanted. The head is not. The blade does most of the work. The magic only augments and it bleeds out slowly, whereas with a staff, any part can be used for attack, so the discharge of magic is more rapid. To answer your question, a staff is neither superior nor inferior. The application is different."

"Excellent. Next question. When you join many fire-felt slats together, do they emit more or less heat?"

"The heat remains constant to the slat." Lavak had read this lesson in one of Drudylan's many recommended books. "That is, all the slats emit an equal amount of heat. When combined, we perceive them to be hotter to the touch, but they are not."

"Very good. Let's continue with fire-felt. Why does water placed in an enchanted pitcher boil, but sticking your finger in the same pitcher when it's empty not burn you?"

"Water reacts to magic, not the pitcher. Its mass fills the container. It's fluid and so contacts a large area of the pitcher's interior surface. A person's finger doesn't. Somebody would need to stuff their entire arm in and somehow have their skin touch every part of the pitcher's inside to feel a hint of heat."

"Why, then, can you wrap your fingers around a fire-felt arrow and only feel warmth? Why don't you get burned? Why must the arrow strike you hard for its full effect to be felt?"

"The arrow is passive until shot. Unlike a container, where the enchantment is in flux due to the shape of the container, an arrow's magic is at rest. It's when the arrow comes to an abrupt stop the magic is discharged."

Drudylan nodded. "Wonderful. Next question. If an iron-like arrow is fired at iron-like armor, which will be defeated?"

Lavak thought for a moment before speaking. "It depends.

There are several factors to consider such as the strength of each enchantment, including age, the skill of the enchanters who made them, and so on. If everything was equal, arrow and armor would negate each other."

"Now, time for a simple test on the reading material I gave you the other day. How did the order first discover godspear was magical?"

Lavak rubbed his chin as he dredged the information from his memory. Drudylan had furnished him with a stack of books to study. None provided straightforward details regarding enchantment. A paragraph on one page referenced a footnote in another book, which in turn alluded to an ascendant's memoir in yet another book. The trail to learning enchantment was a winding one. "It was by accident. At the time, jarnium grindings were used as an additive to darken clay. One day a potter was throwing a bowl on his godspear wheel. He lost control of his creation and the bowl collapsed. In a fit of rage and frustration, he flung the clay aside and threw the wheel into his kiln. After he regained his composure, the potter checked the kiln, and to his surprise, the wooden wheel wasn't marred by fire. It had luster and was stronger than before. It was weak compared to today's standard of magic, but it was the first crucial step in uncovering the godspear's secret."

"Correct. After the discovery, the order refined the process begun by the potter into what we know as enchanting today. Next question. After it was realized the combination of water, fire, godspear and jarnium created magic, what did the order try in its search for other constituents having the same effect?"

"Everything," Lavak said.

"Indeed. Everything was given to experiment. Beeswax. Grave dirt. Goat's milk. Horse dung. Cat vomit. Deer hooves. Gutter slime. If you can think it, it was probably attempted in enchanting. It's how the order came to learn of the six elements." Drudylan slapped his legs and grinned. "Looks like my neck is safe for now."

The workshop door opened, and Volstrysa strode in. "Is it

done?"

"A masterpiece from an apprentice," Drudylan said proudly. "He's a quick study. See for yourself." He stepped aside to allow Volstrysa room.

Volstrysa took the beetle from Lavak and examined it for several minutes. "Impressive. The detail is extraordinary. The best I've seen in a long while."

"Thank you." Lavak's lips tingled as if on the brink of turning numb. Something ice-kissed was hidden inside Volstrysa's robes.

She laid the beetle in Lavak's waiting palm. "Now that you have passed your first trial in enchanting, you may begin the next. Are you ready?"

Lavak nodded and followed her out. Drudylan gave him a congratulatory pat on the back as Lavak left.

In the anteroom, Lavak found his old attire replaced with new robes. The cloth was of finer quality, with stitching and embroideries of gold he'd only seen adorn the supreme's and prime's attire. "You were in need of better clothes. Your old robes were becoming threadbare." Volstrysa removed the robe from the peg and held it before him.

Lavak removed his apron and hung it on the peg before accepting the robe from the supreme. His head began to throb. He winced under the robes as they slipped over him, pain raging in his mind. There was magic somewhere in his new robes. Despite the intense throbbing, he regained himself. He wanted to appear unruffled before the supreme. She didn't know of his ability, and Lavak intended to keep it that way.

Why was she using magic on him? He'd been nothing but compliant with her and given Volstrysa no reason to question him. Was she scheming for another reason? He had no answer. Until he did, he'd allow Volstrysa her deceptions. Meanwhile, he'd need to find the enchantment and remove it before the aching became unbearable.

"Follow me," Volstrysa said with a smile.

They left the workshop and proceeded to a nearby building. Lavak had seen this place many times from the spire. From his view on high, its design was obvious: six spokes converging at a central hub. The spire itself functioned (by intention or not) as a large sundial, and when its shadow fell on this particular building, the bells of the city tolled three.

They strode to the hub door, framed within thick blocks of stone. Volstrysa rapped on it. The door opened to reveal a wiry old gentleman with fanning gray hair. His arced spine left him with a perpetual hump as he motioned Volstrysa and her charge to enter. From behind a white cloth mask covering the lower half of his wrinkled face came a raspy cough.

Inside, six more doors branched from the hub, entrances to each of the six spokes. Every door was identical in size and shape but were either painted white, red, blue, black, purple or green.

"Each of these doors leads to an element lab." Volstrysa swept her arm in a grand gesture to encompass all the doors. "As you can see, their color denotes what each wing is dedicated to." She pointed at the red door. "Fire-felt. In there, eldrite crystals are infused with items to give the properties of flame." She flicked a hand at the black door. "That is where objects are imbued with iron-like from jarnium powder, brought from the quarry in Kyrkynstaag. The purple door leads to the labs where suspension magic is applied."

Her information was rudimentary, and Lavak was grateful for the overly simplistic lesson because he only half-heard Volstrysa's words as he struggled amid the pains of magic emanating from his robes to seek answers to new questions regarding her intentions for him.

"Influence lies behind the green door. It comes from our valdsker mine. It's the rarest of all elements. It's highly sought after and, therefore, highly valuable. It's also the most difficult to master enchanting. Even with skilled hands, the magic it yields is not always predictable.

"There was a time, long ago, when wars were fought for the

elements. The instability from constant turmoil had loosened the Ascendancy's hold on the people. The order was in danger of falling. After many bloody conflicts, the supremes convened to draft the first modern laws of the Ascendancy. Azazura was divided into three domains, each ruled by a supreme. Each domain possessed two elements. It was agreed domains would exchange elements to further the order's cause. A chest of kalatite from Morivar is exchanged for a chest of noxstone from Dorsluin. The only exception is valdsker. It demands a three to one exchange due to its rarity and power. Morivar has become quite wealthy because of it.

"Elements can mix in their natural state without incident. They're inert; however, if they mix and enchantment is attempted, explosion occurs. The godspear is ruined along with weeks of effort and preparation. This room is a neutral space. It prevents contamination by isolating each wing. Here you must choose which element you will use for enchanting. Once you do, you can only enter that wing until the process is complete and you begin a new enchantment. It's vital that elements are kept isolated at this stage of enchanting.

"This will be practice for you, Lavak, so you may understand the ways of magic. The enchantment you give is unimportant, only the knowledge gained matters, however, it's impractical to empower something like your pendant with fire-felt or ice-kissed, as those offer no useful properties to ornamentations. I suggest iron-like or airy as your first trial."

"Influence," Lavak said.

Volstrysa's eyes widened in surprise. "Influence? Are you sure? It can be fickle for the practiced and aggravating to the uninitiated."

"I'm the transcendent, aren't I?" Lavak said. If he truly was exceptional as she claimed, she shouldn't question his choice. "It should be an easy task."

"Very true. I hope you're right." She turned to the old man. "A new enchanter."

The old man nodded, the gesture exaggerating the hump between his shoulders. "Certainly, Supreme," he said with a cracked and fragile voice. He coughed violently until the fit ended with a disgusting gag. Upon lifting the mask from his face, a thin stream of spittle dangled from dry lips. The old man spat it to the ground and straightened his body to a less crooked state. "Come with me." He hobbled to the green door, opened it and passed into the hall beyond.

Lavak began to follow until he noticed Volstrysa remaining fixed in the hub's center. "You're not coming?"

Volstrysa shook her head. "No. I spent enough of my life within those walls. My throat can't tolerate the scratching dust. I've matters of state to address, anyway. Go on. You're in capable hands."

The old man closed the door, separating Lavak from Volstrysa. He removed an apron and mask similar to his own from a hook on the wall. Several more hooks hung there, each burdened by aprons and masks or robes.

"Take your robe off," the old man said. "Hang it on the hook." He waited as Lavak complied. "Now, put these on." The apron went on easily, but Lavak was uncertain how to don the mask. "Like this," the old man said, a hint of irritation in his rasping voice. He slipped it over Lavak's nose and mouth and tied the four strings attached to it behind his neck and head. "You'll get used to the air, but keep the mask on. Exposure to your throat and lungs will feel like broken glass, and the damage is permanent." The old man motioned to a broom leaning by a bucket. "Before you leave here each night, shake your clothes. You shake them good, until no more element comes off. Any valdsker shaken loose you sweep up and put into the bucket. Understand?"

"Yes. Are you the master enchanter?"

The old man wheezed a laugh before stifling a cough. "No. Just the sweeper. Dust goes everywhere. I sweep. I clean. I don't enchant. Not anymore." He quieted another cough.

They passed through a series of doorways on their way to the far end of the passage. With each new door opened, a thicker cloud of glittering, fine particles assaulted them. Lavak's eyes stung and watered. He now understood the old man's warning. The air was polluted, and to breathe it invited malady. The old man coughed again. Lavak retied the strings so his mask was tighter against his face. A thin layer of the dust already clung to his clothes. At least the ache in his head had lessened and continued to diminish the more distance was gained between him and the robe. He wondered if he'd chosen poorly with influence as his first enchantment. Had he ditched the robes only to subject himself to more torment in what lay ahead?

At the final door, where the stagnant air was choked by valdsker dust, the old man knocked. A wiry fellow in his sixth decade, his head shaved like those of the clean-pated aspirants a fifth his age, opened the door. His apron and mask were immaculate, albeit coated in green dust.

"I was told to expect you." His voice was hoarse, and as he spoke it sounded as if he struggled to keep a cough suppressed. "I'm Master Enchanter Corundra. Influence is my specialty."

Possibly the man responsible for the enchantment sewn into my new robes. "An honor." Lavak bowed in respect. "Volstrysa, I mean, Supreme Volstrysa only just asked my choice of enchantment. How could you be expecting me?"

Corundra shrugged. "In her infinite wisdom, the supreme probably informed each master enchanter to expect you. Or, by the same unmatched wisdom, she suspected you'd choose influence. Now, let me see what you've brought."

Lavak displayed the beetle in his hand.

"A unique piece. I've never seen a beetle before. A bit ghastly for jewelry, perhaps. I'm not sure you could persuade anybody to wear it. However, since this is an exercise in enchanting, it doesn't matter. Your craftsmanship is remarkable, but whittling godspear is only one step in the process. What you're about to undertake here is the most important. I cannot overstate that enough. What you do in the next room will determine the potency of your item's magic.

"You've chosen influence as your first enchantment. Normally, I'd refuse to permit an amateur from wasting valuable element on an initial attempt. However, considering your unique situation, I'll allow it. Before we proceed through the next door, what do you know about valdsker?"

"Not much," Lavak admitted. "It's rare. Morivar possesses the mine. It's used to enchant influence. And, if it's what is in the air, I find it quite irritating."

Corundra's gruff laugh was phlegm-laden. "All true. Especially the last point. You haven't been exposed long enough to have it seep under your clothes and abrade your skin. It itches awful. You'll get used to it. Or, you'll go mad. I recommend always wearing your mask.

"Usually, aspirants are sent to the quarry or mine before they're allowed to enchant so they gain an understanding of an element's source. Since your situation is unique, I'll give you a brief lesson instead.

"We mine valdsker, or rather, those who owe the Ascendancy mine it. They don't know what it's for and they know better than to ask. It's our secret. Not theirs. Valdsker is difficult to extract. Jarnium is easily distinguishable in rock layers. Noxstone is—"

"Where does noxstone come from?" Lavak asked.

"Hmm. I've some work ahead of me. Aspirants usually know such things already. I'd have thought Volstrysa would've given you a syllabus before sending you here. I wasn't expecting to be your guide through academia."

"I've been working on finding a cure," Lavak said, agitated. Corundra's tone was bordering close to that of a grackle. "No formal schooling has been offered to me, and if it were, I'd only take it if it meant finding that cure. I'm here because Volstrysa thinks learning enchantment will help my endeavor. If you've a problem with my disparity of education, I suggest you speak to her about it."

Corundra stared blankly at Lavak, clearly taken aback. He

chuckled and coughed. "You've some fire in you. I like that. Very well, Transcendent. Please accept my apologies. Now, where were we? Ah, yes. Noxstone. It's the element used in suspension magic. Dorsluin has rights to the mine. As I was saying before, noxstone is easily extracted. The deposits are often clustered and impossible to miss once uncovered.

"Valdsker, however, isn't valuable simply because it's the element for influence enchantments. Valdsker is stubborn. It doesn't readily expose itself. eldrite and kalatite are minuscule, but they're crystals. They sparkle when any light passes over them, making them easy to find. Valdsker hides. Most often in other mineral deposits. Valdsker has to be hunted, not mined. To find it, rock is chipped away and each piece broken apart, ground down and the crushed particles scoured. The process is tedious."

"If it's so tedious and valuable," Lavak said, "isn't it wasteful to have it floating in the air?"

"Yes, but unavoidable. And we reclaim as much as possible that's lost to the air. We've a way of purifying reclaimed valdsker to remove any contaminates such as dust and dirt. That's enough about elements for now. Time for a more practical lesson. Follow me."

He led Lavak into a large room. It was similar to Drudylan's workshop, with many tables dedicated to the craft, but lacking the larger woodworking tools. Several aspirants and ascenders hunched over workbenches. None acknowledged Lavak when he entered, but Lavak knew them all by savor.

"Here, you'll embed valdsker into the godspear. The concept is a simple one, but technique is the challenge. Let me show you." Corundra slid onto the stool of the nearest unoccupied worktable. Set on the table was a large glass jar, half full with fine green powder. "Your piece," he demanded, holding open his hand. Lavak dropped the beetle into Corundra's palm. The master enchanter surveyed a row of small tools at the far edge of the table: spoon- and spatula-like instruments of varying sizes, with some thin as needles and others wider than the broad side of a butter knife. He chose a spoon close to the width of a quill nib and set it beside the wooden beetle. Removing the lid from the jar, Corundra took a pinch of valdsker and sprinkled it onto the beetle.

"You take this," Corundra said, holding his selected tool up, "and force the element into the grain of the godspear." He pressed the back of the spoon slowly but firmly against the beetle, rocking the tool gently side to side. "You continue this until the entire piece is imparted with the valdsker." He lifted the spoon instrument. The dust was no longer on the surface of the wood. Now it was within the tight grain of the godspear, marked by a pale, translucent patch of green. "When you've finished the first embedding, begin again. Apply a second and a third and a fourth. As much as necessary."

"How many are necessary?" asked Lavak.

Corundra shrugged. "That depends on you. If you do a poor job and don't embed every bit of wood with each pass, it may take dozens of coats. If you're careful and take your time to do it correctly, it may be as few as five."

"How will I know when I have enough?"

Corundra pointed to the jar. "When this beetle is as green as the valdsker in there." He slid off the stool and gestured for Lavak to sit.

Settling onto the stool, Lavak picked up the spoon and repeated what he was shown.

CHAPTER 13

Shutters dangled from broken hinges. Windows with panes of cracked glass, or no glass at all, sat neglected in crooked walls. Only bare gray wood framing the windows remained. Clapboards curled and split, unseating nails. A rickety door split nearly in half threatened to break apart as Zirrin knocked on it, wobbling with each hit of his fist.

Ralm waited a step behind Zirrin. This was their third visit today, their third eviction, the third squalid location and third desperate occupant. This was Zirrin's profession, his grim task. Shadowing him reminded Ralm of the times he trailed Brun. Except with his father, the work was usually guiltless. People who fell from favor here, who struggled and failed to maintain status, who were forced to sell their magic for food, were unwelcome in all but one circle. Without magic, a person rolled down the Hillside and landed atop the heap of dispossessed unfortunates clogging the ninth circle.

A woman in simple clothes stained by countless hours of begrudging labor opened the door. Midmorning light shone on frizzy hair and in every wrinkle etched upon a troubled face. Her eyes, large but weary, flashed with recognition and dread upon seeing Zirrin.

Without preamble, Zirrin held a letter before her and said, "Morva Dulnith, I hereby serve your eviction. You're to vacate these premises by noon tomorrow or be found in violation of the law."

"I knew you were coming." Tears pooled in her eyes. "I didn't think it would be so soon."

"I'm sorry, Morva." Zirrin rested a comforting hand on her frail shoulder. "I wish it were different."

She nodded. "Me too. When my husband died, I had to pay for his funeral. I didn't have enough money. I had to sell our magic."

It was the third story Ralm heard today. Different circumstances, but the outcomes were all the same. People struggled. Decent people. Good people. Honest, hard-working folks who only wanted to earn a living and raise their family. For every wall they climbed over, two more obstacles blocked them. Zirrin's appearance was the culmination of their misfortunes.

The sound of children playing came from inside the home. Morva wiped her eyes. "If it was only me, I think I'd be fine. But my children. I can't bear the thought of having them in the ninth circle. It's no place for them. I fear for them. I may have to send them to an orphanage." She leaned against the door frame and sobbed, unable to continue.

"I understand," Zirrin said. "Morva, I may be able to help, if you are willing."

"I'll do anything." She dried her eyes and wiped her nose with a sleeve.

Zirrin produced a small envelope. "I can't let you stay here. The orders are final, and if you're still here tomorrow you'll be imprisoned and your children taken. You'll likely never see them again. However, I can keep you in the eighth circle."

"How? Please, tell me." Hope filled her glistening eyes.

"There is an address inside this envelope. Take your children and go there. Take only essentials from this place, you'll have room for nothing else. You'll need to work to earn your stay, but at least you'll stay within the eighth."

"Work?" Morva asked, suspicion heavy in her voice. "What sort of work? When the money ran out, I tried everything to pay the bills." She glanced into the dim of the house before returning her attention to Zirrin. She whispered, "I tried everything. It was awful. Those men. Those stinking, vile men. I felt as if I was betraying my husband's memory. I can't do it again, Zirrin. If that's the kind of work you'll have me do, I'd rather take my chances in the ninth."

"It's not like that at all," Zirrin said. "I'm sending you to an inn. You'll clean the guest rooms, do laundry, help in the kitchen. In exchange, you'll be provided a room for you and your children to live in. As a servant, you'll not be required to own magic. Just present the letter inside this envelope to the innkeeper. He'll see to the rest."

Morva's hand went up to her mouth as she gulped. "How can I ever repay you?"

"There may come a day when I need a favor. When I ask for it, you are to oblige."

Her lips bent into a faint smile as she nodded. "I will. I promise."

Zirrin raised a finger. "There is one last thing. Your medallion. I must have it to give to the order as proof of your eviction."

"Yes, of course." She retreated into the house. A moment later she returned and gave two medallions to Zirrin. "Here's mine, and the other was my husband's medallion. I meant to return it after the burial but was so grief-stricken, I forgot. I suppose I won't be needing either now."

"No, you won't. Where you're going, you'll stay inside, away from the order's eyes. There will be no more traveling between circles for you."

"The ninth is nowhere I want to go." She sighed and stared into her home. "So many memories here. Good and bad."

"Change is the one constant, Morva. Your memories can go with you. Take the good ones. They're not confined to this place."

"Thank you, Zirrin."

"Now, dear Morva, collect your children and things and go."

Zirrin gently pushed her into the house and carefully closed the rickety door.

Three visits, three evictions, three arrangements. The first home they went to that morning was for a man who was short one enchantment. Having only two magical items put him in violation and at risk of eviction. Zirrin offered to give the man a third enchantment in exchange for a future favor. The man eagerly agreed to save his home and status. After proper documentation for a "sale" of magic between Zirrin and the man was completed, Zirrin produced a fire-felt saucer from his pocket. In exchange, the man owed Zirrin a favor.

At the second visit, the owner had failed to pay his taxes. He and Zirrin reached an understanding: Zirrin would pay the man's arrears for a future favor. Zirrin dealt a lot in favors and spent more on his charities than what was returned to him. He worked in a manner oddly similar to the duties of overseer. While an overseer was expected to settle disputes, sometimes through arrangements and compromise, Zirrin molded the will of the state to his own designs. Exactly what those were, Ralm wasn't certain. How he survived and thrived, especially when giving magic to the poor, was a greater mystery. Zirrin explained it as a fluid system. He gave magic away, and if he needed magic, he collected from those owing him—only after they've recovered from whatever tragedy had put them in straits.

Zirrin spun to face Ralm. "Well, that's all the evictions for today," he said more cheerily than the situation warranted. "Here you go." He passed one of the medallions to Ralm.

"I thought unlawfully possessing one was discouraged," Ralm said.

"This is a dead man's medallion," Zirrin said. "It was never recorded as received at the spire or reported stolen or missing. I have her medallion, proof enough of her eviction and forfeiture of residency. I'll make a note in my report the other is lost. However, if you're ever questioned about it, say you're Girg Dulnith. You were believed dead, but it was a mistake. You were taken prisoner by bandits and only recently returned to Dorsluin, where you found your wife and children gone and your home foreclosed. You searched but haven't found them. I doubt you'll need to give such details, but it never hurts to be ready. Now, let's move on."

Ralm hung the medallion about his neck and tucked it under his shirt as they strolled toward the markets. It was his third day watching Zirrin serve evictions. Every morning Zirrin collected the day's notices from a guard at the gate, and every time his work was finished, Zirrin enjoyed mingling with the people in the marketplace.

"It seems you have many favors owed to you," Ralm said as they approached the first row of shops.

"Yes, many." Zirrin flashed a mischievous grin. "Most have gone uncollected thus far. Some I've called upon to juggle favors for others, like the innkeeper. He owed me. He's paying me back by boarding Morva and her children. It's simple bartering, just not in hard goods all the time."

"How many favors are owed to you? And when do you plan to collect?"

Zirrin winked at Ralm. "Those are matters of my business I'm not willing to divulge to you or anybody. Better you not know such things." He tapped his blue-lustered cane, the brass-capped bottom clacking on the broken road.

Ralm had asked those same questions the past two days, and Zirrin had given the same answers. Ralm resigned to Zirrin upholding the mystery. "How do you make your money? The innkeeper owed you, but it's that woman who benefits from his debt. You've gotten nothing from it except a spent favor."

"In the short term, I've gained little. I swapped one favor for another. But I don't plan for the short term, Ralm." He glanced at the spire standing high over the shops. "They're not the only spiders spinning webs."

During the past two days, Ralm had begun observing how

eighth circle dwellers behaved around Zirrin. Some met his gaze and greeted him with a polite nod or wave. Others quickly averted their eyes and hurried away. Ralm guessed those acknowledging Zirrin had paid their debts or had never owed him, while those scampering away were still indebted. Many scampered.

There was a new shop in the market, its design familiar to Ralm. He'd seen it his first day in the city. Yellow and green streamers waved from the roof. Beneath a colorful awning, enchantments covered a table flanked by two hulking guards. A slender man with heavy-lidded eyes stood between them. The gathered crowd was eager to see the wares of this new merchant. Zirrin pushed his way through, Ralm close behind.

"That's it, good people. Only serious buyers at the table. Browsers to the back," Chulvar said. "Please, no shoving. Plenty for all, and if I don't have it, I can get it. I've magic from all the domains. Just what you need to move inward. Don't hesitate. Buy today, or somebody else will."

"Hello, Chulvar," Zirrin said flatly as he reached the table.

The merchant's eyes bulged. His face flushed. "Zirrin. I wasn't expecting to see you today."

"Why not? The eighth circle is my home."

"Certainly. I thought you'd be busy. Hey you, no touching." Chulvar slapped a patron's roving hand, knocking a trinket out of his grasp and back onto the table. "Anybody caught trying to steal or touch without permission will be dealt with by Pup and Cub." He stabbed his thumbs toward the two motionless warriors. His threat was enough to cause all probing fingers to quickly withdraw.

"Finally made it into the Hillside?" Zirrin said.

"Took me some time and many rounds, but yes. Can we have this conversation someplace else, at some other time? I've a business to run now."

Zirrin waved a hand. "Of course. Congratulations on reaching the eighth."

Ralm wiggled between Zirrin and another customer to scan

the table. Many of the items were the same as when he first visited the shop, with a few new additions.

"A friend of yours?" Chulvar appraised Ralm with a hawker's greedy stare. "Climbing or falling?"

"Neither," Zirrin said with a hint of annoyance. "Visiting."

"What is that?" Ralm pointed at a bracelet carved like a chain, the wooden links shimmering a faint black. He marveled at the skill. To nibble godspear into links was no minor feat.

Chulvar cocked his head, one brow buried, the other arched. "What is what?"

"That. That bracelet." Ralm pointed again.

"Are you asking because you're interested in buying, or just interested?"

"Just interested. The craftsmanship in the—"

"Thank you. Please move back," Chulvar interrupted. "Only serious buyers to the front. Thank you." Chulvar's gaze turned suddenly inquisitive. "Hold a moment. Hmm. There's something familiar about you. Have we met before?"

Ralm stiffened. "No, I don't believe so," he lied. Wearing his painted face, he'd traveled enough of the eighth circle to grow comfortable in the presence of both the public and the order. Nobody had questioned or approached him. His disguise was convincing, or so he thought.

The merchant snapped his fingers. "Your voice. I knew I recognized it."

How? Ralm had mimicked the guttural voice of the ascenders. Had it not been adequate? How could Chulvar know?

"Oh! Look at this." A burlap-clad arm reached past Ralm and snatched a brooch from the display. A rotund man with a curled mustache examined the object with fascination, bringing the brooch close to his face, away from the table, away from Chulvar's reach. Other hands pawed at items on the table.

"No touching!" Chulvar warned, his eyes bulging. "Pup!"

The brute on the right stepped forward with a grunt, one

meaty arm extending over the table. Pup gripped the overly curious man by his collar and lifted him off the ground. The man yelped as he dropped the brooch onto the table. Pup hoisted the man higher. All other offenders and would-be offenders cowered. Any magic items in their hands were quickly returned to the table as they stepped back, mouths agape, eyes locked on Pup.

"Let this be a lesson to you all," Chulvar said with a scowl. "Hands off the merchandise, or Pup will be hands on you. Understand?" The crowd nodded fearful understanding in unison. The mustached man caught in Pup's clutches nodded the most vigorously. "All right, Pup. Let him go."

Pup released the portly fellow onto his rump. He flailed, trying to regain his feet and dignity. Pup stepped back and resumed his position beside Chulvar as the crowd enclosed the table again. They shoved and jostled for the nearest positions. Elbows jabbed Ralm's ribs. Feet stepped on his. Jabber was loud in his ears. The commotion was more than Ralm could tolerate. He pushed back those closest to him, trying to exit the mass of bodies, his heartbeat quickening along with his breath. Body heat and sweat surrounded him. Locked in the tangle of bodies, Ralm's patience dissolved.

"Is this all you live for?" Ralm shouted at the crowd. All movement and noise ended. All faces turned to him. "To fight over baubles the order tells you are important? You're so focused on trying to move higher. You do know that's the order's plan, don't you? To keep you competing with each other. To keep your attention from the real problem. The Ascendancy. Magic is nothing more than a distraction." Everybody gawked at him, his outburst chiseling astonishment into their expressions. Something inside Ralm blossomed. The impoverished, the rivalry between citizens, the oppression of the ruling class, he could no longer ignore.

Chulvar glanced about nervously before saying, "Ladies. Gentlemen. Pay no mind to this madman and what he speaks." He leaned across the table and whispered harshly into Ralm's ear. "You're bad for business. Get out of here before I put Cub and Pup on you."

"We were just leaving," Zirrin said. He took Ralm by the arm and pushed through the crowd. Once down the street and far from the magic shop, Zirrin pulled Ralm into a shallow alley. "Boy, you certainly have a way of muddying the water."

Ralm blinked. "What do you mean?"

"Oh, come now. You know. What exactly were you thinking back there? That kind of talk will get you in prison. Or worse."

Ralm lowered his head. "I'm not sure what happened. It was the crowd, the close quarters, the heat, maybe. It all just got to me," Ralm stammered the explanation.

Zirrin shot quick glances down the street. "Ralm, I know what you're feeling. I feel it every day, and there are times when I want to shout my frustrations, too. But I don't, because I know if the wrong people hear me, I'll never see my family again."

"How can you live like this?" Ralm's own frustration simmered. "Living in fear, under the rule of the order. There are so many wrongs here, yet nobody does anything about them."

"It's been this way for centuries, Ralm. It's all people know. But that isn't to say they don't sense things are bad. They do. But these are simple folk. They don't make trouble. They don't want trouble. They want to go about their day's work, go home and wake up the next morning. Maybe not completely free, but freer than a jail cell, which is where they'll end up if they question the order's ways. They're good people. Even the undesirables were once decent folk, but hardships have driven them to darker pursuits. Everybody in the ninth and eighth circles want more, but they're scared. They wait for somebody to lead them. Fear keeps them quiet, but if somebody shows them the way, they'll follow."

"It won't be me," Ralm said. "I've my own problems. I've the godspears to save and a family to find. If they're still alive. This place will need some other fool to lead a rebellion." Ralm started to walk past Zirrin and back into the street. Zirrin raised an arm, barring Ralm's way.

"Ralm, I'm not asking you to do that. Others have tried and failed. They died. I don't want that to happen to you. I'm only asking if you feel a need to express your discontent over the situation, you do it in a more discreet manner. Yelling in the street will only bring attention to yourself. Unwanted attention."

Ralm's spent the return to Zirrin's home in quiet reflection. He recalled the day's events and considered Zirrin's advice and how best he could apply it. He was discontented, and though he certainly didn't intend to cause a rebellion, he did feel a need to voice his frustrations in some manner. But if he couldn't speak them, how?

At the front door to Zirrin's home, raised voices and a baby's cry escaped from inside. Zirrin and Ralm rushed in to find Hilni in the sitting room with a wailing Brella clutched tight in her arms as another woman attempted to pry the child from her.

"You've no right. Give her to me," the woman said.

Hilni pivoted away from the woman, guarding the screaming child bundled against her bosom. "You're not thinking clearly. You need to leave."

"I want her now," the woman demanded.

Zirrin intervened, placing himself between the two women. "Frayna. Why are you here?"

"She's lost her mind," Hilni said as she rocked the infant.

"I've come for my baby," Frayna said as she tried sidestepping Zirrin. "I want her back."

"You're in no condition to make decisions," Hilni said. "Think of what's best for the child."

Tears streaked Frayna's face. "I am. That's why I'm here. I've decided to take her to the orphanage."

"Madness." Hilni put her finger to the baby's mouth. The child suckled it, quieting instantly. "She's better off here."

"It's my decision," Frayna said. "My child. My decision."

Ralm watched from the sitting room threshold, silent and still, uncertain of the details leading to the current drama, certain only a woman half his age and looking twice as ragged was causing a disturbance in Zirrin's home. Her threadbare clothes distinguished her as a ninth circle dweller. How she made it into the eighth, he couldn't guess.

Frayna sent a spiteful glare his way. "Who's he?"

"Nobody," Zirrin said. "Nobody you need to worry about. Now, Frayna, please. Think about what you're doing. We can figure something out."

"I asked you to care for her. You did and I'm grateful. But she's my child, and it's my choice what to do with her."

"The orphanage?" Hilni said. "That's no place for a baby."

Frayna stiffened. "Maybe she'll be chosen by the supreme and made a member of the order. That's a better life than I can give her and better than anything else in the city."

Zirrin grunted his displeasure over her statement.

Hilni shook her head, her eyes fully somber. "The orphanages are overflowing with babies dropped off by parents thinking the same thing. What happens if she isn't chosen? What then?"

"I'll never know," Frayna said.

"That's right. You'll never know," Hilni said. "You'll never know if your child is an ascender or starving in the street. Or if she lived or died. Or a mistress or a prostitute. You'll never know her first words, or what her favorite color is. You'll not know any of it."

For a brief moment, a glimmer of realization flashed in Frayna's eyes. She paused, speechless, then the glimmer disappeared. "I've made my decision. Now give her to me."

"No." Hilni spoke the word like it was forged iron: flat and firm.

"Give me my child, or I'll call an ascender. I know you don't want that."

Hilni glowered at the woman before giving Zirrin a pleading look.

Zirrin frowned and shook his head. "Give her the child."

"But—" Hilni started.

"But nothing," Zirrin grumbled. "The child is hers, and

there's nothing we can do."

Hilni shot Frayna a final menacing stare. She looked upon Brella, her expression changing instantly to adoration and motherly kindness. She cooed the child once more, kissed her softly on the forehead before gently giving her to Frayna. Hilni's eyes glistened with tears as she watched mother and child leave her home. As the door shut, she sobbed, sinking her face into Zirrin's shoulder. Zirrin held her tight, stroking Hilni's head and hushing her. He glanced at Ralm, still standing at the threshold, uncertain if he should stay or leave.

"Frayna was in a rough spot," Zirrin explained. "She was without money and living in the ninth. She asked if we could look after the baby until she recouped. She's gotten better, though I'm not sure by how much. I think she stole a medallion. No other way she could've gotten here from the outer ring. If she's caught with it…"

"What does she mean, she's going to the orphanage?" Ralm asked.

"The order is comprised of orphans," Zirrin said. "It simplifies matters. Without family, ascenders won't have distractions. That's one reason they wear masks in public. If they encounter a family member, resemblances can't be recognized. Orphanages are overrun because so many people hope their children become ascenders just to have a better life. When the orphanages are full, and they always are, children end up on the streets. Many die."

"Where's this orphanage?"

"There are many. Too many," Zirrin said. "But I'd guess if she were to go to an orphanage, it'd be the one in the north quarter of the ninth."

Ralm bolted out the front doorway. Zirrin voiced his protest to his leaving, but Ralm didn't care and he didn't stop to argue. On the street, he scanned both directions, hoping to find Frayna. He didn't. Sprinting toward the gate leading to the ninth circle, Ralm expected to intercept mother and child before they reached it. The gate came into view, but still no sign of Frayna. Ragged breaths left his mouth as he paused, hunched over with hands on knees, sweat collecting on his painted brow. Two guards stood watch at the entrance to the ninth. They stared blankly ahead, spears slack at their sides. Ralm gathered himself and strode by as if he'd done so hundreds of times before, while inside fearing he'd be stopped simply for being there. He wasn't, and after he reached the squalor and filth of the ninth, out of the guard's view, he dashed for the north quarter.

He found Frayna, stepping quickly, a mere forty strides from the orphanage. It was a dismal place of stone and wood, squatting wide along the outer wall of the ninth. Light cast from within highlighted grime-smeared windows. Behind a rusted iron fence dozens of children, some barely crawling and others nearing adolescence, played and loitered in a courtyard overtaken by weeds, wearing clothes either too loose or too tight on their delicate frames.

"Frayna. Wait," Ralm called.

She looked back, eyes narrowing when she saw him. "Leave me alone. This is none of your concern."

Ralm ran past her, spun and stopped, blocking her way. "I know it isn't my concern, but I'm concerned for your daughter."

"Move aside, or I'll call the guard." She tried moving around Ralm. He stepped in her way.

"Please, just a moment." He struggled to speak, still breathless from the pursuit. "Just one moment and I'll never trouble you again."

Frayna glared at him from over clenched teeth, glanced to the orphanage beyond, then back at Ralm. "You have your moment."

Ralm nodded. "I know how you feel. I heard what you told Zirrin and Hilni. I heard what they said to you. I understand your feelings and their feelings. But I want to ask you something, and that will be it. I'll not bother you again."

She smacked her lips. "Ask."

"You're willing to give up your daughter so she may have a chance to become an ascender, but look around. Look at the despair in this place. What if she isn't chosen? Do you want her out there?" He pointed to the courtyard. A girl no older than five rolled a chunk of broken cobblestone in her hand like it was a toy. "Or in the street? Do you want her growing up, doing anything she can to survive? Stealing. Prostituting. Or worse."

"Maybe she'll be chosen. Maybe she'll be in the spire instead of the street," Frayna said and pushed by Ralm.

"And maybe she'll spend the rest of her life asking why her mother abandoned her," he said as she passed.

Frayna stopped, her gaze fixed on the orphanage before her. "Don't you think I've thought that hundreds of times already? Do you have children? Do you know what it's like to think of nothing but them every waking moment of the day?"

"No. I don't. My wife and I were hoping to have children someday."

"You'll know then," Frayna whispered, almost too softly for Ralm to hear. "You'll know the true meaning of sacrifice after your child is born. You'll know your life comes second to theirs and you'll do anything to protect them, even if it means giving up your life so they may live, or giving them up because they'll be better off than if they were to stay with you. I've done things, horrible things, just to earn a few rounds to feed and shelter her, but it wasn't enough. There's not much a woman of my standing can offer. I've no skills. All I can offer is what men want."

Morva's confession to what she'd done just to feed her children echoed in Ralm's mind. "Don't be ashamed, Frayna. You did what you had to for her, but you don't have to do this. You're taking a big chance. Look at all those children. Don't you think their parents had the same hope? Is this place better than what you could give her? At least with you, she'll have her mother. She won't be alone. She'll be loved."

Frayna sniffled and wiped her nose with the back of her hand. She stared at the children in the courtyard: discarded, filthy and forgotten. Her gaze fell upon the child in her arms. "I don't know what to do."

"We'll work something out," Ralm said, his voice low and soothing. "Take her back to Hilni. Let her care for Brella while you reconsider. I'll speak to Zirrin. I'm sure he can arrange something."

"I already owe them so much." Her words wavered as they left quivering lips. "I can't ask them for more."

"You won't need to. They want to help. They're good people. Please. Just one day. If nothing can be arranged, then—"

"Fine. Fine." Frayna turned to him with dewy eyes. "One day." She strode toward the gate, sobbing.

Ralm didn't follow. She needed time alone. The woman was burdened enough with guilt and regret. Him being with her would only worsen her feelings. Instead, he studied the orphanage, its dreary state a reflection of his mood. What an awful place for a child to live.

"Hey, got any rounds?" a familiar voice came from his side.

Ralm snapped his head to find Rill standing a few paces away, his hair more tussled than the last time they'd met. His shirt may have been white once but was now so dirty and stained it was impossible to be certain.

"I'm afraid not," Ralm said.

"Sprig thinks you do." The boy tilted his head and stepped aside, revealing the young girl who guided Ralm his first day in the city.

"Hello, little Sprig," Ralm said through a smile.

Sprig smiled back.

"We remember you. Sprig remembers you being nice to her, though you were dressed like somebody not so nice. Sure you haven't got any rounds?"

"How do you remember me?"

"We know where you went, remember? Since then, I've watched the place and figured it out, figured out who you were by watching you come and go." Rill beamed pridefully.

"That's very clever."

He jabbed his thumbs at his chest. "That's me."

"Pleased to meet you again, Rill. And you too, Sprig. I'm glad you like the name." She smiled again but shied away. "So, you live here at the orphanage?"

"Did," Rill said. "There ain't no room for us in there anymore. Cribs and beds for the little ones. When kids get too old, they get pushed onto the street. We still come back for food when it's around."

"There isn't room enough for everybody?"

"Nope. So me and Sprig roam the city looking for food, just like the others. There's supposed to be some extra scraps of bread today, so we came for it. Looks like others heard the same. No bread here. Oh well. Maybe there's some fish guts out on the docks."

A sickening feeling welled within Ralm at the notion of these children fending for themselves. "There's always a chance the order will come."

"Ha. That's a funny one. They come once a year, and when they do, they want a baby. When a kid starts crawling, he can wave those dreams good-bye." Rill cocked a brow. "You sure you got no rounds?"

"None on me. Sorry."

Rill shrugged. "Not for me to worry. Tell you something. If you ever need a guide or anything and got some rounds you wanna toss, I'm willing for the work. Sprig too. She's good at getting places, and me, I'm good at lots of things."

Ralm grinned. The boy was certainly confident. "Very well. If I have any needs you might help with. Should I come back here to find you?"

"Nah, we're hardly here, unless there's food, which ain't often." He scratched into the dirt with his toe the letter X. "Just put this in the window of that place you're at. Sprig and me go all over, and we'll see it when we're about. Don't forget the rounds." Before Ralm could reply, Rill and Sprig disappeared behind the corner of the orphanage.

Ralm meandered back to Zirrin's home. He passed through the gate, displaying his medallion with a casualness which surprised him. The guard's gazes flicked to the medallion long enough to acknowledge its validity before returning to their idle stance. The encounter should have set Ralm uneasy, but instead he dismissed the interaction without care, his thoughts elsewhere. He returned to Zirrin's home to find Hilni in the hall, Brella in her arms. Hilni radiated delight.

"Isn't it wonderful?" she said. "Frayna brought her back. She brought her back. Did you have something to do with it?"

"I, um—" Ralm wasn't certain what he should say.

Zirrin emerged from the sitting room. "If he did, then I owe Ralm a favor."

"Where's Frayna? Is she here?" Ralm asked.

Zirrin frowned at Ralm's question. "No, lad. She's not. Said she had something to do. She asked us to look after the child."

"When is she coming back?" Ralm asked.

Zirrin shook his head. "She didn't say."

Ralm met Zirrin's and Hilni's eyes, both brimming with joy at the baby's return. Ralm should have felt the same, but something leaden had settled over his mood and he didn't know why.

CHAPTER 14

It was rumored Taloon Taltaw was back in the city. Zirrin left his home to find him. It had been weeks since he first mentioned the name and days since Ralm asked of his whereabouts. Ralm had given up asking. The man was dead or lost somewhere, he concluded. What reason was there to nurture hope only to have it wither and die?

When Zirrin left that morning after sharing the news of Taloon's return, Ralm begged to accompany him in his search for the elusive man. Zirrin refused. He sternly refused.

"Taloon is a cautious fellow," Zirrin explained. "He doesn't trust many people. I doubt he trusts me, but if I show up with you, well, we can forget any help he may offer."

On other days Zirrin left Ralm at his home, Ralm became quickly bored. Reading and rereading Zirrin's journals, idly conversing with Hilni or alternating between staring out the window and staring at the burning chip-brick was all he had to do. Each pastime was fleeting in his restless and tedious existence. Today was different. Something else held his thoughts, a new venture which overshadowed even the prospect of finally meeting Taloon. Today was the day he began poking the beehive to see how loud the buzzing grew.

He watched from the sitting room window as people strolled

down the street, attentive to their own needs, pursuits and lives, all of them too preoccupied with daily burdens to focus on the greater scheme binding them with invisible chains. An elderly gentleman in frayed robes shambled past his window. Ralm had seen him pass many times before. According to Zirrin, the old man possessed five enchantments and needed one more to move to the seventh circle. On his aged face Ralm saw the hunger which came from being so close to reaching his goal. Behind intense eyes at having seen thousands of days come and go was a mind surely consumed with uncovering the answer to one elusive question: how to acquire the sixth enchantment?

How, indeed? The old man was locked. To buy another enchantment required money. To have the money required selling an enchantment or plying a trade. Neither was an option. Any skills once possessed to earn rounds had deserted him: hands were no longer steady, wits no longer sharp and tongue no longer clever. The man was in an unenviable position. Ralm knew this because Zirrin told him as much. Zirrin was well informed about those who owed him.

The old man was far down the street now, nearly out of view. More people ambled by, all driven by the same need. A woman, one arm hooking a basket of herbs, the other leading a young boy, loped past. Her aspect was of undeniable desperation. Not as intense as the old man's, but her eyes revealed a struggle to feed her family while saving enough to relocate further into the city.

All these people. All caring about themselves. All competing in a tournament of the order's design.

He glanced at the red X in the corner of the window. The work Ralm planned was better suited for somebody streetwise. Paying Rill was worth his price. He knew the city far better than Ralm. When he'd arrive, Ralm didn't know. Rill only told him to place the mark in the window and he'd come. The details of the arrangement were muddy, at best.

A presence crept behind him. Ralm didn't need to turn

around to know Neva stood there. She came and left like a breeze. Before Ralm knew she was there, she was already gone. But not this time. She waited silently for him to acknowledge her.

"Are they done?" he asked.

She nodded. Hair swayed at her waist. The svelte girl glided out of the room and upstairs. Ralm followed, not nearly as quiet no matter how hard he tried and how often he practiced. In her room, on her bed, lay a stack of paintings. Neva gestured to the top painting. In the foreground were dozens of city dwellers, their facial features distorted. Looming behind them was the menacing image of an oversize ascender, complete with a grotesque golden mask. He stretched a dark hand over the people.

"Neva. It's perfect. Absolutely perfect. This is just how I imagined it," Ralm said. She swayed side to side at his praise. Ralm fished a round out of his purse. "Here. You've earned it." Neva stopped swaying, shook her head and raised a slender hand. "Please. I can't expect you to do this for free," he said. She continued shaking her head in refusal. "Use it for supplies. Twenty paintings must've used a lot of supplies. Take it." She paused, as if to consider his reasoning. "I may need more of these," he said, nudging the money toward her. After a moment, Neva tenderly removed the coin from his palm and nodded. "Thank you." He examined the remaining paintings in turn, each with similar symbolisms as the first. One painting showed all of Azazura. Slashes crossed it. Blood dripped from the wounds. One red line parted the Risc, jarring Ralm's memory of the place and the wild man who helped him cross it.

"Neva. I once knew a man who couldn't hear, but this didn't mean he couldn't speak. Instead of using words, he used his hands. For example, to say he was hungry, he put a hand to his mouth." Ralm performed the gesture.

Neva went still. She gave no reaction, and with hair veiling her face, Ralm couldn't read her expression. Then, Neva responded with a spate of hand motions. Ralm couldn't follow her fingers. They moved too fast. She was practiced in sign language.

"Slow down. Slow down," Ralm said, grinning. "I don't know much. Just the basics. How do you know about this?"

"I taught her," Hilni said from the bedroom doorway.

Ralm spun in surprise. "I've been here weeks and never saw you do any signing."

Hilni shrugged. "You're never around when we do. Most of the time it's unnecessary. I ask Neva a question and she nods yes or no. Neva dear, please leave us for a moment." Neva did as told and quietly left. Hilni closed the door behind her. She moved close to Ralm and peered around him to the paintings on the bed. "I know you asked Neva to paint these." Ralm began to speak his defense. Hilni held a silencing palm outward. "I'm not mad. Neva may be young, but she can make her own decisions. She'd never have agreed if she felt uncomfortable about it. That's reassuring to me. It means time has healed her, or maybe your request has finally allowed Neva to express herself about the tragedy."

"Tragedy? I don't understand," Ralm said.

Hilni knelt beside a stack of paintings leaning against the wall. She flipped through them slowly. "Neva was five when it happened. She was there when the riot started. She was with her brother. He was a protester. People were starving and demanding food. Scalamar ordered food be brought and distributed. When the food never arrived, things turned violent." She stood, a painting in her hands. She held it before Ralm.

Red. So much red in the painting. A river of it flowing down the middle of a street Ralm recognized, not far from where he stood. At the edge of the painting flames engulfed shops, made vivid by yellow and orange paint blended together, capturing the untamed fire's ferocity.

"Neva hid a ways back from the uprising," Hilni continued. "But Hraad didn't. He was in the middle of it, shouting against the order." She laid the painting down and knelt to skim through the stack again before she lifted another painting, this time the portrait of a man. His tawny mane hemmed plump cheeks and hopeful eyes.

"Hraad was like you. He opposed the way things were. He wanted change and died because of it. Neva watched the low guards kill him and many other rioters."

"Is that why Neva doesn't speak?" It was all Ralm could manage to ask. He hadn't expected a horrible layer of the Paladas family history to be peeled back and exposed to him. Hilni was right. It was a tragedy. He'd never considered such terrible misfortune to have visited this kind and giving family. During his stay with them, there had been no mention of a son.

Hilni shook her head. "No, that's from a different time. But Zirrin was there. He tried stopping the Low Guard. He ran to Hraad's defense. The Low Guard beat him too, but spared him, leaving him with a leg that would never fully heal." She swallowed as she stared at the painting. "Hraad died believing in something greater than himself, but he died needlessly. Hraad spoke openly against the Ascendency, and in return, the order made an example of him." Hilni raised her head, her tear-choked gaze falling on Ralm. "I know what you're trying to do, Ralm. I do. I support it. Your ideals match Hraad's. Just promise me one thing."

"Anything," Ralm's voice cracked.

"Never reveal yourself. That's how you end up dead." Hilni set the painting beside the other on Neva's bed.

"I won't."

She laid a gentle hand on Ralm's cheek. "I know it was you who convinced Frayna to bring the baby back. I owe you for that."

Tears gathered in the corners of Ralm's eyes. "No, you don't. You've given me so much. You've treated me like family, even when you didn't know me. It's I who owe you."

"You saved that baby's life, Ralm. You truly did. It's a debt that can never be repaid." She leaned close and kissed his forehead. "You've become like a son to me. And just as I supported my other son, so shall I support you." She hugged him, and Ralm hugged her back. Rivers of tears flowed down both their faces.

There was a knock at the front door. Ralm and Hilni separated and wiped their eyes. They hurried downstairs, and Hilni opened the door. Nobody was there. Ralm craned his head out the doorway, peering left and right. Still nobody. Perhaps somebody knocked on the wrong door, realized their mistake and left.

"Psst. Psst." It came from the corner of the house.

Ralm stepped outside and edged to the corner. He peeked around it to find Rill standing there, a mischievous grin on his face.

"Good of you to finally call me," Rill said.

"Ralm, is everything all right?" Hilni asked from the doorway.

"Fine. Everything is fine. I'll be in shortly." Ralm waited until Hilni shut the door. "Why didn't you wait out front?"

Rill leaned against the side of the house and folded his arms across his chest. "Brings too much attention. No need for me to be standing where every eye can see."

"That was smart."

"Smart is what I do." Rill grinned. "So, what job do you need me for? Pickpocketing? Eavesdropping? A little of both?"

Ralm cleared his throat. "None of those. I need you to hang some paintings around the city. Preferably in areas with a lot of traffic. Put them where they'll be most seen. Spread them throughout the city the best you can."

Rill rubbed his chin. "Hmm. Gotta admit, I wasn't figuring this as the job."

"Is it too much for you?"

Rill shot Ralm an offended expression. "No job is too much for me. It's just, not what I was expecting, that's all. And it's a bit more of a hassle than most things."

"What do you mean?"

"Purse snatches and sneak-abouts are easy. You cut and run before you're seen, real quick and such. But hanging these, it's gonna take time. I need to find a spot, wait until no eyes are around and nail them up. There's a bit of scouting involved, plus carrying of paintings, hammers and nails. It'll slow me down."

"Hammer and nails?" Ralm echoed, though it was more him scolding himself. Of course, how did he expect the paintings to be hung without nails? A foolish oversight on his part. "I don't have any."

Rill slapped his forehead. "How you thinking these are gonna stay? Hold them up with hopes and wishes? You ain't done this kind of work before, have you? It's a bit of a hassle, but I can get them. It'll cost extra, though. And about that." He held his palm out, dirt caught in the creases of his skin. Ralm dug into his purse and dropped two rounds into Rill's hand. "All right. Give me those pictures. I'll have them all up before two nights have passed."

Ralm went back inside, retrieved the paintings from Neva's room and returned to Rill. Burdened with artwork and money, the boy darted down the street, nearly colliding with Zirrin in his haste. Zirrin gave the boy no regard. His gaze remained fixed on the street immediately ahead of him. As he neared, Ralm joined him by his side, anxious to hear any news.

"Well?" he asked, drawing Zirrin's eyes to his.

Zirrin flashed a quick smile. His eyes twinkled briefly. "Well, what?"

"Your contact. Taloon. Is he here?"

Zirrin looked over each shoulder, up and down the street, then past Ralm. "No. I don't see him here."

Ralm smirked at Zirrin's playful mood. "Then where?"

"Come with me."

They strode down the street, Ralm matching Zirrin's determined but not overly suspicious pace. Passing into the ninth circle, they entered slums harboring the forgotten, the unclean, the unwanted. The condemned festered in the ninth, their dreams discarded and lives disdained. Robbers. Rapists. Prostitutes. Murderers. Orphans. All those considered unsavory by society dwelt there. Trapped. The ninth was a hope-swallowing quagmire few escaped.

A withered old man staggered past in a tattered loincloth and nothing more. He turned to Ralm, hand held out expectantly. Ralm shook his head and the man continued on. Beggars loitered everywhere. They gathered thickest around heavily trafficked gates and markets where coin flowed easiest. Another of the downtrodden stumbled across Ralm's way, reeking of wine and feces. With each passerby, Zirrin gave careful pause and plenty of space. Ralm understood his reasons. One never knew their intentions. Were they coming close to beg or to steal? Maybe to kill.

Ralm didn't share Zirrin's caution. Zirrin traveled these areas daily. Perhaps he'd experienced enough during his outings to become wary. Ralm felt no fear in the slums, or revulsion at the squalor. There was ample unpleasantness here. Certainly enough to concern him, yet he wasn't wary. Instead, the abundant want ignited a fire inside him. The quality of these lives, or lack of, brewed within him an anger never felt before. He cast a venomous stare at the spire. The order had built a city where those with power ruled and those without suffered. A society where the benefits of magic should be shared by all was instead reserved for the privileged. The Ascendancy amassed wealth and power by exploiting the godspear. It horded magic and tossed a few meager crumbs for the masses to fight over. If magic was given to all, the city would prosper. Each person could live unfettered. Citizens would help neighbors, rather than pursuing a selfish course.

Ralm stepped over a puddle of urine, the acrid stench assaulting his nose. Nearby, a woman huddled against a wall. A boy shivered beside her. Ralm clenched teeth and fists at the sight.

Zirrin led him through a market. Overripe fruit and vegetables were haggled over at a table between an irate patron and callous merchant. Further down, a man sold alive but sickly chickens missing many feathers. Quickening pace, Zirrin and Ralm weaved around denser collections of bodies amassed near vendors with tables sparse of goods. It wasn't until they reached the southern gate when Zirrin stopped, ignoring the sentries standing there as much as they ignored him.

"Down there is where we go," he said.

He pointed to the city's waterfront where long warehouses squatted by the docks. Behind them, a myriad of small fishing shacks crowded together, all with chimneys belching gray smoke into a blue sky. Docks teemed with people: fishmongers and merchants, sailors and anglers. Bins filled with the day's catch awaited sorting. Longboats and rafts mobbed an inadequate amount of moorings, while galleons anchored off shore, their hull's displacement too great for the shallows.

"He wants to talk to you," Zirrin said. "Taloon is very interested in what you have to say."

"Can he be trusted?" Ralm asked. The stink of fish assailed his nose. Men trudged by, casting suspicious glares from their weathered faces.

Zirrin shrugged. "You need help. It usually outweighs trust."

"So we can't trust him?"

Ralm waited for Zirrin to reply. He didn't, and for the first time since entering the ninth, Ralm was wary.

CHAPTER 15

It was a strange sight—a ship out of water, perched away from the dock's edge, its bulk leaning port side. The hull was clean, scrubbed free of barnacles and waterline stains. Where stern and rudder once occupied was now a gaping hole, hewn and cleaved by ax or some other edged tool. In it, a door sagged so out of square as to appear dripping from the hinges supporting it. The chipped and faded words *High and Dry* were barely visible along the sun-bleached keel.

Ralm and Zirrin followed a series of sloped planks linking the dock to the tavern's entrance, the warped boards moaning under their weight. Zirrin pushed the door open without hesitation. A thick, acrid cloud of pipe smoke escaped, lingering at the entrance until a stray breeze dispersed it. They entered, greeted by gloom and more smoke smelling of sour mint. Beyond the gray haze, a few hanging lamps lit the dim surroundings. Tables and chairs leaned with the crooked hull. No effort had been made to modify the furnishings and set them level.

Zirrin strode directly for a bottle-cluttered bar. The barkeep nodded as he approached, frown heavy on his face as he poured ale from a keg into four mugs. Zirrin slid onto a stool, and Ralm sat beside him. The stool wobbled under him.

The barkeep finished his pouring and brought two drinks to a pair of scruffy fishermen in twill jackets seated in a corner. They stared suspiciously at the newcomers until the drinks landed on the table. Each grabbed a mug and slung it to his lips. The remaining ale was served to a couple of uniformed seamen in the opposite corner of the tavern. Ralm tensed upon seeing servants of the order. A sudden urge to leave bloomed inside him. Only the prospect of finding the elusive Taloon helped wilt his fears.

"What's your drink?" He was a lean man with hollow cheeks. A tapered mustache extended beyond the width of his face. A small patch of whiskers hanging from his prominent chin did little to hide a deep cleft. His eyes were both dark and glinting, as if first gathering in lamplight before reflecting it. "And you best be drinking. If you plan to just sit here, that'll be a round for each of you." His was the oddest accent Ralm had yet heard. While others in Azazura spoke a heavier dialect than Vidreyans, the barkeeper's was almost lilting in its tone.

"Two of what they're having." Zirrin gestured to the sailors.

The barkeep nodded. "Two pig swills." He poured the drinks as he stared at Ralm with those dark-glinting eyes, eyes brimming with query and appraisal. "You sail in from another domain, or you a groundpounder touring the docks?" He slid two foamy drinks across the bar.

"A groundpounder, I suppose," Ralm said.

"You suppose?" The barkeep wrinkled his nose. "You either are or aren't. When somebody ain't being direct, it means they're hiding something. Is that what's the doing here? You hiding something?"

Ralm shifted uncomfortably under the barkeeper's scrutiny. He glanced to Zirrin, seeking aid, and found only a man sipping his drink. "Not exactly."

"Not exactly?" the barkeep echoed. "Quite the mysterious customer you are. How about it, men? Mysterious, eh?" he said loudly so all in the tavern heard. Ralm's eyes darted to the sailors. They showed no interest in anything except finding the bottoms of their mugs. The fishermen locked eyes onto Ralm briefly but otherwise remained silent about the matter. The barkeep rubbed his chin. "Well, if you aren't inclined to say where you're from or what you're hiding, there's one more question. Best if you're honest with it. Best for you. Why are you here?" Ralm shot a desperate glance at Zirrin, hoping for assistance. "The question is for you. Not him," the barkeep snapped, startling Ralm.

Lowering his voice, Ralm said, "I'm looking for somebody to help me get past the blockade."

The barkeeper's eyes narrowed into a piercing stare. His lips pursed and remained fixed for several long moments before finally bending into a smirk, then parting completely as a boisterous laugh spilled from his mouth. "Get past the blockade? You hear that, everyone? He wants to get past the blockade. He's a madman, as crazed as any illkin."

An urge to shrink from embarrassment (and unwanted attention by the sailors) gripped Ralm as the barkeep bellowed. The feeling passed quickly as the thought of what was at stake strengthened Ralm's resolve. He slammed a fist on the table. "I didn't come here to be laughed at. And I didn't come here to be ridiculed by a barkeep. This is a waste of time. Come on, Zirrin." Ralm stood abruptly and kicked his stool back. It skidded and toppled over. He was about to leave when the barkeeper's hand fell on his, pinning it to the bar.

"Hold there." All jest vanished from the barkeep's demeanor. "You've a bit of temper in you? Takes a little stoking and your fire burns. That kind of behavior will get you in trouble."

Ralm jerked his hand free. "It's frustration. Not temper. I've important matters to do and no time for your banter."

"All right. All right." The barkeeper's voice eased into a soothing tone. All traces of mockery were gone. "Who were you looking for to help get you through the blockade?"

Ralm glanced at Zirrin, who now seemed invested in Ralm's exchange with the barkeeper. He nodded consent to Ralm. "I'm looking for Taloon Taltaw."

The barkeep nodded. "Ah, Taloon Taltaw. Now there's a madman. If anybody knows about the blockade, it's Taloon. You know the tale of Taloon?" Ralm shook his head. "Well, straighten that stool and put it to use." He waited as Ralm righted the stool and sat back down. "Taloon was a simple sailor, quite happy shipping cargo between the lands. One day Taloon meets an upstart." His eyes flicked quickly in Zirrin's direction before returning to Ralm. "This man told Taloon his theory, an idea that went against all Taloon believed. The upstart told Taloon there was no monsters in the sea and the blockade wasn't there to protect Azazura from invasion. No, indeed. He explained on good authority there was an island out past all them ships, a place where trees grew so large as to touch the sky, and from those trees magic came. Of course, old Taloon didn't believe him at first. Who would? It went against everything Taloon was told since he was a lad. But something kept nibbling at Taloon's brain, and it wouldn't stop. The more he thought about it, the more it started making sense. Maybe that upstart was onto something. After a lot of thinking, Taloon decided to break through the blockade and find out for himself. He gathered a crew of the craziest, most suicidal men he could find, fitted his boat for the job and sailed across the sea." The barkeeper leaned across the bar and whispered to Ralm. "Know what happened?"

"No. What?" asked Ralm, thoroughly engrossed in the barkeeper's story.

"Taloon never got past the blockade. The boats saw him coming. When he got close, they attacked. Taloon escaped and made it home, but the order was wise to what he'd done. The Ascendant ordered his boat sunk. Taloon loved the sea, so he built another ship, but the order put a hole in it before she could be launched. The order wanted Taloon away from the sea for good. Now water never touches the boat, except when it rains. It's forever on dry land. Instead of it being for sailing, it's for drinking and it's where you're sitting now."

Ralm scanned his surroundings. He'd mistaken the rigging

and pulleys hanging about the place as decorations. They weren't. They were vital components for a ship. "This is Taloon's ship?"

"This is Taloon's ship," the barkeep said quietly.

"Where is Taloon now?"

The barkeep poured himself a drink and grinned. "With his ship. Instead of captain, he's barkeep."

"Taloon?"

The barkeeper tilted his head slightly in acknowledgment. "At your service."

Ralm blinked. "Why the game? Why fool me?"

"No fooling, lad. Taloon was vetting you. Taloon needs to make sure of your intentions. Luckily, Zirrin was here. If you'd come alone, Taloon would have Trips put your backside to the dockside."

"Trips?"

Taloon pointed at the two sailors. "Trips and Wyss. And those other two are Quay and Ongol. Don't mind their uniforms. None have worked in years."

"So, you've a crew for a landed ship?"

"Crew. Staff. They look after the place when Taloon's gone, or they just stay for the drink."

"The drink ain't worth staying for," grumbled Wyss. "But it's better than nothing."

"They've no place else to go," Taloon said. "The Ascendancy has seen to that."

"Captain," Trips said. "Want me to stand by the door in case an actual customer comes along? I'll send 'em walking."

Taloon smirked. "The best thought you've had in a year, Trips."

Trips mumbled something only he could hear and waited by the door, peeking through a slit for anybody coming up the planks.

Taloon rubbed his hands together. "Zirrin returns with a guest who asks old fool Taloon to be foolish again. Is Taloon understanding correctly?"

Ralm nodded. "Except for the fool part. I'm from the island.

The trees, the godspears, are dying. I sailed with my wife and her brother to Azazura to find help in stopping the beetles destroying them."

"How did you get past the blockade?"

"By accident and by tragedy," Ralm said. "We sailed with watchers, ascenders, who tried murdering us during the voyage. I fell overboard. I don't know what happened to the others. I washed ashore the next morning, or I think it was the next morning."

"Interesting," Taloon said. "Getting back will not be so easy. A lone body may slip past the blockade, but a ship, well, a ship will not be so easily overlooked."

"Zirrin mentioned you may be willing to try in a De' laNir."

"De' laNir." Taloon repeated the words slowly. He rolled the letters in his mouth. "You mean a Delaner? Is that it?"

Ralm shrugged. "If it means a fast flying ship. I've known it as De' laNir. That's how it was named in the stories I heard growing up."

Taloon snorted. "Stories do that. Little changes here and there go a long way. Maybe where you come from they're called De' laNir, but Taloon knows them as Delaner, named after the inventor, Ascender Delaner."

"I'm fine saying it my way," Ralm said. "The less association with the order, the better."

Taloon released a hearty laugh. "Now, that's an agreeable attitude. Taloon will call them De' laNirs from now on, too."

"I need a ship. I need a captain. I need to get back to Vidrey."

Taloon's laughter faded. "You're making a deep request, lad. Taloon tried once and failed. Taloon lost his ship. If he tries again and fails, Taloon may lose his life." He looked about the tavern with sorrowful eyes, his gaze resting briefly on each relic marking his former life: gaffs and nets hanging from walls and fishing poles leaning into corners. "You know, lad, old Taloon's been living a lie. He's a sailor pretending to be a barkeeper. Taloon's seen enough of this place. Taloon's had solid ground under his feet for too long.

Taloon will help. Taloon still has the itch to scratch, to see what's beyond the blockade, and if Taloon dies trying, well, better than dying the slow death here on land."

"You'll help?" Ralm asked.

Taloon's dark, glinting eyes met Ralm's. "For a price. Taloon can't be doing it for free. If you can get a De' laNir, Taloon will captain it. He'll catch the wind for you. When all is done, Taloon keeps the ship. But Taloon won't be risking himself to get it. Acquiring the ship is up to you."

Ralm frowned and slowly nodded. "That's fair. Now all I need is to find one."

"Finding is easy. There's one out in the bay right now," Taloon said.

"There is?" Ralm abruptly stood, excitement rippling through him. "Where is it? Can I see?" He was like an eager child awaiting a gift.

Taloon strolled to a window and pointed beyond. "Certainly. She's right there."

Ralm rushed outside, crossed the zigzag of planks and bolted across the dock to stand at its edge. Sea foamed and misted below his feet as waves slapped dock supports. A cool breeze swept by him as he gazed upon the water where small and large fishing vessels sailed or rowed along the coastline. Zirrin and Taloon came up beside him. "Where is it?" Ralm asked. He should have seen it by now. De' laNirs were magnificent, unlike any other ship, with billowing sails and gilded figureheads, or so the stories told, yet nothing unusual drew his attention.

"There." Taloon pointed at a brig anchored one hundred paces from shore. Soldiers and sailors milled about on deck. "Not the brig, but what's alongside it."

Ralm strained his eyes. Beside the brig was a barge, or what may have been a barge. It was half the length of the brig and as flat and boring as the boards used for its construction. There were no billowing sails. No gilded figurehead. It was unremarkable, with no resemblance to anything from the stories.

"Are you sure?" he asked. "It doesn't look like a De' laNir."

"You've seen many De' laNirs, have you?" Taloon asked.

"No, but the stories always made them sound so grand."

"Ah. Yes. Well, stories do that," Taloon said. "They make things sound better than they usually are. And each time a story is told, the details become grander and grander while the truth becomes smaller and smaller. That's why they're stories."

Ralm stared at the flat boat with mounting disappointment. "It isn't very impressive."

"Never judge by appearance alone." Taloon chuckled. "That's a mistake many make and all regret."

"It's enchanted? I see no shimmer to it." Ralm squinted.

"The water affects it. Something of an illusion. Light reflecting off the sea distorts the ship's true appearance. Taloon thinks the order prefers it that way. Keeps less attention on the ship. If you get close, you'll see it. Though Taloon doubts that will ever happen."

"Where's the rest? I thought there was a fleet of them. Maybe there's an easier one to reach somewhere else."

"Perhaps long ago there were more," Taloon said. "These days, there's no need. The blockade relies on stationary vessels and De' laNirs are expensive to build. The ascendant maintains one as a symbol of his power, but they're seldom used for anything other than display. Taloon did see one sail once, long ago, and it was a sight. Oh, such a sight."

"You've never piloted one?" Ralm asked with a sinking heart.

Taloon shook his head.

"Could you, if given the chance?"

"It's a ship, lad. But it's also something else. Under full wind it doesn't sail like a normal ship. It handles differently. But, to answer your question, Taloon could sail her. As you can see, getting to her is the trick. She's moored off shore. One reason is because she has a long keel, a very special keel. She doesn't take shallows. The other reason is security. Keeping her in the deeps prevents thieves from trying to steal her. And from what Taloon knows, her magic is a dinner bell for illkin. Imagine her being docked. Illkin would swarm her constantly. Taloon supposes it wouldn't be a bad way of drawing them out and dealing with them all at once. Strange. Why didn't the order ever use the De' laNir for that purpose? It could eliminate the illkin threat." He rubbed his chin thoughtfully. "Regardless, getting to her will be the trick. The brig next to her has one purpose: protect the De' laNir. If the men aboard see anybody coming close, arrows start flying. Once, Taloon watched a fishing boat with a broken rudder drift near. The amount of arrows pelting the fishermen was astounding. In the hundreds. When the ship drifted close enough, soldiers boarded and killed every one of the fishermen still alive before sinking the boat. That's how protective the order is about the De' laNir. So, as Taloon said before, getting it will be the trick."

Ralm surveyed the distance between land and ship. Swimming was possible, but foolhardy. If he managed to reach the De' laNir undetected, he'd be too exhausted to fight or try stealing the ship. And operating a ship, magical or not, was beyond his abilities. Ralm would need help, which meant either everybody swimming to reach the ship, or everybody riding in a boat. The former meant finding people willing to risk their lives, the latter meant the same but in a boat easily seen from the brig even during the darkest hours of night, all under a hail of arrows. "I'll need time to come up with a plan."

"Taloon's heard that very phrase spoken dozens of times before and the result has always been the same. Failure."

A commotion further down the dock arrested their attention. Two dock workers probed the water with long poles as curious onlookers gathered around. Ralm and Zirrin edged closer to see.

"Looks like another one," Taloon said before heading back to the *High and Dry*.

"Another what?" Ralm asked.

"Seen enough of them in Taloon's life, don't care to see any more," was all he said before slipping back into the tavern.

"That's it," one of the workers said, stirring his pole. "Almost got it looped."

"Easy. Don't poke it," the other worker said between grunts. "You don't want it popping or it'll reek worse than ten-day-old fish."

"I have it. Get your loop around the legs," the first dock worker said.

His assistant complied. "Got it."

The two men heaved up their poles and stumbled back as they dragged a body from the water onto the dock. Onlookers either gasped or retched meals onto the seagull-sullied planking. Ralm and Zirrin exchanged troubled glances. The body was pale and bloated, but they both recognized the corpse.

Frayna.

CHAPTER 16

Ralm meandered quietly down the street, head lowered in somber reflection. People brushed his arms as they passed, some hurriedly weaving ahead of him, others striding in the opposite direction. He paid mind to none of them. His thoughts were elsewhere, at the fire burning outside the city. That's where she was. Frayna. Her corpse, once swollen from water, now immolated, soon to be nothing more than ash for the wind to carry away. Ash, mingling with the ashes of other recently deceased. Her ashes mingling with Wirgan's. His remains were out there too, though he'd been burned days ago. Zirrin had informed Ralm as much. The pile of dead, rotting in the sun, was set ablaze when the foul stench and swarming flies infiltrated the city. Wirgan and Frayna. Two people briefly entwined in Ralm's life. Two people, soon to mix together before scattering forever. Life. Death. Water. Fire. Air. Simple in their individuality. Complex when their strings tied together.

Zirrin had arranged her funeral. Calling upon some favors owed to him, Frayna's body was removed from the docks and taken to a local woodworker where a coffin was built. Few of the poor were given such respect. Few could afford a coffin. Money was better served on the living, so most of the ninth and many of the eighth's residents who perished were laid bare upon pyres, their scant possessions left to families or filched by strangers. Zirrin refused to allow Frayna that final indignation. She was burdened in life. She'd be free in death.

Burning bodies was a strange concept to Ralm. Unlike Vidrey, there was no room for graves in the outer rings of the city and no place to plant a tree (though Azazurans clearly followed different customs and didn't plant trees with their dead). Ashes were easily dispersed and easily forgotten. Only memories lingered after, and they occupied only the mind. For the wealthy, for the affluent, for those inhabiting the inner rings, patches of land were dedicated to cemeteries, though it was rumored many widows could no longer visit their husband's graves. They had sold their magic to pay for the plot and, along with losing their spouse, lost their prestige.

A churning in Ralm's stomach forced him to the side of the street. He stopped, bent over and leaned against a wall. Guilt roiled in his guts, buzzed in his mind, ached in his heart at a realization. He was responsible for Frayna's death. He may as well have pushed her into the water himself. At the orphanage, he had persuaded her to return Brella to Hilni. Little did Ralm understand the impact of his words. He was offering Frayna a way out, devoid of regret. He'd simplified the matter for her. Had she left the child at the orphanage, she may have chosen to live, to watch her child grow from a distance. Perhaps one day she would have climbed out of her pit of despair, escaped the shackles of poverty and rescued her daughter from the orphanage.

Ralm had altered her course. By convincing Frayna to give the child to Hilni, she glimpsed a future where she was unneeded. Hilni and Zirrin could feed and clothe the baby, raise and protect her. Frayna wouldn't need to improve Brella's conditions. She could never match what the Paladas family provided her child. Ralm persuaded Frayna into irrelevance.

Her suicide was unquestioned. Witnesses reported seeing her standing at the edge of the dock staring blankly at the sea. There were concerns for her behavior, but nothing more. Nobody intervened. People involved themselves first with their own interests. To pry into the matters of another was, if not rude, an inconvenience. Best to ignore it, better to let people sort their own problems out. Focus on oneself. There was, after all, the inner circles to inhabit. To reach that goal, one must distance compassion and scorn sympathy. Apathy permitted Frayna to plunge into the Cryptic Sea without interruption and be swallowed by cold, dark waters. She was hauled out not for the dignity of her remains, but because a body floating dockside was bad for local morale.

Bent boles make poor poles. The simple philosophy endured in Vidrey. Outcomes to an overseer's decision meant compromise for all parties involved. Since his arrival in Azazura, the results of Ralm's choices had more serious consequences, most notably the deaths of Wirgan and Frayna.

If he were to make more choices, he'd need to consider all possible repercussions. Ralm wouldn't risk more lives.

The turmoil in Ralm's stomach lessened. He straightened and returned to the flowing mass of people in the street, his guilt diminishing but not disappearing. Faces materialized and dissolved in the crowd around him, each unique: bearded, clean-shaven, short hair, long hair, crooked noses, cheeks blemished with rashes, scabs, boils, blisters and warts. But the eyes were the tying thread. Within them was held a silent hunger for magic. Hard work meant money earned, and money earned meant magic bought. With enough magic came movement into an inner circle. The further inward, the better living, the better housing, the better food, the better everything.

A pair of guards passed Ralm, faces rigid, eyes locked forward. He didn't flinch. He didn't fear them, and as his gaze drifted upward to the always looming spire, Ralm's eyes narrowed in anger. Hands balled into tight fists at the towering presence, ominous and dark, a constant reminder to the people their place was on the ground, scurrying like ants while the ascendant observed from above, untouched by their struggles. Untouched because of chance, chosen as a child to become something more than an orphan, to mature and forget his roots in favor of power absolute. How easily the wind may have blown in another direction and the ascender of today would never have been anything except another orphan.

Fists loosened as a bout of frustration overtook him. His plan to find a cure was simple, or so he once thought. Landing on Azazura's shores had led to one complication after another. Frayna's death was a potent sting on its own, but the same day he discovered something else equally deflating. The De' laNir ship, which he imagined so many times as something beyond marvelous, was instead something less than boring. Stories he believed historical unraveled to morsels of truth with generous portions of exaggeration. And to worsen matters, reaching the De' laNir was currently impossible.

A new choice revealed itself. Was he to accept the way things were in the city, or not? If Ralm did not, he'd continue his efforts to find a way home and ignore the struggles of those around him. If he chose the opposite, he'd put the needs of the Azazurans before his own people. Both mainlanders and islanders were in danger. An overseer's first duty was to his people. The tenet was simple and straightforward back home. Here it held new meaning and new complexity.

Ralm didn't notice at first, but as he brooded through the city, a pocket of emptiness surrounded him. The throng of people around him vanished. No elbows jabbed him, no shoulders rubbed his. The space between him and the people had expanded to a few steps in every direction. Ralm, caught in his own thoughts, didn't notice his island of isolation, or that the people had given way for an approaching ascender, until it was too late. Ralm collided with the robed figure.

"Watch where you're going, flea," hissed the ascender. His hood was drawn down over his golden mask. One hand gripped a purple-hued staff.

"You'd have seen my coming better if that ridiculous mask and hood were off." Ralm's words were wrapped with the same malcontent simmering inside him.

Bystanders' mouths gaped in surprise at Ralm's blatant disrespect for the ascender's office. Potential witnesses to the developing crime darted away before they were further involved.

The ascender paused, as if uncertain how to react. "You bend to me." He brandished the staff. "And you will do so now."

"I'll not bend to you," Ralm bellowed for all nearby to hear. "You don't control me."

The ascender thrust his staff, the butt striking Ralm square in the chest. Ralm staggered back, his hand rubbing the pained area. The ascender twisted the staff in his hands, studying it as if perplexed. He jabbed again. Ralm tried to dodge the strike, but the staff nicked his shoulder. It was a minor blow, feeling no worse than a dozen other bruises Ralm had endured falling from trees as a boy.

Again, the ascender stared at his staff. Ralm couldn't see his eyes under the mask, but the manner in which the ascender examined his weapon suggested something wasn't happening as expected. He stepped forward and gripped Ralm's face, his thumb digging hard into Ralm's cheek. The ascender turned Ralm's head side to side, evaluating him. "What are you?" he asked, his voice harsh and accusatory.

His question troubled Ralm. He didn't ask who. He asked what. "A man, just as you," Ralm said, recalling Scalamar's words about ascenders wearing masks to deceive the people into believing they were more than human. To declare the ascender a man was defiant and satisfying.

The ascender pulled his hand away and stared at his fingers, now stained with Ralm's face paint. Rubbing thumb and index finger together, he rolled the smear of paint between them into a loose ball. Ralm felt suddenly exposed. If the paint was on those fingers, it was no longer on his face. His disguise was compromised. How much of his true identity was revealed? Was his face merely smudged, or was his dark skin showing through for all to see?

"Stay where you are," the ascender commanded. "You're under arrest. Guards!"

Ralm shoved the ascender, sending him into a stagger. He tripped on the bottom of his robe and fell onto his backside, his head striking the ground with a thud. Ralm bolted into the throng of people. He heard the ascender call for the guards again. Ralm slowed, mixing into the swirling mass of bodies, fighting the urge to run. If he did, he'd bring attention to himself. Best to blend in, resist the instinct to flee. He kept his head low, avoiding eye contact with those around him. If any paint was absent from his face, he'd be mistaken for an illkin, which may incite panic and draw more attention to him.

The guards he'd passed earlier sprinted by as they raced to the ascender's call. Ralm turned away, hiding his face. They went by without noticing him, focused solely on heeding their master.

Ralm had scant moments for escape. Soon the ascender would order the guards back in his direction with a description of a feature sure to set Ralm apart from the crowd. He scolded himself for his brash and hasty actions. Nothing good would come of this. And now he was more a target than ever.

He returned to Zirrin's house before the alarms reached Pigeon Lane. Ralm checked each direction, made certain nobody was watching and slid through the front doorway. He closed the door, leaned against it, shut his eyes and sighed. His encounter with the ascender was ill timed and poorly handled. If the authorities hadn't given searching him priority before, they certainly would now. He was now known by them, known for what he truly was. Dark skin marked him illkin among the people, but dark-skinned, communicative and disguised revealed his true origin to the Ascendancy. It wouldn't take long for them to fit the pieces together.

He waited by the door, expecting alarms to ring close, followed by the tromp of boots as Low Guard rushed the door. When neither was heard, he went upstairs to Neva's room. The door was open. He knocked on it anyway before entering. She stood at an easel, the brush in her hand sweeping across the canvas. She looked up through the long hair concealing her visage and, seeing her work defaced, immediately set to correcting Ralm's disguise. She assembled her paints and within moments repaired the damage.

"Thank you, once again," Ralm said softly as she applied some powder over the paint. Neva nodded slightly. "I have another job for you, if you're interested." Neva stopped, her hand hovering by his cheek. "Can you paint me something showing how the Ascendant controls the people with magic?" Neva nodded vigorously. The request seemed to thrill her, though if she were smiling, her hair concealed it.

She finished touching up his cosmetics as the sound of the front door shutting reached her room. Ralm thanked her again and returned downstairs, finding Zirrin in the sitting room peeling off his coat.

"Lots of excitement happening out there," Zirrin said, tossing his coat over the back of one chair before flopping into another. "I don't suppose you have anything to do with it."

Ralm shrugged as he stared at his fidgeting feet. "I don't know. I guess it depends what the excitement is about."

A bottle of wine and four glasses on a silver tray waited on the table beside Zirrin. After pouring into two glasses, he slid one across the table, his gaze on Ralm. "It seems somebody out there bumped into an ascender. Actually bumped into one of those snakes." Zirrin grinned, sipped some wine and grinned some more. "Good." He dabbed the corner of his mouth with a finger. "Too many people give too high regard to that kind. Always paying them more respect than they deserve, bowing and scurrying away. It's enough to make one mad asking why."

Ralm sat across from Zirrin and took the offered wine. He brought it to his nose and the aroma wafted in. Wine seemed the beverage of choice in the city, or at least in Zirrin's home. Wine and tea. For breakfast and mid-afternoon, a warm cup of tea was a favorite drink for Hilni. For lunch, dinner and the late evening, wine was preferred. He'd seen Zirrin drink mead once, after the proxy. Otherwise, it was always tea and wine. Ralm sipped from his glass, the sour tang flowing over his tongue and cheeks. He craved a mug of sweet Vidreyan mead. "Isn't that what's expected? Show them reverence."

Zirrin flicked his free hand at the air. "Why? Why should they be courted so? Do they shower us with riches? With food? Do they bring the rains and sun? Do they command the night? Do they speak to animals?" He shook his head and gave a long exhalation. "No, of course not. The only thing they provide, and the people grovel before them because of it, is who lives and who dies, who is jailed and who remains free."

Ralm snorted. "Free. Free? Is this what people consider free? To live in fear, under tyranny? To spend their lives racing about, the spoils of their efforts given to the Ascendancy, all the while trying to scrounge enough to purchase enough magic to move to an inner circle. You call that free?"

"Certainly not. But people are born into it. It's all they know. Generations upon generations know of nothing else. Those in power tend to stay in power." Zirrin stared into his wine somberly. "You come from a place far different from what is here. You see with fresh eyes what most here cannot." He leaned forward, set the glass down and matched Ralm's gaze. "There's a fresh rumor out there about an encounter between an ascender and a man. A painted man. I know of no other in the city who paints his face." Ralm began to deny his involvement. Zirrin waved a hand and silenced him. "I don't know what happened, but whatever it was worried the ascender. To put fear in an ascender is no small accomplishment." He reached into a pocket, removed two glass jars and placed them on the table. "Paint. For Neva. I used to be able to buy these openly, but now it's best not to draw attention. Too many prying eyes with too many loose lips. It's inconvenient, sneaking about to get something as simple as paint, but it's worth it. I want her to keep painting."

"Zirrin, are you implying—"

"I'm implying nothing except this: you're angry at the Ascendancy. Channel your anger into something useful. Something more than paintings. They're a start, but not an end. Do something more. Do something for the people."

Brun's words, the axiom he'd repeated throughout his life, resounded in Ralm's mind with inescapable relevance. The overseer's first duty was to the people.

"Boles and poles," Ralm whispered.

"Indeed."

Ralm strolled to the window. Night was gathering, the first stars beginning to glitter in a blackening sky. Vidrey was somewhere under those same stars. What were the islanders doing at this very moment? Were they preparing for dinner? Or were they watching more godspears die? Perhaps neither. Perhaps both. Vidrey was far away, and there was nothing to be done about it. All he could do was make a choice and accept the consequences.

His gaze dropped to the lowest window pane. He'd need to put another *X* in it soon.

CHAPTER 17

Lavak flexed and contracted his fingers to work the pain out of them. Embedding valdsker into godspear was tedious work, and gripping the slender spoon-like tools for long periods of time cramped his hands. With a long sigh he leaned back and admired his work. The beetle lay before him, tight honey grain hidden inside the element of valdsker, green as the jar situated at the far edge of the worktable, the once-smooth surface now gritty. It had taken three days to complete his work, far longer than Lavak originally anticipated. The first coat consumed five hours of his time. The godspear hungrily absorbed the fine powder without delay. After the first coat, only the faintest tinge of green was seen in the wood grain. Lavak attributed the lengthy effort to his novice skills. He expected the next embedding to proceed more quickly. It did, but only slightly. He resisted every temptation to hurry. Meticulously, he pressed the valdsker into the wood and rocked the tool back and forth, forcing it into the grain just as Corundra demonstrated the first day. Each scribed line in the beetle's carapace, every bend in the barbed legs, required delicate attention. On several occasions, Lavak regretted crafting such a detailed object. If he'd known the embedding process was so time-consuming, he'd have opted for a simpler design.

His pains and patience instilled in him new respect for enchantment. He now understood why magic was so valuable.

Godspear was only part of the price. Enchantment, and the craftsmanship it required, was a skill unmatched by any other in the land.

"Excellent work," Corundra had praised him earlier that day.

"I suppose," said Lavak. "I was hoping to have it done in four coats. To beat the masters."

Corundra folded his arms across his chest. "Now listen to me, I told you it could take as few as five coats. That wasn't a challenge. Different objects take element differently. The finer the detail, the more passes will be needed. Remember, it doesn't matter how many times you do it, just that you do it right."

"But I'm the transcendent, this should come naturally to me."

The old enchanter snorted. "Is that so? And who told you such foolishness?"

"No one. Everyone. I thought—"

"There's the problem, you're thinking too much. And you're letting all this transcendent talk fill you with worry about living up to the name. Here's my advice. Don't listen. It will only make things worse, and you'll get nothing for it." Corundra glanced at the beetle. "You chose a rather complicated first piece. I don't mean just the carving, but the influence as well. Not many are bold enough to try it, and few are given the chance with untested skills. Be proud of what you've done because it's more than most have a chance to do."

"What are we?" the voice asked, dragging Lavak's mind to the present.

He didn't answer and didn't bother searching for the source. During his time in the workshop under Drudylan's tutelage, the voice hadn't sounded at all. Lavak first considered his imagination finally at rest, but as days blended together he realized it was because of the room's noise. Hammers and files in Drudylan's workshop made for a distracting atmosphere, drowning out thoughts and hushed voices alike. Here in the elemental halls, tools worked quietly. The strange spoons and tiny spatulas were inaudible no matter how hard they were used. The voice visited

Lavak frequently during his time here, but he didn't indulge. The voice, however, seemed irritated by this and persisted with its asking. Ignoring it was almost impossible. This unseen, invasive entity first entreated, then demanded, Lavak's attention.

He stood and arched his back, stretching sore muscles. It was late. The other enchanters, including Corundra, had retired hours ago. There were no windows here, no tempted drafts to blow and scatter the precious valdsker. Without windows, time was a vague concept. Only an enchanter's work measured the progress of hours.

Lavak tenderly wrapped the beetle inside a linen. He added it to another linen—stuffed with treasures—tucked under his shirt.

Night greeted him as he exited the enchantery. Guards at the door gave him no recognition, their stony gazes fixed forward. Overhead, stars peeked through wisps of clouds plodding across a tranquil sky. Ahead, lamps aglow in windows dappled the spire. At its peak gleamed a pinhead of faint light: Volstrysa's chamber. She was still awake, possibly waiting for him to either examine his completed work or entertain him. Her interest in him was becoming more obvious, not just because he was the transcendent, or his training as an enchanter, but more romantically as well. Subtle gestures, casual touches and embraces lasting far longer than he considered appropriate were but a few of her flirtations. Lavak may have lived on an island his entire life and may have had little dealings with the opposite sex, but even he was not oblivious to Volstrysa's coquetting. She made clear her intentions.

He entered the spire and started the long ascent up the stairway. Volstrysa had offered him unlimited use of the lift, but Lavak preferred taking the stairs. He didn't like being inside the box, at the mercy of two men who probably cared little for him. A mere slip of the handle, intentional or not, while he was mid-spire would be all that was needed to send him plunging to his death. Besides, the lift would take him directly to Volstrysa's chamber, the last place he wanted to go tonight.

The stairway spiraled upward like a coiled snake. Every thirty steps brought Lavak to a new landing, marked by a symbol engraved into the stone floor. A corresponding symbol on the armored sleeve of the high guard stationed at each landing denoted his rank. Every thirty steps brought Lavak to a higher-ranked guard, more esteemed and deadly than the last.

There was a difference between guards and ascenders. The latter moved freely between spire, city and domain. The former did not. He understood only a little about the rank structure of the High and Low Guard. High Guard were the order's elite warriors, charged with protecting the spire and its occupants, especially the ascendant. Low Guard were the army beyond the spire's walls, assigned with maintaining peace and enforcing laws in the city and throughout the domain.

He was neither ascender nor guard but was given privileges few in the order were granted. He moved about the spire freely, and he hadn't earned it. Volstrysa lavished him with attention while ignoring many of her other underlings. He was reviled here. Kuldahar had said as much, but Lavak felt it, too. Contempt blazed in soldiers' glares. Bitterness hung thick around ascenders.

Continuing up the spire, his leg muscles began to ache. Lavak reached another landing and paused to catch his breath. The high guard didn't look at him. He stared ahead with almost unblinking eyes, rigid as a statue. The savors of iron-like and airy mingled with Lavak's senses. Both magics were woven together, forming a breastplate both strong and light. Lavak climbed higher, leaving the guard and his savor behind.

On trembling legs he stumbled down the curved passage leading to his lab. Volstrysa told him to see her immediately upon his completion of the embedding, but other matters tugged Lavak toward his lab first. He pushed open the door, lamplight from the passage spilling into the dark room. Lighting a candle, he shut the door behind him.

Settling into his chair at the table, Lavak stretched his legs and relaxed awhile before retrieving the two balls of linen he'd smuggled from the enchantery. He opened the one containing the beetle, his reminder a cure was still needed for the godspears. The glass box housing the lone beetle was nearby. Lavak distanced his work from it, fearful the insect might somehow escape to feast upon his efforts. Beside the box, a small bowl filled with beetle frass Lavak had been collecting drew his attention. He slid the bowl close and probed the contents with a finger, the texture silken to his touch. Minuscule crystals glittered in the light. There was a riddle hidden inside the droppings, but Lavak didn't know the question, therefore, he couldn't pursue an answer.

Unfolding the second linen presented Lavak with a meager yet inviting display of magic: the cap for a walking stick fashioned from suspension, an airy bracelet, a single glove lined with splints of iron-like, an ice-kissed arrowhead and a fire-felt spoon. Their savors mixed like the aromas of a hearty stew. Lavak touched nothing, as if a child deciding which treat to sample first.

Kuldahar's suspicions of Lavak pilfering the cup from the kitchen had acted as a warning. Magic was too closely monitored in the spire. Although the evidence was destroyed, Lavak couldn't risk being almost caught again, though his desire to experiment with his abilities was irresistible. Fortunately, he'd found a stash of magic that, by his estimate, was overlooked if not entirely forgotten, by most.

Hidden in the bottom drawer of Corundra's desk was a trove of magic. Lavak had been unaware of it until one evening when Corundra warned him of the folly of wasteful enchantment.

"Let me show you what impracticality brings," Corundra said as Lavak tediously applied the second layer of valdsker to the beetle. "Come here."

Corundra led Lavak to his desk. The aged enchanter eased into his chair and pulled open the bottom drawer, revealing it to be almost brimming with an odd assortment of small magics. Corundra rummaged until finding a suitable example to hold before Lavak.

"See this stylus?" he asked. "See its luster?"

Lavak didn't respond immediately. He was mesmerized by Corundra's hoard. It had been there, mere feet away, the whole time he'd been embedding, and Lavak hadn't realized. He'd sensed a savory mixture nearby but attributed it to the other aspirants and ascenders sharing his workspace or perhaps the possessions of enchanters in one of the other element wings.

It was impossible to visually determine the stylus's nature of magic. The luster was absent and only when the faintest of savor tickled his senses amid the assault of the drawer's other savors did Lavak realize held within was an ice-kissed enchantment. Despite knowing this, Lavak shook his head. Corundra was about to teach a lesson, and Lavak wasn't about to reveal his ability.

"Of course not," Corundra said. "It's weak. Very weak. Amateurishly weak, actually, because it was created by an amateur. But that isn't the point. Plenty of novice enchanters make weak enchantments. The point is the application. Now, understand that all first-time enchanters are allowed to make whatever they want. It's not the item which is important, but the practice. However, the enchanter who crafted this stylus did so with the belief that using ice-kissed would keep the user's hand from sweating. Evidently, the enchanter had written a lot during his time as an aspirant and found it difficult to hold onto his quill due to sweaty fingers and a wet palm. Is that practical?"

Lavak shrugged, uncertain how to answer. He was only partially listening to Corundra's lecture. His attention refused to stray from the drawer's contents for more than a moment.

"No! It's not practical," Corundra continued. "How many people suffer from moist hands while writing? Very few, I suspect. Those writing atop a fire and those with something to be nervous about writing. My point is, magic should be for something useful. Something practical." He shook the stylus in his hand. "This is neither."

Corundra dropped the stylus back into the drawer before sliding it closed. His lesson was over, but Lavak learned more than the elderly enchanter intended. He now knew of a supply of magic he could loot. Likely, Corundra didn't keep inventory of his stash, and if he did, Lavak doubted he did so with regularity.

Now back in his room, Lavak could experiment at his leisure. He studied each enchantment before finally deciding on the bracelet. Immediately the magic coursed into him upon his touch. His stomach fluttered as the bracelet turned to dust. Lavak grew instantly restless. His heart raced. He rose from his chair, anxious to move, and found his muscles responded quicker than usual. Arms raised in a blur of motion. He crossed the room quicker than he could blink. Eventually, the magic dissipated.

It seemed the enchanter attempted to give the glove's wearer more resilience when striking targets. He drained the magic and the godspear disintegrated, but the leather and stitching remained. Energy rattled Lavak's innards. But there was more. He felt confident to the point of brash and borderline belligerent. Lavak wanted nothing more than to find somebody to fight and was tempted to approach the guard on his landing and slap him across the face to incite something violent. It was an unaccustomed feeling. He'd always avoided confrontation. Concentrating, he quieted the urges before directing the magic down his arm. His hand trembled. Lavak punched the wall. Stone cracked beneath his fist. He felt no pain. No bones broke. No scraped knuckles. No blood.

When he siphoned the spoon, Lavak was uncertain what he should do with the fire-felt magic. Instantly, his body was covered in sweat. Malicious thoughts passed through his mind, unspeakable acts against friend and foe alike Lavak found great joy in pondering. He turned to one of the bookshelves, hoping for inspiration. Though he disapproved the destruction of books, igniting one would prove a satisfying experiment, but as he reached for one, the magic leapt from his fingers and seared the binding. Lavak stared in disbelief at his hand. The magic had left his body and traveled unseen through the air. The malice occupying his thoughts a moment earlier, now gone.

If fire-felt behaved in such a manner, would ice-kissed? A pitcher of water on the table was to be his target. Lavak drained the arrowhead, the chill of magic running the course of his spine causing him to shiver. There came with the sensation a sudden, overwhelming paranoia. The fear of his thefts being discovered overtook Lavak along with the certainty at any moment High Guard would break down the door and arrest him. Desperate to be rid of the feeling, Lavak pointed at the pitcher and the ice-kissed flushed from his body. Frost collected on the pitcher, and when Lavak peered inside, the water within was frozen. Gone from his body was the magic and paranoia.

He was becoming fatigued by the repeated transference of magic. Despite his weakening state, Lavak wanted more magic.

There was still one item left: the cane tip of suspension. He drew out the magic. Though it ricocheted inside him, a serenity ensconced Lavak. He felt calm, unaffected and untouched by troubles. Even when thoughts fell upon the godspear plight, he experienced no anxiety over it and no urgency to find a cure. He was at peace. And what better way to experiment with suspension than on the creature responsible for giving him anything but peace these past weeks? Lifting the lid of the jar, Lavak pointed a finger at the beetle and unleashed the magic. The beetle immediately went still as the comforting sensation departed Lavak. Replacing it was the worry he'd thrown too much magic at the small insect and killed it, but after a few minutes, the beetle returned to its usual pursuits.

A mild throbbing crept into Lavak's head. He tried to ignore it, tried to keep his thoughts on the beetle, but couldn't. He willed sore legs to carry him to a shelf where a box once containing leaf samples rested. Inside lay a single button. Too small for any person's clothing, the button seemed intended for a child's doll were it not for its green luster. Had Lavak discovered it lying on the floor, he'd have thought as much and questioned its usefulness, but this button had been sewn into his robes. If Lavak hadn't sensed its presence, he'd have never known it existed. Even with knowing magic was near, it took him over an hour to locate it, pinching each inch of fabric, feeling for irregularities until finding a hard lump inside the supple cloth's hem. With a knife he'd excised the button. The button fell to the floor with a soft plink. He dared not touch it with bare skin, fearful of how influence may affect him. If his head throbbed when he was in vicinity of influence, how might the magic affect him once absorbed? Would he go mad? Would it kill him?

More questions followed. Why would Volstrysa use it on him? He'd never shown her resistance. If anything, he was compliant. They both aimed for the same goal: to save the godspear. Or was this how she kept underlings in control? Were similar buttons sewn into the clothes of all ascenders and aspirants of the Crimson Spire, unbeknown to them? He hadn't sensed any, hadn't felt the throbbing in his head, when others were near. They carried other magics Lavak detected, but were those enchantments powerful enough to conceal a small amount of influence? Doubtful.

He was aware of Volstrysa's reputation. It was uttered directly from the mouths of ascenders. The Dark Mistress. A name earned for her raven hair and seductive ways. Lavak experienced her charms firsthand, but considered Volstrysa's affections merely polite and hospitable, as a host providing food and shelter for a guest. Did she behave this way with others in private, or was he the exception? If he was one of many, why use influence on him when he sensed none hidden on other ascenders?

"What are we?" the voice asked, this time louder than in the past.

Lavak ignored it.

Other voices and laughter, familiar and cruel, outside his head, echoed down the passage beyond his door, and with them, a distinct mixture of savors. These voices would not be easily ignored. Lavak slumped in anticipation of the oncoming, inevitable disturbance before a curiosity gripped him and with it, a spontaneous gamble full of spiteful promise. He plucked the button from the box, disregarding his former apprehensions. The magic surged into him, thin but powerful as it snaked up his arm and into his chest. The button dissolved into a gray smear of ash on his fingertips. Lavak shuddered as new, untested magic pulsed through him with more energy than expected from such a small object. It swirled in his chest and mind, giving him a clarity he'd never experienced before. He saw the world through new perspective and discovered alternate meanings hidden inside all he surveyed. He pondered deeply the trivial, enthralled by complexities oft overlooked in the common and everyday. Books on shelves revealed patterns. Every crack in the stone walls surrounding him eluded to a dozen reasons he'd never considered prior. The influence receded and settled in his stomach. His superior clarity vanished. It happened quickly. He hadn't a chance to absorb any of it and was left to wonder what sight he'd been gifted and what he'd missed. Still, he was alive and sane, his fear abated and the influence inside waiting to be unleashed.

The door swung open and slammed hard into the wall as Kuldahar, Eberan and Jaquista strolled in just as Lavak wiped the dust from the spent magic off the table.

"Looks like we're not the only owls in the spire." Kuldahar sneered as he ambled to Lavak. "Though we're the only ones deserving of roosting here." He bumped into Lavak's chair with deliberate force.

"Yeah, not all of us can get here without paying our share," Jaquista said.

Kuldahar leaned against the table. He glowered down at Lavak. "Quite true. Most of us have to work to reach this level. Hauling chamber pots and sweeping floors, spending hours in the kitchen peeling potatoes. Meanwhile, some get to enjoy their unearned place without so much as a blister to show for it."

Lavak glared at him. He was reliving his childhood: bullied and teased, but now, instead of the color of his skin, it was for jealousy. "Why do you torment me? What have I done to you?"

"You don't belong here." Kuldahar's eyes narrowed. "You're

here because you're a freak to be studied. You weren't orphaned, you weren't selected by the supreme and you weren't trained. You're Volstrysa's pet. I was her favorite, but then you came and now she gives you all the attention."

"She used to give me attention too," Jaquista said. Eberan nodded agreement. "But now you're here, we're ignored."

"You see?" said Kuldahar. "We've been cast aside. Someday, you will be too."

Lavak didn't sense influence on the grackles. Volstrysa's power over them didn't require magic. This made them more dangerous. They were acting on their own free will. So if not use influence on them, why him? The question begged for an answer Lavak couldn't provide yet. "You taunt me because I'm favored by the supreme, yet say I will be forgotten by her in the future. Won't her casting me aside be enough, without you hounding me?"

The three ascenders exchange perplexed glances, telling of minds dismantling the logic in his words. It was the same on Vidrey. His superior reasoning often left grackles dumbfounded. Kuldahar punched the table. Just like back home, Lavak's intellect left grackles frustrated to the point of violence. He regretted having tapped the iron-like already.

"At least with you here, I won't need to coddle you once it's my turn to go to Vidrey," Kuldahar said through gritted teeth. "From what I heard by other ascenders, your importance is greatly exaggerated. Rumor is you have no abilities and watching you is a waste of time, fit for a wet nurse and an insult to ascenders. All this talk of you being the transcendent, when in reality you're nothing but a powerless freak."

"Look at this," Eberan said, picking up the godspear beetle.

"Don't touch that," Lavak cried and immediately regretted the outburst. Displaying concern for anything, whether it be person or possession, was a sign of weakness. Grackles preyed upon the weak.

"Let me see that." Kuldahar snatched the beetle from Eberan.

He studied it for a moment before chuckling. "This? This is what you made? Every aspirant tries to make something artistic for their first attempt. You craft this hideous creature. You truly are a freak."

"Give it back." Lavak tried plucking the beetle from the ascender's hand, but Kuldahar dodged his attempt and held the piece just beyond Lavak's reach.

"You want this?" Kuldahar teased. "You want your ugly little trinket back?"

Don't show interest. Pretend you don't care. Lavak crossed his arms. "Never mind. You're right. It's ugly and I'm a freak. I don't belong here. I shouldn't be trying to save the godspear. After all, it's only the Ascendancy's power at stake. I'm sure you've everything under control. You've got a cure already, haven't you? You're just keeping it for yourself until the perfect moment to unveil it to Volstrysa."

Kuldahar grinned, undaunted by Lavak's prodding. He dropped the beetle into the bowl of excrement. "A perfect place for it."

Lavak stared at his work submerged in beetle frass. A small cloud of fine dust mushroomed over the bowl from the sudden disturbance. The influence within him unseated, hammering his chest with every quickening heartbeat. He gripped Kuldahar's wrist. Magic violated the ascender's body in a surge, transferring out of Lavak. "Go away," Lavak commanded.

Kuldahar stared blankly at Lavak for a moment. Eberan and Jaquista stared too, mouths agape. Lavak wrested his grip free from Kuldahar. After a long moment, Kuldahar blinked and toddled out of the room without speaking a word. Eberan and Jaquista exchanged confused, wordless looks before following him. None of them looked back at Lavak.

Lavak smiled the faintest of smiles. The influence hadn't killed him, but had aided him. Ordering Kuldahar away was a satisfying experience, but it paled compared to the brief moment of lucidity Lavak experienced when the influence poured into him.

Was all influence as fleeting in its effect? Or, would it last longer if siphoned from an enchantment larger than a button? Lavak's thoughts led his gaze to the bowl where the beetle lay submerged.

Removing the beetle, he gently shook the bulk of droppings from it. He rubbed, blew and brushed away the dust. Despite his efforts, a stubborn film of excrement clung to the godspear. The imparted green hue was now dulled by feces. His work was ruined.

Washing it may help, but doing so would take with it some of the valdsker he'd so agonizingly applied. Kuldahar had dealt him more insult with the simple action of discarding the beetle than any words could ever do. Why had he commanded Kuldahar to leave? It was a waste of magic. Kuldahar deserved humiliation. Ordering him to clean the floor with his tongue would've been a delight to witness.

"I was informed you were here," Welnaro said from the threshold, irritation heavy in his voice. "You were to report to the supreme immediately upon your return to the spire. I don't like being sent to look for people. That's a job for aspirants."

Lavak remained seated, his back to Welnaro. He wanted to tell the prime about his chosen pupil's repeated tormenting but decided against it. Likely, Welnaro was aware of Kuldahar's behavior. He probably supported it, for whatever reason Welnaro justified. A complaint to this man would only bring tenfold more reckoning from his subordinate.

"I'm not feeling well. I needed to rest a bit. I'll go up shortly."

Welnaro grumbled about the disrespect at speaking to him with Lavak's back turned.

Lavak twisted in his seat and hung an arm over the back of his chair. Welnaro glared at him. Gripped in his hands was a peculiar staff. It matched the prime's height and was fashioned from godspear, but it was unlike any magic Lavak had seen before. Welnaro's staff was dual lustered.

"That's a clever way of applying two magics on one item," Lavak said. He'd meant it as a compliment, but unintentionally added a note of condescension to his voice.

Welnaro wrinkled his nose and scowled at Lavak's observation. His grip tightened on the purple-and-red-lustered staff. "A practice dating back centuries. It's the only way to combine magic. Every aspirant older than ten knows this."

The insult wasn't lost on Lavak, but he was too curious to care. "Prior to enchantment, the staff is split lengthwise? Then, each half is imbued with magic? Afterward, the two pieces are rejoined, held together by those leather straps?"

"It's the only way to combine magic," Welnaro repeated gruffly. "As I said, every aspirant beyond the age of ten knows this."

"And the enchantments, fire-felt and suspension?"

"I'm not your teacher. Don't waste my time with elementary questions you should already know."

"In a fight, you first strike with suspension. Once your opponent is stunned, you finish them with fire-felt. Is that the principal behind it?"

One of Welnaro's gloved hands slipped off the staff and curled into a fist. "Or I beat them to death."

The threat wasn't lost on Lavak, but he was too fascinated to care. "I'll go see Volstrysa shortly."

"She's waited too long already. Don't mistake your place here, islander. And don't abuse her hospitality. It can be relinquished as easily as it was given."

"My stomach is unsettled. I feared an embarrassing situation if I visited her before it quieted."

The squeak of the staff's leather bindings being forcibly squeezed preceded Welnaro's harsh words. "Be quick. If I have to come look for you again, not even the supreme will spare you from my wrath." He slammed the door with enough force to rattle jars on shelves.

Left alone again, Lavak stared at the beetle. He wasn't ready to see Volstrysa. He was exhausted and dejected. Days of effort had been undermined in a moment by a petty ascender, stealing any vigor he'd reserved for the remainder of the evening. Some food and a long sleep was all he wanted now and not necessarily in that order. He closed his eyes as weariness overtook him.

"What are we?" the voice asked, but now it sounded different. Louder, like before, but also in harmony with another unseen speaker.

He sighed. His other tormentor. Unlike Kuldahar or the grackles back home, this one he couldn't escape. It was in his mind, probably was his mind, succumbing to madness. He wanted to give the voice an answer, if for no other reason than to allay it so he could have peace. Until recently, Lavak didn't have an answer. He didn't know who "we" were or "what" they were meant to be, but during his moment of clarity with the influence he'd glimpsed some insight.

"I am Lavak. Lavak Splinterfist."

"Splinterfist," the voice echoed. "Splinterfist. Splinterfist. We are Splinterfist."

"No. I am Splinterfist. Not you. Who are you?"

"Splinterfist." It spoke slowly, as if adjusting to the fit of the name. "We are Splinterfist."

Lavak snarled. This wasn't his intention. He'd hoped giving the voice an answer would silence it. Instead, the voice was more vocal than before, more distracting, more maddening. "Who are you?"

"Splinterfist," the voice said. "We are Splinterfist." A strange symbol flashed briefly in his mind with the voice's declaration: two facing crescents and between them a pair of letters trailed by a singular number. It vanished without imprinting his memory.

"I am Splinterfist!" Lavak screamed. "I am. Not you. Now be silent and bother me no more."

And there was silence. The voice didn't reply. It was gone, to Lavak's relief. He released a long breath. Was this insanity, or was he so fatigued he dreamed while awake? Maybe it was better to see Volstrysa now. His mind and the rest of him could use more tangible company.

Lavak was winded by the time he reached the spire's peak.

Sweat beaded on his face. His lungs burned. His legs ached anew. He ignored all of it in his attempt to outrun the voice in his head. It had yet to return, but Lavak dared not hope he'd been successful in its banishment.

He glanced at the stolid guard at the door, wondering how the man could so easily traverse the daily climb without succumbing to exhaustion. Lavak composed himself before requesting entrance. The guard knocked loudly on the door, and Volstrysa's voice came from the other side, bidding entrance.

She sat by the fireplace, a trio of fire bricks glowing brightly within the stone confines. Her hand cradled a glass of wine while an open book rested on her lap. "Come closer." She set the glass down on the table beside her. "I've been expecting you. Have you finished it? I'm eager to see."

Lavak glanced at the beetle with its lackluster sheen in his hand. "Yes, but there was a problem."

She rose and placed the book on the table alongside the wineglass before gliding close to him. "Let me see." She took the beetle from him and examined it. Her frown was brief, almost unnoticeable in the dim light. "It's all right. Embedding is the hardest part of enchantment. Nobody masters it immediately. It's still good for a first attempt." The disappointment in her words was unmistakable.

"You don't understand. Kuldahar—"

Volstrysa pressed a finger to his lips. "Shh. Let's see what happens after the enchantment is complete. There's no time to make another. A storm is coming." She pulled her finger away. "Lavak, you should have some wine. To celebrate your creation."

He paused, ready to refuse her offer, but remembered she believed him still under her control through the influence button. He nodded and Volstrysa poured him a drink. "Here. Take it and drink." Lavak swallowed a tart mouthful. Was this how the Dark Mistress earned her name? Kuldahar's words about him once being her favorite echoed in his mind. Was it true? Was Lavak simply the next to fall into her web?

"I know you've been busy trying to save your trees," she said. "You've been put in an unreasonable situation. The fate of your people rests with you. It's a heavy burden. Has learning to enchant aided in your endeavors?"

Lavak nodded slowly. "A little, but the cure still eludes me."

"I'm sorry for that. Enchanting was perhaps a necessary distraction." She pressed the beetle into his palm. Her fingers caressed his. "But it's still an admirable piece you've made."

"I'm grateful for the lessons, though I fear if the godspear perishes, they'll be of little use."

Volstrysa stroked his cheek with the back of her hand. "Quite true. I'm confident you'll solve this problem. However, we need to make preparations should the godspear die out."

"Preparations to save my people?"

She smiled. "Yes, but there are greater things at risk than just your people. I know you don't want to hear that, but it's true. Azazura hangs in the balance. I've ordered all enchantment of godspear be reduced to half its usual production. If we can't save the trees, we must save every piece of godspear we can and use it wisely and sparingly. The enchanting workshops you spent your time in recently are usually very active, with three or four workers at a table instead of one. Far different from what you experienced. It's one of many adaptations I've employed to mitigate the diminishing godspear."

"You speak as if they're already doomed." Lavak fought to keep the edge off his words.

Volstrysa shook her head, the ends of her ebony hair sweeping across her breasts. "No. I want to see them live. I won't deny magic is what gives the Ascendancy its power, just as I won't deny I've no desire to lose that power. However, I must plan for all outcomes. To do otherwise would be foolish. Don't you agree?"

Lavak wanted to shake free of his charade and tell Volstrysa saving the godspear was all that mattered, but her mention of plans reminded him he was supposed to be under her influence. What outcome for him did her plans entail?

"Come." Volstrysa pulled his sleeve and led Lavak to her bedchamber door. She opened it and sauntered in before disrobing. Underneath her ascender's clothing a silken nightgown hung loose over Volstrysa's slender frame. She moved to the bed, her hips swaying with each light step, and sat seductively on the edge. Volstrysa lifted her gaze to Lavak, her eyes lustful. She patted the space beside her, inviting Lavak to join. At that moment, Lavak's thoughts were on Melindi. He didn't want to betray her, no matter how she felt about him. In the depths of his heart, he believed they could be together one day, however, he still had to operate under the pretense of being in Volstrysa's control. If he wanted to keep his true abilities with magic a secret, Lavak needed to maintain the deception.

He stepped inside the room and closed the door behind him.

CHAPTER 18

"Everything all right?" Rill asked, his cagey gaze darting left to right.

Ralm nodded. "Everything is all right. Why?"

Rill peered around Ralm, into the street beyond the alley. "It's just, I thought we'd do this at Zirrin's place."

"There's too many eyes looking for me," Ralm said. "I can't risk having them looking toward his house. I've already endangered him too much."

The boy's restlessness lessened. "All right. Just thought maybe something was wrong, that's all."

Ralm cast his own wary glance into the street behind him. City folk padded by, unconcerned with mischievous dealings in blind alleys. "The Ascendancy has a particular interest in finding me. The fewer people I'm connected to, the better."

"It's some uproar they're having. That about you?" Rill's voice dropped to a whisper. "Are you the Painted Man?"

Ralm brought a finger to his lips. "Shh. It's a secret." Whether the order or the people had given Ralm the epithet, he didn't know, but *Painted Man* conjured mystery and fear, which fueled many of the rumors burning throughout the city as of late.

The boy's eyes lit with excitement. "It was you. They're saying you defied an ascender. He tried arresting you, and you scared him so bad he went running to the spire, wetting his robes and screaming all the way. Bad dice for him."

It was surprising to hear how his brief encounter with the ascender had blossomed into an exaggerated tale in such a short time. Rill wasn't the first to retell the story to Ralm, and his was not the most embellished. One of the more grandiose tales circulating involved Ralm changing into a wild boar and chasing the ascender up the side of the spire. "It didn't happen like that. Some words were exchanged, along with a few blows. It was over as fast as it started."

Rill's eyes dimmed with disappointment. "Well, it has people talking, anyway. And from what they're saying, the order is going to put a bounty out on you if they don't find you right quick. Then all sorts will be hunting you."

"Which is all the more reason we need to remain watchful. I don't want you getting found any more than myself."

"Needn't worry on me. They ain't caught me yet." Rill grinned and folded his arms across his chest.

"They haven't had a reason to catch you," Ralm said. "But if they learn you're helping me, they'll chase you until you're too tired to run."

Rill shrugged, dismissing Ralm's warning with his own brand of confidence. "Let me cry myself to sleep over it like I cry about not having a mom or dad." He snapped his fingers. "Hold on. I don't cry over that."

Ralm smirked and shook his head. The boy was more self-assured than Ralm was on his best day. "Just be careful. For me."

"I'm always careful." Rill winked. "Now, what have you got for me?" Ralm slid a roll of paintings from inside his shirt and passed them to Rill. The boy thumbed over the edges, counting. He cocked a brow at Ralm. "Six? That's all? Not as many as last time."

"They'll have to do." Ralm tossed a round to him. "That's all my money. Guess this'll be your last job for me until I get more."

Rill tucked the roll of paintings under an arm. "I hope they last longer than the others you had me put up. The ascenders had them torn down within a day."

"I expected as much. Hopefully they were up long enough to serve their purpose."

"If you mean getting other folks painting, they sure did."

"What do you mean?"

"Well, a little bit after them first paintings were taken down, I started seeing others. Different places, different times. They weren't special like yours. They were…" He gazed at the sky as if he'd find the right word there. After a moment, he snapped his fingers. "Amateurish. That's it. Real simple. But their meanings were clear enough. Guess whoever saw yours got…" He struggled to find the proper word, searching the sky again, along with the walls and ground.

"Inspired?"

"That's it. They were inspired by your paintings. Sometimes they're on paper, sometimes right on the walls. Figure that. Painting on the walls. That takes some dice, doesn't it? Chance getting caught while standing there putting paint on a wall. Not sure even I'd run that risk."

His information was unexpected. Ralm's intent for the paintings was to give himself an anonymous voice to decry the injustices of the Ascendancy. They were meant as a catharsis for his frustrations. He'd never anticipated others would mimic his actions. "Well, I hope whoever is doing it is as crafty as you and doesn't get caught."

"If they're like me, they won't. But aren't too many like me." Rill stalked to the rear of the alley, where shadow perpetuated despite the radiance of day, and was swallowed by it.

"There certainly aren't," Ralm said with a smile.

He was more cautious returning to Zirrin's home than on previous outings. The city watch had grown more aggressive in their random interrogations of street travelers. With Ralm having assaulted an ascender, every guard was more vigilant, more apt to question a person on a whim as much as a suspicion. He flitted from one dim alley to the next. If a patrol approached, he hid. Unmoving.

Not breathing. Still as a corpse.

Returning to Zirrin's home, he was lured into the sitting room by the soft glow of lamplight and activity. Zirrin sat in his favorite chair. Opposite him the merchant Chulvar was seated. Engaged in conversation, they abruptly halted upon Ralm's entry. Crossing the threshold, he was startled by the two brutes standing inside the sitting room to either side of the doorway. He hadn't expected to see Chulvar there, much less the intimidating forms of Pup and Cub.

"Ralm. Come in," Zirrin said. "Don't be alarmed. Please, have a seat."

Glancing between the seated men and the hulking men, Ralm scuttled to an unoccupied chair.

"A pleasure to make your acquaintance again." Chulvar stood and shook Ralm's hand, a reserved smile on his lips.

"Likewise." Ralm sank into his chair. He hadn't expected Zirrin to be entertaining company, but the stacks of books and journals encircling the room were tidy. He looked to Zirrin. "I'm—"

"Wondering why they're here," Zirrin finished. He motioned to Chulvar, then Pup and Cub. "Chulvar is here at my request. The other two gentlemen, well, they go where Chulvar goes."

"Hired help, of a sort," Chulvar added, settling back into his chair.

"At your request?" Ralm echoed. "Am I interrupting? Should I go?"

"No." Zirrin waved his hands. "We've been expecting you. Waiting for you, actually. You're the reason Chulvar is here." A glass of wine on the table beside Zirrin was in need of refilling. Another rested by Chulvar and was almost as empty. Two more glasses, unused, sat beside an uncorked bottle. Zirrin poured wine in one of these and handed it to Ralm. "Would either of you like some refreshments?" he asked Pup and Cub.

"No. Thank you," Cub said. "We don't drink while working."

Zirrin shrugged and frowned. "Very well. More for us." He leaned back, one finger running along the brim of his wineglass as he gave Ralm an inquisitive stare. "There's been quite a bit of gossip going through the circles lately. People are talking about a man who defied an ascender. A man who not only lived, but escaped." Ralm shifted in his seat. The conversation was already making him uncomfortable. "A painted man. They say he paints his face to disguise himself from the ascenders and can change form at will." Zirrin chuckled at this last remark. "Gossip does have a way of flourishing with every added dose of exaggeration."

Hilni entered carrying a platter of sliced cheese. Her arrival momentarily suspended their conversation. "Good evening, Ralm." She set the platter on the table before turning to Cub and Pup. "Are you sure you don't want anything to drink?"

"No. Thank you, ma'am," Pup said. "We don't drink alcohol while working."

"We have water and goat milk," Hilni said.

The two warriors glanced to Chulvar for permission. The merchant nodded his consent.

"Goat milk will be fine," Pup said.

"Water for me. Goat's milk doesn't sit well in my belly." Cub rubbed his stomach to emphasize the discomfort.

"That's too bad, dear." Hilni reached up and patted his cheek softly. Cub smiled and blushed. "Help yourself to some cheese."

"Thank you, ma'am," Cub said.

"Very much appreciated, ma'am," Pup said.

"Please, call me Hilni."

Ralm waited until she left the room before speaking, his voice firm and low. "You and I know the truth of it. That's all that matters."

Zirrin grinned and shook his head. "Oh, but it's quite the opposite. The story is inspiration for people, and the grander it is, the more it spreads. Of course, the embellishments about you growing twice your size and squashing the ascender under your boot are laughable, but regardless, the story is being told."

That was a new version of the story Ralm hadn't heard before. "It's just a way for people to pass the time. They'll forget soon enough."

"No, they won't," Zirrin said. "There's a special kind of power to it."

Ralm sipped his wine. "A power?"

"Yes. I intend to add to the story and continue to add until the Ascendancy is no more."

"You've drunk too much wine, Zirrin. Your head isn't clear. A story can't topple the Ascendancy."

Zirrin set his glass on the table. He reached between his hip and the chair arm and retrieved a folded paper. Opening it, he revealed one of the first paintings Neva had drawn for Ralm. "I know who made this, and I know who she made it for. Just as I know the man she painted it for is frustrated by what he sees. I know this is his way of expressing his frustration." Zirrin gave Ralm a weighted stare before drinking the last of the wine from his glass. "You've poked the beehive, Ralm. Now the bees are buzzing. Like it or not, you're now a target. The order is casting nets and soon will draw them in. You can't hide forever. Sooner or later, they'll catch you. But there is a way to avoid being caught. End the Ascendancy. Remove it and you remove the threat to you."

Ralm sneered. "No. I told you already, I'm not your revolutionary leader, no matter how much you want me to be."

"You've frightened the order, Ralm. Whatever happened between you and the ascender put the order on its heels. We need to carry that momentum until the order falls on its back."

"You'll need to carry it without me. I don't like the order, it's true, but this isn't my fight. I've the godspear to save. I don't have time for what you're asking."

Zirrin's gaze drifted to the window. "Are the trees more important than those people out there?"

"Those people?" Ralm asked cynically. "Those people only care about one thing: magic. And they'll do anything for it, including undermine each other. Why should I care about those people?"

"Why should you care to save the godspear? It's the source of magic. To save them would only continue to feed power to the Ascendancy. Saving them will only have people continue their pursuit of magic. Abandon your desire to save them, Ralm, and you'll rattle the order to its foundation."

"I'm only one person, Zirrin. What I do or don't do has little effect on the world."

"Oh?" Zirrin cocked an eyebrow. "I think the people would disagree. There's excitement over the Painted Man." Zirrin poured himself more wine. "I ask only you speak to a few of them. You're not from here, Ralm. You see what is happening from a different perspective. That may be useful to sway opinion. Your skills as overseer would be invaluable in that endeavor. You could enlighten them."

"Overseer? I wasn't a very good one. I'd likely be more detriment than good."

"You were enough an overseer to rise and face the threat against the godspear. That alone is worthy of merit."

"I did so against the wishes of the council." Ralm stood and moved to the window. He stared absently through it. "All I want to do is find a cure, find my family and return to Vidrey."

"What if that happened right now? What if you had the cure in your hands, your wife and her brother next to you, and you managed to return to your island? Do you believe you could simply go back to living your life as you did before, knowing what you now know? Do you believe the order would allow it? Do you think they'd allow you to live knowing what you know, knowing the truth about Azazura?"

"You speak as if they know who I am, who the Painted Man is. They don't."

"They don't…yet," Zirrin said.

Ralm sighed. His shoulders sagged. "I never expected things to get so complicated."

"Of course you didn't," Zirrin soothed. "And how could you have guessed things to be as they are? You were never told the truth about the godspears, or the hold magic has on everything here. You were sheltered and content. Then all that changed. Sometimes, Ralm, things don't happen as we want them to. Sometimes, plans take a terrible turn. What we expect to happen never happens. Plans slip through our fingers like sand. But sometimes, the unexpected turns out to be better than what we wanted."

"What do you gain from the Ascendancy's end? You have more to lose than most if the order is removed. You've made a good living from it so far."

"I've lost more than you realize. We all have." Zirrin's features stiffened, his gaze hard as stone. "And make no mistake, my business may be entwined with the Ascendancy, but that doesn't mean I'm comfortable about it. Do you know why I trade in favors? It's because I feel guilty about how people are treated here and my part in it. I take no pleasure in evictions. If there's any way I can ease somebody's suffering, I will. Better I be the one giving them the papers than somebody less compassionate. But I can't live on my charities. That's where favors come into play."

Ralm studied Zirrin, and in that hanging moment a quiet understanding developed between them. Zirrin opposed the order, but rather than do so openly, he deprived and undermined through his favors to people. Ralm's eyes found Chulvar. "What about you? I thought you made good money selling godspear. If the Ascendancy falls, so will your profits."

Chulvar swished wine in his mouth, swallowed and spoke. "You've no idea the regulations involved with being a merchant here. The rules and guidelines, fees and taxes. My profits are sliver-thin. It's enough to discourage an entrepreneur from trying. What have I to gain, you ask? Peace of mind I gain, along with higher profits and lower costs. Those make happy customers. All will benefit."

"Not if the godspear are gone. There'll be no more magic," Ralm said.

Chulvar shrugged. "There's more than magic to sell. I don't

care what lines my tables. What matters is how much I have in my purse at day's end."

Ralm turned to Pup and Cub. "What about you two? You're paid for your services, but you think freely. What are your opinions on all of this?"

They glanced at each other, their lips locked in stern half-frowns.

"Been kinda boring lately," Pup said. "I reckon we can use a change to things around here."

"Yep," Cub agreed. "Maybe even see some action. More than just shoplifters, that is."

Zirrin held his hand up. "Let's hope not. Better if we have a peaceful transition."

Cub tapped the cudgel hanging at his hip. "You can hope for peace all you want. I plan for the alternative."

"Me too," Pup said. "In either case, we're in. And at no charge."

Chulvar gasped. "No charge? Mercenaries not charging? Madness, but I welcome it. You'll save me a bit of coin at the shop." He was sitting forward now, his rump on the edge of the seat.

"Hold on, there," Cub said. "Our fee is waived for this thing you're doing with Ralm, not for you needing us at the table."

"That's right," Pup added. "We still have bellies to fill, too."

Chulvar slouched back into the chair, disappointment clear on his face. "You certainly fill them. With some to spare."

"You think we like being hired muscle?" Pup asked. "We do it because we're big and there's need for our services. But I don't want to be a warrior forever." He thrust forward his hands. "I want to use these for something more than hurting and killing. I'd like to be a baker someday." He kneaded the air as if it were dough.

Chulvar snickered. "It would be my luck to hire a killer with a conscience. What about you, Cub? You wanting to be a baker as well?"

Cub shook his head. "Nah. I burn bread."

"At least half of you are sensible," Chulvar said.

"I'd like to be a toymaker. Build things to make children happy," Cub confessed.

Chulvar thrust his hands up. "Next time I hire thugs, I'll make sure they're career thugs."

The tromp of boots thundered down the street. Zirrin hobbled to the window and peeked out. Ralm moved beside him. Outside, seven Low Guard assembled before Zirrin's home, their attention focused on the house across the street.

"Get back," Zirrin hissed, anxiety thick in his voice. He dulled the lamp.

Ralm retreated to the seclusion of the room's dim interior.

"What is it?" Chulvar asked.

"Low Guard."

"Here?" Chulvar sprang from his chair, his heavy-lidded eyes bulging. "I knew it was a mistake coming here. We have to get out."

"We have to fight." Cub balled his hands into fists.

"Yes. Fight." Pup's club was already in his hand.

"You have to stay calm. All of you," Zirrin said.

Ralm peered over Zirrin's shoulder. Outside, the Low Guard advanced on the house across the street. One knocked on the door. Nobody answered. There was no second knock. They burst through the doorway, disappearing inside. Minutes passed without signs of movement before the Low Guard reappeared. Two gripped the arms of an elderly gentleman, his face locked in terror. Two more Low Guard carried strange devices built from wood, metal and cord. The old man cried as he was forced to the ground and his hands tied. Dragged to his feet, he was roughly led away. Silence and stillness returned to the deserted lane.

"The fool," Zirrin said as he continued to stare at the empty street. "I warned him not to try selling it at the market."

"Sell what?" Ralm asked.

"His invention. He claimed to have discovered a way to preserve meat. Something about using low heat and circulating air."

"That sounds marvelous," Ralm said. "Why would the Ascendancy care about such a device or why he sold it?"

Zirrin turned to Ralm. "Because such a device threatens the order. It challenges magic. The enchanted box in my kitchen, it does the same thing his invention does, but its magical. Mundane things capable of doing what magic does are threats to the Ascendancy. I'm not talking rudimentary items like these window panes. It's impractical to craft those with magic. I'm talking about contraptions which stir people to question the usefulness of magic. Which would you buy: the box in my kitchen for two thousand rounds or his invention at a fraction of the cost and doesn't deteriorate as magic does?"

"His invention, of course."

"Exactly. The Ascendancy can't have that. It decides if there can be an alternative to magic or not."

"At the expense of progress?" Ralm said. "We have all manner of inventions on Vidrey, many employed for the harvest of godspear. Why haven't the watchers called the Ascendancy on us?"

"You're isolated. You've no knowledge of magic. You're not a threat. And your inventions make godspear production more efficient, which benefits the order. They wouldn't interfere where profit and power are concerned. Tell me, do your people prune?"

"Certainly. It's necessary. Many plants and trees would grow unruly if we didn't."

"It's the same here, except instead of plants, the order prunes people's ideas. We're living in a stagnated society, Ralm. Whenever new growth appears, the order snips to keep it from flourishing. This is one of many injustices by the Ascendancy."

The injustice recently witnessed stirred Ralm's defiance. "All you want me to do is speak to people?"

Zirrin nodded. "Yes. I'll arrange everything. The who, the when and the where." Zirrin winked. "I do have favors to collect."

Ralm's gaze reached the four men in turn. Somehow, he'd been pulled into a conspiracy to overthrow the Ascendancy. Zirrin was right about one thing: if Ralm returned to Vidrey but left things as they were in the city, he would forever be haunted by the decision. Too many people were suffering. He sat and sipped some wine. "What do we need to do?"

Hilni returned with the warriors' drinks. She was about to quietly leave again when Zirrin stopped her. "My dear, that roast we've been saving. The one in the box."

"Yes, what of it?" Hilni asked from the threshold.

"Get it cooking. We've hungry guests here, and it's going to be a long night."

"But Zirrin, we were saving that for a special occasion," Hilni said.

His eyes lit with vigor. "This is a special occasion, my sweetest. We're on the eve of revolution."

CHAPTER 19

Volstrysa was stiff as a statue sitting in her chair: back straight, hands resting on her lap. The pinnacle of dining etiquette. Morning's first light pierced the stained-glass window behind her, spraying prismatic splendor over a clean set of enchanted plates and cups neatly arranged on the table. Aromas of warm bread and sizzling bacon filtered through the floorboards from the small kitchen one level below. Usually, the most esteemed aspirant was tasked with feeding and serving Morivar's highest-ranking official, but Volstrysa had ordered a different cook for today's breakfast. From the pleasant scents greeting her nose, she'd chosen the replacement well. No hint of burning food caught in the air.

A stirring came from her bedchamber: sounds of a body rolling over her plush bed, the swish of a blanket cast aside, the soft groan one gives while stretching away the stiffness of a night's well-earned rest. Moments later, Lavak stumbled out in wrinkled robes, hair matted on one side and tousled on the other, his eyes red from sleepiness.

"Are you hungry?" Volstrysa asked. "You must have worked up an appetite after last night." Lavak nodded sluggishly. "Breakfast will be served shortly. Please, sit." Lavak shambled to the table and dropped heavily in the chair opposite her. "Did you sleep well?"

He rubbed his eyes. "Yes, what little sleep I got. Last night was my first."

"It didn't seem like your first," Volstrysa lied. "Not to worry. There will be more opportunities for you to build your stamina."

"More?"

"Yes, much more. You can't expect me to be satisfied with just once, not with your talents." Another lie. Lavak's inexperience made their first coupling a clumsy act. He was a man, but naive like a child in many ways, especially in the art of lovemaking. She'd guided him last night, leading his fingers over every curve of her body, whispering into his ear her carnal desires. The act was not sensual, not erotic. But her time with him wasn't for pleasure. If she wanted a satisfying experience, there were dozens of more suitable candidates to fulfill her desires. Her seduction of Lavak was necessity. "I hope you got enough rest. Today is special for you. I want you to have all your wits."

"Why is today special?"

"The next step of your enchantment is today. After this, only one thing remains and you'll have your own magical item. Your first." She giggled. "It's exciting, isn't it?" A soft knocking at the door interrupted her, but Volstrysa's pleasant demeanor didn't stumble. "Ah, that must be breakfast. Enter."

The door swung slowly open. The aspirant Melindi scuttled inside, the tray in her hands piled high with bacon and steaming bread while a flask of wine teetered near the edge. She bowed her head, her focus entirely on serving the meal. She shuffled to the table. Volstrysa studied her and Lavak. She'd been informed they were spending an unusual amount of time together. She wanted to know why. Was it simply because their ages were so close? Or was there something more?

Lavak hunched over the table, wrapped in his robes, staring into his lap, unaware of Melindi's presence. Volstrysa examined her, knowing without seeing what her robes concealed: a supple and firm body, unmarred by wrinkles. Youthful, like Volstrysa once had been.

Melindi rested the tray on the table, her attention still on it.

She set the flask in the table's center, then sliced and served bread. The first piece she laid on Volstrysa's plate. It was when she placed the next slice on Lavak's plate that her eyes found him. Melindi hesitated. Her hand trembled. The butter knife and plate rattled in her grasp. Lavak glanced up and met her gaze. His mouth gaped, his eyes widened, and within them churned a sea of surprise and apology and a silent plea for her forgiveness. The exchange was brief, but to Volstrysa, the moment told her everything. Lavak averted his gaze, glancing quickly at Volstrysa with eyes now guilt-laden, before focusing on his lap again. Melindi finished serving the bread and bacon and stepped back, clutching the empty tray tight to her bosom.

"Can I do anything more for you, Supreme?" Melindi's words wavered as they left her mouth in a controlled rush.

Volstrysa nibbled on some bacon and chased it with a sip of wine before answering. She chose her next words carefully and purposefully. "My lover looks cold." Her words issued a rustling of fabric as Lavak and Melindi both squirmed under their robes. "Stoke the fire to warm him."

"Of course, Supreme," Melindi stammered before striding to the fireplace and blasting the chip-bricks with air from the bellows until they glowed an intense orange.

"Do you know him?" Volstrysa asked. "My lover, that is." She didn't fail to emphasize the stinging word.

Melindi straightened and turned to face Volstrysa. "Supreme?"

Volstrysa shot a quick glance at Lavak. He was hunched lower now, body sunken below the table until only his shoulders and head were above it. "Surely you must have seen him in the spire."

"Yes, ma'am. I was assigned to his care when my superior fell ill."

"So you do know him?" Volstrysa asked.

"Yes, Supreme."

"Strange. You've never mentioned her to me, lover," she said to Lavak.

Lavak said nothing. He was bundled tight in his robes, head stooped low.

"Will there be anything else, Supreme?" Melindi fidgeted through every word.

"Yes. As you can see, my lover is still too cold to prepare his food himself. Spread butter over his bread."

Melindi shifted awkwardly at the request. Volstrysa delighted in the aspirant's rueful nod. Melindi leaned over the table and scraped butter from a dish with a knife. She dragged the blade slowly across the warm bread, careful not to tear the food despite her quaking hand. Throughout her task, she remained an arm's length from Lavak, never glancing at him once, eyes on the verge of watering. When finished, Melindi stepped back. "Will there be anything else, Supreme?"

With Melindi and Lavak beside each other, Volstrysa appraised them. Each was visibly uncomfortable being in the other's presence. Lavak continued scrutinizing his lap, his face flushed. Melindi absently swayed side to side, shifting her weight between feet as if waiting for permission to flee. There was awkwardness in the air. This aspirant's relationship with Lavak extended beyond mere caregiver.

"Does the supreme require anything more of me?" Melindi asked.

Volstrysa didn't answer immediately. She toyed with thoughts on how to draw out the aspirant's unease and make Lavak less comfortable. She tired of the game, however. There was still much to do today. "No. You may leave." Volstrysa flicked a hand but inwardly wasn't so dismissive.

Melindi bowed and departed at a hurried pace, snatching the tray as she exited, her cheeks crimson. She chanced a quick look at Lavak as she passed, a gesture which served to only confirm Volstrysa's suspicions.

When breakfast was over, she and Lavak shared a bath.

Staves of fire-felt lined the interior of the copper bathtub in the corner of her bedchamber, keeping the water hot and soothing no matter how long it sat. She washed his hair and body and instructed him to do the same for her. He obliged but said nothing.

"I'm not mad," she whispered inside the steam. "About that girl, I mean. It's all right if you know each other."

Lavak didn't reply.

"You're embarrassed. Is that it? You don't need to be."

Lavak didn't reply.

"You belong here, Lavak. You understand, don't you? No matter what happens, you belong here. With me."

She dried his naked body and dusted his skin with lavender powder. He slipped into his robes and she into hers.

"Take your beetle," she said before entering the lift.

Outside, she led him to one of the largest structures hemming the spire's courtyard. A cluster of four towering chimneys sprouted from the center of the brick building's roof. No smoke exited the stacks, but a shimmering haze over them suggested an intense heat was escaping.

"Do you know the order once attempted transporting entire godspears across the Cryptic Sea?" she said as they crossed the courtyard.

Lavak didn't shrug. He didn't offer any acknowledgment.

"Dozens of ships were used," Volstrysa continued. It was interesting history, at least, to her. "The trees were hauled into the water and tied to the ships, but the godspears were too large and heavy. Many trees sank and took the ships tied to them down as well. The order did manage to transport three of the largest godspears to Azazura before abandoning the effort."

Lavak's disinterested nod was almost imperceptible.

Upon entering the building, they were greeted with a rush of sweat-inducing air. A massive furnace, constructed from layers of brick stacked wide and high, occupied the cavernous room like an ominous centerpiece. Its girth dominated the floorspace. Brick stacked upon brick, rising, penetrating the roof before branching into chimneys. Soot hung in the air with a choking presence and gathered in corners with black permanence, unspoiled by the fiery glow leaking from the furnace.

Perspiration was already beginning to collect under her arms and along her back. To stay here for long in ascendant robes was ill-advised. She had no desire to spend the rest of her day in sweat-sodden clothes. She guided Lavak closer to the furnace, its heat more oppressive with each step. An aspirant, barely twelve years of age, wearing a loin cloth, thick leather gloves and sandals, worked the furnace. Sweat glistened on his skeletal form. Any perspiration dripping off him splashed on the floor and immediately evaporated.

Of all tasks given to aspirants, feeding the furnace was the most trying. Body weight shed rapidly. Constant drinking of water was vital to avoid dehydration and death. It was grueling work, but any aspirant surviving his yearlong courtship with the furnace emerged a different person both physically and mentally. Wills strengthened. Confidence soared. Bodies toughened. Rising to ascender could not be achieved without first enduring this infernal matrimony.

Volstrysa recalled her time feeding the fire, the blisters and scars earned during her marriage to the brick beast. Days of relentless heat were followed by nights shivering in her room under layers of blankets because everywhere but near the furnace felt frigid. When her year was finished, she was nothing more than a cadaverous reflection of herself. Three months of eating seven meals daily passed before she was at proper weight again.

The aspirant opened a small metal door at the base of the furnace and fed in a chip-brick, taken from a nearby stack of hundreds. Using an iron rod, he pushed the chip-brick further in and closed the door. He dunked his bald head into a barrel of water. "Supreme," he said, beads of water running down his face. "You honor me."

Volstrysa nodded curtly. "We've something for the furnace."

"Certainly. Anything for our most highest," he said.

Lavak held open his hand, revealing the beetle. The aspirant gave it a curious but brief study before placing it on a metal table beside the furnace. "There's a few in there now ready to come out. Brace yourselves."

He opened a steel door framed within the bricks, the squeal of its stout hinges lost in the fire's roar. A gust of heat shot out. Volstrysa's eyes burned, the moisture in them instantly stolen. The aspirant grabbed a pair of tongs from the table and used them to remove a bowl of absolute black from the furnace.

"The fire," Volstrysa said directly into Lavak's ear so she could be heard over the furnace, "is what gives enchanted godspear its ebony color. As the wood is charred, the elements melt and infuse with the wood grain, bonding them together." The aspirant plunged the bowl into a trough of water. Steam hissed on the surface. "Water from the Cryptic Sea. The quenching rapidly cools the godspear, locking the element in place. At this point, godspear and element are one."

The aspirant removed a charred plate from the furnace and dipped it into the trough. Water sizzled on the surface. With his tongs, he set Lavak's beetle on the rack inside the furnace and closed the door.

"Should be just a few moments," he said before dunking his head into the water barrel again.

"Excited?" Volstrysa asked.

Lavak shrugged but said nothing.

Volstrysa struggled not to frown. The first enchantment was a momentous process for every aspirant, but if Lavak was excited, he didn't show it. He was aloof. His interest was lacking. By now, Lavak should have been enamored by her. Every man after a night of coupling would be like a puppy, clinging to her side, watching her, waiting for praise, trying to steal a kiss at every chance. Lavak behaved the opposite. He kept a distance from her, spoke only when addressed and averted his gaze. Was his emotional disconnect the product of another? Was the aspirant Melindi to blame?

For a moment, Volstrysa questioned her actions at breakfast. Perhaps exposing Lavak to Melindi while in her presence had been a mistake. There was no doubt something had developed between him and the aspirant. Volstrysa didn't know if it was romance or friendship, but she needed to remedy the problem. Lavak wasn't yet enthralled to her. That needed to happen. Soon. Eventually the other supremes would discover Lavak was in Azazura.

Beads of sweat merged to become a steady rivulet down her back. Volstrysa ignored the persistent swelter and smiled through her discomfort. "What about those?" She pointed to the stack of chip-bricks. "You probably never imagined they were used for this."

"Do you hoard them all for enchanting?" Lavak asked. "On Vidrey, everybody receives chip-bricks to heat their homes and cook their foods."

"Most are necessary to keep the furnace burning. The people do well enough with firewood. Occasionally, if we have surplus, we'll auction them. They're quite popular among the people and sell for a hefty price."

"Wasteful," Lavak muttered.

"Wasteful? How so?"

"You burn so many chip-bricks just to enchant. Why not build a furnace of fire-felt and use that instead?"

Smart boy. The order had been enchanting thirty years before having a similar inspiration. Lavak thought of it in only minutes. "Although fire-felt is hot, I'm afraid it isn't hot enough to melt elements. Chip-bricks are, however."

The aspirant, busy removing the bowl and plate from the trough during their conversation, now said, "It should be ready now." He opened the door and reached into the furnace with the tongs.

Another blast of heat struck Volstrysa. For a moment, she considered forgoing the propriety her position demanded and submerge her head in the cooling barrel of water. She didn't, remembering not only the decorum she was expected to maintain, but also her triumph over the furnace many years ago. She wouldn't let the heat, no matter how uncomfortable, have the better of her.

A quick sizzle and puff of steam rose from the water as the beetle fell in. A few moments later, the aspirant fished around in the trough and removed Lavak's work, setting it back on the metal table. Black and dull, the beetle seemed a mockery of itself.

Volstrysa studied Lavak as he puzzled over the piece before saying, "One final step in the process remains. Come. Let's get out of here before we start to melt."

Outside the air was cool relief. Volstrysa flapped her robes, separating them from the clinging sweat on her skin. Lavak appeared equally relieved to be away from the heat and took several deep breaths of welcomed fresh air. Volstrysa led Lavak back to the spire, but instead of going through the front entrance, she led him to the rear. Two High Guard stiffened to attention at their approach. One swiftly opened a narrow iron-like door set into the spire's base. Down a short flight of steps Volstrysa and Lavak went, into the lowest level of the spire where a strange latticework of iron straps spanned the width of the room. Upon this, an assortment of godspear items equally dull and black as Lavak's beetle lay: weapons, bowls, plates, cups, armor, chests, doors, ornamentations and more.

"Set your piece on the iron," Volstrysa instructed. "Be certain at least some of it touches metal."

"Why?"

Volstrysa pointed up. "That answer is at the top of the spire."

"Is it safe to leave here?"

"Nobody will tamper with it or steal it, if that's what worries you."

Lavak rested the beetle where two bands of iron intersected. They left the lower level and entered the spire through the conventional entrance and rode the lift back to the supreme's perch. Upon exiting, instead of heading for her chambers, Volstrysa opened a door to a balcony overlooking the breadth of her domain.

"You can almost see the Balk from here," she said as a steady wind snapped her robes. "It's a beautiful view, but don't get too close to the edge. There are no railings to keep you from falling. A sudden gust could throw you over."

Lavak inched nearer the edge and peered over. A strong wind buffeted his robes, and for a moment he struggled against a force threatening to lift and carry him off the balcony. He scrambled backward and pressed his body against the wall.

Volstrysa looked westward. Dark clouds marched toward them, lightning and thunder tucked in their gray folds. She pointed to an iron rod as thick as her body and twice her height projecting upward from the spire's peak. "That rod runs down the length of the spire and connects to the iron banding where you placed your beetle. When the storm arrives, lightning will strike the rod and travel down it." She raised her voice over the howling wind. "Anything touching the iron will receive the lightning's charge. That's how the magic is activated."

"Is it safe to be in the spire when the lightning strikes?" Lavak yelled, the wind blowing more fiercely now.

"Yes. Let's go inside now. You don't want to be out here when the storm arrives."

Volstrysa ushered Lavak into her chambers under the advancing storm. Lightning flashed, brightening the sky in heraldic warning of a thunder certain to follow. First was an ear-piercing crack. Riding behind it was a boom which shook and rattled baubles and trinkets and anything else lacking significant weight. Being so high and so close to the source, the thunder was near deafening in the supreme's chambers.

Volstrysa wrapped Lavak in her arms and pulled him onto the bed. She kissed his neck as a lightning bolt split the clouds outside her window.

CHAPTER 20

Looking through the grimy window, Ralm was reminded of home. Beyond Dorsluin's docks, the Cryptic Sea's placid waters glistened in the waning daylight. It was a sight he'd beheld many times from the shores of Vidrey. There were boats here and many more people moving about, but the scene left him homesick nonetheless, wanting to return to his birthplace. His heart quivered at the thought. He ached to see Brun and the mighty godspears again—whatever condition they may be in—to pick apples in the orchards, or tend the beehives, all while sweet aromas of hundreds of dinners cooking throughout the village mingled in the air.

All of it would have to wait.

He turned from the window, his eyes adjusting to the dim interior of the warehouse. This was where he was needed, in this cavernous room where the slightest of sounds echoed off walls caked in a decade's worth of dirt. Here, in this place somehow still reeking of fish long after the last scale had fallen to the floor and was stolen away by a starved rat. Here, where seventeen men and nine women sat on busted barrels and warped crates, whispering among themselves as they waited for the meeting to begin.

Ralm traced his footsteps on the dusty floor, amused by the history they told. His footprints meandered and stopped, shuffled and paced back and forth, over and over through the dark corners of the warehouse and across a floor now lit by slanting, diffused sunlight. They appeared to belong to a man confused or lost, or perhaps somebody who had misplaced something and searched everywhere to locate it. They were, in truth, tracks made by a troubled and restless man.

Zirrin separated from the blurry distance at the rear of the warehouse and strolled to Ralm, his feet stirring dust clouds hanging low in the air. "We're just waiting on Taloon. Then we can begin."

Taloon had arranged the location for this first meeting. He'd known of the warehouse's vacancy and suggested using it, insisting it was a perfect location. The noise from the docks would hide any sounds made inside, preventing eavesdroppers from hearing any conspiratorial plans. The warehouse's location also served another purpose. Everybody from the city was allowed access to the docks. The road connecting Dorsluin to the piers was the only means of passage for merchants and sailors intent on selling their catches and goods. The constant flow of traffic would prove valuable in concealing Ralm and the others' movements, even in daylight.

"I saw your bed in the back corner," Zirrin said. "Are you sure you want to stay here instead of my house? Hilni is in grief over it. She insisted I bring two loaves of bread for you." He gestured to Ralm's bed, which was little more than a straw-stuffed mattress. "And I'll admit, I think it's an unwise decision to be all the way out here by yourself."

"It would be less wise to remain at your home," Ralm said. "I can't risk your family any longer. We both agree the Ascendancy will find me eventually. I'd rather it happen here in isolation than bring trouble to your doorstep."

Zirrin smiled, his eyes sparkling despite the dim. "You have my thanks for that. But I know the risks and accept them."

"I know how you dislike uninvited guests, especially those who overstay their welcome."

"Ralm, you know that doesn't pertain to you."

"I know, but I feel I overstayed. Especially with everything happening."

The warehouse door swung open. Pale light flooded the inner vastness as Taloon entered. He pushed the door shut with a grunt, coughed as wisps of dust assaulted his face, allowed his eyes a moment to adjust and found his way to Zirrin and Ralm.

"The satisfaction of using this location is delicious." He grinned as he gave the place a quick survey.

"It's perfect, just as you noted," Ralm said.

"No. Not just about that," Taloon said, spreading his arms wide. "The former tenants were fishermen. When they could no longer afford to pay the rent to their landlord, the ascendant, they were evicted. The rent is too high for most people, but instead of lowering it to something affordable, the ascendant has chosen to keep the rent high, thus the place has remained unoccupied. Quite fitting it's now used to undermine the owner."

Ralm resisted smiling. Taloon was correct. There was a certain satisfaction in using the Ascendancy's own assets against it. That, however, brought with it a new level of risk. At any moment a prospective tenant or somebody in the Ascendancy conducting a random inspection of the place may discover them. Still, it was the best Ralm and company had at the moment and the rewards currently outweighed the risks.

Zirrin clasped his hands together. "Shall we begin?"

Ralm gripped Zirrin's elbow and pulled him to a whisper's distance. "Do all these people owe you favors?"

Zirrin stared at Ralm, his lips and brow bent downward in puzzlement. "Favors? No. Why do you ask?"

"I don't want people here because they owe you and are repaying a debt. If this is going to work, it needs to be done with people wanting to make change."

The confusion dissolved from Zirrin's face, replaced by a wide grin. "My boy, I'm not entirely sure what overseers do, but I think you do the job well. I'm of the same belief. Yes, these are all people frustrated with how things are. As for collecting favors, it was the only way to get them out here."

Not reassured by Zirrin's reply, Ralm straddled a barrel beside Taloon. Nearby, Chulvar sat upon a crate. Pup and Cub lingered by the doors.

"Ladies. Gentlemen," Zirrin began, his voice booming, "I've summoned you here so we may finally begin what we've thought in secret for so many years." Nervous mumblings passed between the crowd. "We talk about our problems, and to some degree, I think we enjoy complaining about them. It gives us something to discuss over dinner. But talk is all we do. I for one am tired of it. The time has come for action. Are we to live our lives as we always have? Oppressed? Or are we finally going to change the way things are, to make the lives of not just us, but our descendants, better? For too long we've groveled beneath the Ascendancy. My friends, you're all here because you owe me favors. I'm collecting on those now."

A man approaching his seventh decade rose on unsteady legs and addressed Zirrin.

"You loaned me fifty rounds, Zirrin," he said. "You expect me to spill my blood to repay that debt?"

Others in the crowd grumbled doubts and concerns.

Zirrin frowned. "No. I don't want any blood spilled. With luck, there won't be any bloodshed. However, if the time comes, I expect you to fight so your loved ones will be free." Zirrin glared at the old man as he sat again. "But I'm getting ahead of myself. That isn't the reason I'm collecting. I've a guest here." Zirrin pointed at Ralm. All heads turned in his direction. "This is Ralm, and he has something to tell you. Listen to him and I'll consider your debt repaid."

Ralm strode to where Zirrin was standing, aware each pair of eyes in the place followed him. He was visited by a memory from Vidrey: during the Fall Festival when he assumed role of overseer. It wasn't so long ago, yet it felt like innumerable years had passed since that night.

"My name is Ralm Willowsong. I come from an island beyond

the blockade."

"Is this why you brought us here, Zirrin?" a woman asked, standing abruptly. "To listen to the lies of this man?"

Zirrin was about to speak, but Ralm silenced him with a raised hand. He said, "I speak truthfully, madam. I've no reason to deceive you."

"Why should we believe you?" she asked, wagging a finger at him. "Men tell lies easy enough. Lies, and for what? For wealth and wenches? You're wasting our time here. Hurry up so we can go."

"Why do you believe what the Ascendancy tells you?" Ralm asked. "What proof have they given which makes you blind to anything else?"

"Everybody knows there are monsters in the Cryptic Sea and unknown horrors beyond," another man blurted. "The blockade protects us. The supreme protects us."

Ralm met his gaze. "If sea monsters are so dangerous, how is the blockade immune to their attacks? Have you personally seen these sea monsters or the horrors beyond?"

The man stuttered as he struggled to form a reply. He glanced to his neighbors in the crowd. They offered no support. "Have you?" he finally asked Ralm. "What proof have you to say otherwise?"

"I've crossed the sea in a small boat and survived. As for proof, you will be shocked by it, but once you see, you will believe."

"Where is it?" the man asked, turning to the crowd. They nodded their agreement. Bolstered by this, the man said, "Let's all see this proof so we may judge for ourselves."

"Before I show you, let me explain my origin. The island I come from is where godspear, what you call starwood, grows."

A frail man of advanced years, who until now remained silent, asked, "How can you have no magic, yet claim to come from an island where the magic grows."

"The godspear are not magical," Ralm said. "They are trees. When the lumber is brought to Azazura, the Ascendancy enchants it. The lie is they make magic from the stars. It's one of many lies the order tells you."

"And we're to believe you, on your word?" the frail man asked.

"On more than my word," Ralm said. "Have you heard the rumors about the Painted Man?"

A woman stood. "I have. They say he was attacked by an ascender, but rained lightning down upon the ascender and killed him."

"I heard," began another woman, "the Painted Man picked up the ascender and threw him across the city and out into the sea."

A man spoke next. "Nah, that's not what happened. The Painted Man grew twice as tall and squashed the ascender underfoot."

"None of those stories are true," Ralm said.

"And how would you know?" the first woman asked.

"Because I am the Painted Man," Ralm said. Gasps and whispers raced through the crowd. "It's true I opposed the ascender, in a manner of speaking. But no lightning rained down, he wasn't thrown into the sea and I certainly didn't grow twice my height and squash him. What I tell you is truth, but you see how quickly lies spread and how easily they're believed? The Ascendancy has been spreading lies about itself and everything else for years."

The crowd stirred at the news. Many countenances were locked in astonishment.

"If you are the Painted Man, tell us what really happened," somebody from the rear of the crowd said.

"I crossed paths with him in the street," Ralm said. "He attacked me with his magic. It didn't work on me and I ran away. That's all."

"Impossible," a man said as he rose to his feet. "Nobody, not even illkin, are immune to magic."

"I don't know how or why I wasn't affected, only that I wasn't," Ralm said. "And I can prove it." He'd anticipated skepticism.

Zirrin stepped forward and raised his cane. "You all know what this is. You all have a good idea what it can do." He removed the brass ferrule and leveled the bared cane tip to Ralm's chest. "Are you ready?"

Ralm wasn't ready, uncertain the outcome of the demonstration. Sure, he'd avoided suffering the ascender's magical attack, but he hadn't tested his theory since. Perhaps his immunity had been accidental, caused by the ascender delivering a glancing blow which resulted in the magic not discharging. It was too late now to reconsider. "Ready."

"I'll try not to impale you," Zirrin said with a smile.

He jabbed the cane at Ralm, the tip striking square in his chest. There was a brief hiss as the enchantment released and a quick stab of pain from the impact, but Ralm received no crippling wound, magical or otherwise.

Silence enveloped the warehouse as those in attendance weighed what they just witnessed. Outside, dusk had arrived. A calm settled over sea and shore. Occasional voices interrupted the inner quiet as the few fishermen remaining dockside tended to the day's final tasks before going home. Taloon lit a lantern and set it on a barrel, its soft glow guarding against the pressing gloom. Long moments filled with murmurs and shuffling feet passed before anybody spoke.

"It's true," the aged man said. "Spiders in spires. It's true."

Ralm said, "There's more proof I can give. I'm about to show you why I'm called the Painted Man. What you're about to see will surprise you. It may frighten you. Understand, I'm from a place where all the people are like me. We're not illkin. I am not illkin."

With a rag from his pocket, Ralm proceeded to wipe the layers of paint off his face.

CHAPTER 21

He departed before dawn. Slipping his robes on slowly, fearful the sound of cloth rubbing skin may wake Volstrysa, Lavak glanced nervously at her lying in bed. She didn't stir. Her chest rose and fell in slow rhythm, the sign of deep sleep. Carefully, he lifted the latch of her bedchamber door and gently opened it to stifle any hinge squeal. Volstrysa still didn't stir. The door gaped enough for him to slip through, and after he did, Lavak gingerly closed it behind him.

The violent storm from the night before had passed an hour ago, leaving a cool calm in the air. Beyond a chamber window, streaks of gray entwined ribbons of gold in the sky, a hint of morning's approach. Lavak tiptoed across the room and, with as much care as before, opened the door and left.

With need for stealth over, he dashed down the spire's steps. He startled high guards at each landing. Either they were dozing or deaf not to hear his footsteps echoing down the coil. When Volstrysa woke and found him missing, she'd question them. By then, he'd be out of the spire, away from her. High guards cast him disapproving stares but made no effort to stop Lavak. Descending the spire was never met with opposition. The ascent, however…

His haste was spurred by the weaving of many events. First, he wanted to find Melindi and explain about the prior morning. Volstrysa had sabotaged any potential relationship Lavak might have with her. The entire scene was a contrivance arranged by the supreme. Melindi needed to understand his arrangement with Volstrysa. He was a captive of sorts and Volstrysa his keeper using magic to sway his mind. Melindi must know this and understand although he'd shed the influence from his clothes, the charade must still be maintained, which included obliging Volstrysa when she wanted to bed him.

After that awkward breakfast, at the furnace, Lavak struggled to behave as expected. Melindi remained in his thoughts. He couldn't shake his guilt or erase her image from his mind. Her final glance to him before leaving his company was embedded in memory. Her expression harbored a tempest of emotions. Anguish. Bewilderment. Heartbreak. Her care for Lavak was evidenced in her bright eyes, eyes brightened further by the glisten of restrained tears as she fled the supreme's chamber. That moment betrayed Melindi's words to him in the garden days earlier, when she convincingly refused his affections. Why Melindi misled him, he didn't know. He didn't care. All he cared about was the chance for them to be together, though it was at risk, and Volstrysa with her ruinous jealousy was to blame.

Volstrysa. She was becoming more present in his life, and Lavak resented it. Resented her. When he first arrived in Azazura, she occasionally visited him to engage in light conversation before leaving him to his work, often not speaking to him again for days. Since placing the influence in his robes, her attitude had changed. Her demands of him increased. She expected he give all attention to her. On Vidrey, he'd have relished it. Here, she irritated him. The godspear cure was secondary to her; Volstrysa's interest revolved around him. She was comely and intelligent, but there was falsehood to her nature. The supreme was too accommodating. She behaved as if the world ebbed and flowed around Lavak and agreed with his most banal comments. Was this how the Dark Mistress operated? Was this her method of seduction? Had Kuldahar been treated similarly? Eberan? How many others? Was he just the next?

A subtle warning nagged Lavak his was a unique circumstance, that Volstrysa's interest in him was of a different strain. He'd detected no influence on her other subordinates, so why use it on him? Yet, he was no subordinate, as she repeatedly avowed. He was—

Of course. The explanation was clear. He was the transcendent. She was maneuvering him. Volstrysa may not be aware of his emerging abilities, but she believed they would one day manifest. She was aligning herself with him. When his power was finally revealed, her invested time would be rewarded. It's why he was isolated, given his own lab, catered to by her. Volstrysa couldn't risk another interfering with her plans, including and especially Melindi. Her involvement had been accidental, an unforeseen introduction prompted by a sickened superior. Volstrysa had revealed her childish ways and her selfish desires at breakfast. More importantly, more ominously, Volstrysa was now aware of Melindi and Lavak's mutual affinity.

Their coupling only complicated matters. Lavak was hopeful he and Melindi might share a future together. Until then, he was compelled by pretense to spend his nights in rapture with Volstrysa. Despite his guilts, Lavak enjoyed his newfound experiences with a woman's flesh. He only regretted it was Volstrysa instead of Melindi. His only justification: when he and Melindi were finally together romantically, he'd be practiced in lovemaking and not some blundering fool.

Such an absurd arrangement, sharing his nights with a woman he was indifferent to and spending his days pining for somebody forbidden. The situation was so cruel and comedic Lavak laughed as he passed the high guards stationed at the main entrance.

Daylight was painting the spire's gray peak a luminous silver when Lavak scampered outside. He didn't have much time. Volstrysa would be waking soon. She'd discover him gone and search for him, first asking the guard outside her chamber door for information. Her sentry would eagerly report Lavak's passing, feeding Volstrysa all the knowledge she required. Lavak could almost hear time taunting him.

Last night's rain had cleansed the city and lent gloss to every surface, no matter how tarnished or drab. Puddles speckled the courtyard. Cobblestones gleamed slick. The air was purified and enlivening. There was tranquility in the moment, when dawn's calm lingered and the racket of daily happenings was yet to arrive. Lavak may have enjoyed it if not for the urgency driving his steps.

He bolted for the dorm only to find its doors locked. With sinking heart, he headed for the gardens. Melindi wasn't there. His plan crumbled and Lavak berated himself for foolishly ever thinking it plausible. Dejected, he ambled to the spire's rear. At least he could examine his enchantment. That plan, too, collapsed, because when he arrived, two high guards stood rigid at the door, shields and weapons at their sides. Wet hair plastered haggard faces. Small pools of water at their feet were growing slowly larger from the steady drip of their uniforms. These men had been at their post all night, enduring hard rain without shelter. The scowl carved into both men's countenance revealed the underlying discomfort of being soaked to the skin. Lavak reached for the door, but one guard stepped before him, blocking his way.

"None are allowed inside until the supreme arrives," the guard said sternly.

"But I've an enchantment in there. It belongs to me." Lavak regretted how his words sounded leaving his lips: weak and pleading.

"The enchantment maybe, but the starwood belongs to the Ascendancy." He shifted, the act releasing from his garments a sudden, miniature downpour which pattered between his feet. "You need to wait."

Lavak ignored the savor emanating from the guard, his thoughts trained on other matters. He'd hoped to take his magic before the others arrived and sneak away to hide for a while, preferably with Melindi. He had no desire to see Volstrysa today.

Hopefully, she'd be too busy with other concerns to bother with him, granting Lavak a day's respite. With nothing else to do and nowhere else to go, Lavak chose a spot several paces from the guards and leaned against the spire to wait.

The first aspirant arrived within the hour. Lavak had seen him before: a boy one third his age with a round face. His robes flared and bunched unflatteringly about his rotund frame. He arrived with a determined step which faltered upon noticing the guards. It appeared he, too, was anxious to inspect his completed work. He paced between the guards and Lavak, wringing his hands and muttering to himself.

"How long before the supreme arrives?" the aspirant asked the guards.

"She'll arrive when she's ready," the guard said with obvious irritation.

"Maybe I should go get her."

The aspirant's remark drew haughty laughs from the men. "You go right on and do that."

The boy paused in consideration of the guard's advice. "I'll wait, I suppose."

"You're smarter than you look." The guard grinned before his expression returned to its former stoic visage.

Lavak groaned silently to himself over the probability of seeing Volstrysa today.

More people arrived soon after. Aspirants and ascenders huddled expectantly around the door. When they pressed too close and grew anxious, the guards issued stern warnings any order member touching them or the door would be claiming their magic with broken fingers. This quelled those gathered and dispersed them into small groups (the aspirants seeking their own kind and the ascenders mingling with others of equal rank) far from any risk of injury.

Lavak lingered at the fringe of a swelling group of aspirants, his anticipation for magic overpowering his desire for isolation. He recognized most of the faces from either the spire or the atrium. If he ignored the robes and shaved heads and the many savors swirling around him, Lavak might have imagined he was back in Vidrey waiting with villagers for the Fall to commence. The excitement in the air was identical.

"I was hoping you'd be here," a voice came from beyond the nearby assembly of aspirants. Lavak didn't need to look to know the speaker. Kuldahar. "Since the supreme favors you so highly, I expect your enchantment will be the greatest ever created." The aspirants stepped aside to allow Kuldahar passage, trepidation on their downcast faces.

"Or ever to be created," Eberan said, trailing Kuldahar by a step.

Lavak sighed. He needn't turn to face them to know Jaquista accompanied the pair. They usually ran as a pack. "It may have been, but we may never know because of you."

Kuldahar smacked his lips. "See that, boys? Let the freak into the spire, give him all he wants and before long, he's thinking he's better than the rest of us."

"Only better than you, Kuldahar," Lavak said.

Kuldahar came to within a stride of Lavak and raised a fist. Those aspirants and ascenders closest quickly terminated conversations they were engaged in, transfixed by the scene bordering on violent. Lots of eyes watching. No mouths speaking. People enjoyed a good altercation, and this was worthwhile entertainment to pass the time until the supreme arrived. "I don't know what you did to me before. I don't remember anything after entering your room, but Eberan thinks you did something. He can't explain what, he just knows you did something. For that, you're going to bleed."

"He dares threaten a Splinterfist," the voice said, a harsh whisper in Lavak's mind. "He is jealous of us. Jealous and fearful."

"Be quiet!" Lavak shouted. One nuisance at a time!

"Don't try to silence me, freak." Kuldahar sneered. "You're

not better than me, and you certainly can't tell me what to do."

"Leave him alone!" Melindi said as she marched in the bullies' wake.

"You here to fight his fight?" Kuldahar's glare shifted between Melindi and Lavak. "Is that it, freak? You need a girl to defend you?"

"No. That's not why I'm here." Melindi grinned impishly. "I'm here because I wanted to tell you I got the stains out of your blankets. Next time it happens, don't hide them. Bring them to the laundry right away. The stains come out much easier when they're fresh."

Kuldahar's complexion blanched, then blushed. His eyes darted left and right, finding many ears that just heard Melindi's words. His cheeks puffed. He glared at Melindi. "Remember your place, Aspirant."

"I do. It's in the washroom removing your stains."

Snickers escaped the crowd, drawing Kuldahar's attention away from her. He opened his mouth as if to speak, then quickly shut it. His departure was so swift, Eberan and Jaquista ran to catch up.

"What was that?" Lavak asked, unable to conceal his amusement.

The grin lingered on Melindi's face. "He wets his bed," she said loud enough for all within the immediate area to hear. "He's done it for years and always managed to keep it a secret. Well, until now."

Lavak's smile crossed the span of his face. "You may have just made an enemy."

"I'm not afraid of him," Melindi said.

"Here she comes," an aspirant shouted.

Volstrysa strutted to the door with Welnaro closely following. Lavak crouched slightly so the heads of others obscured him from Volstrysa. The scattered groups of ascenders and aspirants merged into one large mass to surround their supreme leader. Volstrysa addressed them, her features, gestures and speech abundant with pomp.

"Members of the Ascendancy, you've worked hard to produce magic we and all people of Azazura cherish. You ascenders are the finest crafters in the land. Your work is without equal. Your enchantments people treasure most of all and pay dearly for.

"As for the aspirants, some of you are nearing ascension. Your enchanting skills have improved greatly over the years. Others have only begun training. New lessons will be learned today as you behold your enchantment. Admire it not for the magic within, but for the wisdom gained in its creation. Through discipline and practice you'll become an ascender and enchant the things all those in the land desire. Keep to your studies. Be mindful the teachings of your superiors."

Volstrysa swept her gaze across the gathering. "Many of you have been working hard to find a cure for the godspear. It's no secret our production of magic has decreased as we ration and prepare for what may be troubling times ahead. However, I have absolute confidence you'll discover a solution and save the godspear, thus saving the order. Whoever does will gain personal favor from me." Eager murmurs pulsed through the crowd. "And once a cure is found, production will resume in full.

"The season of storms has begun. There is still godspear to enchant, despite its limited supply. Our work isn't complete, but today, bask in your accomplishments." She nodded to a guard, who swung open the door. Volstrysa entered, swallowed by the interior's dim, followed by Welnaro. Ascenders obediently filed in behind, trailed by anxious aspirants.

"Melindi," Lavak began as he joined her at the back of the line. "About yesterday, I—"

She presented him a cautious smile. "This isn't the time for that."

Melindi stepped down into the dark bowel of the spire. Lavak, puzzled by her ambiguous remark, was compelled to follow.

The smack of recently excited metal assailed his nostrils and tongue as Lavak reached the foot of the steps. It was soon overpowered by the tang from dozens of newly enchanted items. People huddled close to the iron latticework in search of their personal treasures. The room's temperature rose sharply from the influx of bodies. Ascenders and aspirants jostled and jockeyed to the front, eager for their magic. Across the iron bands, a dazzling display of prismatic luster shimmered in the lamplight, lending vibrant colors to an otherwise dismal area. Lightning had charged the elements and fused them permanently with the godspear. What was once charred wood was now magical and luminous.

It was a simple matter to differentiate the works done by masters and apprentices. Those crafted by skilled hands shone bright, while the duller-sheened marked the inexperienced. Each was valuable to the Ascendancy. Aspirants were always awarded their first enchantment. For the rest, and there were many, magic was distributed where required. Arms and armor went to both low and high guards, depending on quality (High Guard always received the finest of enchantments). Artistic pieces were sold to Morivar's wealthier residents, while lesser-quality items city merchants acquired.

Nausea gripped Lavak. His heart raced as dizziness threatened his balance. Legs weakened, trembling almost uncontrollably. He propped himself against a wall. Melindi tended to him immediately.

"What's wrong?" she asked.

"I…I don't know." Lavak did know. It was the savors. The mixture of enchantments in such a confined space was overwhelming.

Melindi pressed the back of her hand to his forehead. She held it there for a moment and frowned. "Your skin. It's clammy."

His breathing turned quick and shallow. Claustrophobia struck him. "I need fresh air," he struggled to say. Melindi started to hook her arm around his for support when Lavak stopped her. "The enchantments. Get our enchantments."

"They can wait. You need out of here."

"Please. I'll be fine. For a moment. The beetle. It's mine. Influence." He'd intended the description to be more coherent, but basic speech was challenging at the moment.

Melindi hesitated, worry etched into her features. "I'll be right back," she said and was gone, threading her way through the crowd.

The urge to vomit came suddenly and passed just as quickly, replaced by a fit of shivering. His head throbbed, a dual attack spurred by the presence of influence and his racing heart.

"What of the Splinterfists?" the voice asked in its rasping whisper. "What of us?"

"Knots." Lavak groaned. "Be quiet."

"What of the Splinterfists," the voice asked again.

No ascender or aspirant seemed to notice Lavak's behavior. All were too involved in praising their own work and comparing it with their peers'. Melindi returned and helped Lavak up the steps. He glanced back a final time. Among the thronged ascenders and aspirants stood Volstrysa. Despite all the activity surrounding her, the supreme's attention was fixed on Lavak and Melindi. She glared as they climbed the stairs, the scowl on her lips and scorn in her eyes unmistakable. Lavak turned away and felt Volstrysa's stare drill into the back of his head.

Each step away from the concentration of magic brought a modicum of relief. Lavak's ailment lessened. By the time he reached the uppermost stair, he felt almost normal. When sunlight warmed his face, Lavak was well enough to walk without Melindi's support.

"You should rest a moment," she said.

"Not here," he said. Lavak pointed in the direction of the gardens. "Over there. I want us to be with the trees." And as far from Volstrysa as possible.

They walked with deliberate ease to the gardens. The magic's effects were mildly uncomfortable now. His nausea was gone, though he was still a bit unsteady on his feet.

Volstrysa concerned him. At her insistence, he'd learned enchantment. She undoubtedly expected to share with him the moment he first handled his newly enchanted godspear. She was owed that and he'd denied her.

"How are you feeling?" Melindi asked as she helped him to sit on plush grass beneath a dogwood.

"Much better. I don't know what happened." It was a lie he hated to tell her, but Lavak feared sharing his secret may endanger Melindi. His tie to magic was unique. If those of dark repute learned of it, they may try to use him for their own gains. And if he did tell her his abilities, should he tell her of the voice? Was there a voice? Or was he going insane? How would she react to all of it? Ultimately, he decided the less Melindi knew, the better.

"Do you think you're well enough to look at your work?" Melindi asked.

"I almost forgot all about it, I was in such a bad state. Yes. I'm well enough to look."

Melindi reached into her robe and withdrew the beetle. He pulled the sleeve of his robe over his hand before Melindi dropped the beetle into his palm. If she thought it was strange behavior, she kept it to herself. Lavak examined the luster, or lack of. Sunlight filtered through the dogwoods, its rays striking the beetle but giving it no brilliance. Its charred appearance was gone, replaced by the unimpressive green found on dying lichen. His first attempt at enchantment was of questionable success.

"I've never seen influence look like that after being charged," Melindi said.

Lavak snorted. "It's testament of my failure. Perhaps Kuldahar was right."

"Don't be so unforgiving. Enchantment is difficult. It takes the best ascenders years to master the art."

"I fooled myself. All the talk of me being transcendent filled me with overconfidence. I believed it and thought I could accomplish anything with ease."

Melindi touched his knee gently. "Some of the best things in life we must work for. If everything was easily gotten, what appreciation would we have for anything?"

Her words softened the sting of the lesson, if only slightly. "It's Kuldahar's fault. Because of him, this ended up in beetle droppings. I tried cleaning it."

"Kuldahar has a way of making everything difficult. Just use this as experience on what not to do. And when at all possible, keep things hidden from that bed wetter."

They both chuckled at Kuldahar's expense.

"I want you to have it."

Melindi shook her head. "I can't. It's yours. It's your first. You should keep it as a memento."

"I already have a memento." Lavak motioned to her pendant hanging from his neck. "If you don't want it because it's different—"

"Different is good. I like different." Melindi smiled as she reached for the beetle, then paused. Her tone straddled playful and serious when she asked, "You're not going to use its magic on me, right?"

"Of course not. I'd rather sway your emotions the natural way," he said with a grin. Did the beetle hold any magic at all? It lacked luster and he suffered no headache.

"I'll cherish it always," Melindi said. "It will make a nice necklace."

"Around your neck, anything would be nice. Even a nasty-looking, poorly enchanted beetle." He suddenly realized he'd unwittingly imitated Ralm with the gesture. Cyji's slothful husband had somehow mustered enough ambition to whittle a necklace for her. Lavak's situation was not entirely dissimilar. "Melindi, about yesterday—"

She pressed a finger to his lips. Her touch sent his heart racing. "There's nothing to say."

As much as he didn't want to, Lavak pulled her finger away.

"Yes, there is. It wasn't how it appeared. I'm not Volstrysa's lover. I don't have feelings for her. But I have to pretend I am, because, well, it's complicated."

She smiled weakly. "I know. I'm not upset. I truly am not. She has a reputation, and you've been in her company quite often. It was only a matter of time before something happened. You're a man, and men have needs."

"I don't need her. I need you."

"No, you don't."

"I do. And I think you need me. I saw how you looked at me. You were upset."

"I was surprised. I didn't expect to see you there, that's all. It was my first time serving the supreme breakfast. I was told to prepare a meal for two, but I thought Prime Welnaro was the second at her table, not you."

"It's just—"

Melindi pressed her finger to his lips again. This time Lavak didn't push it away. "Let's not speak of it again. I'm not upset, and you did nothing wrong. Understand?"

He didn't understand. Did he misread her yesterday? Was he still so naive to the ways of women? The situation confused and frustrated him. He looked into her bright eyes and instantly was lost in them. Confusion and frustration melted away. He nodded yes.

"Good," Melindi said with a satisfied smile.

They sat in the shade of the dogwoods, contented by the silence around them and the unspoken understanding between them. The more he learned of Melindi, the more enraptured Lavak became with her. She was all he could ever want in a companion.

"She endangers us," the voice whispered.

Lavak winced at its unexpected and unwelcome return. He forced a smile. The voice wouldn't ruin his precious time with his cherished Melindi.

CHAPTER 22

"Well?" Rill looked up at Ralm and waited for his deserved praise.

"You did an excellent job." Ralm patted the top of Rill's head.

Rill beamed. "I always do."

Sprig edged out from behind Rill and shyly smiled to Ralm.

"Hello, little Sprig," Ralm said. "Have you been helping Rill?"

Sprig nodded and slid behind Rill again.

"You delivered all the papers?" Ralm asked.

The pride in Rill's features faded slightly. "All, except this one. It got ripped, so I thought it was no good anymore." He raised a hand, a crumpled page clutched in his grungy fingers.

Ralm flattened the paper. The words on it called for action, urging citizens to unite and protest the Ascendancy. "That's fine. You did well."

Again, Rill beamed. "I'm just wondering. I can't read. I don't think lots of people read so good. What makes you think anyone will see these and care?"

His was a valid question. Ralm spent many days writing and rewriting, copying the words to each of the hundred identical works. His fingers still ached from the effort. "I don't expect everybody to read them. But I expect at least some to generate enough interest for folks to gossip, even if they do so in private. Words float farther than silence."

"If you say so. I'm just the messenger."

"And what a messenger you are." Ralm rubbed the boy's head again.

"All that will do nothing for me right now," Chulvar said, drawing Ralm's attention away from Rill.

The merchant stood before the crowd: a menagerie assembled within the warehouse of faces young and old, men and women, all with hopeful eyes trying to break through a thick, invisible wall of despair. These people yearned for encouragement, and they came here seeking Ralm to give it to them.

"I can't afford to pay my occupancy fees because I'm not selling my enchantments," Chulvar continued, his cheeks reddening. "I can't support your cause if I can't operate my business. Do you have any rounds to loan me so I can continue my trade?" He held out an open palm expectantly.

"Remember, Chulvar, you were among those who approached me about starting this revolution. I didn't ask to lead, yet the burden has become mine. If I'm to lead, you must accept and follow my plan, no matter the distress it might cause. That is, unless you want to be leader."

Chulvar's waiting hand dropped to his side. "I'm just a merchant. I can't lead. There's no profit in it."

Ralm smiled. "I'm a simple man from a simple place. I'm no more qualified than you." His gaze swept across the sixty or so faces of the crowd. "By now, there should be triple this amount of people gathered," he said more to himself than anybody else.

"What's that?" Rill asked.

"Nothing," Ralm said.

He instructed his followers during each of the previous three meetings to recruit more people. His expectations were too high. Though new members were joining, they were not coming in numbers Ralm had hoped. Sometimes only one new person accompanied a current member, and sometimes none at all. Many of the new members came to see if the rumors about Ralm were true:

that he was the Painted Man and was immune to magic. He still wore the paint, which Neva had donated and instructed Ralm how to apply himself. As for demonstrating his immunity, Zirrin was absent the past few meetings, lured away on business and favors. People had to take Ralm's word, or the word of witnesses. Their reactions to this were always either skepticism or disappointment.

"Ralm," said Rill.

People wanted the system to change, but expected others to do the work for them. Their passivity was inexcusable. Do nothing, but gain everything from successes. Do nothing and risk nothing should the attempt at change fail. Ralm understood the reasoning. Inaction was safety. People nailed their existence to security, but what good was existing, even if safely? Existence was living, not thriving. It was surviving another day, repeating it again the next day and the next, until all the days combined into a lifetime no better than the first day and the world was left no better for those whose days were yet to begin.

"Ralm," Rill repeated.

Hopefully, the latest posters would spark more interest in the revolution and rouse people from inactivity.

"Ralm," said Rill again.

"What do you want?" Ralm said, irritated the boy had pulled him from his thoughts.

"I know how to get more people here," Rill said.

"Oh? I'll take any advice you have," Ralm said and partially meant it. Desperation was setting in as time was running out. He wasn't above listening to the wisdom of a child, especially one who'd spent his life on the streets of Dorsluin.

"Those posters you have me hanging up." Rill's tone bordered on apologetic. "They're nice and all, but it's like I was saying. Lots of folks don't read, and even if they did, the Ascendancy tears the posters down before people have a chance to see them."

"I can't stand in the middle of the street and shout about it, Rill. You've any better ideas?"

"Actually, I do. I know lots of orphans. I know lots of other people, too. Like the ladies who walk the streets and are always talking and laughing with men."

Prostitutes. Ralm didn't doubt Rill knew the proper name of their profession. The boy was simply being polite by not directly naming them as such. "Yes, what about them?"

"You see, orphans and those ladies don't care for the Ascendancy. Especially in the outer circles where the Low Guard can do just about whatever they want to whoever they want. You want people, the right people, to know about what you're doing, then you've got to get to their ears. They got to hear about it. Not read it on a poster. Orphans are all over the place. They can say things while in a crowd, make people think somebody important is talking about it instead of an orphan. And those ladies, well, they talk a lot already. And they like us orphans. Lots do. Always giving us cakes and stuff. Except for that mean old snorter on Waterrun, but we don't need to involve her. The others, though, they'd help. I know they would."

"And what would they expect in return?" Ralm asked. "I can't afford to pay all those people."

"I think they'll help just because."

Ralm was skeptical. If every orphan operated like Rill, they'd expect payment. And what he knew of prostitutes, they're services weren't free, either. His purse was empty of rounds. He couldn't afford Rill for another day, much less a city's worth of orphans. However, he'd come to trust the insight of his young friend. "See what you can do about it, but tell them they'll be doing it for free. Make sure you explain that to them."

Rill nodded. "I will. I'll be clear like glass about it."

The people gathered were growing restless at the delay, marked by the rustle of clothes as the bodies they covered shifted anxiously. There were still chores to be done: fires to feed, dinners to cook and children to tuck into bed. Every minute spent waiting on Ralm was a minute better spent elsewhere.

"We are what we allow ourselves to be and what we limit

ourselves to be," Ralm said to the crowd. "Chulvar. You say you're just a merchant. You're more than that. You're willing to abandon familiar comforts in exchange for what lies beyond the unknown." Chulvar gave a respectful nod. "All of you are already more than what you consider yourselves to be. Just coming here proves it. Don't limit yourselves. Believe you can be more. Believe one person can do great things. One can do much, and many working together can accomplish extraordinary feats." Several heads bobbed agreement. "I don't accept leadership willingly, but I don't hide from the burden, either. If anybody here is willing to lead, you're welcome to it. Come forward now, or anytime, and I'll step down without protest. Do any of you want it?" He waited. None argued for the position.

"We follow you," came a voice from the crowd.

"You're our leader," another spoke.

"What do you require of us?"

"I require nothing," Ralm said. "It's our cause which requires. There's an end, but to reach it requires many steps. Chulvar, if you can't pay your fees with rounds, barter instead."

Chulvar shook his head. "Bartering is illegal within the city. He'll never agree."

"Yes, he will, because all other merchants will be bartering as well. I have negotiated with most of them already." Chulvar's eyes bulged at the news reaching his ears. "I have visited their shops and spoken to them. I needed their opinions on the matter and their views on the Ascendancy. This was not easy. I couldn't ask these questions directly. No merchant admits his misgivings openly. However, they do like to talk when making a sale and indulge in a great range of topics to a potential buyer. This, Chulvar, I'm sure you know already."

"Of course," Chulvar said. "When making a sale, you need to sell yourself to the customer first."

Ralm nodded. "Sometimes merchants will say whatever is needed to make a sale, even if their words are lies. While untruths about an item or service isn't admirable, what a merchant speaks regarding his own beliefs is something else. They'll agree with a customer all day if it gets rounds in their hands. Merchants boast and brag during a sale, but more so after they've closed shop and had some wine. I sought them in taverns and got their tongues wagging after a few drinks. Though they remain secretive about much information and some may be lies, one needs only peel off the bark on their words to find the truth. I discovered merchants all share a common resentment toward the Ascendancy. They're forced to pay outrageous fees to continue business. With some coaxing, I persuaded them to avoid the transaction fees entirely through barter. This removes any records of a trade and still allows for profits, albeit in a different form. Investigations by the order over missing inventory will be claimed as lost."

"What of the fees and taxes?" Chulvar showed interest, but the tone of his words was lathered in skepticism.

"The key to success is freezing the money flow. It's fluid. When rounds stop moving, it loses value." Since his arrival, Ralm had learned the fundamentals of commerce in Azazura varied drastically from Vidrey. After relocating to the warehouse, he'd devoted a large share of his time studying and understanding Azazuran economics through observation and books loaned to him by Zirrin and Chulvar, though the latter's contributions tended to focus more on bookkeeping and accounting. While still informative, Ralm struggled to remain interested in the often boring and always tedious principles of recording. "Once everyone is bartering, the need for money will disappear. If taxes and fees are to be paid, it will be done in trade. This one step will be effective in shaking the foundation of the Ascendant's power. The Ascendancy will feel the effects and may try to end it through more presence on the streets. More eyes from the spire will watch transactions being made. This we can also circumvent if it reaches that point."

Enthusiastic murmurs passed through the crowd. All were in support of Ralm's plan.

"As for magic, if you want it for yourself, then get it. But do not feel you must own magic to elevate your status. Buy it to elevate your happiness."

Chulvar shook his head. "I enjoy dealing in rounds. It's simple. What am I to do, trade a magical pitcher for ten chickens? Soon, I'll have more chickens than I care for."

"It's a temporary solution, Chulvar," Ralm said. "Not one long lasting. It's only to rattle the order."

A woman of modest dress spoke from her place amid the crowd. "Magic is expensive. What do any of us have to trade for it? I would need to barter all I own and still not have enough."

"The market determines the price. Demand drives the market. If the pursuit for magic to gain status is removed, fewer will buy it. That will increase supply, which will lower the price of magic."

His reasoning satisfied her. She nodded her approval, though ever constant in Ralm's thoughts was the increasing rarity of magic due to the godspear plight. His plan wouldn't last long if all magic disappeared, but then, neither would the order.

"This is not all. We must rally the outer circles. They've fallen into disrepair. We are told taxes are used to maintain the streets and walls, to pay guards to protect us. Yet walls and streets crumble. Those paid to protect us are instead our keepers. Authority is abused. Taxes don't benefit us. The money goes to the spire and little, if any, finds its way back here."

"Who needs walls anyway?" a voice in the crowd bellowed.

"You're right," agreed Ralm. "The walls separate us, divide those who have from those who have not. They should be torn down. So let's give those in power a message. Let's prove taxes are unnecessary because we'll furnish our own maintenance and protection. We'll work together as a community to rebuild what has fallen, clean any garbage that collects, fix what is broken. Remove the debris of collapsed buildings and replace it with gardens to grow food so none go hungry again. Together, we can overcome. We'll no longer rely on the empty claims of the Ascendancy. Instead, we'll rely on ourselves and our neighbors. It may start small, but as we work toward our goals, more will join, and the more who flock to our cause, the more powerful we become. It is our unity the Ascendancy fears. It's why they divide us with walls and with pursuits of magic. In unity we prevail."

Though only sixty in number, the applause from the crowd was louder than ten times that amount.

CHAPTER 23

Basara crumpled the letter in his fist. It was delivered that morning by courier, an urgent report from one of his many spies abroad. The news was bad. Bad enough to topple his plans if left unchecked. The transcendent was in Morivar and had been for some time. Volstrysa kept him hidden and only by her careless parading of Lavak was his presence discovered.

"Spiders in spires!"

He almost laughed at the archaic expression. It was almost as old as the order, with roots tied to the scheming of the earliest ascendants. Plots and conspiracies, assassinations and betrayals, daily pursuits of supremes outwitting their peers to gain advantage. It almost doomed them all. A schism in the order led to decades of war between domains. Chaos ruled as citizen and ascender alike perished by flame and spear. Even ascendants were not immune—usurped by subordinates, thrown from the soaring heights of chamber windows or slain in battle by rival ascendants on the Bloodstained Plains. Supremes rose and fell in the span of days. Sometimes hours. Orphanages lay deserted, the children conscripted to fill Ascendancy ranks.

Order didn't come then, just as it didn't when the spires were gutted of occupants, or when all the magic in Azazura was squandered, or when blood trickled instead of flowed. Order didn't come when the fleas, beset by famine and war, united against the Ascendancy and demanded a new system of government. None of it was deemed important to the squabbling supremes.

Only one event cured the mortar in the Ascendancy's foundation: Kyrkynstaag's bid to claim Vidrey as its own. The desperate attempt by the then ruling supreme mirrored Basara's present circumstance: a woefully insolvent domain. He'd planned to collect as much godspear as possible, enchant it and eliminate Morivar and Dorsluin. It was an ambitious plan, one Basara framed his own upon. However, his predecessor made two critical mistakes Basara would not. First, he announced his intentions. Why? Basara couldn't say. Arrogance, perhaps. Records of the time were lost. The bold declaration spurred the other ascendants into swift action and by a two-to-one ruling, laws were established to restore peace and preserve the Ascendancy's power. Those laws still remained. Laws forbidding supremes from assassinating other supremes. Laws outlining when wars could be waged. And laws preventing Kyrkynstaag, or any domain, from seizing Vidrey as its own.

Basara thought himself a clever spider, weaving his web of deceit. The laws keeping the order in balance with strict forbidding of coups did well to preserve the Ascendancy in the past, but they were antiquated, meant for a more turbulent time. His plan simplified matters and nullified the laws: dissolve the triumvirate, eliminate the division of wealth and bestow it all upon Azazura's only ruler. Of course, new laws would need to be enacted. Primarily, laws protecting him from harm.

His ravenous beetles were efficiently culling the godspear in Vidrey. They were, perhaps, more efficient than Basara had anticipated. It appeared the godspear would be eradicated completely. If a few more could be harvested before that happened, the better to increase his surplus and power. But Basara possessed a stockpile of hidden godspear, and if the beetles consumed every last tree on the island it was of no import to him. That was his predecessor's second mistake: greed. Basara learned from this error and reined his greed, mindful it didn't ensnare him. Unlike his predecessor, Basara was content with not having all the godspear on Vidrey, as long as his rivals had none at all. With that arrangement, he'd gain absolute control of Azazura.

Yes, he was a clever spider, but he wasn't the only one. There was another, with her own web. The Dark Mistress was laying silken threads, and at their center, a man who could unravel Basara's own web, and along with it, his plans.

He cared nothing for the transcendent. Kyrkynstaag had long ago dismissed him as an oddity. Lavak demonstrated no powers. His inability to commune with godspears was a subject of ridicule and jest from his spy's reports, the notion of Lavak harboring some innate power was scorned throughout the spire. Only Morivar had insisted on his continued observation on the island. Volstrysa's fascination with Lavak concerned Basara. It seemed a frittering of hours, unless the Dark Mistress's lusts extended to primitive freaks. No. There was something more. Volstrysa possessed knowledge exclusive to her. Otherwise, why would every crimson watcher sent to Vidrey commit so much time to Lavak? His own watcher, along with Dorsluin's, joined Morivar in observing Lavak while there. Although Basara couldn't attest to Dorsluin's motives, his were simple: if Morivar was interested in Lavak, so should he be. It wasn't wise to ignore where spiders built their webs.

There were many spiders spinning webs, some in his own spire. He sensed the growing agitation in his ascenders. They were dissatisfied with his rule and questioned his methods. He needn't spies to know this, only keen eyes and sharp ears. His was a precarious position hard fought and harder kept. To be supreme ascendant at Basara's age brewed contempt in senior ascenders. So long as he lived, they'd continue as mere ascenders, forced to obey the orders of a boy, whom, in their eyes, was undeserving of the office.

The only reason he'd not yet become ensnared in any webs was because Basara hadn't chosen his successor. Keeping the spire without a prime was risky. If ill fate befell Basara, there'd be nobody to replace him. Chaos would ensue. Basara knew this, as did all his underlings. This universal understanding was why the lack of a prime assured Basara's survival. No amount of infighting in a prime's absence was worth the risk of disrupting the order's power. The ascenders, as disgruntled as they were, accepted Basara's decision to remain without a prime. For now. But patience was thinning. None, save for Regnidon, knew Basara's true plan. If they did, he'd likely have already been tossed out a window.

That threat was still distant. There was a new, more pressing matter to contend with first.

Basara sensed the assassin's presence behind him. There was no flirtation with his dagger at Basara's back like the last time the Dirge visited, but knowing how easily the assassin could reach Basara was a point of concern sharper than any blade.

"Did you enjoy my report?" the Dirge asked.

"It was entertaining," Basara lied. It was less a report and more a poem. He turned to face the assassin and recited a verse from the Dirge's macabre musings. "Two fishes flopping on the shore, two fishes will swim no more." The Dirge smiled proudly. He may have been a gifted killer, but his poetry was lacking. Basara knew better than to voice his criticisms. He liked his neck as it was—without a slice across it. "I've another fish for you."

The Dirge arched a brow. "More ascenders on remote islands?"

"No, but it will require your art of infiltrating spires."

The Dirge rubbed his chin. "Sounds expensive."

"With you, it always is."

"I'm worth it. You get what you pay for. You want a job done right, you get me. You want it done sloppily, if at all, you get somebody cheaper."

There was no arguing with the assassin. He was right. He was skilled in bloodletting and equally talented in keeping his true identity and past a secret. Few lived who were aware of the Dirge's existence, and none knew his origin, including Basara. One theory put the Dirge as an orphan who learned his craft in the streets, enforcing for local merchants. It was one of many potential possibilities. "This particular target is no ascender, though he acts as one."

"An impostor?"

"Of sorts. His name is Lavak. The Dark Mistress has grown fond of him. She keeps him close to her."

The Dirge grinned. "Another one of those, eh? She has a way of using her guiles on the men in that spire."

"We all have our gifts. Hers is seduction. Yours, a blade."

"And you? What is your gift?" the Dirge asked, his eyes piercing Basara like the dagger on his belt.

"I'm a visionary."

"A visionary? What vision do you have?"

The Dirge was setting a trap, as if the verbal exchange was another one of his hunts.

"Soon, you'll be employed by the most powerful man in Azazura," Basara said, offering the assassin a morsel of tantalizing insight.

"Those two I dispatched, they stood in your way of this?"

"They were obstacles in need of removal."

"What of the island? I'm quite curious of it now. Is that part of your quest for power?"

Basara waved a dismissive hand. "It's soon to be of no importance. Regnidon is seeing to matters there." Had the Dirge disobeyed his orders and explored the island? Basara carefully sculpted the two ascenders' murders, delivering the Dirge there at night so he didn't see too much. If he'd explored Vidrey, the assassin wisely kept it to himself, but Basara arranged for as little time as possible for the assassin to wander Vidrey freely. "Soon, there'll be nothing there to tease your curiosity. It would be best if you struck it from memory and did your job."

The grin held on the Dirge's face. "As you wish. This Lavak.

He's an impostor. He's in Volstrysa's company. What else should I know about him?"

"I thought you studied your prey. I see no reason to disclose information you'll learn on your own."

"The reason is because I want to know what kind of job I'm accepting. I don't know this Lavak. Am I being contracted to slay a lamb or a bear?"

"You're the deadliest assassin in Azazura, yet you sound hesitant. Fearful."

"I'm neither. It's a matter of cost. If this Lavak is the kind who frequently gets drunk and stumbles into alleys, it will be an easy kill. But if I must spend weeks watching and waiting for an opportunity because he's the captain of the High Guard who is never without escorts, that changes things. I'm planning a holiday and don't want to see it delayed."

"A holiday?"

"Does it seem so unbelievable?"

"I thought you enjoyed your work."

"I do, but even I need rest on occasion. Now, this Lavak. Lamb or bear?"

"Very much a lamb. Perhaps the easiest pay you'll ever earn."

"Why mark him? Is he another obstacle?"

"Yes, he is." The islander's journey to Azazura had alerted Volstrysa and Zenteezee to the beetle infestation on Vidrey, a fact Basara hoped to keep secret until the godspear were gone. By then, it would've been too late for either supreme to act. Lavak's arrival in Azazura was unwelcome, but Basara discovered opportunity in the transcendent's unexpected presence. He strode to his desk, slid open a drawer and removed a tattered scrap of indigo cloth, which he passed to the assassin. "Once you've killed him, leave this near the body."

The Dirge turned the cloth over. "What's this stitching in the corner? A partial Dorsluin emblem? Ah, I understand now. You want to blame them for the assassination. Hoping to start a war?"

The counterfeit had been effortless. Not even Zenteezee would recognize it as fake. "No. I simply want Volstrysa's anger and attention on Zenteezee." With her distracted, it would be one less pair of eyes watching Basara's movements. If war erupted between Morivar and Dorsluin over Lavak's death, it would only aid Basara. The two domains would weaken each other, assuring Kyrkynstaag a swift victory over both.

"I trust payment has been arranged."

Basara nodded. He'd emptied the treasury for this kill. The auction for the influence had been a failure with the final bid only forty thousand rounds. To worsen matters, Pelnaniv had been right about the taxes and fees: commerce was slowed to a near standstill. With nothing in reserves, the city was bankrupt. His plan was at risk. He needed to act soon. Basara couldn't afford to pay the Dirge for any more surprises.

ABOUT THE AUTHOR

Born a woodsman's son, Dean spent much of his life in the forests of eastern Connecticut. While his peers spent Saturday mornings watching cartoons, Dean was out with his father cutting, splitting and stacking cords of wood to sell. It was these weekend "retreats" which instilled in Dean a deep appreciation of the woods and all the splendor they held.

Lightning Source UK Ltd.
Milton Keynes UK
UKHW022204270420
362420UK00009B/220

9 781734 033236